About the Author

Born in Vietnam of unknown parents, Martha Bertrand was brought up in a cold and spartan orphanage in the north of France. Having won a scholarship, she completed her secondary education in Paris. Gripped with the irresistible urge to travel, she then moved to Britain to learn English, graduated, trained as a teacher and taught for twenty years before fulfilling her first ambition that was always to be a writer. "With nothing known about my family, I am the head of a new dynasty with my name indelibly carved at the top of my family tree."

To Yvonne,

With my very best wishes,

[signature]

No Requiem for a Dead Pirate

Martha Bertrand

No Requiem for a Dead Pirate

Olympia Publishers
London

www.olympiapublishers.com
OLYMPIA PAPERBACK EDITION

A CIP catalogue record for this title is available from the British Library.

ISBN, 978-1-80074-588-9

First Published in 2022

Olympia Publishers
Tallis House
2 Tallis Street
London
EC4Y 0AB

Printed in Great Britain

Dedication

To my husband who has been my staunchest supporter, my PA, my IT manager and my best friend.

Acknowledgements

I would like to acknowledge the excellent Pirates of Nassau Museum, George Street, Nassau, Bahamas, which gave me the inspiration to write this book.

Prologue
Part I

Pirates of Cove Island — The late XVIIth Century and early XVIIIth Century saw the golden age of piracy. Men and boys who wanted to better themselves often gambled with their lives by becoming sailors in the King's Navy. In 1689, the onset of war between England and France, soon to be followed by Spain, encouraged the existence of an alternative navy which fought and plundered enemy's ships with the full blessing of the King.

Led by men like Sir Henry Morgan, Bartholomew Roberts and Edward Teach (Blackbeard), pirate ships roamed the West Indies and raided almost every ship they encountered. But despite their brutal and reckless existence, these pirates had a conscience and when, for example, Bartholomew Roberts captured an English frigate called the *Onslow*, they found a clergyman on board who was on his way to become the chaplain of Cape Corso Castle. Rather than use their usual force to coerce him into service, the pirates courteously invited him to join their crew, '*promising him he should do nothing for his money but make punch and say prayers*'. Eschewing their generosity, the chaplain politely declined and was subsequently allowed to rejoin his ship with almost all his belongings, for the pirates kept nothing that belonged to the Church except three prayer books and a bottle-screw.

These were difficult times for those left behind on land and if a husband did not return home, the unfortunate wives had to find some way to survive. Facing much reduced circumstances, many were forced to seek employment in town or country houses. Others, of a more adventurous disposition, disguised themselves as men and boarded ships in order to seek their fortunes alongside privateers and pirates.

It is in this social and domestic upheaval that we meet Anne Bonny, a bored and frustrated housewife who escapes a loveless marriage by eloping with a pirate. This is the story of a fearless opportunist who sought her fortune and freedom by going out to sea, armed only with the courage of a man and the boldness of a sailor.

Part II

The Cross of Madeira — Woodes Rogers is Governor of the Isle of New Providence with only one purpose in life, to fight the war against pirates. One day however, he receives the news that a Spanish galleon has been intercepted and robbed of her treasure — including a jewel called the '*Cross of Madeira*', destined for the King of Spain — by one of the most successful pirates of all time, Captain Bartholomew Roberts. To avert another war with Spain, the Governor promises to reward handsomely whoever recovers the treasure and catches the villain, dead or alive.

Part III

Ten years later — Anne Bonny's baby is now a young lad. Of an age to understand his true origin, his adoptive mother finally reveals to him who his parents really are. Suddenly, it all becomes clear to him why he has always had this yearning for the sea. Should he stay home and work on the farm or answer the call of the sea and break his mother's heart? A letter from a stranger will give him the answer.

Behind The Story

The idea for the book 'No Requiem for a Dead Pirate' came whilst Martha Bertrand was on holiday in Nassau, The Bahamas. There, she took her young sons to the Pirates Museum.

Learning about pirates turned out to be a fascinating experience, but what was even more thrilling was to discover that two notorious pirates were actually women, Mary Read and Anne Bonny. There is nothing like a good mystery to fire up the imagination and whilst Mary Read died in prison of tropical fever, nothing is known about the fate of Anne Bonny.

This book is thus an attempt to give Bonny a life beyond the prison walls which, we hope, will not end on the gallows.

Although the book is largely a work of fiction, certain elements and characters are drawn from real life events.

The Pirates' Prayer

Thank you, Lord, for opening our eyes to the beauties of this world
For the wondrous light of the sun and the freedom of the sea
For the wind that steers our ship and the food that we receive
Let us sail in your faith and pray in your name
And should we sin in pursuit of honour and glory
Forgive us all our trespasses
Forgive us our greed and excesses
And let us sail in your faith and pray in your name

Amen

Part I
Pirates of Cove Island

Chapter One
First Voyage at Sea

It was the hour past midnight. In the sheltered creek of Nassau on the Isle of New Providence, sloops waited indolently in the sleepy harbour.

Nearby, two dishevelled sailors chatted idly at the bottom of the gangplank of a sloop named the *Kingston*, when they were alerted by a shuffling noise. Immediately, they turned their heads and watched two unsteady silhouettes advancing towards them. Despite the thick darkness cut only by a narrow streak of moonlight beaming across the bay, they instantly recognised the tall imposing frame of their captain leaning heavily on a mystery companion. As usual, too much rum had got the better of him and Jack Rackham staggered about, feeling the worse for wear. Rather blasé about such a familiar sight, the two sentries sighed.

"Well, here he goes again, Calico Jack, the most feared pirate of the West Indies!" one of the sailors snorted. "Look at him. My wife's scarier than him!"

"Aye," his companion riled. "He's got his sea legs on land again!"

As the two figures approached the ship, the unusual appearance of the stranger, dressed in baggy trousers and an oversized shirt that hung rather loosely on his solid frame, aroused suspicion among the two guards and their hands immediately fell on their pistols.

"Who goes there?" one of them hailed.

"Arrgh! Can't you see, you dummies. It's me… your captain!"

"Aye, but who's your companion?"

"A new recruit, if that's any of your business. His name's Alan Bonny. He's a bit young and a bit green but he's a strong lad and a darn sight smarter than you lot, so get out of my way or I'll slice you in half!"

"Aye, aye, Captain!"

Knowing better than causing grief to their captain when he was soaked with rum, the sailors quickly stepped out of the way and watched the unlikely pair scramble up the gangplank.

At the top of the gangplank, Rackham stopped to catch his breath.

Then, still leaning heavily on his companion, he asked between gasps of air, "Come on, lad, take me to my cabin."

"Where's that, Captain?"

"There! Up there!" Rackham replied impatiently, pointing at a narrow flight of stairs leading to the top deck.

Struggling to push the captain up the steps, young Bonny tripped and fell on top of the captain.

"Damn it!" Rackham groaned. "You useless rogue!"

"Hey! It ain't my fault!" the lad cried out.

"Come on!" the captain roared. "Get me up those damn steps, you idiot, or I'll make you scrub the decks for the rest of your days!"

The two finally made it to the captain's cabin, a rather cramped space, Bonny noted. A brief glance was enough to inspect the whole of its content. Immediately to the left of the door, he spotted a narrow berth nestled against the wall adorned with a red curtain that ran the whole length of it. Adjacent to it stood a small table just below the porthole with one single chair pushed against it. A brass lamp hung so low from the ceiling that he could touch it without stretching his arm. On the table itself, a small and narrow white porcelain tray, containing an ink well and a thin stick that looked like the remains of a quill, fitted snugly in a groove carved inside the edge. Spread over the table and held down by small blocks of wood was an old parchment map detailing the extreme contours of South Carolina and the numerous islands that formed the Bahamas with a thick black cross on the spot that marked Nassau. To the west of the map, Alan's sharp gaze spotted a much bigger island and mumbled the name to himself, Cuba. On the floor, tucked between the table and the wall, he stared with glee at a magnificent sea chest that seemed to be bursting with stolen treasures. On its lid, he could clearly see two large initials tarred in black, JR. He imagined it full of pieces of eight — even gold doubloons if Jack Rackham was as rich as he boasted to be — and bursting at the seams with sumptuous clothes. The lad's train of thought was suddenly interrupted by the captain's loud moans and groans.

"Arrgh, that wretched rum!" Rackham growled, dropping his full weight onto the narrow berth. "It'll be the death of me…"

With one last grunt, Jack Rackham tossed his body towards the wall and within seconds, he was gone, dead to the world.

The young lad glowered at the captain, wondering what had happened to the colourful and brash character he had seen cheering, singing and sometimes even dancing in the middle of the tavern, flashing his money around and grabbing any pretty maid willing to be his companion for the night. But… he suddenly thought, what about him? Where was he supposed to sleep?

"Er… Captain? Where am I going to sleep?"

The captain grunted in his sleep.

"Go and grab yourself a hammock. I'll see you in the morn…"

Stepping outside, Bonny felt the unnerving silence seize him with a sudden fear. Furtive steps shuffled around the quay, invisible and threatening, as if ready to pounce and kill. But in reality, nothing moved except for the heavy cables of ships ready to sail towards their next unpredictable adventures.

For as long as he could remember, Bonny had harboured dreams of running away to travel to the end of the world, to escape the servitudes of a life on land that would yield nothing but hardship and beatings. Then, quite by chance, at barely eighteen years of age, he had met Rackham in a tavern, the *Cock 'n Bull*, where the flamboyant pirate, in the manner of a stage actor, re-enacted all the fantastic escapes he had made after each raid. And nothing excited him more than telling all and sundry how he had raided a Spanish galleon returning from the New World, laden with gold, silver and jewels, using impressive words and plenty of arm action for maximum effect. Captain Rackham was loud, brash and at times somewhat scary. Not everyone was taken in by his ripping yarns, though all listened avidly, riveted by his wild stories, sometimes gasping in awe, and other times shaking their heads in sheer disbelief. Then, he had spotted young Alan who seemed listless and aimless. In want of new hands for his ship, the captain had accosted him and bragged all the more about his wild adventures at sea. He had chinked his gold chains and flashed his large gold ring that boasted a huge blue topaz, in front of the young lad's eyes, telling him there was a lot more where these came from. To convince him even more, the captain had thrust his head closer still to Alan's face, and, at that moment, the young lad thought he had caught a glimpse of a sea chest glittering with gold in the captain's dark brown eyes which sparkled with excitement and suspense. Then, another time, Rackham sprung out of his chair, marched up and down the tavern, and started singing a well-known pirate sea shanty, urging everyone to join in. As he passed a table set a little further away from the bar, he grabbed the barmaid who had just deposited a round of drinks, and together, they swirled on the wooden floor, despite her faint protestations. As he did so, his long dark hair, tied in a pony tail, swung erratically under his old tricorn.

Despite the excitement of it all, young Alan had remained circumspect. The thought of going into battle and swinging from ship to ship to plunder and kill did not appeal to him one bit. No, guided by his Bohemian soul, he just wanted to go and explore exotic lands he had never seen before. What finally swayed him to risk it all and join a pirate's crew was the irresistible lure of riches which Rackham described to him with such verve and passion that he was momentarily blinded by the glitter of gold. Throwing caution to the wind and forgetting all thoughts of battles and war, there and then, he decided to run away from home.

Exhausted, he made his way to the main part of the ship and entered a wide open space full of wooden beams with hammocks suspended in between. Instantly, a vile stench hit his nostrils and almost made him sick on the spot. Struggling to breathe, he rushed back onto the main deck, gasping for air. When he had quite recovered, he looked for somewhere to settle. There was nothing on the deck but coils of cables piled up in several corners of the bridge. His eyes heavy with sleep, he decided to settle next to one using it as a pillow, by the prow so as not to be disturbed, and quickly fell into a heavy sleep.

***

It seemed that he had only been asleep for a short while when a sharp voice cut into his dreams.

"Hey, sonny! What are you doing here?"

Alan was too sleepy to respond.

"I think we've got a stowaway!" someone yelled.

"Well, stowaway or not, we've got no room for layabouts! Get up, you lazy devil!"

The man who spoke started kicking Alan. The painful blows were enough to stir the young lad into action.

"Stop kicking me, you stupid fool! That hurts!" he protested, unaware of the several faces peering down at him until he had his eyes quite open.

As if he had rehearsed the moment many times before, the burly sailor broke into a spontaneous jig.

"Oooo! That hurts, oh deary me, I must tell my mummy!"

The pirates burst out laughing. With their mocking jibes, their hideous faces and their vulgar laughter, Alan could barely contain his anger. He jumped onto his feet and warned, "Get away from me or I'll call the captain!"

"By the devil's teeth!" riled the ringleader. "He's no stowaway, he's a friend of the capt'n! Watch out, lads, he could be our next leader! Ah, ah, ah!"

Again, all his mates joined in the laughter. Eventually, one of them enquired, "What's your name, lad?"

The young recruit darted defiant looks around him before replying.

"My name's Alan Bonny, I've just joined this ship... and who might you be?"

Instead of a reply, the ringleader drew his cutlass.

"Freddie Main's the name, and if you want to join our crew, you've got to prove yourself. Come on, draw your weapon and show us what you can do!"

Alan stood rigidly on the prow, knowing that he did not have a weapon to draw. He had not expected such a fierce response from the sailor but he did not panic yet for the named Freddie Main was obviously playing the big guy in front of his mates. Fearless, young Bonny stood up to him.

"What do you want?" he asked, jerking his head back in sheer defiance.

The pirate's expression changed, as if a cloud had thrown a dark shadow on his sardonic smile. He narrowed his eyes and began to growl like a dog.

"I want to play," he snarled.

Dennis Macarty, the pirate's best pal without whom Freddie Main would only be half a man, heckled, "Come on, Freddie, make him dance!"

Taking pity on the young boy, Indigo John, who was surveying the scene from the rigging, shouted, "Leave him alone!"

"Not yet, Indigo, not yet! We need to see how good he is!" Freddie Main retorted. "If he can't move his feet, he can't dance, and if he can't dance, he can't fight, so he'll be no good to us... Come on, lad, put them up!"

Alan stood up to face his challenger. Taking a deep breath to swell up his chest, he stared at Freddie Main straight in the eyes and harked back, "I don't have a weapon and only a coward would fight a man with no weapons!"

Ignoring the lad's remark, Freddie Main lunged several times forward, forcing young Bonny to pounce about and jiggle on the spot. The pirate continued with his sadistic game for a while until, as quick as a flash, Bonny seized one of the mate's cutlasses, squared himself up to his assailant and roared, "All right, matey, if that's what you want, come and get it!"

Stunned by the unexpected fierceness in the lad's response, Freddie Main suddenly stopped… then roared with loud laughter. He hit himself on the sides, looked at his opponent and mimicked in a high-pitched voice, "Oooo… I'm so scared! You want to have a bit of fun? So do we, don't we, lads?" he riled, turning his head towards his mates.

"Aye, aye," a chorus of male voices replied.

Far from being intimidated, the young lad wielded the cutlass in front of him and threatened, "You may have your bit of fun, but not over my head. You want to see what I can do, then I'll show you, but I'm warning you… you'll never have the chance to see me fight proper… because you'll be dead!"

Freddie Main whistled with admiration at the young man's fearless stance.

"You may speak with smart words, lad, but here, pretty words mean nothing! Only the power of your arms and fists can save you from certain death, either against me or any other threat," he warned.

All around them, shipmates gathered on the deck, ready for a bit of entertainment and a good laugh. Some men climbed onto the rigging for a better view. The ship was now well out to sea and the swell of the ocean rocked the ship and made every man unsteady. Dark clouds whirled around in the sky, whisked by a heavy breeze that kept pushing the ship towards strong currents and sandbanks that Pete Atkins, the helmsman, struggled to avoid.

Back on the main deck, totally oblivious to the whims of the weather, the pirates waited for their bit of fun. Egged on by his mates, Freddie Main gesticulated wildly, wielding his cutlass while roaring like a demented beast, before suddenly lunging forward for the kill. Alan Bonny responded in kind, never flinching, youth and agility being his only allies. By contrast, Freddie Main plodded heavily on the wooden deck. A stout man with a heavy frame and a large belly that hung loosely over his belt, the rogue was at least half a century older, making him heavy-footed and often short of breath. Nevertheless, he felt superior to the young lad who had to use both hands to hold his cutlass; and all the time, he snarled and sneered, and openly mocked his victim, until suddenly, growing more complacent, he found himself pinned by the sharp point of Bonny's cutlass against the bulwarks.

"Right, matey, satisfied?" Bonny growled, his teeth clenched.

He held the pirate at the end of his cutlass for a few more seconds, staring menacingly in the pirate's eyes. They were no longer mocking but wide open in shock. The sailor's mouth opened and shut a few times but no sound came out. His lips trembled as he tried to find words to placate the young lad, but each time, his words came out in broken syllables. Fearing a humiliating end to his own fight, the pirate tried to humour young Bonny.

"Hey, lad, I was only joking! I tell you what… You go and scrub the deck and I'll fetch you a good measure of my share of rum!"

Bonny was quick to retort, "Only after I've scrubbed the deck with your foul blood!"

Upon which, he slashed the sailor's chin with a swift swipe of his cutlass. Freddie Main winced in pain while the rest of the pirates gasped in horror.

Immediately, two of the men drew their own cutlasses. Straight away, Alan squared up to them, his eyes staring hard.

"All right, mates!" he yelled. "Who's next?"

Alerted by the commotion, the captain emerged from his cabin. Immediately, some of the shipmates shuffled in front of Freddie Main to hide him from view.

"What's going on?" the captain enquired, undecided whether he should sound angry or simply curious. "You know the rules about fighting on board!"

A tense silence hung over the deck. The captain darted quizzical looks around, trying to figure out what his men had been up to, then he looked more distinctly at the suspicious group of men standing by the bulwarks, and through their legs saw Freddie Main slumped on the deck. As if responding to a silent order, the shipmates shuffled out of the way. Freddie Main was slouching against the bulwark, pressing his chin with his hand as small rivulets of blood trickled through his fingers.

"What's the matter with you, Main? Did you hurt yourself?" the captain enquired with some concern.

"That's all right, Capt'n. I was… I was just shaving and the razor slipped," the pirate bluffed.

The captain glowered at him with an incredulous eye and riled, "Well, next time you shave, make sure you don't use a cutlass!"

A few feet away, Alan drew a long breath through his dilated nostrils, and, as a way of declaring victory, he threw the cutlass he had borrowed onto the deck. One of the pirates stepped forward to retrieve it and quickly withdrew to mingle among his mates so as not to draw remark. The captain threw a quizzical glance at young Bonny and warned, "And you, my lad, if you want to learn how to use a weapon, make sure you pick someone you can trust."

Then, turning on his heels, he retreated to his cabin once more. The pirates watched him disappear up the narrow staircase, after which their eyes locked onto Bonny where they stayed, fixed and menacing. Far from being intimidated, the lad threw a cold stare at them before swaggering off. Freddie Main racked his throat and spat on the deck. Then, he turned towards the lad and muttered through his clenched teeth, "I've not finished with you, blasted little devil!"

But his words were lost in the wind, and Bonny greeted his menacing stare with a defiant grin.

The storm that had been threatening for the last few hours finally abated. The dark clouds scurried off towards the distant horizon, to chase another day. On board the ship, the atmosphere remained tense and the young recruit who, only a few hours ago, was wandering listless and carefree through the streets of his home town, had to keep his eyes open, remain on his guard and constantly look over his shoulder to protect his back and his life.

Chapter Two
A New Hand on Board

Following the morning incident, Captain Rackham reminded his crew of the rules aboard his ship. He had written them down on a piece of parchment paper which he kept rolled up in his cabin, and, on that July morning, with the sun beating down and burning the back of his neck, he stood on the upper deck, scanning the faces of his men standing to attention on the deck below, and set about spelling out the rules.

"Article One, Every man shall have an equal say and vote in the affairs of the ship. He shall have an equal share of the fresh provisions and liquors at any time seized and shall use them as they please, except… and I repeat… except that all liquors shall be prohibited prior to a planned attack.

"Article Two, Every man shall be treated fairly with duties and chores equally divided and fairly distributed according to the state of his body and health.

"Article Three, Every man shall receive an equal share of the prizes, clothes and treasures seized. But if a man defrauds the company to the value of even one dollar, he shall be marooned and if any man robs another, he shall receive ten lashes before being put ashore where he shall be sure to encounter hardship.

"Article Four, Each man shall keep his piece, cutlass and pistols at all times clean and ready for action. He that shall desert the ship or his quarters in time of battle shall be punished by death or marooning.

"Article Five, None shall strike another aboard the ship. All quarrels shall be settled on shore by the means of pistol. If both miss their aim, they shall take to their cutlasses and the first man to draw blood shall be declared the victor. You'd do well to remember that… all of you!

"Article Six, Every man who shall become a cripple or lose a limb in the service shall have eight hundred pieces of eight from the common stock, and a proportional amount for lesser injuries.

"Article Seven, The Captain and the Quartermaster shall each receive three shares of a prize; the Master Gunner and Boatswain, one and one half shares as shall the carpenter; other officers, one and one quarter. All others shall receive one share each.

"Article Eight, None shall game for money, either with dice, cards or any other means.

"Article Nine, Musicians shall play only by day, by night on request only, and they shall have a rest on the Sabbath Day."

At the end of the reading, Captain Rackham rolled up the charter and waved it at his crew, scouring their faces with supreme authority. "These are the rules. These are *our* rules! By the very fact that you accepted to board this ship, you have vouched to abide by them. Anyone caught breeching these rules will be instantly dealt with. So let it be a warning to you all!"

Rackham scrutinised closely the faces looking up at him from the main deck, searching for a nervous twitch that would betray the slightest sign of dissention among his men, but all remained standing rigidly still and in complete silence.

***

There were about forty men on board, most of them ruffians who had absconded from Royal Navy ships, one such being that rogue of Freddie Main. Previously a marine on the *Swallow*, he had on two occasions received twenty-four lashes for drunkenness and insubordination. After surviving battles and beatings at sea, with only a fistful of groats to show for his pains, the surly sailor had been left with a bitter sense of justice and a burning desire for revenge. Angry and dejected, he 'ran' and joined forces with a bunch of pirates whose sole purpose in life was to pilfer and grab anything they could lay their filthy hands on, a scheme that suited him perfectly despite knowing that he was most likely to end up on the gallows rather than in the green and pleasant land of England. And he had help for he immediately paired up with one of the most despicable, belligerent and ruthless pirates of the lot, Dennis Macarty.

However, these two aside, there was a hard core of trusted hands in charge of the ship, and these were, Dave Ryan, the quartermaster, Pete Atkins, the helmsman, and a certain Indigo John, in charge of the rigging, named so after the blue coat, exquisitely embroidered, he had robbed from a French naval officer.

One particular mate stood out from the others for the very fact that he categorically refused to touch any alcohol. His name was Mark Read and he was a loner. How he ended up on the *Kingston*, no one knew. His aloof manner, bordering on arrogance, kept him at a firm distance from his rowdy mates. Often seen scouring the main deck with hawk eyes, he was compared to a barometer, speculating on the general mood, the overriding tension on the ship and the atmospheric pressure at sea. Woe betide anyone foolish enough to disturb him when he was in one of those contemplative moods.

While most of the shipmates sought riches and riches only, there was one notable exception. 'Boy' Jennings, named so because of his youth, was a tall lad whose plain mousy hair was cut through by a rebellious streak of bleached hair, on the left-hand side of his head, a family trait inherited from his mother's side. So far, he had refused to give his age for fear of being treated like a cabin boy. Of polished manners and calm resolve, he had planned to become an officer in the King's Navy, had he not been captured and coerced to become a pirate, before he even had the chance to earn his first commission.

Finally, to ease the mood, unwind the men and cheer up the crew, someone with a musical inclination had been allowed on board. His name was Ned Hornby, a Welshman by birth, who owned a concertina and a deep rumbling voice that often crooned to the mournful tune of 'Longing for the Land of my Fathers'. Being short and stumpy, and quite old for a pirate, many wondered why he should want to risk his old age for a dangerous life at sea. Every time the question was put to him, Ned Hornby nodded his head and smiled condescendingly, reacting to the question by asking another, "Would you like me to play you a tune?"

Solely the captain knew the actual truth, for our old minstrel was an inveterate gambler who did not have two groats to his name. With no other skills with which to earn a living, the only alternative opened to him would have been a life on the streets playing his concertina and begging for his keep. He also knew that the cold English weather would soon send him on his way to the celestial choir of angels; and it was while he mulled over his fate that he had decided he wanted to stay a little longer on God's earth, be it as a petty thief, a hopeless gambler or a timid pirate, if there was such a thing. And he was in luck for Captain Rackham was in desperate need to recruit more hands for his next voyage. To entice the old crooner, instead of being given arduous chores on board, the captain had insisted that all he wanted from the old dear was for him to act as his manservant and play a bit of music.

***

Several days passed without the single sighting of a ship. During their idle moments, of which there were many, some of the men sat in small clusters around barrels or on the deck itself, playing cards or games of dice while discussing various boarding tactics. Others simply smoked while gazing dreamily out to sea in a rare moment of plenitude.

At this very moment, Ned Hornby was sitting near the bowsprit, with his back against the wind, playing his concertina that wailed some nostalgic aria until he was almost reduced to tears. Fed up with his sentimental crooning, Dennis Macarty threw an apple core at him.

"Hey Ned! Can't you play something a bit more cheerful?"

"You wanna dance?" he harked back. "I'll make you dance!"

And he started.

Two wooden feet and a bottle of rum
Is all you need for a little bit of fun
Blackbeard's lost his ship and all his mates
His head's hanging above the ocean waves

As soon as they heard the first few notes, some of the pirates sprung onto their feet and began to sing through the repertoire of popular sea shanties. Then, they locked arms and swung their legs together, pulling and shoving each other to keep up with the brisk tempo. Some, having enjoyed a few swigs of rum beforehand, decided to ignore the music altogether and launched into a spontaneous chorus of bawdy songs, howling to the wind and scaring the fish.

As usual, Captain Rackham was nowhere to be seen. While his crew carried on the merriment, grating his ears by hammering their feet onto the wooden deck, he was stretched out on his berth, trying to keep his head above a thick alcoholic haze. But the noise proved too much, so he put his pillow on top of his head and fell into a deep sleep.

Back on the main deck, Alan Bonny, the new hand, observed bemused the noisy display of pirates at play. Itching to join in, he tapped his foot on the deck, but that was all he dared do at this stage for he sensed that his shipmates were not yet ready to welcome him, especially after the Freddie

Main incident. Just as he thought of it, he spotted the very man with his mates prancing about like a rogue wave out of control. This was a relief for whilst the pirate was busy making a public display of himself, at least he was not scheming and plotting to seek revenge against him.

However, as soon as the music stopped, the pirates regrouped in their clusters and the tension returned. Shapes and shadows moved furtively against the glare of the sun, touching each man with an invisible hand as sinister as if the spectre of death had descended onto the deck, carefully selecting its next victim. The salty wood creaked and the cables whistled in the wind. Some superstitious pirate had once decreed that if the wind howled through the cables without the sails moving or flapping, it was a sign that something terrible was about to happen and ever since, each time the wind blew over their tetchy heads, the pirates threw a quick glance at the sails in the hope of detecting the slightest movement or swell in the open canvas. And so far, no malediction had struck.

The constant noise and tension on board gave Alan the impression that someone was stalking him with murderous intent. Feeling nervous and jittery, bordering on paranoia, he kept jerking his head from side to side and over his shoulder just in case someone was waiting to pounce on him. He had no friends, not even a casual ally, and with the captain out of action, Alan felt at the mercy of the entire crew who looked as if they could not wait to get the better of him. Repeatedly, and subconsciously, he found himself pacing the top deck with a predatory look upon his face, constantly checking the pistol that the captain had given him, while scrutinising the moves of every shipmate. This was not at all the kind of life he had expected. What he needed, he decided, was a mate, a strong ally who would side with him and make his life on board slightly more tolerable.

From afar, he had observed Mark Read whose quiet confidence and independent streak set him apart from his more needy shipmates. His tanned complexion seemed rather smooth for a mariner and his shoulders, although large and well developed, looked round and plump rather than muscular. Nevertheless, he liked the quiet authority he seemed to exert around him. After a few days of keen observation, Alan felt confident enough to make a direct approach.

"Hi there! And who might you be?" he asked.

"Mark Read's the name," the sailor replied dryly.

Undeterred by the curt response, Alan engaged in small talk to sustain his attention.

"Mine's Alan Bonny…"

"I know," the sailor cut short.

"Oh… you know?" Alan reacted with a coy smile, pleased to have made his mark on a fellow shipmate he secretly admired. "So… how many ships have you attacked, then?"

"Three or four…"

"Did you get lots of gold, jewels, clothes and things…"

"I got the same share as everybody else!" Read cut in sharply.

"So where do you stand during an attack? Do you fire the cannons?"

"You don't know much about the trade, do you? Otherwise, you would know that it's better *not* to fire the cannons because if you want to seize the ship for yourself, it's not a good idea to smash it to bits and let her treasures sink to the bottom of the sea!"

Alan threw an admiring glance at the sailor, impressed by his knowledge of warfare.

"So, what do you use to attack?"

"Grenades, stinkpots, pistols, my cutlass and whatever else I can carry…"

"Do you kill or take prisoners?"

"Depends on the enemy. Sometimes they'd rather be killed than be tortured or forced to become pirates… But from what I saw the other day, *you* certainly don't intend to take prisoners!"

"Too right I don't. I often give the impression of being weak, feeble and naïve. I could tell straight away that none of them was going to take me seriously, and I reckoned that if I didn't get the better of that dog Freddy Main, I'd end up being kicked around and used as everyone's dogsbody, and that, mate, is not what I came here for!"

"So, why have you come?"

"Need you ask? Same as you probably. Get rich quick so that I can disappear and live happily ever after…" Then he scanned the deck with disdain and added, "…and leave all those dogs behind!"

"And… I'm not a dog?" Read enquired with a quirky smile.

"No, not you, you're as rough and ready as the lot of them, but there's something different about you, though I can't quite work out what it is."

There he stopped, suddenly absorbed in a thoughtful pause. Then he asked, "You don't drink, do you?"

"Nope, but only because I want to sell my share of rum so that I can make my fortune quickly and live to enjoy it rather than die in misery. As they say, a pirate's life is a short but merry one… but me, I don't want to hang like a dog, not me, I've got plans I have."

"You're a smart guy, you are… You and me, we'd make a good team…"

"Forget it!" Read cut in sharply. "No team for me! I'm in it for myself and myself only! I don't care about anybody else!"

Bonny was not ready to give up.

"Well, I still think we would make a good team. Besides… I like you…" Then whispering in his ear, "I could even fancy you!"

Mark Read took a step back in shock.

"Stop that bloody nonsense!"

Undeterred, Alan Bonny continued by eyeing him up and down.

"Have you ever been injured?"

Read had heard enough. He started walking away.

"Don't worry! I'm not gonna touch you!" Bonny hailed. "I just want you to be my friend… I need an ally… you could do with one too!"

Read stopped in his track.

"No, I sure don't! And anyway, what is it to you if I have a few scars here and there?" he declared non-plussed.

"It means… no extra pieces of eight for you, hey! Well, me, I've got a scar," Alan boasted. "Right here." He pointed at his left shoulder.

Read chose to ignore the remark and turned his head towards the sea. He really could not care less, what ailments other people had; all he wanted right now was to be left in peace.

"D'you want to know how I got it?" Alan continued unfazed.

"Nope," Read retorted dryly.

Deaf to his stern rebuff, Alan told him anyway.

"I got it in a fight with a kitchen lad who worked for my father."

He looked at his companion to study his reaction but to his annoyance, the pirate remained stubbornly impassive and kept staring at the sea with utter indifference.

"Anyway," Alan continued. "From now on, I'm gonna say I got it from a cutlass during a battle. Sounds better."

Having failed to make his mark, Alan eventually left his companion gazing silently at the sea, and wondered off towards the main deck, determined to try again later.

Not far from there, Freddy Main was playing cards on an upturned barrel with his mates. As soon as they spotted Alan stroll on the bridge, the group of them growled and hissed. The young lad glared back at them with disdain.

"Oooo! I'm so scared!" Freddy Main scoffed, making his mates roar with laughter.

***

As the days went by, the captain could not help noticing a rapprochement between young Bonny and Mark Read. To him, it seemed inevitable that the two should strike a friendship for they both looked the same age, displayed the same aloofness towards their more primitive shipmates and seemed rather reluctant to mix with the rest of the crew. However, there was a notable difference between the two, in that Mark Read was one of the most experienced hands on board, while Alan Bonny barely knew how to hold a cutlass. One day, he decided to call them over.

"Read, why don't you teach young Bonny the rudiments of sword fighting? He's never been to sea, never seen battle, and he really ought to learn how to use a cutlass with just one hand; and also, how to fire a pistol without blowing himself up! Here's a spare cutlass!" the captain said, throwing the weapon at Bonny, who managed to catch it by sheer reflex reaction.

"Aye, aye, Captain!" Read agreed.

"And…" the captain added. "Don't spare him!"

Then he left the deck abruptly. Bonny looked at his mate and frowned. "What did he mean by that?"

Read replied with a cryptic smile. "Raise your cutlass and you'll find out… But first, let's go on the upper deck where it's quieter. We don't want to get those dogs going, they'll be too glad to join in the fight, especially against you, and before you know it, they'll have you dangling and begging for mercy from over the side of the ship. Come on, let's go!"

As soon as they reached the upper deck, Read assumed position and yelled, "En garde!"

Baffled, Bonny stared at his companion. "What? What does that mean?"

"It means 'get ready to cross swords'…"

"What? All that in just two words?"

"Don't worry about it. Just raise your weapon; always remember to stand sideways so you don't expose your chest; you see, you've got to make yourself as thin as possible to minimise points of impact so as to protect your vital organs…"

"Bloody hell, Read! I just want to learn to fight! Not become a sword fighting champion!" Bonny exclaimed.

Exasperated, Read retorted, "You're learning to fight for your life, you dummy! Come on! Right foot forward, left arm up behind your head for better balance, and lunge forward… like so."

As he explained the moves, Read leapt forward, with his cutlass stretched out in front of him, forcing Bonny to jump out of the way.

"Hey!" he protested. "Give me a chance."

"I'm afraid, in battle, you won't get a second chance, so you have to be quick on your feet, sharp as a knife, and ruthless with your enemy… like this!"

Before Bonny had a chance to react, Read had lunged forward once more. The sharp point of his cutlass caught Bonny's loose shirt and tore it open. Instantly, loud cheers rose from the main deck. In sheer panic, Bonny dropped his cutlass, grabbed the loose flaps of his shirt and ran along the main deck towards the brig. Puzzled by his mate's strange reaction, Read gave chase.

"Hey!" he hailed. "Where are you going? We've only just started!"

In an instant, they both disappeared below deck. Once they were out of sight, Bonny stopped to catch his breath. Read looked at his mate and asked, "What's up with you? Why did you run away?"

Bonny took a deep breath and replied, "I didn't want those dogs to see…"

"See what?" Read enquired, as puzzled as ever.

Bonny hesitated for a moment, then letting go of his torn shirt he replied, "This!"

Opening his shirt wide, Bonny revealed a pair of plump breasts suspended high and firm in all their glorious naked beauty. Read stared, speechless.

"By the devil's teeth," Read stuttered in shock. "You're… you're…"

"Aye…" Bonny replied in a matter-of-fact way. "But don't tell those dogs... no one needs to know..."

"Aye," Read parroted, still stunned. "No one needs to know..."

Leaving his mate to recover from the shock, Alan continued in a matter-of-fact way, "Anyway, I'd better go and change my shirt." Then he chided, "That was a bit reckless of you. You could have killed me up there with your wretched cutlass."

"Don't be silly," Read said dismissively. "I know exactly what I'm doing. I'm like a cat, I know when I want to play and I know when I want to kill. But... why? Why are you masquerading as a man?"

Bonny thought before replying. Then, he slowly owned up to his status. "All right, if you really want to know... my name's Anne... Anne Bonny. I've always dressed up like this. My father made me. You see, he was forever chasing petticoats, and one day, he got his wicked ways with one of our maids. Unfortunately, he got her with child and that's how I was born. Of course, his wife was furious with him, and when she saw that he wouldn't change his ways, she left him. However, I had an older brother who died when he was only a little child and to hide his shame, my father made me take his place. So he dressed me as a boy."

"Poor you." Read sighed in sympathy.

Bonny looked down at her breeches and feet, and sighed, "Don't worry about it. I'm so used to it that sometimes I forget what I am. Anyway, this is between you and me. For the rest of those dogs, I'm Alan Bonny, all right?"

Then, Bonny had a sudden thought, "What about the captain? Do you think I should tell him?"

"Hell no, Bonny! Don't you realise what this means?" Read exclaimed, somewhat panicked. "Pirates are extremely superstitious. If they discover you're a woman, they'll have you thrown overboard! As far as they're concerned, women are not just a nagging menace, they bring bad luck too! No, no! Nobody must know or it will be the death of you!"

"Unless..." Bonny decreed with a cheeky grin. "...unless I seduce the captain."

"Hell, Bonny!" Read exclaimed, rather outraged. "There's no stopping you, little hussy! First with me, then with the captain!"

"It's called 'survival instinct'...! Oh well, too bad." She sighed. "I thought Rackham might like to have a woman on board his ship. Imagine the kudos that would give him. I can just see him boasting in the *Cock &*

Bull, "And yes, Ladies and Gentlemen! The bravest pirate I ever had on my ship turned out to be a woman! Ah! Ah! Ah! He's not a bad sort, really; he's brash and jolly, a bit lazy, yes, but who doesn't want a slice of a good life without having to work too hard for it, hey? And — surprisingly — unlike most pirates, he doesn't enjoy killing. No, not Calico Jack. He's only in this business to get rich quick and run away with the rum and gold, and, quite frankly, I'd run away with him too!"

Suddenly, behind them, the two mates heard muffled steps. Slowly and quietly, they shuffled behind one of the wooden pillars, just as the large frame of Freddy Main appeared in the doorway.

"There he is!" he screamed, pointing at a silhouette half-hidden in the darkness. "Get him!"

Out of the semi-obscurity, invisible hands fell heavily on Bonny's shoulders. Others grabbed his hands to tie them with a rope before dragging him all the way to the top deck where an impromptu audience had formed.

Brandishing his cutlass, Read ran after the men and confronted the pirate, "What do you want with him?"

"*Him*?" Freddie Main riled. "That's no '*Him*'!" He turned towards the shipmates. "That '*Him*' here is a woman!"

Instead of a spontaneous revolt, the men stood stunned in the kind of silence that is only heard when a death sentence has been passed.

Disappointed by their dumb reaction, Freddie Main cut Bonny's shirt open with his cutlass.

"There!" he shouted as if suddenly vindicated. "Alan Bonny is a woman and we don't want no woman on board our ship because they bring back luck! And, they can't fight either!"

Out of the blue, a voice heckled, "This one can! Remember, she gave you a nice close shave with her cutlass!"

Everyone turned their heads to see who had spoken. Standing on a pile of cables next to the main mast, Boy Jennings stood legs akimbo and with his fists dug deep in his sides.

Ignoring him, Freddie Main continued, "Men, we need to hold a trial," he declared. "Because this woman here, this impostor, is no more a pirate than my grandmother's a duchess!"

A howl of laughter greeted his remark.

"And if he's not a pirate," Freddie Main continued. "He can only be one other thing, a spy!"

At these words, the laughter stopped abruptly. Freddie Main narrowed his eyes, clenched his teeth and drew his cutlass. Bonny did not flinch. She stood rigidly still, looking straight ahead, her hands holding on firmly to the loose flaps of her torn shirt. Wielding his cutlass, the pirate suddenly pointed it at Bonny's chest and declared, "We don't want no women on board our ship, cos women are bad news, they don't just bring bad luck… They take up too much space. They eat our food, drink our rum and grab our share of gold! In my mind, they're only good for one thing… and that's to walk the plank."

"Yeah! Yeah!" a chorus of voices cheered. "Walk the plank! Walk the plank!" they chanted.

"You're nothing but a coward, Freddie Main!" blasted Bonny. "Because you can't fight unless you have ten men fighting with you. Remember how you crumpled under my cutlass. Your eyes were wild with panic… and you were shaking, yes, Freddie Main, you were shaking with fear! I bet you didn't tell that to your mates. Pitiful you were, yeah, pitiful. Even now, you have the sad look of a dog about to hang. Well, Freddie Main, I'm ready to fight you any day…"

"Shut up, you stupid wench!" Freddie Main harked.

"Make her fight or walk the plank! Make her fight or walk the plank!" the pirates chanted again.

"No, she won't!" a lone voice yelled.

It was the captain.

"Leave her alone," he shouted. "Whether she fights as a man or a woman makes no difference to me as long as she's willing to fight. And you, Freddie Main, you know that Bonny is not afraid to put up a good fight against you or anybody else, so you'd better keep your hands off her or *I'll* make *you* walk the plank!"

"Women bring bad luck!" he blasted.

"Aye!" Dennis Macarty interjected. "We've got to get rid of her!"

"Forget that bloody nonsense! My advice to you all is, forget the fact she's a woman. Treat her like any other shipmate, and I don't want to hear another word about it, understood?" The captain scrutinised each and every face. All stood still and remained in complete silence. Satisfied, he finally declared, "The matter is closed!"

Following this incident, Anne Bonny no longer attempted to conceal her true identity. However, she carried on wearing her men's clothes simply because at sea they were more practical. At first, the other mates kept their distance, but gradually most of them grew to accept her as one of theirs, although they were all agreed on one thing, whether a man or a woman, they could never trust her.

***

Several days passed with no quibbling, no fighting, and not the single sighting of a ship. In the gentle swaying of a tropical breeze, the *Kingston* glided smoothly across the ocean waves. Sitting on his favourite spot, near the prow of the ship, Ned Hornby picked up his concertina, threw a furtive glance at Anne Bonny and began to sing, "*Did you not promise to marry me…*" Immediately, the rest of the crew joined in.

Anne Bonny turned her head in the direction of the music, wondering whether it was a taunt to tease her. When Ned Hornby saw her looking at him, he winked at her and smiled, then carried on singing. Her head dulled with boredom, she scoured the bridge in search of her mate. A mere few feet away, Mark Read was leaning against the bulwark in sheer contemplation and smoking a clay pipe. The more she saw him, the more she liked him. His long and wavy hair floated freely in the wind, as detached and carefree as his attitude towards the rest of the crew. Anne noted with pleasure how handsome he looked with his powerful shoulders, his strong arms and the permanent look of determination etched on his face. Before she realised what she was doing, she was walking towards him.

"Hi!" she greeted with a friendly smile.

"Hi!" Read replied, with his usual detached manner.

"You know…" said Anne hesitantly. "I still want us to be friends."

Slowly, Read took his pipe out of his mouth, looked at Anne straight in the eyes and stated dryly, "I told you before, I don't need a friend."

"Maybe… but here, everybody needs an ally."

"I've got everything I need," he flatly stated.

"But I never see you with anybody."

"That's right. Like I said, I've got everything I need."

"Pity. I could do with some company…"

Overhearing the short exchange, a sailor riled, "What's wrong with you, Mark Read? You don't fancy the new shipmate, hey? Pass her over to me, I'll have her!" Thomas Clark jeered. "Hey Ned! Play us a frisky sea shanty, I wanna dance with me new partner!"

As he spoke, the sailor jumped to his feet with his arms outstretched towards her. Instantly, Anne drew her cutlass. She squared herself up to the sailor and threw her head back in a show of defiance. In a brusque movement, she swung her cutlass above her head, "The only thing I'll dance with, matey, is your filthy dog head!" she roared.

"I'll have your teeth before you have my head, you wench!" retorted the sailor.

"To replace your own rotten teeth? Ha! Come on, then, old dog, come and get them!"

In a sudden move, the sailor lunged towards the woman and their cutlasses clashed above their heads. Pushed by the momentum, his body threw hers violently against the bulwark. Having anticipated his attack, Anne retaliated by kicking the sailor between the legs. As the sailor gasped in agony, she sent him flying on the ship deck with a violent kick on the shoulders. Seeing their comrade humiliated by a woman, Freddie Main waved to his mates to surge forward. Together, they drew their cutlasses and began to advance towards Anne, their jaws jutting forward and their eyes deadly, fixed on their prey.

"You may win over one of us, but you won't win over all of us," Freddie Main growled. "You're on your own, wench…"

Suddenly, a blade slashed the air in front of her.

"Not quite!" a firm voice cut in.

Anne jerked her head towards the voice and saw Mark Read by her side, with his cutlass stretched in front of him. As she turned her head, she caught sight of Dave Ryan and Boy Jennings standing on the upper deck with their hands resting on the balustrade.

Of the two men, Boy Jennings was the most worried. He did not like the way things were turning out, and he feared that someone might get killed. He looked at Dave Ryan and said, "We've got to intervene before the stupid fools kill each other. You're the quartermaster, tell them to stop!"

Dave Ryan shrugged his shoulders with indifference and scowled. "None of my business… let them!"

Both men fell silent as they watched Anne edge her way cautiously towards the bulwarks to make sure no one could surprise her from behind until she came level with her unexpected ally. With their backs protected, Bonny and Read threw a conniving glance at each other before squaring themselves to face the surge of pirates who glared at them with wild eyes and teeth showing.

Dave Ryan soon realised that if he did not intervene, blood would be spilled.

"That's enough!" he shouted. "Leave her alone!"

"I've got her cornered, I'm not gonna let her go this time!" Freddie Main growled.

"If you don't stop now, I'll get the captain!" the quartermaster insisted.

One of the shipmates, a Scott named Angus MacDonald, tried to pacify the angry pirate. "Dinnae bother, man!" he warned. "If you get killed, you'll nae get your proper share of things!"

Suddenly, the captain emerged from his bolthole.

"Are you men fighting again?" he asked, exasperated.

Immediately, most of the pirates put their cutlasses away.

"Not fighting, Capt'n, not us. We was just comparing our cutlasses to see which one was the sharpest," replied Freddie Main, swivelling the bare blade in the sun so as to throw blinding rays in the eyes of his adversaries. Then, he slid his weapon back in his belt and swaggered away.

The captain espied the gathering with suspicious eyes, then beckoned Anne to follow him.

"Come here, lass, I've got a job for you."

Reluctantly, Anne followed the captain up the narrow steps to the top deck. Once inside the captain's cabin, Jack Rackham closed the door with a firm hand and warned, "I need to warn you, Bonny, you've got to try and keep out of trouble. These men are ruthless and they'll stop at nothing."

"It's not my fault, Captain. Freddie Main's set on revenge, and there's nowhere for me to hide on this ship."

"Of course it's your fault. You shouldn't have roughed him up the first day you came on board."

"He started it!"

"Anyway, I don't want to hear any more about it!" he cut sharply.

Having made himself clear, the captain paused to think. He tapped his foot on the wooden floor, cupped his hand around his chin and coughed once or twice to clear his throat. Then, he looked straight in Bonny's eyes and suggested in a softer tone, "If you want somewhere safe… then… there's always my cabin."

"Thanks, Captain, but I'm not afraid of the guy. I can handle him.

Besides, I've got an ally now."

"Who's that?"

Anne looked askance at the captain, wondering whether it was safe to reveal her friend's name. As she pondered, the captain's eyes shone with a glint of compassion, and the heavy frown on his forehead showed more concern than anger.

"Mark Read," she admitted reluctantly.

"Mark Read?" repeated the captain. He paused and looked at Anne even more intently. "Well, I want no more trouble. Read is one of my best hands and I certainly don't want to lose him in a stupid fight against stupid men like Freddie Main!"

"Like I said," Anne declared stubbornly. "I'm not afraid of him. I've never been on a pirate ship before but I know how to deal with dogs, and so should you! You're the captain, you're the boss, so it's down to you to sort him out."

Surprised by her sudden aggressive stance, the captain raised his voice.

"Now, you watch what you say! These dogs happen to be my men! And another thing, I may be the captain but I'm not the boss; everybody is the boss here…"

"What's the point in that?" Anne riled.

"It's perfectly simple. We're all in it together, we loot and we share the loot but someone has to sail the ship and that's my job as the captain. Understand?"

"I've never come across a system like that. At home, my father is the boss and everybody has to obey him or they're kicked out! You're too soft, you are."

"I really don't care what your father does…"

"He's a lawyer," Anne cut in abruptly.

The captain looked quite taken aback by her remark. He peered at her with different eyes as it suddenly dawned on him that the woman standing in front of him was nothing like she appeared to be. First, he thought he was dealing with a lad, then a lass. Now, a simple remark had revealed a glimpse of her background, and far from being the uncouth layabout he had encountered in a noisy, malodorous tavern, she was a smart girl, probably educated, and most likely from a well-to-do family with a gentle disposition and refined manners. What on earth was she doing on his ship? More to the point, why was she so aggressive? He wanted to find out, but right now, he

42

had to warn her about the danger she created for herself by being so ruthless with his men.

"You watch your steps, Anne. You're more bloodthirsty than the worst of them!" the captain reprised. "Well, we, pirates, don't operate that way. We're more like equals, that way we have more freedom… and we can have more fun too. Talking of which, I want you to lay off that guy Mark Read."

Anne grinned, flashing her beautiful white teeth with contempt.

"Why should I? Like you said, captain, we're all in it together so we can have more fun!"

Suddenly, the captain snagged her arm, pulled her towards him and said, "I want my bit of fun too!"

Anne looked at him coldly in the eyes and said, "Well, that may be so, Captain… but not with me… not with me."

Upon which, Anne wrenched her arm out of his grip, turned abruptly towards the door, and stormed out of the captain's cabin.

Chapter Three
First Sighting

A loud cry from the crow's nest woke everyone up from their afternoon slumber.

"Ship ahoy to starboard! Ship ahoy to starboard…!"

A sudden rush of heavy feet hammered the main deck. Jack Rackham grabbed his long glass, peered over the horizon and soon spotted a schooner.

"Yeah… Yeah…" he muttered with glee.

"What do you see, Captain?" Pete Atkins hailed from behind the enormous ship wheel.

"Ah! Ha! From her slow speed I fancy she's laden with a sizeable bounty. Gentlemen, I see a feast coming towards us, a feast that's gonna last a good, few days! And you won't get thirsty, gentlemen, for I can already hear the sound of the best Caribbean rum sloshing around in that fat belly of hers! Atkins, Get onto her!"

"Aye, aye, Captain!"

Ned Hornby rushed towards the main mast.

"Shall I hoist the flag, Capt'n?"

"No, not yet. I want to get a closer look first to see who's manning that ship."

It was a well-known ruse for pirates to use government flags in order to approach merchant ships without raising suspicion. This time, however, Rackham knew he would have no need for such a subterfuge for, with his right eye still peering through his long glass, he had already identified his new prey.

"Well, my oh my! If it isn't our old friend Tisdale!"

"You mean the landlord from the *Cock 'n Bull*, Captain?" the quartermaster queried.

"The very same, my man, the very same. Ned, hoist the flag!"

"Which one, Capt'n?"

"My flag!"

Ned Hornby opened the wooden box bolted to the deck next to the main mast, stored away his concertina inside it and hurriedly unfurled a black flag picturing a pair of cutlasses criss-crossed below a ghostly white skull.

Jack Rackham turned to his quartermaster.

"Dave, you're in charge of the lower deck. Indigo John, get your men onto the rigging and let out all the cables ready for boarding!"

Indigo John was a man built like a giant but blessed with the agility of a mountain goat. Following his captain's orders, he waved to his men and together they gathered near the rigging.

"Mark Read, get your men on the stern and Boy Jennings, get yours on the bowsprit!"

Trampling heavily on the wooden deck, the men rushed to their stations. Anne watched the men climb the rigging with the speed of spiders crawling on their webs to retrieve their prey. From the upper deck, she observed with a keen eye Boy Jennings and Mark Read gather their men, telling them where to stand. She felt excited, overwhelmingly so. Her heart pounded hard in her chest. Her hands were trembling with anticipation and clammy with sweat as she braced herself for her first encounter at sea.

"What about me, Captain? Where shall I go?" Anne asked expectantly, cutlass already in hand.

Jack Rackham threw a swift glance at his new recruit.

"Don't ask me... Choose your team!" he told her.

"Aye, Captain!"

Anne rushed along the main deck towards the stern and met up with Mark Read.

"Officer!" she hailed. "You've got one extra man on your team!"
"Well," her companion riled. "I hope you're as good as your bluff!"

***

A few leagues away, at the sight of the Jolly Roger, the merchant ship reacted swiftly. All her sails had now been rigged in an attempt to increase her speed and make good her escape.

"Captain, she's running away!" Dave Ryan shouted.
"I know. I see it. Atkins, quick! Prepare to come about! Indigo John, rig all the sails!"

***

45

The ship made a sharp about turn north-east and began to chase the schooner. Helped by a strong breeze, the *Kingston* pounded the waves, skimming over green lagoons and sunken wrecks festering with nurse sharks. On the deck, the pirates waited at their post with their jaws clenched and their eyes scowling fixedly on their prey. In this tense moment, all that could be heard were the cables whistling, the salty wood creaking and the waves pounding hard on the hull, throwing large sprays of water upon the deck and drenching the pirates as they stood rigidly still.

As the *Kingston* gained on the schooner, the tension grew among the men. Some began fidgeting nervously with their weapons, counting them, checking them and loading them. Standing by the rigging, Indigo John swelled up his chest in nervous anticipation and reached out for a cable to steady himself. On the stern, Mark Read stood erect, his arms folded tightly across his chest, while next to him, Anne stood, legs akimbo, with her fists on her hips and a gleeful smile on her lips.

Still holding his long glass, Jack Rackham kept his eye keenly trained on the schooner.

Suddenly, a loud bang tore through the air and a huge spray of water whooshed a few feet ahead of the ship.

"They're firing at us!" Ned Hornby shouted in panic.

"Shall we fire back, Capt'n?" one of the gunners asked.

"Only if you want to sink the bounty!" the captain replied in a sarcastic tone. "Don't panic, it's only a warning shot. She's running away which means she doesn't want to put up a fight. Indigo John, Boy Jennings, Mark Read! When we board, you and your men, seize the crew and throw them into their own brig. If they fight, fight back but remember, Tisdale is an old mate, so spare him and spare his crew if you can."

"That's not a proper way to fight!" a voice objected.

The captain turned around to find his one female shipmate scowling at him.

"Well, that's how we do things here. We want to stash up treasures, not dead bodies!" he riposted. "If you want blood and proper fights, go and join Black Bart's crew!"

"Black Bart? Who's he?"

As he spoke, the captain kept a wary eye on the other ship, trying to anticipate her next move. He felt sure she would not fire again for she

46

seemed more concerned about keeping her precious cargo intact. Lighter in weight, the *Kingston* was fast catching up on her, taking the wind out of her sails by lining up straight behind her. Before long, the *Kingston* was able to manoeuvre herself beside the schooner, whose sails stood tall and imposing next to them. They were so close now that both crews were able to eyeball each other.

"Men! Get ready to board!"

Leaning against the bulwark, Jack Rackham hailed to the other ship's captain.

"Ahoy, Henry, my friend, I salute you! Good to see business is thriving!"

"Get away from me, Jack Rackham, you thief… and you'd better keep away from my rum!" Henry Tisdale roared.

"Henry, my friend, I've a whole crew dying with thirst and you know your rum is the best in the whole of the Caribbean. Now, let's make a deal!" Rackham bantered jovially.

"You go to hell, Rackham!" Tisdale cursed.

"Be at peace, my friend, we don't want no blood and we don't want no fight," he bartered, detaching every syllable to show that if the repartee was delivered in a light-hearted mood, he was extremely serious in his intentions.

"I tell you what…" he continued. "I help myself to your excellent provisions and rum and we let you go without firing a single shot, what do you say?"

Then turning towards his men, he shouted, "Forward!"

Immediately, the pirates grabbed the ropes and swung on to the other ship's deck where they quickly overpowered the crew. Indigo John seized Tisdale and brought him to the captain, arms locked behind his back.

"You robber! You thief!" Tisdale shouted before spitting at the captain. "You won't get away with it! And don't you dare ever set foot in my tavern again, you damned pirate!"

Jack Rackham flailed his arms in mock disappointment.

"Henry, my friend, that's no way to speak to your best customer! Besides, we don't want to blow you to pieces and we sure don't want to harm your crew. We just want to have a bit of fun. And while we're at it, why don't you join us, hey?"

The pirates laughed.

"Go to hell!" Tisdale cursed again.

"As you wish, my friend, but whether we go to hell or elsewhere, I figure that we'll all be jolly merry when we get there and that'll be all thanks to you!"

The pirates punctuated the captain's remark with loud laughter.

"I'll have your skin one day!" Henry Tisdale swore.

"And I'll have your rum today!" The captain chuckled before turning to his men.

"All right, men!" he shouted. "Put the planks in place and prepare to transfer the barrels and any provisions you can find."

When all the loot had been transferred, Jack Rackham ordered, "Leave them one barrel and some food to keep them going till they reach port."

"No!" a voice protested. "We take everything!"

Visibly surprised at being overruled so blazingly, Rackham jerked his head around. His eyes fell on Bonny who was standing firmly behind him with a mean look upon her face and her cutlass pointing directly towards Tisdale's crew.

"Don't be satisfied with half, take the whole lot I say!"

Rackham took a deep breath and spat back, "I say we've taken enough."

"And I say we take all of it!" Bonny riposted with fire in her eyes.

Rackham inhaled hard and blew furiously through his nostrils. Nobody had ever interfered with his command. He wanted to slap Bonny across the face and bring her to submission, but there was no time for that. He threw a furious look at the contemptuous woman and declared sternly, "You'll do as you're told or I'll throw you on Tisdale's ship so that he can take you himself to the authorities!"

"Forget it!" Tisdale riled. "I'm not having any of your filthy rejects on my ship!"

Ignoring his remark, Rackham ordered, "All right! Everyone back on board! Lift the planks and wave nicely to Mr Tisdale and his most generous crew."

"Hurray! Hurray!" the pirates cheered.

Furious, Tisdale brandished his fist at Rackham and barked, "I'll make you pay for this, Rackham! With your blood or your gold, fear not, I'll make you pay for this!"

The captain received the threat with a loud bout of laughter. Then, with a friendly wave, he bade, "So long, Tisdale my friend! See you back at the *Cock 'n Bull*! In the meantime, we shall drink to your utmost generosity and your good health!" Rackham jeered.

Upon these words, the *Kingston* fled with every inch of canvas open to the wind as the high seas robbers cheerfully waved their scarves, neckerchiefs or handkerchiefs, mocking the stunned crew and singing a few choice words of farewell. Even when his silhouette was close to disappearing, Henry Tisdale could still be seen gesticulating like a mad man and cursing the pirates.

***

Back in Nassau, the robbed innkeeper wasted no time to gain justice. He went straight to the authorities where he reported his ordeal, determined that the Governor of the Island should hear about it. With a bit of luck, he would have them caught and hanged, like all the other sea dogs who had dared pilfer his precious rum!

Meanwhile, oblivious to the looming threat, the *Kingston* sailed merrily away. Ned Hornby resumed his position by the bowsprit and started playing a cheerful song on his concertina while the captain ordered Pete Atkins to set sail for Cove Island.

Before retiring to his cabin for a well-earned rest, the captain threw a tired glance at Hornby and shouted, "Enough of that racket, Ned, I need to rest my head. Take your turn in the crow's nest, and no more singing!"

"Aye, aye, Capt'n, I'll just sing a short one, then."

"No!" the captain protested. "Not even a short one!"

"Oh, go on, Capt'n, just a short one to lull you to sleep, hey?"

"If I hear another sound from you, Ned Hornby, I'll throw your music box to the sharks!"

Vexed, the sailor huffed and puffed and grumbled all the way up to the crow's nest.

***

Moments later, Ned Hornby squeezed his short portly frame inside the crow's nest where, overcome by the effect of the celebratory rum, he soon fell into a heavy slumber.

The rest of the crew were in no better state. Moaning and groaning, they lay about, stretched out on the deck or sitting up against the bulwarks. No one, not even the captain or the quartermaster, seemed in a fit state to do anything, no one… except two shipmates with cunning eyes and shrewd minds, Mark Read and Anne Bonny. Each had quite a different motive to remain sober. Mark Read wanted to hide his share of rum without being seen, while Anne Bonny simply wanted to seduce him.

Making the most of the boat's complete inactivity, Mark Read slunk below deck and hid the rum in the hollow compartment he had carved between the floorboards and the hull. The access was through an invisible panel on the lower side of the ship. Storing his bounty away with the rest of his treasure, he roughly estimated that he had several gold doubloons worth of various merchandises.

Suddenly, he heard some footsteps approaching. Quickly, he replaced the wooden panel and as he struggled to move heavy coils of cables in front of it, Anne appeared.

"What are you doing?" she enquired, craning her neck to see what he was up to.

"These cables are in the way. I'm trying to move them out into this corner."

"Let me help you," she said, noticing his shifty look.

"There's no need. It's done. It'll be all right there," Read replied sharply. "I'm going back on deck; I need some fresh air," he then added.

"Me too," Anne echoed. "But not just yet…"

As they were walking towards the narrow staircase, Anne suddenly turned around and faced her companion. Mark stopped dead in his tracks.

"What's the matter?" he asked, with a quizzical look on his face.

"Mark… Mark…"

As she whispered his name tenderly, Anne grabbed his shirt, pulled him towards her and planted a kiss on his luscious lips. To her shock, instead of relishing this tender moment, Read pushed the woman away from him. Anne stared at him, puzzled.

"Why, Mark? Why won't you let me get close to you?" She sighed.

Unmoved by her doe-eyes and soft whispers, Read remained on his guard.

"You're wasting your time. I'm not interested so get your hands off me!" he blurted out.

"I can't!" Anne answered back in sheer frustration. "Ain't I good enough for you?"

"I said I'm not interested. So keep away from me," Read stated coldly.

"What's wrong with you? They're all queuing upstairs to have me! Why not you?"

"First, there's Rackham! Everyone knows he fancies you…"

"I don't care!" Anne retorted. "He's not gonna go far. He likes rum too much. But you…" she said, looking at Mark with doleful eyes. "I've been observing you… and unlike this bunch of layabouts, you're more with it. You've got your head screwed on proper and if anybody's going to make a fortune out of this business and survive long enough to enjoy it, it'll be you. I like strong men because I want to go far and I won't go very far with him…! But with you…"

"All right, Anne! I think it's time I came clean with you. Give me your hand!"

"My hand? Make up your mind, Mark! One minute you push me away, and the next you want to…"

"Shut up and give me your hand!"

As he spoke, Mark Read grabbed her hand and thrust it against his chest.

"There!" he said.

"What? What are you doing…? Oh my God!" Anne exclaimed.

"That's right!" Mark stated plainly.

"Oh my God!" Anne stuttered in complete shock. "You're… you're a woman too?"

Chapter Four
A Pirate's Story

A month had gone by since Anne first boarded the *Kingston*, under the assumed name of Alan Bonny. She had done so expecting a life full of adventures, excitement and riches. Instead, she discovered that pirates were a ruthless bunch of murderers and pilferers, that their captain was the weakest cog in the wheel and that the only shipmate she was keen to woo turned out to be a woman!

Pondering over her fate, she looked at her mate and asked downhearted, "Why…? Why are you dressed up like a man?"

Her friend could not help but smile.

"I don't know why you're so shocked. You did the very same thing. Remember? You came on board this ship as Alan Bonny."

"Only because I figured that it was the only way I'd get on board."

"Why were you so desperate? Are you on the run from the authorities or something?"

"No, I'm on the run from my husband," Anne confessed with a big sigh.

"I was right then. I knew you were running away from something or somebody…"

"No, you didn't. You don't know anything about me."

"What I mean is… for a young lass like you, with a mind sharp as a knife, I reckoned there's got to be something spectacularly wrong with your life to be running away like this."

"Well, now you know. What about you? Why the disguise? And by the way, you're good, you really look the part."

Read smiled with gratitude this time.

"Same reason as you, probably."

"So… who are you?"

"My real name is Mary Read. I've always dressed up like this, ever since I was little. My mother made me. I had a brother, you see, and my grandmother used to give my mother money towards his upkeep, but the little beggar died, didn't he? My mother didn't seem all that bothered by his death; she was more concerned about losing the income, so she made me take his place. It's all right… I'm used to it; besides, it's good fun and I get to travel and make good money."

"Wow! I can't believe how similar our stories are," Anne exclaimed. "Does anyone else know?"

"Nope, they haven't got a clue! I swear like them, I fight like them and I give as good as I get."

"But…" Anne continued, still bewildered, "how did you end up on the *Kingston*?"

"Trust my luck! I joined the crew of this Dutch man-of-war that was sailing to the West Indies. And then — typical! — no sooner had we got there than we were attacked by pirates who looted the ship. Then they let the crew go…"

"It sounds just like Rackham!" Anne interrupted.

"As a matter of fact, it was him. And that's how I ended up on the *Kingston*."

"But why did they take *you* and nobody else?"

"Because I was the only one who could speak English… Anyway, what was wrong with your husband?"

"In one word… not much of a man!" Anne chuckled.

"That's one word?" Mary teased.

"Okay, it's more than one word but that's what he was… not much of a man…"

There she paused to look at Mary. As the friends faced each other, relaxed and carefree for the first time in months, Anne noticed that Mary's features appeared smoother than ever. Now she understood why everything about her seemed at odds with her adopted gender, the round shoulders that were plump rather than muscular, the waist that seemed too much taken in under her belt, and her smooth skin never grazed by a growing stubble, even first thing in the morning, despite Mary's dark hair. It all made sense now, and Anne could not believe how she had been fooled for so long, considering her own circumstances. After a while, she stopped looking at her friend, rolled her eyes towards the ceiling and sighed with contempt. "My husband was a good for nothing, always drunk or at sea, so he was never there… not that I wanted him around… Anyway, I was so bored that I got myself a job in a tavern which turned out to be the *Cock 'n Bull* and that's how I met Jack Rackham."

"And you're going to stick around with him?"

"Might as well. Where else can I go?"

"He fancies you, you know," Mary intimated.

"He fancies any woman... he's a real man... but I fancied you." She giggled. "However, now that I know who you are, I might try my luck with him."

The two women looked at each other, serious for a moment; then they burst out laughing.

"I wouldn't bother if I were you. I mean... Jack Rackham, he's only a small fish, ain't he? And the way he always lets the crews go... One of these days, one of them's gonna come back and beat him real good."

"Yeah, I know... but I'll take my chances. You should have seen him in the *Cock 'n Bull*... He looked so brash, so strong. He was so much fun to be with then... Now, just look at him, totally wasted. Sometimes I wish I was with Blackbeard."

"Not likely! He's dead!" Mary cut in sharply.

"Is he? So why did Rackham shout his name at me?"

"He didn't. He said *Black Bart*, that's Bartholomew Roberts. Now, *that's* a real man! The best of the lot, I say."

"I'd like to see that... What makes him so good, then?"

"Apparently, he has great self-discipline which he imposes ruthlessly on everyone else sailing on his ship. What's more, he's rumoured never to drink alcohol."

"Not even rum?"

"Never touches the stuff! That way, he always has his wits about him, not like all the other pirates who often fight when they're totally drunk out of their brains."

"Wow! What a man! That's my kind of man."

"Well, don't start getting carried away because you're more likely to meet Black Beard than him!" She chuckled.

"But you told me Black Beard was dead."

"That's what I mean," Mary added with a wry smile. "Black Bart's mainly involved in the slave trade so he sails mostly around the coast of Africa."

"I'd love to meet him, though," Anne replied dreamily.

"Yeah, well... for now, you're stuck with Rackham." As she said this, she smiled and her whole face lit up. Anne Bonny stared at her, letting her thoughts run away with her. Pity she's a woman, she's so handsome. After a pensive pause, she queried tentatively.

"What about you? Have you got a special mate?"

Mary returned her searching stare. She flicked back her unruly mane of long dark hair, exposing her features radiating with love. The heavy frown that she had cultivated to make herself look more masculine had disappeared and her stern expression had melted into a soft glow. Like the rarest black pearls, her dark brown eyes sparkled with mythical wonder. Mesmerised, Anne envied her beauty, her inner peace and serenity. Reading her friend's thoughts, Mary smiled.

"Er… so… You've got plans?" Anne asked coyly, unable to decide how to interpret her friend's enigmatic smile.

"Plans? No, not me. We pirates are a superstitious lot; making plans is tempting fate… it's bad luck… just like learning to swim. I will eventually settle, I know that, though where, I haven't decided yet. I love the sea too much, you see, that's my problem. Whenever I've been on land for a few days, I feel trapped. So, I hang around ports, pacing the quay and itching to get aboard a ship. By then I've passed caring what kind of ship I join; I just want to go, sail away, smell the sea because whenever I stand in the fresh sea breeze, I feel so clean and so free. After the stench of London, the poisonous fog, the grubby buildings and grotty streets, believe you me, the sea is the best place you could ever be, so much light, it's just a wide-open space that makes you dream… I love it."

"So, you're from London?"

"Yeah, but I left home when I was fifteen to be a footboy on a man-of war and I've never been back since… not that I'd want to for that matter."

Suddenly, a voice boomed from the narrow staircase.

"Hey, you two, all hands, on deck, we're heading for Cove Island."

It was Dave Ryan, the quartermaster. The two women jumped on their feet and hailed together, "Aye, we're coming!"

But before she could make another move, Mary stopped Anne.

"Please, don't tell anyone about me."

"You bet I won't. We're mates, ain't we?"

Re-assured, Mary agreed wholeheartedly, "Aye, we're mates… and my name is still Mark Read!"

The two women began to make their way towards the main deck. As they ran towards the steps, Anne felt a strong grip fall on her shoulder.

"Just a minute! I want a word with you."

It was the captain. In a sheer reflex reaction, Anne freed herself with a sharp blow in his ribs.

"What do you want?"

Jack Rackham growled and pushed her in the direction of his cabin. Once there, he slammed the door behind him. He was seething with anger and Anne had to turn her head away to avoid his foul-smelling breath. Rackham ignored her reaction, grabbed her chin, looked at her straight in the eyes and growled, "You're spending too much time with that fellow Read. I've told you before, keep away from him!"

Anne stared back at him defiantly. "Cool it, Jack! He's just a mate."

The captain was getting increasingly agitated with rage. "Drop him or I'll maroon him!"

"That would be a really stupid thing to do! He's your best hand! You said it yourself!" Anne retorted. "There's nothing going on, Jack, but if you don't believe me, ask him to his face!"

"All right, I will!"

Rackham opened the door and yelled, "Read! Come here!"

No sooner had Read stepped into the captain's cabin than he hit her with a direct question.

"So… what's going on between the two of you?"

"Nothing! Absolutely nothing! We're just mates."

"I don't believe you!"

"Well… you'd better had because… I'm a woman too!"

The words hit Rackham like a blow on the head. What was going on? He, the captain, had no idea of the true identity of two members of his crew. Was this some kind of conspiracy? Were they spies on a mission to hunt him down to bring him to justice? As the captain of the *Kingston*, he suddenly felt that instead of whiling the hours away with surplus measures of rum, perhaps he should pay closer attention to his crew. He remained silent for a while, too shocked for words. What about the rest of the crew? How would that superstitious lot react when they discovered that there was not one, but two women on board? In front of him, Anne stared back at him with sheer arrogance, studying his shocked reaction with her arms folded across her chest, and waiting to see what he was going to do about it. The truth of the matter was that Rackham simply had no idea. Unable to find an instant solution which would settle the matter, he paced his cabin nervously, his right hand rubbing his chin as he tried to work out what he should do or say next.

Eventually, he turned to Read and asked, "What's your name?"

"My real name is Mary Read but I'm quite happy to be known as Mark Read. It makes no difference to me," she replied, holding her head high to show that she was in full control of her somewhat irregular situation.

Jack Rackham continued to stare at her, then on the spur of the moment, he reached out for her shirt and peered inside it.

"By the devil's teeth!" he exclaimed. "What're you doing on my ship?"

"Don't you remember? You took me hostage." Mary sneered.

Ignoring her remark, Rackham declared abruptly, "I don't want no trouble… You're gonna have to go!"

"And let your best man go?" Anne interrupted. "Well, you've done some pretty dumb things in your time, but that would be the dumbest of them all! If you get rid of her, you're gonna get caught, Jack Rackham, and mark my word, you're gonna hang!"

The captain turned towards her and ground his teeth, "Well, I suppose, you can stay, but on one condition… as far as everybody is concerned here, you are Mark Read… And no messing about with the rest of the crew, understood?"

"No fear of that, captain!" Mary decreed firmly.

Then the captain turned towards Anne and scowled at her. "And same goes for you, Anne Bonny!"

The young woman pulled a face and scoffed back at him, "Don't you worry yourself, Jack Rackham, I wouldn't have any of them as my dog!"

***

The *Kingston* was now less than an hour away from Cove Island. Bored rigid, the pirates soon reverted to their old ways. Knowing that the captain was yet again out of sight and probably comatose on his berth, they started playing cards, using for stakes handfuls of groats or their share of rum. Up in the crow's nest, Ned Hornby risked singing another tune while down below the pirates' voices began to rise louder and louder. Unwilling to take part in the illicit activities, Mark Read sat alone, on the prow of the ship, in a stubborn silence that made the other shipmates all the more wary of him.

Suddenly, the lone pirate heard a commotion coming from the main deck. He turned his head and saw Boy Jennings involved in a heated argument with another pirate.

"I didn't cheat. You cheated!" he blurted out.

"No, you did, I saw you! That card never came out of your pack, it came out of your belt!" Freddie Main barked back.

"You're calling me a liar?"

"Stop it, you two!" Angus MacDonald intervened. "You're gonna wake up the capt'n!"

"You owe me!" Main growled menacingly.

"I don't owe you anything!" Boy Jennings riposted. "You're the one who cheated!"

"You owe me ten groats and I'll get them, even if I have to fight you for it."

"Well, fight it will be!" Boy Jennings pledged defiantly.

At the sound of this, Read panicked. Boy Jennings was only a young lad. A clash of iron with Freddie Main, that bulldog of a brute, twice his weight, was sure to finish him. In the middle of the affray, Ned Hornby's voice shouted, "Land ho! We're approaching Cove Island!"

Anxious, Read jumped on his feet and made straight for the captain's cabin. He banged loudly on the door.

"Captain! Captain! They're fighting. You've got to stop them!"

After a short silence, a sleepy voice enquired from behind the door, "Who's fighting?"

"Freddie Main's challenged Boy Jennings to a fight. He's gonna kill him, I know it! We've got to stop him, Captain," he pleaded.

"Stop who?" the voice replied, mildly concerned.

"Freddy Main, of course! Captain, you've got to stop the fight."

Eventually, the captain opened the door. "Well, calm down, they can't fight until we get ashore anyway. That's the rule," he declared calmly.

"They don't care! They're still gonna fight!"

"Good. That young lad Jennings could do with more practice. He's still too heavy on his feet."

"But he's sure to get killed by that dog Main!"

"There are no dogs on my ship!" the captain remonstrated. "Anyway, why should you care if Jennings gets killed?" he asked with a cryptic smile.

Realising that he was not going to get anywhere with the captain, Read threw a dark look at him, turned on his heels abruptly, and rushed back onto the main deck. There, he made straight for the reviled pirate and blurted, "You're a liar, a murderer and a cheat!"

Freddie Main turned around to see who was addressing him in such insulting terms, and when he saw Mark Read, he burst out laughing. Calling out to his mates, he chortled. "You know, sometimes I wonder what kind of crew I've joined. By the look of Read and Jennings, I sometimes feel I must be on some kind of nursery ship or something. I mean, look at them two, still wet behind the ears and not long off their mothers' nipples..." Then drawing his cutlass, he pointed it at Read's lips and mocked, "See, there's still milk dripping from your lips, lad..."

Read drew his pistol.

"Don't you make fun of me or I'll blow your brains out!"

Changing his aggressive tone to a softer one, Freddie Main gently tapped the pistol with his cutlass.

"Sweetheart, I thought I'd tell you... it's not loaded yet..." He chortled.

A loud burst of laughter punctuated his remark.

"All right!" Read shouted. "You think you're better than me, don't you? Well, let's put you to the test! I challenge you to a fight on land."

Freddie Main laughed again. "Sorry, sonny boy, I've already got an appointment with Master Jennings here."

"I don't care. I'll fight you first and I'll fight you good!" Read vouched forcefully.

"As you please, me lad, as you please... Now, if you don't mind, I've got a game to finish."

Read threw himself at him and grabbed him by the scruff of the neck. "You're gonna fight me or else..."

Main retaliated with a powerful swipe of the arm that sent Read crashing onto the deck. "Never fear, sonny, I'll fight you all in good time... and I'll fight you to the death!"

Having said this, he spat on the deck, readjusted his shirt and belt, and went back to his game.

***

Moments later, the *Kingston* dropped anchor close to the shore. The captain came out of his cabin and went straight onto the main deck to give his orders to land. The cockboat was lowered into the sea and minutes later, Freddie Main stepped ashore closely followed by his mates.

A spell on land was always a welcome break from the constant tension at sea. Whether he had apprehension or fear in his belly, Freddie Main did not let it show, and for now, the pirate was busy chatting away in a light-hearted mood, bantering loudly with his other mate, Dennis Macarty. Together, they boasted about the shares they had received from the last raid. Feeling in a jokey mood, they hailed Bennett, a simpleton, and asked him what he had got the last time round, knowing full well what the answer would be. Clearly embarrassed, Bennett dropped his head, jutted his jaw and curled his lips before answering, "A frock!"

Once again, the pirates rolled with laughter while at the same time holding on to their sides and complaining, "My ribs hurt!"

Digging for remains of his pride and self-esteem, Bennett emitted a sarcastic giggle and grimaced back at them.

"All silk, mind! Of the finest silk!" he added, keen to upgrade the derisory value of his useless prize.

Then the conversation, as always, turned to rum, and more to the point, when they would next get it. They were becoming more rowdy, frustrated and impatient, and wanted to celebrate here and now, and not when the captain would be sober enough to land and stand on his own two feet.

As for Freddie Main, he had already decided what he was going to do with his share of things. Upon his return to Nassau, he would make straight for the *Cock 'n Bull*, and enjoy the full pleasures of life holding a girl in one hand and a glass of rum in the other. As he bantered more, rubbing his hands with gleeful expectation, he suddenly felt a sharp prod in his back. He jerked his head around frowning angrily, ready to challenge whoever dared trouble his peace. Mark Read was standing a few paces behind him with a cutlass in one hand and a pistol in the other.

"Not now, lad…" Main growled dismissively.

Read lunged towards him and blasted in his face, "Now I say!"

Freddie Main glared at his challenger before pushing him out of the way. He muttered to himself, incomprehensible sounds that blew out of his mouth like clouds of spit coming out of an enraged bull. Then, he glared at Read again with his fists clenched in anger.

"And I said not now!" the ruffian barked back.

Read ignored the rebuke and instead of walking away, he squared himself up to his foe and threatened, "You take one more step and I shoot!"

Main stopped dead in his tracks. For a few seconds, he said and did nothing. Then, all of a sudden, he swivelled on his feet and wielded his cutlass.

"Arrgh!" he roared, charging towards Read.

Immediately, the other shipmates ran into the nearby trees for cover, knowing that loose shots were often the cause of much injury.

From there, they watched Freddie Main and Mark Read cross swords, with Read still holding on to his pistol. At first, Main seemed to have the upper hand over his more agile assailant. As luck would have it, he had spotted, in the sand right behind Read, a large dead branch. Using the force of his formidable arms, he drove his adversary closer and closer towards it. Feeling invincible, he was now grinning with the smell of victory already twitching his nostrils. Just as he expected, Read stumbled over the piece of wood and fell backwards, letting go of his cutlass and pistol.

Immediately, Main lifted his cutlass with both hands and harked, "Pity you had to die so young!"

Read saw the blade flash into his eyes and thought that his last moment had come. But he was not ready to die; this was not his fate, nor his destiny. Something urged him to react, a cry from the head or perhaps from the heart, so he rolled quickly onto his side, grabbed his pistol and shot Freddie Main at point blank range. The shot hit the pirate right under the chin. The force of the blow shattered part of his skull and splattered bits of his brain onto the warm sand. The pirate's body froze, his eyes fixed into the void and his mouth opened wide, howling a silent scream as an unstoppable flow of scarlet blood poured down his throat. Read scrambled quickly out of the way, and with his mouth baying, he watched Freddie Main's body crumble down onto the dead branch, where it lay, silent and still. Stunned, Read dared not move. Then he got up slowly, unable to take his eyes off the inert body, expecting it to bounce back and slay him on the spot.

Around him, nothing moved, not even the branches of palm trees which normally swayed gently into the sea breeze. In the stony silence echoed the smooth lapping of the ocean waves cascading onto a beach, deaf and dumb to the poignant dramas that were brutally acted out upon its very shore. Standing still, Read looked around, expecting men to come out from all corners of the beach, but there was not a soul around. Everything stood still. Then, he began to hear something. He pricked up his ears. It was the gradual sound of hesitant steps crunching the hot sand as men emerged from everywhere to come and gawp at the scene.

***

Boy Jennings had watched the whole fight from the ship's deck with his hands clasped nervously onto the bulwark. Standing next to him, hands on hips, the captain eyed him peculiarly. He suspected that something was up between Jennings and Read despite never having seen them together. He muttered some thoughts to himself. Why would Read want to risk his life by fighting against a brute of a man like Freddie Main unless it was to protect Boy Jennings? He wondered and wondered more. Then he turned towards Anne who, pre-empting his question, declared quite flatly, "Don't ask me, Jack, I know nothing."

Chapter Five
Battle at Sea

Cove Island lay above water like a bleary eye in the crooked head of Eleuthera, a long and narrow strip of land which curled around its small neighbour like a large sea snake slumbering just above the water mark. Hidden from view and sheltered from the open sea, Cove Island was invisible to the naked eye for its thick vegetation shaded by clusters of tall palm trees blended perfectly with the rugged contours of Eleuthera. Jack Rackham had stumbled upon it quite by chance when looking for Blackbeard's lost treasures reputed to be buried on the island. Finding the place deserted of all human life, he had decided there and then to make it his base. Like a retriever with a good nose for lost treasures, he was determined to get his hands on those old and battered sea chests, and nothing, not even the bad luck that went with having two females aboard his ship, would distract him away from his goal.

When the captain finally landed on Cove Island, followed by Bonny and Boy Jennings, he was met by several shipmates advancing slowly towards him. They looked angry, thirsting for revenge. Slowly, they formed a semi-circle around him with their cutlasses and pistols in hand. The captain had to think fast to appease his men for he knew that his next move would decide whether he would remain captain or be dealt with swiftly to join Freddie Main in his grave. Behind him, Bonny and Boy Jennings had already reacted by drawing their own cutlasses.

Remaining as calm as possible, Rackham raised his arms and declared, "All right, men, I understand how you feel. We've lost a friend and one of the most stalwart members of our crew. However, whatever happens to us, life goes on, but only if we let it. So, let's bury Freddy, pray for his soul and get on with our lives…"

There, Rackham paused to scan his men's faces and study their reactions, hoping that they were with him rather than waiting to slay him.

"So, Mackay and Bennett, get the shovels. Once the matter is settled, we'll be able to move on to the important business of sharing the rum and the loot! We all deserve a break, and we might as well make it a merry one."

The men did not respond. Their aggressive stance stood firm. Eyeing each other, trying to detect a hint of a complicitous sign, they remained silent, rigid with their teeth clenched and their fists clasped tightly around their weapons. The crippling suspense could not last. Someone had to make the first move… and someone did.

"Aye, aye, Capt'n! Let's get on with it. I'm getting thirsty!"

All eyes turned towards the man who had just spoken, darting the same vengeful looks reserved only for traitors. It was Ned Hornby.

"Aye! I'm getting thirsty too!" Indigo John echoed.

His cry was followed by the rest of the men. The captain, hugely relieved, shouted in turn, "Come on, lads, let's get down to business!"

Immediately after Freddy Main's burial, the captain gathered his most trusted hands and together they dragged the stolen cargo onto the beach. At the sight of it, the pirates instantly regained their good humour. They formed a tight circle around the captain, pushing and shoving each other to have a better view of the bounty; and there they stood, wide-eyed and mouth gaping, their hands shaking with greed. Growling with impatience, they watched the captain unpack a quantity of coins, some of them gold; silver watches and other pieces of jewellery, many of them encrusted with precious stones; boxes of silk stockings, refined clothing, lace hats and other valuable merchandise. As was the custom, the captain passed the dice around so that whoever threw the highest number could get the first pick. It now came to Stan Bennett's turn. The pirates mocked and jeered as they speculated on his likely prize.

"Hey, Bennett, what do you want this time? Silk stockings or a pretty hat to go with your beautiful frock?"

Roars of laughter broke out as the hapless pirate stalked away with an exquisite pair of pantaloons.

As the game of luck proceeded, two of the pirates who had already collected their prizes sneaked quietly away and climbed into the rowing boat to return to the ship. One was Mark Read and the other Boy Jennings and together, they quickly off-loaded Read's secret stash of wealth to transport it somewhere private on the island. And while this was going on, their mates, unaware of their missing colleagues, counted and compared their shares before celebrating raucously with the help of Ned Hornby and his concertina, and copious measures of rum.

Soon however, their stomachs began to ache for food, so they staggered about the island firing wildly at anything that moved while others collected pieces of driftwood and dead branches to build a campfire on the beach.

As the flames crackled and sparks flew into the sultry sky, the pirates sat on the beach toasting their good luck and their good fortune. The evening rolled on, with many of them lying about on the beach, unable to enjoy the spectacular sunset that blended the turquoise sea into the blazing red sky. And while their merry voices and loud snores drowned out the exotic songs of roosting birds, the sun sank into the ocean, turning the island shadows into thick black contours silhouetted against the flaming colours of the crepuscular sky.

Not far from the campfire, Ned Hornby sat against a palm tree with his concertina resting idly in his lap. He was snoring. Around him, noises of people moving furtively through the bushes failed to awake him. Every now and then, moving shadows were caught in the moonlight and soft whispers rose and died away in the warm breeze. A small group of die-hard pirates did not care if it was getting rather late. All they wanted to do was to carry on celebrating. One of them, spotting Ned Hornby slumped against a palm tree, threw a piece of driftwood at his head.

"Hey, Ned!" Jonas Crabtree shouted. "Come and join us. We want to drink and be merry, but we can't do that without the happy wailing of your most revered concertina. Come on, get yourself here!"

Ned Hornby woke up with a start. He looked on the ground to see what had hit him, then around him to see if he could catch the culprit.

"Come on, Ned. I wanna dance!" Crabtree insisted.

As he spoke, the pirate stood up, shook out his newly acquired silk frock and started dancing around the campfire with his limp partner, urging everyone to join him.

Back at the tree, Ned Hornby moaned and grumbled something under his breath.

"Hey, Ned!" someone else shouted. "What about your favourite song, *Would you like to squeeze my concertina…*"

"Naaah… I only sing that one to the ladies," he replied grudgingly.

The whole gathering burst into laughter.

The dancing pirate hailed, "But I've got one! Right here!" he joked, parading in his new frock. Then he burst into an impromptu song.

Will you dance with me tonight?

In your silk ribbons and tights
I may have had too much to drink
But I'll give you a diamond ring
And hope you'll stay by my side
To forever be my wife.

Roars of laughter followed the little ditty, with some of the pirates rolling in the sand clutching their sides.

***

After a few days of continuous merriment, the pirates began to get itchy feet again. On one particular afternoon, it fell upon Indigo John to stand at the top of the small hill to look out for passing ships. As he was busy scanning the horizon, he suddenly caught something white in the tail of his eye. Immediately, he narrowed his eyes to better focus on the large object now gliding over the horizon. He had not been mistaken. There she was, in full sail, a French man-of-war.

"Ship ahoy! Ship ahoy!" he shouted, running down the hill pointing north-east.

Immediately, men rushed in from all directions, ran to the top of the hill and concealed themselves among the trees to take a better look at the man-of-war without being seen.

The captain fetched his long glass as the pirates crowded around him.

"What a beauty!" he exclaimed in admiration. Then, after a short pause, he calculated, "She's going east which means… By the devil's teeth! I swear she's fully laden with priceless treasures. This could well be our best catch yet…! Right, men, I reckon there's a huge bounty in her fat belly. We're gonna go after her and by tomorrow morning, we're all gonna be rich! But…" He paused to check that everyone was listening. "But…" he repeated emphatically, "it's not gonna be easy. She's well-armed and she's probably got a crew twice the size of ours, so we're gonna have to be brave and fight with all our might to win her!"

"Are we going for the ship as well?" Indigo John queried.

"Well, it will depend how we come out of it, won't it?"

Standing next to the captain, Dave Ryan, the quartermaster, remained circumspect.

"We can't," he muttered, betraying his doubts.

"Can't what?" the captain cut abruptly.

"We can't go after her, Captain. She's too big... She'll blow us to tinder."

The captain studied his quartermaster briefly and mocked, "Losing your nerve, hey?"

"Nope, but I want to live long enough to enjoy my loot."

Suddenly, a commanding voice heckled from behind them. "What are you scared of? You've done it before when you captured that Dutch man-of-war. And I should know... I was on that ship!" the voice declared with bravado.

All turned towards the man who had spoken so brazenly, only to see Mark Read standing there, legs akimbo, looking at them with contempt.

"He's right! We can't let her go," Anne Bonny conceded.

"You're such a blood-thirsty lot you are!" Dave Ryan riled.

"Not really, but we want the good life and that's the quickest way we're gonna get it!" Anne spat back.

The captain raised both his arms.

"All right, enough arguing! Let's take a vote on it," he decreed. "How many of you think we should go after her?"

After a show of hands, the numbers were equally divided. The captain rubbed his chin while he thought of another way to settle the matter. At that moment, one of the pirates spotted Boy Jennings returning from a call of nature.

"Jennings!" he called. "We need your vote. See that man-of-war over there? Do we go after her or not?"

Boy Jennings was undecided. He had been enjoying the prolonged break and did not feel hungry enough to return to battle just yet. He looked at Read who gave him no indication as to which way he should vote. Anne did it instead.

"'Course you want to go after her, don't you?"

"Let him speak! We want *his* vote, not yours!" Dennis Macarty barked.

Boy Jennings looked at the expectant faces around him before finally declaring his vote.

"Of course," he agreed. Then, feeling that his answer sounded rather feeble and weak, he repeated it but this time with gusto. "Aye! Of course we should go after her! What are we waiting for?"

"Yeah! Yeah!" the pirates cheered.

"Right, men, get ready to leave and let's go! And don't take too much stuff with you, we want plenty of space on board to store the next cargo." the captain cautioned.

"Aye, aye, Captain!"

***

When all the men were safely back on board, the captain swiftly gave his orders.

"Indigo John! Dave Ryan! Boy Jennings! Mark Read! At your stations! Bonny, you go with Boy Jennings! And remember, lads, no more rum 'til we've got her! Anyone caught drinking will forfeit his share, is that clear?"

"Aye, aye, Captain!"

***

Unable to tear himself away from the magnificent sight of the French man-of-war in full sail, Jack Rackham lingered on, leaning against the bulwarks. He was already sizing up his prize and, unbeknown to his men, plotting out his future, a future which did not include them. Should the attack be successful and the hoard bountiful, he reckoned, this would be his last sortie as a lawless pirate. Soon, he would be able to lay down his plans and woo Anne to come with him. Once back in Nassau, they would sell on most of their prizes, except for the jewels. He was even contemplating selling the *Kingston* — probably to his quartermaster who was keen to take over as captain — and escaping to Europe where he would travel to Scotland, and style himself as Laird of the Castle. But first, he would have to change his identity, throw away his colourful pants and start to dress and behave like a proper gentleman. He was in luck there for Anne would be able to help him in his social transformation as her father, he had learnt, was a gentleman of the law. What irony, he chortled to himself before putting away his long glass. Anne willing, the lawless pirate could end up with a lawyer as a father-in-law. The thought made him smile, until his gaze veered back onto the man-of-war, and in his fiery eyes he no longer saw an enemy ship set to be plundered recklessly but the fulfilment of a dream he had not dared imagine until now.

His trail of thoughts was suddenly interrupted by Ned Hornby who shouted above his head, "Capt'n! Shall I hoist the flag?"

"Aye! I want those sea wolves to see who they're dealing with and the sooner they react, the sooner we'll be rich!"

***

Several leagues away, the captain of the French man-of-war observed keenly the looming threat. The sloop flying the Jolly Roger with downright arrogance looked derisory in size in comparison with his own ship. Looking through his long glass, Captain Etienne consulted with his officers.

"She's only small, not a real threat. We've got far more cannons, and with the wind blowing west-east, if we move on her starboard side, the wind will push her towards us, making it easier for us to fire at her and more difficult for her to escape."

His officers concurred. Furthermore, they had taken note of the ensign on the flag and they knew exactly whose it was. In the hierarchy of high seas robbers, Jack Rackham rated as a mediocre pirate, a poor leader with slack discipline on board his ship. He would be an easy enemy to fend off and at this moment, the French commander's main concern was simply to engage in a battle that would keep the structural damage to a minimum. He knew Rackham to be a wanted man and he was as anxious as anyone else to rid these waters of his malevolent presence. Following the motto of his ship '*The brave will conquer*', he ordered his gunners to get the cannons ready.

***

Meanwhile, barely three leagues away, the *Kingston* was cruising fast to narrow the distance between the two ships.

"When do we start firing, Captain?" Boy Jennings asked in nervous anticipation.

"When you begin to see the letters of her name on her prow."

"But she'll be on us by then, Captain; why not before?"

"Because if you do, they'll fire straight back and being the bigger ship, they're not gonna miss us, are they? Whereas with our smaller cannons, if we retaliate, we'll probably miss her by a mile."

The French man-of-war's impressive sight often had the effect of frightening off small bounty hunters... but emboldened by a string of easy victories, Jack Rackham was at this moment feeling invincible. As they sailed perilously close to their prey, his men could hear the French officers shouting orders in a language the pirates did not understand. Meanwhile, Captain Jack Rackham had just deciphered the name on the man-of-war's prow, *L'Aventure.*

Suddenly, his men spotted a cloud of smoke and soon after, two cannonballs landed close to the ship with a loud whoosh on their starboard side, rocking The *Kingston* violently. Inside her, the pirates roared menacingly, holding onto the rigging and wielding their weapons. Others cursed and shouted, gesticulating wildly while propped up against the bulwarks.

The two ships were now extremely close. The French captain ordered his gunners to fire a broadside. Seconds later, cannon balls crashed through the bulwarks and decks of the *Kingston*. A few injured pirates littered the main deck. Above them, Indigo John was still in command of the rig; Pete Atkins was holding on firmly at the helm and Dave Ryan continued firing not far from Boy Jennings. Never far from the action, Both Bonny and Read stood on the top deck, on either side of Rackham, waiting for the call to launch the assault.

The ships stood dangerously close, with both crews firing blindly at each other. Above the uproar, the captain and his quartermaster shouted orders as fast as the pistols were fired. Soon, the air was filled with the acrid smell of gunpowder, and a thick yellowish fog enveloped the ship. Ignoring the dangers of being shot and killed, the pirates jeered and postured as they waited to storm *L'Aventure.*

As the ships came within boarding range, the French commander ordered the ceasefire for he planned to capture the pirates alive. His men were lined up on the main deck with their muskets ready to fire. The two hulls were practically touching. As soon as Captain Etienne shouted his command to board the enemy ship, Jack Rackham responded in kind. "Get the planks ready for boarding!"

The men on the rigging threw grenades and stinkpots before swinging towards the enemy's deck. Even before they had landed, they fired their pistols. The French crew retaliated instantly with murderous volleys from muskets and rifles. Several men fell to the deck, mortally wounded. Mark Read and Anne Bonny jumped on the main deck, fighting side by side. Together, they cut their way through the French sailors. Indigo John led the charge on the upper deck in his attempt to capture the French commander, but as they reached the stairs, the enemy discharged their pistols at them. A scream tore through the acrid smoke and Indigo John tumbled down on top of his men, shot in the head. His place was swiftly taken by his best mate, Richard Parry from the Valleys, whose bloodshot eyes saw redder than the blood spewing out of the French officers' wounds.

"Storm the deck!" Rackham shouted.

Richard Parry fired his pistol with one hand and thrust at the enemy with his cutlass with the other. Bonny was still fighting ferociously alongside Read, and together they slashed their way through the press of French sailors. Their pistols empty, they now fought with just daggers and cutlasses. In the midst of the battle, Read spotted Rackham on the upper deck, holding the French commander in an arm lock. Using the thick smoke for cover, the two female pirates raced towards the stairs, but immediately, their path was blocked by more soldiers. They threw a complicitous glance at each other. Roaring with all the fire in their lungs, they threw themselves at the enemy with all their might. The French seemed unbeatable. Regardless, Bonny fought like a tigress. Suddenly, she felt a searing pain in her upper arm. The shock of the blow paralysed her momentarily and she collapsed on the deck. From the upper deck, Jack Rackham shouted for someone to go to the women's aid. Boy Jennings heard the command. He grabbed a rope and swung above the French sailors' heads, cutting down two sailors who were about to slay the pair. Read and Jennings quickly grabbed Bonny and withdrew back to their ship, dodging blades and bullets on the way. Finally, with a cutlass pressed against his neck, the French Commander asked for quarter. Immediately, Jack Rackham shouted at the men below to stop the fight.

The clatter of clashing irons gradually stopped and soon, all that could be heard were the groans of injured men.

"Right, gather the prisoners!" Rackham shouted to his men.

"What do you want us to do with them?" Richard Parry enquired.

"Put them on the *Kingston*, she's so damaged there's no point in keeping her. We'll swap her for this one, that way we don't even have to move the loot."

"Aye, but we've got to move ours!" Read hailed from the bulwarks.

"Do it now, then, and as fast as you can!" the captain ordered. Then, turning to Captain Etienne, he asked, "Have you got a doctor on board?"

The French commander remained defiantly silent.

"Your silence is worth nothing!" Rackham sneered into the Frenchman's face. "If you've got one, we'll find him…!" Then, addressing Boy Jennings and Read, Rackham barked, "You two, go below deck and see if there's anybody down there!"

"Aye, aye, Captain!"

The French Commander watched his men being herded together and transferred onto the *Kingston* in a resolute silence. He reeled at the sheer stupidity of a pirate who was about to let him and his crew go free, albeit on a damaged ship but nevertheless still in one piece. Rather than feeling vanquished, he smirked at the pirate, at the foolishness of his actions, and vouched that, should they ever have to cross swords again, there would be no mercy.

Rackham pushed the French commander onto the main deck and tied him to the main mast; then he, together with Jennings and Read, left to inspect what lay below deck. They proceeded along a narrow corridor and came to a door which they threw open. There, in front of them, a well-dressed man was sitting calmly at a small bureau. The French naval officer turned towards the threesome. Still holding a quill in his hand and without a hint of fear in his eyes, he calmly declared, "*Je suis le docteur.*"

"Good, we need you up there," the captain said. Then turning towards Jennings and Read, he ordered, "You two, you go and help him tend to the wounded."

Chapter Six
The Last Sortie

Once the inspection was completed, Captain Jack Rackham returned to the main deck and walked up to the French commander who was still tied to the main mast.

"I'm gonna make a deal with you," he said. "We let you go with all your men…" At this point, Jack Rackham looked around the deck and added, "Well, I mean, those with life still in them… You can have our ship… I know she's damaged but she's fit enough to take you back to port… and I'll even give you provisions and rum to last you the journey. In return, you go back to Nassau, see the Governor, plead for us, like, say we were forced to become pirates, and ask if he'll grant us a pardon, to me Captain Jack Rackham and to all me mates here."

Through his thick French accent, the Commander replied, "*Zat's an audacious request considering wat you have done to us. I sink zat favour is wors more zan a ship zat's just a wreck…*"

"All right, what else do you want?"

"*Ze bales of cotton next to ze barrels of rum.*"

"The bales of cotton?" the captain asked, surprised. "Is that all?"

"*Yes, just zat.*"

Rackham gave a peculiar glance at the French officer but still proceeded to untie him before shouting, "Ryan, Jennings, Hornby, get some men to help you transfer the bales of cotton onto the *Kingston*! And yes, get the French crew to help as well!"

"How many bales are there?" Ned Hornby queried, always shy of hard work.

"It doesn't matter, just do it!" the captain shouted back impatiently.

At that moment, Read and Jennings glanced at each other and breathed a sigh of relief. Their secret stash had already been transferred ashore in a secret cave that only *they* knew of.

***

Later that day, the *Kingston* limped back to the port of Nassau while the pirates on board their new ship began to celebrate in earnest on their way back to Cove Island. Unbeknown to them, far from feeling wretched and defeated, Captain Etienne had watched his own ship sail away with a wry grin on his face. Noting his curious expression, one of his officers accosted him.

"Commander?" he asked. "Why did you insist on keeping the bales of cotton?"

Captain Etienne looked straight in the eyes of his Second in Command and replied, "That, Officer, is a matter between myself and the King. In the meantime, they'll make good bunks for the men. By the way, have you done a headcount?"

"Not yet, Commander."

"Well, get on with it then."

The officer swiftly departed to carry out the task. Alone again, Captain Etienne surveyed the state of the ship from the upper deck. The sails were badly torn, and parts of the bulwarks had been ripped apart. As long as there was no sudden storm, she would easily make it back to port. His gaze eventually rested on the bales of cotton that had been left on the main deck and he smiled again at the sight of them. Only *he* knew that buried deep inside them, lay hidden sixty gold watches, strings of pearls, precious jewels, and a large quantity of gold doubloons, some of which he had intended to use to pay his crew.

As soon as he landed in Nassau, Captain Etienne made his way to Government House where he requested an audience with the Governor on a matter of the utmost urgency. Governor Woodes Rogers brushed his gilded overcoat, checked his rush collar and cuffs, and greeted the French Commander warmly. In his eyes, whoever was not a pirate was deemed to be an ally. As soon as he met Captain Etienne, he felt even more confident that the fight against pirates could be won, but they had to act fast. He immediately called for one of his most trusted officers, Captain Barnet, and together they discussed the place, the timing and the tactics with which to catch the villains.

Time was pressing as the French Commander was anxious to return to his men, so he came straight to the point. He told of the attack, named the pirates responsible, and far from fulfilling his side of the bargain, he described them as murderers and tyrants, thirsting as much for their blood as they were for their cargo. During the lengthy account of the battle, Governor Rogers listened attentively to every detail and nodded appreciatively every time Captain Etienne gave a piece of information that would help capture the villains. At the end of the meeting, the Governor thanked the French Commander heartily, promising to arrange for a handsome reward to be paid and offering to repair the *Kingston* on his behalf. On that last point however, while expressing his utmost gratitude, Captain Etienne felt obliged to decline the Governor's offer. Indeed, as a point of honour and pride, never ever would a French Commander want to be seen sailing back to France on board a pirate ship.

The following day, the Governor dispatched Captain Barnet to ready two sloops to go and seek out the wanted men. The word of an imminent attack against pirates spread like wildfire and soon, the port of Nassau was heaving with curious onlookers keen to glean the latest gossip, and with sailors eager to seize a chance for glory.

Captain Barnet put his officers in charge of recruiting each hand. He told them to be swift and pick every available man, regardless of their status. With his crew complete, he stood on the upper deck and peered pensively at the ocean. The weather was calm and the sky clear of clouds. A light breeze swept over the harbour, cooling the spirits and ardour of minds and men.

Now the ships were ready, and as Captain Barnet signalled to his sister ship to prepare to leave, he smiled with gleeful anticipation at the prospect of catching, once and for all, that murderous bunch of high sea robbers.

***

Meanwhile, just off Cove Island, a man-of-war lulled nonchalantly on the calmest of waters. Most of the men stumbled onto the beach, with only a small handful choosing to remain on board. The rum had already been shared out and the men sang and drank to their hearts' content. Many hours later, after they had tired their lungs out and lost control of their drinking arms, those on the beach sought shelter underneath palm trees to avoid the scorching sun while those left on the ship retreated inside the hull. Among them, Ned Hornby, who had so far remained sober simply because it was not possible to play the concertina while holding a mug full of rum, was now quenching his thirst copiously. Soon, the last line of a cheerful sea shanty died away on his mumbling lips as his head slowly came to rest on his deflated chest. Presently, the only sound to be heard was the gentle lapping of the sea mixed with the feeble groans of men too drunk to speak and with heads too heavy to sleep. *The life of a pirate is a short but merry one* and that was the fate all seemed determined to embrace, except…

Amidst the utter chaos, three shipmates had kept their heads very much together. Bonny, Read and Boy Jennings had chosen to remain on the ship and from the prow, they contemplated a scene of sheer decadence. It had been two days since the storming of *L'Aventure* and they prayed that no enemy ship would come to disturb their peace for none of the men, not even the captain, was sober enough to take action or control of the ship. From afar, Anne scoured the beach in search of Captain Rackham. Together, they had shared hopes and dreams. Alas, in his hour of glory, he looked a small figure of a man, staggering about and swaying on his feet. Aye, she recalled overhearing, he had his sea legs on land again. She could hear him laugh and sing and hail the others to join him in toasting their good luck and good fortune. She reflected on thoughts she had shared with her companions. Mark Read was right, without his wits about him, Rackham was not worth a groat. The glowing future he had whispered in her ears was too often shrouded in alcoholic fumes. By contrast, in her mind, everything was clear, crystal clear and nowhere did Captain Rackham feature in her plans.

A new life awaited her, just hours, minutes away even, if only the captain would get a grip and exert the self-control and discipline he required to steer his ship away from trouble. With the treasures she had stashed away, she was close to fulfilling her dream of a peaceful and independent life, away from the misery of a pirate life at sea. Suddenly a thought came to her.

"You know… why don't we just leave them to it and go?"

Mark Read and Jennings stared at her quizzically.

"You mean *leave*… Now? With the ship and all?" Read asked.

"Aye!" Anne replied brazenly.

"We can't do that!" Jennings protested.

"Why not? We've got enough loot on board to start a new life somewhere. Is that not what we all wanted?"

Read seemed undecided. She looked at Anne, then at Jennings and said, "We could I suppose. We've got more than we need…"

"No way!" Jennings cut in. "It's their loot as much as ours!" he cried out, pointing towards the beach. "They risked their lives to get it. There is no way we can take it from them!"

"They won't know… they're all drunk!" Anne sneered.

Jennings squared himself in front of her and declared forcefully, "I won't let you do it!"

But Anne remained defiant. "There's three of us, Jennings! The more time we waste arguing, the less chance we have to get away!"

"I'm not going! And without me you won't be able to sail the ship," Jennings decreed, crossing his arms firmly across his chest.

Anne turned to her mate. "Mary," she begged. "This is our best chance. Surely, you must see it? Most of them have already got their loot hidden on the island anyway! We're never going to have an opportunity like this again. What do you say?"

Mary shook her head firmly. "No, Anne, Jennings's right. We can't run away and leave them. Quite besides that, *L'Aventure* is too big a ship for us to sail her alone. We need a full crew."

Anne shrugged her shoulders. "I'm disappointed in you two. I thought you were different, smarter than the rest of them. But you're not, really. You're just like them, like that Freddie Main who couldn't fight without his gang propping him up against the bulwarks. Well, mark my word; one day, you're both going to regret this, you're going to regret the chance you had to get away from those growling dogs to start a new life somewhere nice, in some faraway place where we won't be hunted down."

"You're making a shameful display of yourself, Anne. We are not traitors, and we won't betray our mates. But what you've shown us right now, is that we cannot trust you, and that's a terrible shame," Jennings decreed.

"All right, all right, forget I said anything!" Anne conceded.

"It's too late anyway!" Jennings stated. "We've got company."

The women turned their heads at the same time towards the sea and immediately spotted two sloops sliding across the horizon. At first, the sight of the small ships gave them no cause for concern but just in case, they remained alert, following the ships' movements with a keen eye. Anne went to the captain's cabin to fetch his long glass and soon returned onto the deck. She felt uneasy. These were probably not pirate ships as all pirates tended to operate independently from each other. Only merchant or government ships had more than one ship on the move for protection and safety. Having started his career in the King's Navy, Boy Jennings was all too aware of it and warned his shipmates who both replied that they knew that too. Standing on the prow, they suddenly observed the sloops make a sharp about turn and set sail straight towards them. The three pirates tensed up. Anne looked again through the long glass and suddenly exclaimed, "By the devil's teeth! They're preparing for battle! That French Commander's betrayed us! Jennings, go on land and raise the alarm!" Then, turning to her friend, she shouted, "Come on, Mark, let's shake this lot up!"

Like a man with his breeches on fire, Boy Jennings jumped into the cockboat and rowed as fast as he could to the beach. Without bothering to secure the cockboat properly, he started running about the beach, screaming and shouting, "Wake up, you lazy lot, we're under attack! Come on, get yourselves moving! We're under attack!"

Alas, none of the men were in a fit state to respond. Incapacitated by too much rum, they could barely lift their heads. Suddenly, Boy Jennings heard shots being fired. He looked towards the sea and saw that one of the sloops had accosted their ship while the other was making straight for the beach. He looked about him, cursing and shouting at the men sprawled all over the ground. He felt helpless, but what else could he do to save his mates? The light breeze brought with it the acrid smell of gun powder. Jennings looked towards the sea and saw men boarding *L'Aventure*. He knew straight away that this was no courtesy call and that something was happening that he had feared all along. He had to think fast. If he hung around, he would be captured and tried as a pirate, and that only meant one thing, the gallows. But at only twenty years of age, Boy Jennings was not ready to die. He threw one more glance towards the sea, whispered, "Goodbye, Mary darling", ran up the sand dune and disappeared into the woods.

Back on the beach, the sound of gunfire was enough to stir the ruffians into action. But it was too late. The soldiers landed on the beach and quickly rounded up the pirates. Pushing them with their rifles, they herded them into the rowing boats, ready to take them back onto their ship. Caught in the worse possible state, Jack Rackham surrendered on the spot, barely able to stand up on his own two feet. With his head hanging low above his chest, he was led to the awaiting cockboats muttering wildly to himself. The man who once stood proud among his men now sat in a dumb silence as no more than a common criminal and a condemned man.

Meanwhile, aboard *L'Aventure*, Bonny and Read were frantically kicking the men to rouse them out of their drunken stupor but the inebriated sailors were as good as dead.

The enemy sloop fired two more warning shots. Bonny and Read could tell that the row of well-dressed soldiers lined up on the main deck had one purpose only, to capture all hands, on board and take them back to Nassau where they would be tried and hung, without mercy.

Unafraid, the two women stood near the bulwarks and prepared to defend the ship. They primed their pistols and wielded their cutlasses high above their heads while muttering threats through their gritted teeth.

From the upper deck of his ship, Captain Barnet surveyed the unlikely scene with an easy eye and a cynical smile. Never in the history of piracy had there been a case when all the government troops had to do was to throw planks across the bulwarks and walk onto a pirate ship without drawing a single drop of blood. He smirked with arrogance as he watched the two crazed figures posturing, roaring wildly and wielding their weapons. He had heard the extraordinary rumour that Rackham counted women among his crew, and there they were, screaming at him like two crazed banshees. Eventually, when he had had enough of smirking at the two women pirates, he ordered calmly but with supreme authority, "Seize them!"

Then, with his arms folded firmly across his chest, he watched his men overcome the two lone figures who had tried to resist capture. During the whole operation the worst that happened was that two of his men lost their footing on the planks and fell into the water. The two women pirates were swiftly bundled together, ready to be brought onto his ship, while the rest of the ruffians were marched towards the planks.

A few feet away, by the main mast, a concertina lay idle next to its wooden box, neglected and silent. In the days to come, the merry sea shanties would be picked up by some other crew who would sing them on other ships or other deserted islands. And there, they would carry on the merriment until fate would silence them again. *The life of a pirate is a short but merry one...* except that this time, it might have been slightly too short.

Catching sight of his cherished concertina, Ned Hornby suddenly broke out of the line and ran towards it. His mate tried to stop him and shouted, "No, Ned!"

His cry was immediately followed by a sharp crack and Ned Hornby came crashing onto the deck. Read rushed to his side while Anne screamed at the soldier who had fired the shot, "You stupid bastard! What did you do that for? He wasn't trying to escape! He'd only gone to fetch his concertina!"

The soldier threw a disdainful glance at Bonny and spat back, "What difference does it make… whether he gets it now or later!"

A powerful punch in the face punctuated his remark and immediately after that, the soldier doubled up in agony as Bonny kicked him hard in the groin. Instantly, several soldiers fell upon her.

Behind her, on the main deck, Read knelt down beside Ned. Gently, he lifted his head and rested it on his lap. Struggling to remain strong for Ned, he fought back the tears.

"No need for tears…" Ned uttered, wincing. "Better that way… I was done for anyway." Then he closed his eyes and began to hum his favourite tune.

"Would you like to squeeze my concertina…"

With memories of a happy time filled with Ned's cheerful tunes, Read forced a smile through his tears.

"I thought you only sang that one to the ladies."

Ned opened his eyes, returned a weak smile and said, "I know… I knew, lass, I always knew… You're a good lass… I want you to have my share of things… You're a smart lass and you'll probably find a way to get out of this damn mess… I wish… I wish…"

He tried to lift his head in an attempt to finish his sentence but the effort proved too much. His head fell back in Read's lap and his eyes closed… never to open again.

Mark Read stroked his forehead gently and began to sob uncontrollably while among the prisoners, a pirate was heard to say, "He was the lucky one."

Chapter Seven
To the Gallows

In less than a day, the sloops were back in Nassau with *L'Aventure* in tow. Captain Barnet hoisted the victory flag and at its sight, excited crowds jeered and cheered from the quay as the sloops glided triumphantly into port.

In the depth of the brig, the pirates could see nothing, but they could hear the screeching sound of crowds rejoicing, a deafening cacophony that brought them only distress and fear. They sat in semi-darkness with their heads hanging low, unable to face their shattered dreams.

"I always said 'twas bad luck to have women on board!" Dennis Macarty growled.

"I should've been the captain!" Dave Ryan blurted out in anger.

"You're no better!" a voice retorted in the dark.

Amidst the general anguish, another pirate mourned, "He's not been gone long, but I already miss him."

"Who's that you're talking aboot?" Angus MacDonald queried.

"Ned of course!"

"Dinnae worry, man, he's up there playing tae the angels… and you'll soon be there yourself, singing and dancing next tae him, just like you always did. I bet Ned is mighty glad tae be up there, cos at least wherever he is, there's naebody throwing nae smelly stockings at him!"

In the past, Angus MacDonald's humour had never failed to raise a laugh but in the present circumstances, nobody could bring themselves to even smile. Instead, his remark was greeted with a few grunts of anger and despair. Suddenly a voice enquired, "Where's Boy Jennings?"

"Don't know."

"He wasn't with us on the island."

"And he wasn't on the ship either…"

"Did he get shot?"

"Nope, the soldiers only fired warning shots."

"So… he must have escaped!" a pirate concluded.

"Good on him, I say."

"Aye, good luck to him," someone else muttered.

Slumped against the wall, Jack Rackham was saying nothing, but inside his head, he was cursing the ignominy of it all. Arrgh, you could almost hear him say, that wretched rum. He banged his head against the wooden panel in sheer frustration. "What a life, what a waste!" They heard him curse.

Above deck, Captain Barnet ordered that the women be locked in one of the officers' cabins.

"Which one, Captain?"

"I don't care which one, as long as they don't escape!" he replied curtly. "And make sure they're safely locked up as these two have more guts than the whole lot of them pirates!"

"Aye, aye, Captain!"

And there, the women languished until they were brought to shore.

**

Outside, on the quay, the impatient crowds were being pushed back by a line of soldiers and local guards to make way for those about to disembark. Finally, the gangplank was pushed against the bulwarks. The guards boarded the ship, their arms weighed down by manacles which they promptly affixed onto the pirates' feet. Now the prisoners were ready to disembark. The sight of pirates in irons and chains caused hysterical cheers among the overexcited crowds, demanding an eye for an eye and clamouring for justice. When the rumour began to run that among this sorry lot were two women, the onlookers pushed and shoved even harder to get a better view and when they spotted Bonny and Read, they whistled and jeered as if they had just seen the queens of a carnival.

**

Days after these dramatic scenes, the town crier, dressed in full regalia, marched behind a lone drummer towards the market square where he unrolled the piece of parchment he held in his hands and made the following announcement in his booming voice,

"Oyez! Oyez! Ladies, Gentlemen, Folks of the land and others, on behalf of his Majesty King George and the Governor of this island, I hereby proclaim, "On the sixteenth of November, in the year of the Lord 1720, here in Nassau, the notorious pirate Jack Rackham and his crew will be tried.

"On the twenty-fifth of November, in the year of the Lord 1720, here in Nassau, the women pirates Anne Bonny and Mary Read will be tried.

"No man or woman shall be allowed inside the courtroom carrying pistols, muskets, cutlasses, knives or any other weapons.

"No child under the age of fifteen shall be allowed in during the proceedings and no eating or drinking shall be permitted inside the courtroom.

"Here ends the proclamation. Oyez! Oyez!"

With great ceremony, the town crier rolled up the parchment and marched back from whence he came.

***

The day of the pirates' trial finally came. A festival atmosphere spread all over the town. Quick to profit from the occasion, market traders descended on the town square to set up stall. Around them, curious onlookers rushed through the streets and clogged up the pavement outside the courtroom to gawp at a pitiful line of men in chains dragging themselves towards the building, flanked on each side by soldiers carrying arms.

The first to be tried was Jack Rackham. After each accusation for acts of piracy, grand theft, false imprisonment and murder, he bowed his head in contrition. Stripped of all his pride and brashness, he readily admitted his guilt and even went as far as expressing remorse and regret. No women present in the courtroom, who had known him as one of the most charismatic pirates, could recognise the forlorn figure whose faint shadow lingered limply over the dusty floorboards. There were no doubts in their minds that justice had to be done but they had hoped to be entertained by loud protestations, waving of fists pledging revenge, or at least cries begging for mercy. They had expected him to make a scene and to rile at the judge in the same way he had riled at his victims, but instead they saw nothing, not even a defiant streak in Rackham's eyes, and a disappointed sigh rose from the gallery as the condemned man prepared to hear his fate with a resigned look on his face.

Finally, when the judge passed the death sentence, Captain Jack

Rackham accepted the verdict stoically. And while the gallery heaved with satisfaction at the fitting punishment imposed on the pirate, they interpreted his stoic silence as an act of cowardice from a man incapable of uttering a single word in his own defence to save his own neck. From the bench, the judge kept his eyes locked on the face of the condemned man. However, cowardice was not what he saw, but rather a remarkable display of courage and resilience from a man who was about to face death with his eyes wide open, his conscience cleared and perhaps even his sins forgiven. It was all over for Rackham as he heard the judge conclude his summary with these final words, "… that they, the condemned, shall go from hence to the Place of Execution, where they shall be hanged by the neck, till they are dead…

"And the God of Infinite Mercy be merciful to their Souls."

As the trial progressed, every single pirate was condemned to hang. However, before meeting his fate, Jack Rackham pleaded with the prison authorities to be allowed to see one last time the woman with whom he had shared so many dreams. The prison chief hesitated. This was a condemned man's last request. He could not refuse for as a rule, a prisoner's last wish had to be granted. It was the custom, a tradition that made the executioners appear a little more humane before cold-bloodedly putting a man to death; but at the back of his mind, the prison official could not help thinking, was this a trick? Could this be an attempt to escape in a last bid for freedom? The Governor of the Island was consulted. Luckily for Rackham, Governor Woodes Rogers was well acquainted with Anne's father, a man who had gained a lot of respect as an outstanding lawyer and upright citizen in nearby South Carolina and who, from time to time, came to visit these shores.

After a short period of deliberation, Governor Woodes Rogers relented and gave permission to Jack Rackham to meet up with Anne one last time.

Early in the morning of the twentieth of November, the sound of rattling keys alerted the men that their time had come. The guards checked the irons on each prisoner before leading them out. As they passed the women's cell, a guard singled out Rackham and stayed behind with him while the rest of the condemned men continued their doomed march along the dark corridor, the sound of their chains scraping the cobblestones as if wailing a last goodbye.

In her dark prison cell, Anne was sitting on the single wooden plank that served as a bed, with her back leaning against the wall and with Mary's head buried in her lap. She jumped and took a sharp intake of breath as she saw the dark figure of a man staring back at her through the iron bars. Although the light was poor, she instantly recognised Rackham, the lover who had promised her heaven on earth. As he stood there, barely a few feet away from her, she tried to equate the wasted shadow of the man pitifully gazing at her to the flamboyant character she had met all those months ago in '*The Cock 'n Bull*'. She could not help visualising the gregarious sailor who liked to flash his title of *captain* like a huge shining medallion beating upon his large chest, never less than brash and full of bravado, and who loved to sing louder and drink harder than anyone else in the tavern. It was hard, so hard to think back on those happy times when all she saw standing only a few feet away behind the thick prison bars was a bedraggled and bewildered man on the threshold of death. It pained her so much that for a second, she could no longer bare to look at him. Eventually, Anne lifted Mary's head very gently to rest it on the bench and walked slowly towards Rackham. Then she called, "Jack!" as their hands met on the iron bars. They kept clasping each other's hands so tightly that it hurt. After a short while, Anne felt Jack's fingers move and something metallic slipped inside the palm of her hand. Curious, she wanted to retrieve her hand but Jack shook his head discreetly as if to say, don't look now.

"What is it?" she couldn't help whisper.

For all reply, Rackham simply said, "Something to remember me by."

Anne immediately understood. "It's your ring, isn't it?"

Then she closed her hand and held it close to her heart as if it was the most precious object on earth. The emotion was too strong, too painful and she began to feel the tears flowing again down her pale cheeks.

"Oh Jack…" She sighed.

During all this time, the guard was pacing around them, feeling awkward at this open emotional display. He could tell that the file of prisoners had now left the prison for he could hear their chains clang on the cobblestones outside. The morbid sound seemed to act as a signal and the guard separated the two lovers for the last time.

"Come on, Captain, time to go…"

Anne could not let go of Rackham's arm and when the guard eventually separated them, she shouted in a voice mixed with anger and despair, "It's a terrible shame it had to end this way, Calico Jack… but if you had fought like a man, you needn't hang like a dog!" Then she turned her head away and collapsed in tears with her head in her hands on top of Mary's body, unable to watch the sorrowful captain walk out of her life for ever.

**

On the quay of Port Nassau, people suddenly fell silent as the pirates marched towards Dead Man's Quay, the place of execution at the far end of the harbour. In a last attempt to save the condemned men's souls, a priest hailed out loud passages from the Bible and shouted at the top of his voice words of repentance and contrition, just in case the penitents had not heard.

Among the doomed pirates, stunned in a resigned silence, there was one who had not said his final word. His head held up high by the noose, Dennis Macarty let out a frustrated growl and spat on the wooden slats as he watched a familiar figure push her way to the front of the crowd.

"Argh…" he grumbled to himself. "The wife!"

Not content to watch him die, Beth Macarty had come, determined to nag her wayward husband till the bitter end. She eagerly scoured the faces of the men standing on the gallows and, as soon as she spotted him, she wagged an angry finger and yelled, "That'll serve you right, Dennis Macarty! You stupid fool! I told you not to go with that shameful bunch of robbers! Now, you're gonna die with your shoes on, just like I told you many times before!"

"Argh… I'll yet make a liar of you, Beth Macarty!" the pirate riposted, kicking off his shoes just as the trap fell open beneath his bare feet.

Instantly, a loud cheer rose from the crowd. The public execution over, the good people of Nassau returned to their daily chores and to their ordinary lives, feeling more righteous and absolved of their own crimes.

It was the twentieth of November in the year of the Lord 1720.

Chapter Eight
Second Trial

On the twenty-fifth of November 1720, excited crowds gathered once more outside the courtroom to gawp at the unusual defendants who, it was rumoured, were women dressed in men's clothes. The trial was scheduled for eleven o'clock but from early that morning, women, in particular, jostled, pushed and shoved for position, to secure the best view of the prisoners.

The sultry summer months were finally over and the temperature had dropped to a comfortable degree, but inside the courtroom, the atmosphere smouldered with rumours of hot love and wild passion. Eventually, when the two women were brought in, a sudden hush fell upon the room as people, awestruck, craned their necks to catch a glimpse of the women prisoners. Their curiosity satisfied, whispers of wonder and sheer admiration ran freely along the rows.

"Which one's Anne Bonny?" a voice was heard to whisper from the front row.

"The one with a glitter in her eye!"

"Which one's that?" an impatient voice asked again.

"That one! The smaller of the two! Can't you see?"

As the trial proceeded, the women prisoners listened impassively to the various charges levelled against them. At the end of his summary, the judge asked both defendants if there were any possible reason why punishment should not be carried out.

The public gallery waited with bated breath for the women's reply. They prepared themselves for the wails and the desperate pleas that would tug at the judge's heart and bring the whole court to tears. They waited for the moment when the women would drop to their knees and beg for mercy. Failing that, the very least they expected was to see the women fly in a rage, curse and swear at the judge for it was well known that they both had a fiery temper and that their language was as colourful as their past. But... quite unexpectedly... nothing of the kind followed. Instead, Anne Bonny, who had knowledge of the law because of her father's profession, raised her head defiantly and declared with total self-control, "My Lord, I plead my belly!"

A loud gasp from the courtroom punctuated her statement. The judge nearly fell off his honourable seat. Slightly incredulous, he bent over his desk, straightened his glasses and put on an air of complete puzzlement.

"If this is true, Miss Bonny, this does change the course of events," he declared haughtily.

People bristled in their seats and threw alternate glances between Anne Bonny and the judge, wondering what would happen next. Quite partial to a bit of drama himself, the judge lowered his glasses and leered lengthily at the defendant. All around the courtroom, voices began to whisper louder and louder still. Amid the general consternation, another voice rose.

"So do I!" Mary Read breathed, despite being rendered weak by the fever.

Anne turned towards her friend. Mary had always kept herself to herself and for this reason she had never intimated to a living soul that she had had a lover. Shocked, Anne stared at her friend and exclaimed, "You too?"

A roar of laughter followed her remark. The orderly atmosphere of the courtroom quickly descended into chaos as people heckled, jeered and sneered. Some even cheered. However, Anne remained oblivious to it all and continued to stare at her friend. Could this be the real cause of her illness? She wondered.

The people sitting on the front row could have sworn that they saw the judge jump in his seat when he heard the second unexpected news.

"Well I never!" Someone was heard chortling.

"You'd never think that was an excuse not to hang!" Another laughed.

A woman sitting on the front row was seen nudging her friend before declaring between bouts of laughter, "If you can't keep your hands in your pockets, love, make sure you keep them in your own pants!"

"Naaah...!" Her friend chuckled. "You can't earn a few groats doing that!"

At these words, both women dissolved in a fit of laughter.

As the noise reached fever pitch, the judge lunged for the gavel and banged it loudly in an attempt to restore order in the courtroom.

"Silence in court! Silence!"

Then, he turned to the guards and ordered, "Take them back to the cells and call for a doctor."

He grabbed the gavel again, banged it noisily and declared authoritatively, "The court is dismissed!"

Chapter Nine
A Mysterious Gift

The day after the trial, a doctor was brought to the women's cell. After a brief physical examination, he was able to confirm that indeed, both women were with child. Consequently, in accordance with the law, the death sentence was deferred until the women's confinement.

This was a lucky reprieve which filled Anne with hope. She did her best to comfort Mary by concocting all sorts of escape plans. Assured of her success, she would go to her father in South Carolina and ask him to buy them a passage to Europe, to Ireland where she was sure to find some relatives of hers willing to help them until they got back onto their feet, and while she dreamed out loud, Mary's condition deteriorated by the day. Anne begged the prison guard to call for a doctor so that her friend could be given some medicine, but the guard had retorted that the prison authority did not wish to waste precious medicine on someone condemned to die anyway.

"I don't care what you think, fetch the doctor!" Anne raged through the solid iron bars.

Just to show that he was right, the guard called upon the prison chief and asked for a doctor. The prison chief agreed to the request but when the doctor arrived, he took him apart and whispered a note of caution.

"Listen here, Doctor, these women are extremely canny, and I suspect they might be up to something, so don't let them trick you. And another thing, if one of them is really unwell, spare the medicine and find some cheaper way to keep her going until her confinement."

"Well, Mr Grey, I wouldn't recommend any medicine anyway, not in their condition, but I could recommend a large measure of strong ale for the iron because she's probably feeling the effect of pregnancy. A bit of iron would certainly make her feel better."

"That, I don't mind providing, Doctor, especially if it'll cheer up her last days on God's earth."

The doctor nodded and proceeded to the cell. While the prison guard unlocked the door, he gazed at his patient and even from where he stood, he could tell that the symptoms she was showing had nothing to do with her being with child. Nevertheless, he remembered the words of the prison chief and began his examination.

Mary lay on the wooden planks groaning and struggling to breathe. Her furrowed brow was covered with pearly strings of perspiration and her headache was so severe that even the slightest ray of light acted like a lighthouse beam shining straight into her eyes. Doctor Reed took her emaciated hand to check her pulse, then replaced it gently on the makeshift bed. Even if he had wanted to, the fever was far too advanced for him to be able to cure it with the basic medicine he had available. He looked at the patient and forced a smile.

"Never mind, my dear," he said, trying to sound reassuring. "You're probably feeling the effect of pregnancy," he confided, knowing it to be untrue. "However, there's nothing a good measure of strong ale wouldn't cure. I shall order some straight away." Then he left, gripped with sadness. In the eyes of justice, a pirate was a pirate; but when that pirate became his patient, it was no longer a matter of law, but a matter of humanity. Knowing that he could have cured Mary's illness, he walked away with a heavy heart and a bad conscience.

After his departure, Anne tried to comfort her friend again. "See, I told you you'd be fine… and don't worry… I'll take care of you, and mark my words, we're going to do all the things we said we'd do."

Mary forced a smile. "It's okay, Anne. I don't need a doctor to tell me that I'm not gonna make it…"

"Shush! Don't you dare speak like that, Mary! You're a strong lass and you and your baby will be fine!"

"Anne… you've always been a good friend and I know you're being strong for me…" Then, she reached for her pocket and took something out. "But… just in case I don't make it… take this."

She took Anne's hand and placed something in her palm, then folded her fingers over it.

"What is it?" Anne asked, intrigued.

"Don't look at it now… I know I'm not gonna make it so take it. I want you to have it…"

"But I don't want it… I don't want anything from you…"

"Yes… you must" Mary interrupted. "You must take it. It would be such a waste otherwise, and anyway, you're gonna need it for yourself and your child…"

Anne looked down at her friend. Mary's eyes were now closed, exhausted by the few words she had managed to articulate. Unable to wait, Anne looked at what Mary had given her. It was a tiny piece of parchment folded in four. She opened it up. It had nothing but the contours of a small island which she instantly recognised. "Cove Island," she whispered. On it, there were three crosses clearly marked, one by the beach overlooking Dunmore Bay, and the other two marking spots further inland but not too distant from each other.

Anne looked at her friend again.

"Where the crosses are… is that where you've hidden your loot?"

Mary opened her eyes and pointed at the two crosses inland.

"Those two crosses are, one is where I buried my loot, and the other is where Charles hid his."

"Charles? You mean Jennings?"

"Yes… Jennings, Boy Jennings," Mary revealed with a faint smile.

"My! So *he* was… that's why you came to his help when he was about to be beaten senseless by that brute Freddie Main… but I've never seen you together… how did you manage…?"

"Well, that's the third cross there, the one by the beach. You see, we wanted to find somewhere quiet… you know… so we could get together… and we found this cave…"

"A cave?"

"Yeah, a cave… And in there, there's a tunnel that goes right to the other side of the island. So that's how we managed to get together… but there's something else."

"What?"

"Before he died, Ned told me that's also where he'd hidden his loot."

"Well, that looks a bit too obvious. Someone else is bound to find it before us…"

"Not that obvious. There's a lot of tall vegetation around it and it's in the shadow of three palm trees."

"So… if I know there's a cave there, I should find it easily then."

"Very easily. In fact, you can see the three palm trees from the sea."

"Well, I don't want to take your share of things. It wouldn't be proper, would it? No, what I'll do, I'll hide the map somewhere and when you're well again and we're out of this hole, we'll go back together to Cove Island, hey?"

Mary smiled but sighed at the same time, knowing that she would probably never set foot on the island again. Anne placed the map close to her bosom.

"So… what happened to Boy Jennings…?" she continued.

"He's probably hiding in the cave, which means he might still be alive."

"In that case, Mary, you've got to fight and get better… come on, do it for him."

"I can't… you know I can't…"

Here she paused to catch her breath. Anne mopped her friend's pearly brow with her sleeve and tried to shush her, "Come on, you must rest now."

Suddenly, a loud voice boomed through the prison corridors. "Hi, ladies, we meet again, I see!" someone greeted cheerfully.

Surprised, the women looked up at the same time.

"By the devil's teeth!" Anne Bonny exclaimed. "If it isn't old Tisdale from *The Cock 'n Bull!*"

"Aye! Missus! 'Tis indeed I, Old Tisdale here to help! Here's a small cask of ale like the doctor ordered, courtesy of his Majesty the King. Mind you don't drink it all at once, though, could be bad for you and all…" he warned, looking pointedly at the women's girths.

"Well, you mind your tongue, and we'll mind our girths," Anne reparteed, before adding with some irony, "I bet you're missing us at *The Cock 'n Bull?*"

Henry Tisdale looked about him furtively. The prison guard was busy negotiating the price of a cask or two of strong ale with his assistant. After checking that no one was listening, he replied in a low and mournful tone, "Arrgh! Not quite the same without Captain Jack around. It's a sad business it is, if I may say, very sad indeed. Nobody's singing no more; they're afraid you see. The hangings've done them in. They've all gone into hiding, that's what I think and, pardon the expression, but I wouldn't be hanging around myself if I were a pirate. If I'd risk my life to get my hands on some treasure, I'd want to make sure I lived long enough to enjoy it. Silly really, to have all those gold doubloons, jewels and all, and ending up staring at them from the top of the gallows… it's no good to nobody, is it? As a matter of fact, I wonder what happened to all them treasures, 'cause the rumour goes that Captain Jack had gathered a sizeable bounty."

Anne and Mary threw a knowing glance at each other but said nothing.

"Anyhow," Henry Tisdale continued as if talking to himself, "I'd better be going… I hope you fare all right on my ale, it's the best around, you know. Anyhow, be sure to send for me when you need more!"

Henry Tisdale's hunched figure disappeared noisily down the corridor. Anne grabbed her pewter tankard, filled it with ale and gave it to her friend to drink.

"Come on, Mary, you drink this and you'll feel a lot better."

"I don't want it, I just want water."

"But that's what the doctor recommended, so have some," Anne ordered firmly while bringing the tankard to Mary's lips. Almost immediately, Mary started choking on the bitter liquid.

"I can't, Anne, I can't drink it!"

"But you must!" Anne insisted. "I want you to get better. I've got an idea how to get us out of this hell hole. So, come on Mary, try to drink it."

"It's no use, Anne." She stopped to catch her breath. "You know… you're the only friend I've ever had…"

"And you mine," Anne conceded. "Among that lot of useless pirates, you stood out, you were always the bravest in battle…"

"No, you were…" Mary interrupted.

After a long pause, Anne confided with a quirky smile, "I'll tell you something. I've always secretly admired you. I used to think I was the strongest, the smartest…"

"And the cheekiest," Mary cut in.

Anne let out a little giggle. Then, adopting a more serious expression, she conceded, "But I wasn't, you were… I could have loved you if you hadn't been a darn woman!"

Mary returned her smile, and in that smile, Anne caught a glimpse of a mystical beauty that is only visible to those blessed with love. And she wondered… love and friendship… could they be the same?

Too tired to respond, Mary turned her head away and shut her eyes.

The atmosphere in the prison cell was stifling, leaving the woman prisoners, laid low by the searing heat, constantly gasping for some fresh air.

During the next few days, Mary drifted in and out of consciousness. She groaned with pain and panted with thirst. Then, one night, the atmosphere suddenly turned cooler. In the distance, the women could hear the rumblings of an advancing storm. A few minutes later, although they could not see it, they could hear the tropical rain whip up the deserted cobblestones. Mary's face suddenly glowed with a luminous smile.

"At last..." she whispered with a long sigh... and died.

Immediately, Anne fell upon her friend, consumed with grief. She grabbed Mary's hands and squeezed them hard, desperate to hold on to the remnant of a cherished life that was slowly departing. As she stared at her friend's face, the exquisite serenity which exuded from it sharpened even more the sorrow and pain she felt. Deprived for ever of the only friend she ever had, she felt the weight of loneliness and solitude crash onto her shoulders, heavier than the death sentence itself. The excruciating pain of finding herself suddenly alone stabbed her like a blow in the heart. One poignant thought tortured her relentlessly and without mercy, while her loud cries turned into tears of agony as she suddenly realised that she would now have to walk to the gallows all alone and face death deserted by all.

Outside, the rain continued to pound the pavement. Further away, the thunder and lightning tore through the sky like the loud cries of tempestuous gods roaring angrily as if blaming each other for their own miserable fate.

When she was sufficiently recovered, for the first time since she was a little girl, Anne put her hands together and prayed; and if at that moment the prison guard had been standing outside the iron bars, he would have heard her plaintive cry plead, "*Please God, have mercy on her soul.*"

Chapter Ten
Ruthless thy Be for Freedom thy Win

When she woke up the next morning, her head heavy with sorrow and pain, Anne found herself still clutching her friend's hands. They were cold. She rose up slowly from the hard floor and glanced at her friend. For the first time in her troubled life, Mary looked so peaceful, so serene. It seemed that only in death, her concealed beauty was able to shine through.

Wracked with self-pity and regrets, Anne could only think of one thing, Mary's life had ended, just like her own was about to end, at a mere twenty years of age.

Suddenly, the sound of footsteps and keys rattling on someone's belt alerted the prisoner. She fretted, she wailed, then she threw herself on the iron bars and started calling out, "Guard! Guard!"

The guard responded slowly, unmoved by the desperation he had detected in the prisoner's voice. He was used to it. Those agonising cries of despair, those screams of anguish... and those hands, gnarled and rigid, fighting to snatch back a slice of life, those eyes, rolling wildly and begging for mercy and those faces contorted with that terrible fear of death, he had heard and seen them all many times before; and he plodded along, heavy footed and in no hurry to provide the slightest relief to the doomed prisoner.

"Be quiet, you wretched wench! I've never heard anybody wanting to go to hell in such a hurry. All right, I'm coming! What's the matter now?" he growled.

Anne gripped the bars tightly and wailed loudly, "My friend's dead! Mary's dead!"

The guard shrugged his shoulders and stared back at the prisoner. He had been tricked before and he was not about to let himself be fooled again by two good-for-nothing wenches. From the corridor, he grumbled, "What d'you mean she's dead?"

His cold, dismissive sneer threw Anne into a rage. Unable to stand the sight of him, she tore herself away from the bars and paced the cell frantically, biting her lips and wringing her hands to stop them from shaking. She had almost given up on life when a thought suddenly entered her head. She took a deep breath, steeled herself and pointed at her friend.

"Come and see for yourself… can't you see? She's dead!"

Scowling heavily, the guard peered through the bars and watched the lifeless body for a while.

"She's just asleep!" he barked dismissively.

Anne grabbed the prison bars and shouted in frustration, "She's not! I tell you, she's dead!"

Still unconvinced, the guard peered again through the iron bars from where all he could see was a body lying limply on the palliasse. He fumbled nervously with his keys, still reluctant to believe the prisoner. With extreme precaution, all the time keeping a close eye on her, he unlocked the door and approached the bed with caution. Anne watched him with utter disdain. The repulsive sight of his unkempt hair, rotting teeth and grubby clothes from which emanated an awful stench made her feel nauseous to the point of vomiting. Despite the powerful revulsion she felt towards the guard, she followed his every move, calm and composed; but when she saw his filthy fingers touch Mary's delicate hand, she could stand it no more. She set upon him like a demented woman, drew his sword from his belt, threw him to the ground and impaled him on the hard floor. In a reflex reaction, the guard grabbed the sharp blade with both hands to stop it going any deeper but pinned mercilessly to the floor, he struggled hopelessly to save himself, until all life left his body. Unlike that of the condemned prisoners he had so many times herded to the gallows, he had not seen his own death coming.

Anne stood in the middle of the cell, stunned by what she had just done. Suddenly, she spotted the door wide open. She glanced at the dead guard. No matter how filthy his clothes were, right now they smelt of freedom. Swiftly, she stripped the prison guard of his clothes, put on his grubby greasy hat, bundled her own clothes under her arm and left. Further down the corridor, she came across a small group of guards involved in a game of cards. She greeted them with a deep grunt that came from the back of her throat. One of them hailed, "Hey! Where're you off to?"

Anne froze. She could feel the blood pounding through her veins. She was too close to freedom to fail. Just keep walking and don't flinch, she told herself. So, she spoke with utter confidence, "There's a dead prisoner in the third cell. I'm off to get the doctor."

"Bring us back some beer while you're out," the same guard requested.

"Aye!" Anne readily agreed before walking unhindered out of the prison.

From there, she knew exactly what to do. She had rehearsed this moment in her head over and over again.

Walking at a brisk pace, she made her way down the street towards the town square, and a few minutes later she found herself at the back door of the *Cock 'n Bull.* Checking that no one was looking, she crept down the stairs into the cellar and waited there until nightfall. At last, able to get rid of the guard's malodorous clothes, she quickly changed back into her own clothes and remained still, crouching behind a barrel of ale. In the dark confines of the pungent cellar, she could not help thinking of her friend. She recalled the happier times they had spent together and smiled at the recollection that she had even fancied Mary when she had not known her to be a woman. And… fancy her having her way with Boy Jennings. Well, that was a surprise, him among all the men she could have chosen… Then, her face became sombre again as flashes of Rackham's face, of his alluring smile invaded her mind, making her eyes well up with tears. She had to stop those thoughts coming to her head. She forced herself to think of something else, something more gripping that would hold her attention for a while. She began to think of the last words her friend had uttered. She tried to visualise the beach, the three palm trees, the cave, and the mystery her friend had not had time to reveal, what lay beyond the dark passage?

***

At the end of the day, Henry Tisdale hurried the last customers out of his tavern.

As he went round the public room to turn off the oil lamps, he heard steps coming from the cellar. He stopped and listened. The floorboards creaked. Someone was creeping up the stairs. He held his breath. The steps stopped just behind the wooden door. Nervous, Tisdale jerked his head towards the door and watched it open slowly. With his right hand still holding the brass lamp, he stood silently to see who was coming. When a dark silhouette finally emerged, he instinctively reached for his pistol.

"Who's there?" he shouted. "Show yourself if you're a brave man!"

His voice resonated in the empty room with a frightening intensity.

"It's only me, Tisdale, Anne Bonny," she replied in the friendliest tone she could manage, but unsure of his reaction, she stayed behind the door.

"Don't move!" the innkeeper ordered nervously, pointing his pistol at the intruder.

Keeping her cool, Anne continued, "I've come for your help, Mr Tisdale. Will you please let me in?"

Henry Tisdale thought for a moment. He knew the voice and he knew that it belonged to a ruthless pirate who had once raided his ship.

"I've come to make a deal with you," Anne added.

For reply, Tisdale warned, "Get out of my house before I shoot you!"

"Hear me this once, Tisdale. I've got a deal that'll make you rich." Anne threw in, as a last gamble.

"What do you mean?"

"May I come in?"

"All right, you can come in but first, show me you're unarmed."

Anne walked into the smoky room with her hands held high in the air.

"All I have, Tisdale, are the clothes I'm wearing."

Tisdale looked at her outstretched arms and empty hands.

"That's what I thought. How can you make a deal when you've got nothing?" Then he asked in a brusque tone, "What d'you want?"

"I've come to ask you for a favour…"

"You must be joking!" interrupted Tisdale.

"You owe me, Tisdale. 'Twas me who told Rackham not to kill you when we raided your ship."

"Forget it! I don't deal with pirates and besides, if that fool let me go, that's his own look-out! I owe you nothing, nothing at all!" Tisdale retorted.

"Don't worry, Tisdale, I don't want anything from you! I just want to help. You have a ship bound for England full of merchandise. I want to be on that ship. I know pirates and I know their tactics. If you take me on, I'll be able to protect your ship and her cargo."

"You mean, you want to join my crew?"

"Aye, that's what I mean."

Henry Tisdale scrutinised the woman standing in front of him. With her reputation as a ruthless pirate, he knew she could not be trusted.

"What tells me you're not going to steal my ship for yourself?"

"In my condition! My days as a pirate are over… finished! Can't you see? My baby's due in a few months' time. All I want is a safe passage to England so that I can make a new start with my baby."

Henry Tisdale listened. After all, he was a reasonable man. He looked at Anne Bonny and remained silent for a while. He knew he could not trust the ex-pirate who now stood in front of him as a destitute woman; but she was with child and he could not help feeling sorry for her. He was torn. Eventually, he shook his head.

"Sorry, love, I can't help you. It's too high a risk. I've nothing to gain in this sad business of yours and everything to lose."

However, Anne's next reply made him think again.

"You are forgetting one important thing, wherever there's a pirate, there's a fortune to be made. My shipmates are no longer of this earth, but their treasures remain. If you help me, I promise to make you a rich man."

Tisdale's eyes lit up. This was quite a different proposition. Pictures of sea chests full of gold coins and precious jewels flashed before his eyes. He was tempted... very tempted.

"What's your proof that your deal is genuine?"

"See that ring?" she said, showing the innkeeper Rackham's topaz ring to try and convince him. "Well, I can show you the exact spot where this came from."

"Fine, you tell me where the treasure is, and I might, and I say 'might' take you on."

"So, it's a deal?"

"There's no deal until *after* you've showed me the proof."

"Do you have a piece of parchment paper? I'll draw you a map. Have you heard of Cove Island?"

"Of course I have, but there's nothing there. It's just a big swamp."

"I know... and that's exactly why the island makes such a perfect hiding place."

"I'll go and fetch you some writing paper... Hold on! I didn't know you could read and write."

"Well, people tend to forget that my father was a lawyer. I had a private tutor at home."

"Ah... That explains a lot!" the innkeeper exclaimed.

"What do you mean by that?"

Henry Tisdale ignored her question and left the room. A few minutes later, he returned with a piece of paper and said, "I've got a better idea. Why don't I take you there? Then you can take me to the spot..."

"In my condition, I ain't travelling no more than I need to."

"How do I know I can trust you then?"

"For Christ's sake! Give me that damn piece of paper and I'll draw you a map. That way, you can go and check for yourself; and when you return with the proof, you let me go to England on your ship."

"I might just do that."

"Will you let me stay here in the meantime?"

Tisdale rubbed his chin. This was asking too much. Trading with a pirate was one thing, but hiding one on the run from the authorities was a favour too far that could land him in jail. And what about his wife? If it all went wrong, how would he ever manage to explain away his dealing with a pirate who turned out to be a woman with child? She would never believe him and instead, think he had been up to no good. Tisdale rubbed the back of his head with nervous apprehension. Only a gambler would understand his present quandary, and just like a gambler, he felt a mixture of excitement mixed with profound despair as he contemplated the outcome of risking everything for one last chance to win.

Anne was growing impatient.

"Come on, Tisdale, what do you say?"

Sighing heavily, the innkeeper grabbed his chin, thought for a little longer, and finally muttered under his breath, "Arrgh... what the hell!"

"All right, lass!" he grunted. "Come with me."

Tisdale led the fugitive onto the first floor of the inn. At the top of the stairs, Anne followed her host down a narrow corridor. There, Tisdale stopped outside the second door on the left.

"This'll be the best room for you. The window faces the back of the house, so you won't be seen from the street. You'll be quite safe here. It's lucky my wife's away visiting relatives right now, so you won't be disturbed by anyone... except the cats, mind — we have two cats — and the odd mouse. So, if you hear some noise during the night, don't worry, it'll probably be the cats chasing the mice."

***

The following Sunday, standing outside his tavern, hands on hips, Henry Tisdale looked up to the sky to check the weather. The cloudless sky and calm seas boded well for the short journey to Cove Island. Taking four trusted hands with him, he set sail early that morning without revealing to his crew the true purpose of his trip.

After sailing for about two hours, the crew sighted the long uninterrupted beach that formed the eastern side of Cove Island. According to the map, they should be sailing towards the more rugged western side, something Tisdale was not particularly keen to do as he knew the seabed to be covered with coral reefs and sandbanks. Anxious to preserve his ship, he decided to land on the eastern side, and reach the other side on foot.

"Why have we come here, Captain?" one of the shipmates asked.

"Never mind why," Tisdale replied curtly. "I pay you to sail my ship, not to ask questions. Now, look after her while I go ashore. There's a barrel of rum below. Just help yourself but mind you don't vaporise your little brains with too much rum. I need you to sail the ship back today."

The argument settled, Henry Tisdale lowered himself into the cockboat and rowed ashore. Once he knew himself to be out of sight, he took the map out of his pocket and examined it closely. Following the plan, he quickly reached the halfway point of the island and started to look for a palm tree standing slightly apart from the other trees. Thank goodness the island was only half a mile wide, he thought. Within minutes, he had located the tree. Still holding the map in his hands, he counted ten large steps in the direction of Dunmore Bay. Having done so, he looked about him and found that he was standing on top of a large rock with a sudden drop in front of him. Curious to see what lay beneath, he went down to the side to take a closer look and discovered that the rock itself formed part of the roof of a small cave. The discovery made him wild with anticipation. Hardly able to contain his excitement, he rubbed his hands with glee.

"So," he muttered to himself. "She might have been telling the truth after all!"

Before going inside the cave, he looked around to make sure there was no one about, then he entered the dank passage. Alas, without a torch, the total darkness inside prevented him from proceeding any further. As he began to turn back, he suddenly spotted a small alcove cut deep into the cave wall. Feeling his way about, he stumbled across several small casks. He shook the first one to check its content and heard a sloshing noise. He smelt the wood. That one must be full of rum, he thought. He wanted to shake the others for their contents, but there was no time. On the clear horizon, the sun was beginning to set. Too nervous to sail in the dark, with great reluctance, he left everything in place, vouching to return very soon.

As he emerged from the cave, he was instantly blinded by the brightness of the sun. Suddenly, a harsh voice rang out and nailed him to the spot, "Hands up or I shoot!"

Unable to distinguish his assailant who was standing against the sun, Tisdale threw his arms up. "Don't shoot! Don't shoot!" he pleaded.

"What are you doing here?" the voice asked sharply.

"I was only looking to shelter from the sun."

"No, you weren't! I've been watching you. You're after something that doesn't belong to you."

"Who are you?" Tisdale enquired nervously.

Ignoring his question, the stranger continued, "However, I'll make a deal with you. You take me back to Nassau and I'll let you have what you're looking for."

"How do you know I'm from Nassau? Have we met before?"

The stranger did not answer. Very slowly, Tisdale took a few sideway steps to move out of the blinding sun. At last, he was able to take a good look at the stranger who had his pistol trained on him. Tisdale scrutinised his face and eventually lowered his arms for despite the thick beard that covered most of the stranger's face, he could tell he was dealing with a young man who was in much need of help.

"Who are you?" Tisdale asked again.

"I'm an officer from the King's Navy."

"Are you really?" Tisdale questioned, dubiously. "That's not a uniform you're wearing."

"My ship was raided by pirates. They stole my uniform and left me to rot here. What about you? What are you doing here?"

"Oh… just exploring." Tisdale responded, shrugging his shoulders.

"Just exploring or searching for something? Can I have a look at your map?"

"What map?"

"I saw you holding a map in your hands. Show me the map!"

"I don't have a map!"

"Give it to me or I shoot!"

Reluctantly, Tisdale reached under his belt, retrieved the map and threw it at the stranger's feet. As soon as the officer bent down to pick it up, Tisdale set upon him and wrestled him to the ground. There they fought until the sharp crack of a gunshot tore through the air.

"All right! All right! Don't shoot!" Tisdale shouted in surrender.

The officer held his pistol firmly with one hand while shaking the sand off the map with the other.

"How did you get this map?"

"I found it."

"Where?"

Tisdale was stuck for an answer. Then...

"Just a minute!" he protested angrily. "I thought you wanted me to take you back to Nassau! Well, if you want a favour from me, you're gonna have to pay for it with your silence. So no more questions. I do whatever I came here to do; you help me carry whatever I find and the deal is done, no questions asked. I don't care who you are..." At that point, Tisdale took a good look at the stranger. "Actually, I don't believe you were marooned by pirates. Why should they even bother unless you were one of them? It's more like you came to a disagreement or you're a deserter. Whichever way, you're an outlaw and I'm in a good mind to report you to the authorities."

"You do that and I'll shoot you," the stranger retorted coldly.

"Fine, fine! So we've got a deal, then. And don't you go and steal my ship!"

"I bet your men don't even know what you're up to otherwise they would have come ashore with you to take their share of the loot. So... How much for my silence?"

Tisdale gave him a shifty look.

"All right, you can keep whatever you can carry."

Taking two casks each, the men made their way back to the ship.

Chapter Eleven
A Home Coming

From Tisdale's ship, the sailors observed two figures boarding the small rowing boat. Out of the four hired hands, only two were in a fit enough state to follow the events, Jack Connor and Luke Humphreys.

"Who the hell is that?" Humphreys pondered out loud.

"There's some fishy business going on…" Will Harris commented, clutching a mug full of rum.

Another shipmate, Dave Warren, was slumped against the main mast, unable to hold his head up. With his chin resting on his chest, he kept parroting what he thought he had heard.

"Yeah… fishy business going on…" he mumbled, "and we didn't catch a single fish, eh, eh, eh!"

With his sharp eyes, Connor spotted the two men loading the boat with what looked like small barrels.

"I don't mind betting my last groat that they've been treasure hunting," he said to Humphreys.

Overhearing the remark, Will Harris stumbled towards the bulwark.

"Well, if they have, I want my share of things."

"Yeah, I think we deserve a share of whatever they've found," Humphreys declared.

"Aye, aye!" Will Harris cheered tossing his mug in the air and trying to sound coherent. "I wanna… I wanna… arrgh, what the hell! I'll just have more rum."

Standing next to him, Humphreys watched Harris's limp body slither back onto the deck. As his mate lay comatose at his feet, he chortled loudly, "Aye! By the look of you, you've already had more than your fair share! Ah ah!"

A few feet away, still slumped against the main mast, Dave Warren shouted, "Pirates? I'm not a pirate! I'm an honest law-abiding thief I am!"

"Shut up, Warren! You're squawking like a parakeet!" Connor snorted.

"Nag! Nag! Nag!" Warren sneered, mimicking the sound of a parakeet.

Connor ignored him and turned to Humphreys.

"You're right. I think we should ask for a share."

***

Meanwhile in the small rowing boat, the two men were approaching fast. Having steered the rowing boat alongside his ship, Tisdale climbed the rope ladder first, while his companion followed closely behind him. As Tisdale clambered back on board, he was met by several pistols pointing straight at him.

"Welcome back on board, Tisdale!" Humphreys hailed.

Shocked, Tisdale threw bewildered glances at his shipmates.

"What's this?"

"You've been treasure hunting, haven't you? And we, *your* mates, want our share…" Connor decreed sharply.

For all reply, Tisdale glowered at them and growled, "What are you talking about? You've had too much rum, as usual!"

Making every effort to remain standing still while holding his pistol firmly with both hands, Dave Warren retorted, "No, we haven't. We just wanna… just wanna…"

As he tried to spew out his words, he stumbled backwards and accidentally fired his pistol, missing Tisdale by a whisker.

"You fool! You stupid fool! Let go of that pistol before you have us all killed!"

Laid out on the deck, Dave Warren mumbled, "Sorry, Capt'n, I didn't mean to."

"Right!" Tisdale shouted to the rest of the crew. "If you want to get paid, you'd better get this ship going!"

"Not before you tell us who's your companion…" Connor demanded.

"If you really want to know, not that it's any business of yours, he's an officer from the King's Navy so you'd better behave yourselves… and if you don't want to get into trouble, you leave him well alone, all right?"

Undeterred, Humphreys continued, "If you've found a treasure, we want our share…"

"For Christ's sake! There's no treasure!" Tisdale insisted. "What we're bringing on board are this gentleman's belongings so no funny business, all right?"

105

"Gentleman?" Humphreys reprised, curling his lips with disdain. "What kind of gentleman is *that* that looks like a pack of rags in wigs?" he riled.

"What was he doing on the island all by himself? He was marooned, wasn't he? I bet you he's a deserter," Connor speculated.

"Never you mind," Tisdale harked back. "Get back to your posts!"

"Well, he'd better pull his weight around here," Connor continued. "We've no room for castaways!"

Flat on his back, Dave Warren grunted, "There's some fishy business going on... argh... and we haven't even caught a fish... ah! ah! ah!"

Tisdale kicked him in the side. "Get up, you useless peddler, and get back to your post!"

As the ship sailed back to port, Tisdale observed his new recruit with a keen eye. He certainly seemed to know what he was doing which meant that perhaps he was telling the truth after all, that he really was an officer from the King's Navy. On the other hand, a pirate would be equally adept at sailing a ship.

***

Back in the port of Nassau, Henry Tisdale paid the sailors and gave them leave before returning to his tavern. He offered lodgings to his new companion, but the latter declined, claiming he had some urgent business to attend, so they parted on friendly terms, each carrying a small share of the stolen treasure.

It was beginning to get dark and Tisdale hurried back to the *Cock 'n Bull*. Once there, he soon bumped into Anne who looked him up and down.

"So... I see you've got what you wanted."

"Some of it... but you fulfilled your part of the bargain and I'm a man of my word." He paused briefly to catch his breath, then added, "I'll let you sail on my ship though I won't be on it myself 'cause, thanks to you, I've much more pressing business to do here."

"When is the ship sailing?"

"Not sure. She's being careened right now so I need to go and check on her progress but I'm hoping she'll be ready sometime next week."

"And you've got your crew?"

"Oh aye. Here in Nassau, it's never a problem hiring a few hands. The

106

trickiest part of it, though, is to find a captain who won't run away with your goods and your ship. I think I've found someone though."

With pleasant thoughts running through his mind, Henry Tisdale felt suddenly excited. He rubbed his hands together and declared with gusto, "Right, lass, I'm famished. Can you cook?"

***

Anne looked around the kitchen. It was exactly as she remembered it, with its plain walls, the cast iron range stoked up with wood, and a table and chairs in the middle of the room. At the end of the main wall, a louvre-door led to a windowless room where all the provisions were stocked haphazardly on wooden shelves.

"I'll have some bacon, some eggs and plenty of cheese. There's also a loaf of bread in the larder," Tisdale said cheerfully.

From the corner of her eye, Anne observed the innkeeper. He was presently sitting at the table with his arms resting over the top and his feet stretched out underneath it. He looked happy and contented, and through his vacant smile, Anne was busy measuring his integrity, his trustworthiness and the potential risk he represented to her and her unborn child. Right now, she did not know whether his contentment came from the thought of surrendering her to the authorities to claim the rich reward put on her head, or the vision of sea chests full of gold that made his eyes sparkle with exceeding brightness. Now that he had obtained what he wanted from her, there was nothing to stop him reporting her to the authorities. And in that satisfied smile and nonchalant posture, she somehow knew that he was probably already thinking about it.

Breaking his pleasant thoughts, Tisdale declared out of the blue, "My wife should be coming home soon… that is if she's not been kidnapped by those damned pirates! Mind you, she gives as good as she gets, so they'll have their hands full with her! I'd better warn her about you before she starts thinking I've been up to no good while she's been away. I don't want to be bashed around the head with a brand-new corset!" he added laughingly.

Seeing his guest's look of surprise, he shrugged his shoulders in a sign of woeful resignation and added with a small chuckle, "She's always buying corsets!"

Then, he continued, "So, you're from Ireland…"

"Aye, that's where I started from," Anne confirmed.

"Ireland! That's a fine country, Ireland. In my opinion, the best dark ale comes from Ireland, though myself, I come from Bristol, England. Mind, my relatives have travelled far and wide and I'm not too sure where they all are, except for my youngest niece… she's in North Cornwall; I think the name of the place is Chelmouth, though it don't matter to you, does it now? I've never been there myself, too small really, not enough trade there, so I don't know what it's like… …In the last communication I had from her — quite a while ago now — she said that she had moved to a small croft overlooking the harbour with her new husband. She was a fine girl, you know, with a good head on her shoulders, so she'll have become a fine woman, I dare say…"

"Do they have any children?"

"I don't think so but communications are very slow in these parts, mainly because of those darned pirates, and by the time I get the next letter, she might have had one or two little ones."

Anne listened quietly, feeling targeted, but to her astonishment, Tisdale added, "Unfortunately, people like me need them… they bring more trade than any other ruffians I know… You see, they've got more money burning in their pockets than they know what to do with… and they're certainly not afraid to spend it, oh no! Not them."

"Arrgh well, as they say, *a pirate's life is a short but merry one,*" Anne quoted jovially.

"Anyhow, 'tis late and I've a tavern to run on the morrow, so I'm gonna retire. Mind you put out the oil lamp before you retire. There's a candleholder over there you can use when you're ready to go upstairs. See you in the morn…"

Anne watched his shadow squeeze down the narrow corridor. Her eyes fixed to the ceiling, she listened to his heavy footsteps creaking on the floorboards upstairs. She heard the latch of a door being lifted and dropped again in its metal hook. The groaning planks of a wooden bed rumbled in the darkness and a few minutes later, an eerie silence fell upon the tavern, numbing her body and dulling her thoughts. After a moment lost in vague contemplation, she picked up her wooden plate, brushed it over the sink and left it on the sideboard. Guiding her steps with the flickering flame of a candle, she proceeded quietly up the stairs holding her long skirt in one hand and the candleholder in the other. A free woman at last, she should have felt at ease and carefree, but her steps were slow and heavy, weighed down by the knowledge that her fate rested entirely on Tisdale's good will, his integrity and his unpredictable moods.

***

The following morning, Anne woke up and for a few seconds, she felt confused and lost, not knowing where she was. Outside her window, she could hear a loud rumbling sound. Carefully, she lifted the faded curtain and watched several men rolling barrels over the cobblestones before lowering them down into the cellar. Their task completed, they made their way inside the tavern. After a few words and a final greeting from the men, the calm returned.

Moments later, Henry Tisdale came upstairs to share with his fugitive the piece of news he had just received. "I've just got a letter. My wife's ship is due in port in the next few days. Now, when she returns, you're gonna have to stay in your room till I've explained the situation to her. I don't want her to be running to the town square screaming adultery!"

***

Several days later, Mona Tisdale turned up on the tavern threshold, still shaken and stirred by the violent storm that had caught them by surprise in mid-ocean, tossing the ship as if it were no more than a small piece of driftwood.

"My oh my!" she exclaimed while at the same time struggling to lift herself from the cart. "I won't be sailing again in a hurry! Come on, Harry Tisdale, show yourself! 'Tis your wife that's come bringing you news from people you know and news from people you sure don't wanna know! Come on out, you lazy hoof! Where are you?"

Almost instantly, Tisdale appeared in the doorway, his arms outstretched and his face beaming with a broad smile.

"Welcome home, Mona dear. You're looking better than ever!"

"Get away with you, Harry Tisdale! I've lost a few pounds in weight and I look as good as a vandalised scarecrow." His wife chortled.

Ignoring her rebuff, he continued, "Whatever you say, travel must agree with you, my dear. Now, let me take your travel bag for you. Just come into the kitchen and put your feet up while I make you a nice cup of tea."

"No time for that, Harry dear, I've got to take me new boots off first. They're killing me. To think I spent all that money thinking they'd be better for me bunions, they've made them worse! Ten groats I paid for them! Shocking I tell you! I feel as bad as if the tax man had taken my last groat! Come on, Harry dear, help me get the wretched things off."

Anxious to put his wife in the most gracious mood, Tisdale rushed to her side, put his arm around her ample waist and lifted her off her feet.

"Hey! Watch yourself," she cried out, chuckling. "I'm no feather weight! Come on, Harry dear, put me down before you break both our necks!"

Before releasing her, the innkeeper planted a resounding kiss on his wife's forehead. Mona Tisdale looked askance at her husband.

"What's got into you, Harry Tisdale?" she asked with a quirky smile.

The innkeeper replied, his eyes gleaming with passion, "Nothing, me dear, I'm just full of the joys of spring."

"Well, that may be so, Harry dear, but after that terrible journey I've just had, you're gonna have to postpone those joys of spring until the summer because I'm quite spent!" his wife complained, wiping her forehead with the back of one hand and digging the small of her back with the other. "Just help me get these wretched boots off, will you? And while you make a cup of tea, you can tell me all about what's been happening lately; and from what I've heard from the coach driver, there's enough gossip to keep me entertained till the small hours of the morning."

**

That evening, hordes of revellers ambled noisily through the streets and crashed into the *Cock 'n Bull* with the sole intention of celebrating Mona Tisdale's return.

"Good to see you in such fine form, Mrs Tisdale!" a reveller greeted jovially.

"And how many corsets did you buy this time, Mrs Tisdale?" another enquired cheekily.

Mona Tisdale wagged her finger at him and said, "You watch what you say, Reg Parker, or I'll bash you round the head with one of them if you're not careful!"

A howl of hearty laughs punctuated her remark. Enjoying the merry banter, pals of Reg Parker egged him on to say more.

"Hey, Reg! Keep going! We want to see them pretty corsets!"

More hearty laughs followed. Far from being concerned by the drunken state of his customers, Henry Tisdale surveyed the rowdy scene with a contented heart, for business had never been so buoyant since the latest hangings.

As for Mona Tisdale, however, closing time could not have come too soon. Exhausted by the long voyage, she began clearing the tavern on the stroke of midnight and hurried her customers until the last had been pushed out of the door and into the street.

"All right, you lot, off you go to your homes and your wives… your own wives that is!" She chortled in a merry mood.

After taking care of locking all the doors, Henry Tisdale beckoned to his wife, "Mona dear, let's go in the kitchen, I've got something to tell you."

"What, now? Can't it wait till the morning?"

"No, it can't," her husband whispered firmly.

"Why are you whispering, Harry dear? Anyway, I hope you're not gonna tell me that the business is going to the dogs." She sighed. "I've heard about them hangings and all our best customers seem to be in hiding…"

Taking his wife gently by the arm, the innkeeper made her sit at the kitchen table and began a detailed account of the last few weeks. After he had finished, his wife looked at him horrified.

"What…! She's upstairs now? But we can't have her stay here! Can you imagine? If people find out, we're gonna be in real trouble and we'll all end up in prison!" She panicked.

Immediately, Tisdale put his finger across his lips and whispered even more quietly, "Don't worry, dear. She's not gonna stay for long. My ship's ready to sail, I've got most of the crew and, more importantly, I think I've found someone to sail her…"

"Why are you helping her?" Mona enquired, wondering whether her husband had some 'personal' interest in the woman.

"She's told me where the pirates that were hanged lately hid their loot!" he whispered excitedly.

"And you believe her?"

"Aye. I've been there. I've found them treasures!"

"So why are we keeping her, then? Just get rid of her… and I mean proper! You know what pirates are like. If you don't get rid of her, one day she's gonna come back with all her mates and ask for her loot back! No, you've got to get rid of her!"

A deep silence followed Mona's remark. After a long thoughtful pause, the innkeeper gave his reply.

"I can't," he simply stated.

"Why not?"

"I gave my word."

"Aye! You gave your word to a runaway pirate. As if that's gonna count! I don't know why you're worried. Think about it, Harry; you won't even have to do it yourself. All you have to do is go to the authorities and you'll even get a reward for your trouble," his wife insisted.

"No, Mona dear, I won't do it. I gave my word. We've got the loot and that's good enough for me."

"Don't be such a fool, Harry Tisdale. One day you're gonna regret this and I don't mind telling you but when that day comes, you're gonna wish you'd listened to me, mark my words."

Still arguing over what they should or should not do, the fractious couple retired to bed. Exhausted by her long journey, Mona fell into a deep sleep as soon as her head hit the pillow. Lying uneasily next to her, Tisdale was tossing and turning. In his troubled mind, he relived the conversation they had both had and although he was reluctant to admit it, he knew his wife had spoken sense. But he had given his word and, quite beside that, he felt sorry for the wench, especially as she was with child. Unable to sleep, he kept churning the same thoughts over and over again, his wife was right but Bonny had told the truth and thanks to her, one day he would be rich. What was he to do?

***

The following morning, Tisdale got up at day break feeling every bone creak in his tired body. First, he went down to sort out his cellar, then he proceeded to the kitchen where his wife was busy preparing breakfast. Suddenly, they heard someone hammer the front door down shouting some command. They looked at each other with the same thought running through their minds.

"Don't answer the door, Harry!" Mona whispered, still holding the wooden spoon she had been using to stir the porridge.

"We've got to. Whoever it is, they know we're here. If it's the local sheriff, it'll only make him more suspicious if we don't answer. Best to find out."

All flustered, the innkeeper dashed out of the kitchen and rushed to the cellar door behind which he kept the bunch of keys on a hook at the top of the stairs. He fumbled with the keys and cursed loudly when he failed to pick the right one. He reached the front door and unlocked it. As soon as he opened it, he got the fright of his life. Standing on the threshold of his very own tavern, were five soldiers with muskets in hands.

"Morning, Mr Tisdale. Sorry to trouble you at this hour of the morning but we've an order to search all houses for escaped prisoners!" the officer in charge declared haughtily, pushing his men inside the tavern.

"You don't mean those darned pirates again!" Henry Tisdale exclaimed. He quickly added, "I thought they'd all been hanged!" as loudly as he could so that his voice could be heard upstairs.

The officer ignored his remark and began to organise the search.

"You two, upstairs! And make sure you open all cupboards, wardrobes, check behind doors, and don't forget the attic. You, go down the cellar and check down there; and you stay with me," he ordered pointing at his men, "We'll have a quick look around the bar and the backyard."

In the kitchen, Mona Tisdale fumbled nervously with her apron as soldiers invaded her premises. She jumped every time she heard a door open and close. Shaking with nerves, she followed their heavy footsteps up the wooden stairs with her eyes affixed to the ceiling. They were bound to find their irregular lodger now. In her head, she kept cursing her husband. What a fool! She could not help raging. Why did he not get rid of that wretched woman when he had the chance? Now it was too late. What would happen to them and the tavern when they were caught hiding a fugitive? Mona Tisdale was working herself into a frenzy with anxiety and fear. Drawing strength from the Almighty, she began to mouth silent incantations to God, Jesus and Mary, pleading for forgiveness and mercy. Then, she got hold of herself and started working out a way of getting out of this mess. In order to do this, she would have to come up with some plausible excuse or, better still, plead complete ignorance. In her head, she began to rehearse an explanatory speech. No, she had never seen that woman before, she had no idea she was even in her house. After all, she had just returned from a long voyage from the Continent. How could she possibly have known that a fugitive was hiding in her home? Standing by the cooking range, she listened nervously to the soldiers' footsteps hammering the wooden floor above. Right now, they were rapping immediately above her head. The sound of doors being slammed and creaking in their hinges shook her nerves right to the core. She panicked even more when the steps moved in the direction of the guest room. A latch jumped out of its metal bracket with a loud clang. A door groaned in its hinges and the steps stopped... dead. A tense moment followed. Mona Tisdale waited anxiously, expecting the silence to be broken any second by chilling cries of fear and despair, followed by the sound of a struggle as the wretched woman fought for her life. That's it, we're done for, she told herself. Jesus, Mary, Mother of God! She crossed herself several times and begged for divine intervention. She bit her lips and in a sudden reflex, she covered her ears and closed her eyes tightly shut so as to block out the desperate cries of the fugitive pleading for her life. But as well as she may hear, no sound came.

Suddenly, the kitchen door burst out open. Mona Tisdale, already on the edge of nerves, jumped, dropped her wooden spoon and let out a small scream. It was the army officer.

"You're all right, Mrs Tisdale," he decreed. "There's no one here so you're quite safe."

The sudden release of tension nearly caused her to faint. Struggling to hide her state of high anxiety, she breathed a huge sigh of relief.

"Thank the Lord!" she forced herself to say, putting her hand on her bosom and feeling her heart pumping hard inside her large chest. Almost recovered, she tilted her head sideways and enquired in a thin voice, "Er... are you looking for anyone in particular?"

"Just the one, Mrs Tisdale. Good day to you. I'll have my usual pint later."

Mona Tisdale forced a smile.

"Would you like a drink now, Officer?" she offered congenially.

"Better not. If I start drinking too soon, I'll be chasing not one miscreant but a whole lot of them!" He chuckled.

"Is it a *he* or a *she* you're after?" she ventured.

"Don't you worry yourself, Mrs Tisdale. Sooner or later, we'll catch those darned ruffians. Good day to you, Mrs Tisdale, and thanks for your help."

"No trouble… no trouble at all, Officer."

As soon as the soldiers departed, her husband returned to the kitchen. She rushed towards him.

"What happened? Where is she?" Mona Tisdale asked in sheer panic.

"Don't worry, dear, she's no longer our problem," he replied calmly. "She's gone and you're never gonna see her again."

"What do you mean *gone*?" She stared at her husband intently, almost fearing the answer. "You didn't… did you?" she queried in a trembling voice.

"It's better if you don't know, Mona dear… Her fate is in the hands of God now, so let her be and forget she was ever here."

"I wish I could… but I'm warning you, Harry Tisdale, don't you ever do that to me again!"

Chapter Twelve
Auld Acquaintances

'The less you know, the longer you'll live' was Tisdale's mantra, especially in this part of the world where life often equated to a mere handful of stolen coins, and not always of gold. This was one of the main reasons why he did not want to involve his wife in his private dealings with a wanted pirate. No, he reasoned, otherwise there might be more than the odd corset flying around the tavern!

***

Along the harbour quay, everything stood still. Hiding in the concealed alcove of a warehouse, Anne Bonny stared at the sea where the cold reflection of the moon shone a faint glow above the tenebrous darkness of the waves. Her mind wandered. In this exquisite little corner of paradise, there was a dark place where the fierce rays of the tropical sun burnt like the fires of hell, and right now, Anne Bonny felt the searing heat of terror and fear.

Suddenly, the stillness of the night was broken by a small group of drunken sailors staggering along and singing incoherent words that trickled away in an alcoholic dribble. One of them stumbled in her direction. She squeezed herself even more against the wall and held her breath. Unable to remain on his feet, the drunken sailor let himself drop to the ground, only a few feet away from her.

"Cor, blimey," he whined, "me legs've turned to jelly." Then, rolling himself into a ball he mumbled, "I'll just go to sleep here, see you in the morn…"

"Come on, mate," his friends urged him. "You can't stay here! You're either gonna get mugged or you're gonna get locked up."

While they tried to get him back onto his feet, his mates came within inches of the fugitive. At that very moment, Anne felt a twinge in her heavy belly and let a small plaintive cry escape from her mouth.

Intrigued, the sailors stopped to listen.

"What was that?"

The sailor's call was answered by the lapping of the waves rolling softly against the harbour wall. With no other sound to be heard, his mate drawled, "It's probably an alley cat chasing a rat. Come on, mate, try and walk properly."

"I can't, I can't…" the sailor pleaded, stumbling all over the quayside.

Eventually, his friends picked him up and thrust him up on their shoulders. After a few minutes, they disappeared out of sight and the calm returned.

Alone again, Anne dropped to the ground and sat on the small bag that contained all her worldly possessions. There she remained, huddled in her corner till morning came. She fought hard to stay awake but a few moments later, her eyes closed again and her head slumped against the wall.

At first light, a voice broke into her dreams.

"Hey, you there! You'll have to move, love; I need to open the store."

Startled, Anne opened her eyes to see a burly character with ruddy cheeks staring back at her. She got up abruptly, and mumbled, "Easy, mister! Give me a minute!"

Crowds began arriving and milling around the port. Ruffling her hair and readjusting her skirts, Anne made her way confidently towards the main quay and stopped when she came level with one particular schooner. She read the name, *Kingston*. The ship had been repaired and she looked magnificent. She looked up to the bridge and watched the crew shouting orders at each other as they coiled cables and ropes, and loaded bales of food and merchandise. She felt excited as she recalled the days when she used to set sail as a member of the crew, feeling strong and hardy, and ready to face all sorts of unpredictable adventures. The happy memories made her chest heave with wild anticipation. However, in her present condition, she may not have felt as keen to brandish a cutlass and slice in half a ruffian or two, but her sense of adventure remained as strong as ever. She began to walk up the gangplank with an assured step. Soon, a member of the crew spotted her.

"Hey, lady, you've no business being here!" he hailed.

"Yes, I have!" she replied with confidence. "I've paid handsomely to come on this voyage and I have a letter from Mr Tisdale to prove it."

Another sailor butted in. "What does the woman want?"

"She says she's paid to come on this voyage."

The sailor was visibly surprised. "You must be on the wrong ship, love, we don't take passengers…" he shouted.

"I've paid good money, I can prove it!" Anne insisted.

"I'll fetch the captain," he said, turning his heels.

While he was away, Anne crouched down to look for the letter in her bag. As soon as she found it, she stood up triumphantly and said, "There it is!"

As she looked up holding a small piece of parchment in her hand, she had an almighty shock. There, standing in front of her was a man she had known before. She stared at him fixedly, her mouth gaping in complete surprise. Instantly, all sorts of thoughts raced through her mind. By the devil's teeth, what was he doing here? How did he manage to…? What should she call him? Would it be safe to call him by his name? What about her? He mustn't say her name. She must stop him uttering her name.

The captain showed not a trace of emotion and seemed quite unperturbed by her presence on his ship; but Anne had seen that special spark in his eyes, flashing like a sign of mutual recognition, but still, he did not acknowledge her. He took the letter and threw a quick glance over it. Then, to the consternation of the other sailors, he extended a friendly hand to the newcomer and said with a courteous smile, "Welcome aboard my ship. I'm Captain Jennings… and you might be…"

"Annabel," Anne promptly replied. "Annabel Smith. Pleased to meet you, Captain," she added with a complicitous smile that had all the onlookers even more intrigued.

One of the sailors looked at the captain and enquired hesitantly, "You two… you know each other?"

"No!" both the captain and Anne chorused at once… though they could not repress a reciprocal smile.

***

Later that morning, the *Kingston* was ready to sail. It was mid spring, hence the best time to commence the long voyage back to England. The season of tropical storms had passed and the weather was now at its best, pleasantly warm during the day and soothingly cool at night. A strong breeze skimmed briskly over the ocean waves, steering the *Kingston* over green lagoons and in between coral reefs and sand banks.

Among the crew, experienced sea dogs like Luke Humphreys, Jack Connor, Will Harris, Dave Warren, and the helmsman Paul Hastings, felt only answerable to Charles Jennings, the captain. The rest of the crew muddled through a set of orders and chores. They consisted mainly of a handful of gunners and a mixed gang of tinkers, tailors, joiners and carpenters, pedlars and others, not to mention the indispensable ship's mascot, a rotund cat named Basil. His main job was that of a mouser and, judging by his ample girth, he was extremely diligent in his designated role. As usual, he was sitting on the prow of the ship. With his ears pricked and his piercing eyes open at half-mast, he gazed at the scene and licked his paws with the nonchalance and aloofness of a lord, impervious to the frantic activities that went on around him.

***

The captain led his new guest below deck. Raising his head, Basil took note. He opened his eyes nice and wide and followed keenly the pair disappearing down the narrow steps with his tongue still sticking out. Immediately, a picture of the galley flashed before his eyes. It must be dinner time. His tummy rumbled in sheer anticipation and swung from side to side as the pampered moggie darted across the deck, weaving blindly around the sailors as if chasing a pack of mice. Almost tumbling down the steps, he arrived below deck just as the captain was opening the door of his cabin. The latter had to stop him from entering by wedging his foot in the door.

"Not in here, Baz! Go and look for mice in the galley!"

The captain closed the door. At last, they were alone. Lost for words, the two companions stared at each other, unable to stem the wave of emotions that made their eyes glitter with welling tears. Then, unable to speak, they fell in each other's arms.

"Boy Jennings!" Anne cried out.

"No more Boy Jennings, please!" he corrected with a smile. "*Captain* now!"

"All right, *Captain*! I can't believe it's you! I'm so glad you're still alive! I was so worried when I didn't see you being taken with the others, I thought they might have killed you."

"Well, they didn't. I could see we were doomed so I hid in the cave that

Mary and I found. By the way, how's my darling Mary?"

"Oh, Jennings, you don't know… you really don't know?"

Charles Jennings stared at his companion with pleading eyes.

"What?" he asked, with lines of sorrow already forming on his forehead. "What's happened to her?"

Anne bit her lips.

"She didn't make it… she died… of tropical fever, while we were in prison together."

Jennings's face froze in shock.

"Oh my God! What about…" he stuttered, "what about our child?"

Overwhelmed with emotion, Anne could not bring herself to speak the words the captain was so reluctant to hear, so she lowered her gaze and shook her head. The captain understood too well. He let himself drop on the bunk and buried his face in his hands. After a short while, he raised his head again and said, "Poor Mary… She was such a good woman… now I've lost her, and my child… We had so many hopes… so many dreams…"

Captain Jennings stared blankly into the void, his eyes heavy with sorrow. Anne sat on the bunk and put her arm around him.

"It's a sad business, Jennings… she was beautiful and she loved you to the last. But you and I, we're gonna pull through…"

Jennings did not respond.

"For Mary's sake," Anne added.

At these words, Jennings turned his head to look at her.

"What about you? How did you get out?"

"Well… It was thanks to Mary that I got out… Without her, we would both still be waiting to be hanged… then she died," Anne continued with a big sigh. "Then, one of the guards came to check on us and… I gave him a feel of his own sword. The door was wide open so I took his clothes and walked out. After that, I went to hide in Tisdale's cellar. Then, I made a deal with him. I told him where some of the treasure was buried and in exchange, he let me…"

"What!" Jennings interrupted. "You've told him where the loot was?"

"Not all of it! I only told him where one place was, that's all."

"I hope you're telling the truth, Bonny, because I'm through with pirates! I want to start a new life."

"So do I, Jennings, so do I!"

"I never wanted to be a pirate in the first place," he confided. "I hated it and so did Mary. We had plans together. We were going to settle down, have a family and be happy…"

"But you can still do that," Anne told him. "You'll find someone else… You're a fine young man."

"Anyway, it doesn't matter now. What does matter however, Anne…"

"You're gonna have to call me Annabel," she interrupted.

"I'll try to remember, *Annabel*. Anyway, I want to make one thing clear, there are no pirates on this ship, understood?"

"Don't worry, I've no wish to be found out. The old Anne Bonny is dead. I'm now Annabel Smith and I'm determined to stay alive for the sake of my child."

"Well, let's forget about the past. We've got a whole new future ahead of us and prosperous it will be!" Jennings declared with conviction.

***

A week passed with no incident to declare. The warm tropical breeze steered the *Kingston* towards mid ocean where the waves were high, splashing the prow with a cooling spray. Annabel Smith stood on the main deck, lost in her dreams. It was the first time since her capture that she was able to enjoy the sunlight, the fresh air and wide-open spaces without fearing for her life. She filled her lungs with the iodine air, felt the salty spray on her weary features and scoured the magnificent view that she had so longed for while she had been cooped up in a dark and dank prison cell. Watching the distant horizon, she wondered what lay ahead, and when the ship passed Cove Island, she turned her head away, shielding her eyes with her long flowing hair. At that moment, a violent pang gripped her stomach and ripped her heart apart. The sudden flow of painful memories made her swoon and she felt faint. She gripped the bulwarks tightly to catch herself.

The captain spotted her.

"You're all right?"

Annabel jerked her head back, looked at the captain straight in the eyes and replied, "I'm fine, thank you. Just a little seasick, that's all."

"That's not like you."

"I know… it must be my condition."

***

Annabel Smith surveyed the scene from the main deck with eyes full of nostalgic memories. The *Kingston* crew seemed remarkably tamed compared to the rowdy company of pirates. The ruffians were a cheery lot, and despite their frequent arguments and fights among each other, she missed their fractious banter and raucous laughter, and their hearty singing that swelled the sails with their unleashed bravado and pride. Where was Ned Hornby when she was feeling sad and forlorn? Poor Ned, he was probably playing his concertina to the others, cheering them up on their way to the stars.

Brought up as a Catholic by her Irish father, who himself had often swayed away from the righteous path, Anne wondered whether God the Redeemer would be kind enough to forgive her old shipmates and give them the rest and peace despite their dishonourable past. Meanwhile, down here, alone to face her destiny, she missed them dreadfully, and above all, she missed her old self, the outrageously brash and fearless Anne Bonny who flirted like a loose mistress, fought like a wild tigress and shouted like a common fishwife. On one occasion, forever outrageous and brash, she had even flashed her breast to other pirates who had taken the unfortunate decision to storm her ship. She smiled as she recalled their shocked reaction.

By sailing on the *Kingston*, she hoped to revive those memories and recapture some of the exciting moments she had lived through on previous journeys in the company of Mary and Calico Jack, and other likeable rogues like Stan Bennett and Ned Hornby. Here, though, the atmosphere was dull, so dull. On board a merchant ship, from ship boys to old hands, all were responsible for the welfare of the cargo and its safe delivery. "Anyone caught drinking out of hours will forfeit a portion of their pay proportional to the crime." The captain had declared with authority.

A few feet away from the main mast, Dave Warren and Will Harris were presently involved in a game of poker which they played on top of a wooden cask full of rum, and when they heard the rule about drinking on board, both looked at each other, pulled a face, grumbled in their beards and played their next card.

Meanwhile, Annabel Smith paced the main deck, wondering what to do with herself. Her newly-found freedom had an unexpected bitter taste. Not far from her, two ship boys were busy playing a game with some small bones. Suddenly, she spotted a discarded concertina resting on top of a coil of rope. She picked it up and stared at it fondly. She even thought she recognised it. Lost in her thoughts, she had quite forgotten where she was for a moment until a voice interrupted her trail of thoughts.

"Could I have my concertina back, please?" the voice requested politely.

She turned around, half expecting to see Ned Hornby, but the man she saw was a middle-aged peddler on crutches with a wooden peg for a right leg. She smiled at him and readily handed the instrument back to him. As a way of thanks, he returned a wide toothless grin.

***

It was April in the year of the Lord 1721. The weather was beginning to heat up but soon, the ship would be sailing in the middle of the Atlantic Ocean where the wind was strong and chilly, the waves wild and choppy and the sea spray high and icy.

Despite the strong currents, The *Kingston* sailed on, cutting through the waves with determination and pride. Standing on the quarterdeck with his long glass tucked under his arm, Captain Jennings scanned the horizon and hoped for a trouble-free voyage, thanks to the recent purge of pirates. He knew his chances were good for Blackbeard had been killed during a boarding and countless other pirates had been hanged at Port Royal or Nassau. But the path was not as yet clear. There remained a great threat that hung heavily over every ship that dared cross the sea, for out there, in the heat of the sun, in the wind and rain, roamed a redoubtable pirate, whose name was enough to make the bravest of sailors shake in his sleep. He was reputed to be more ruthless and deadlier than Blackbeard himself. His name was Bartholomew Roberts, a man whose life bore a strong parallel with Jennings's own past. Born in a tiny village in south Wales, he had hoped to become a gentleman officer of the King's Navy. But his ship was seized by pirates and Roberts, just like Jennings, was forced to join the pirates' crew, a life to which he adapted so well and with such skill that he soon gained the reputation of being the most successful pirate of them all. Never one to be described as common and ordinary, he strived to stand out from the crowd and distance himself from the common lot that formed his crew by parading in a rich crimson long coat and a wide-brimmed hat adorned with a red feather. At present, he was known to be involved with the slave trade and for this reason, Captain Jennings hoped that the pirate would be sailing off the coast of Africa rather than here in the North Atlantic Ocean. By the Grace of God, the twain might never meet.

***

Back on board, one of the shipmates had been observing Annabel Smith for some time. He thought he recognised her from the time he had stood in the public gallery when two women pirates had been tried. Not that he had wanted to waste his time standing in a packed airless courtroom, but his wife, the gossip queen of Bay Street, Nassau, had dragged him along because she felt it her duty to witness the momentous occasion. Unlike her rascal of a husband who could never do anything right, the righteous Mrs Downing always swept her house clean every day, did her laundry on a Monday and went to church on a Sunday. That was why Bob Downing was a carpenter at sea.

Just as the captain walked past him on his way to the quarterdeck, he tried to grab his attention.

"Capt'n!" he whistled through his missing front teeth. "Might I have a word with you?"

"Yes, what is it?" the captain replied in a brusque tone.

"I think I know who that lady is."

"Who?"

"Her there." He pointed. "Her name is Anne Bonny… you know… one of Rackham's women."

"Is she?" the captain replied, feigning complete ignorance. "How can you be sure?"

"I was in the courtroom that day, in Nassau, you know… They're all dead now, all of them pirates, hanged and all, except her and her mate because they were both with child… aye, I was there when she said, 'My Lord, I plead my belly!', aye, that's how she put it… I was there and it's her!" he insisted.

The captain looked at the woman passenger then at the sailor. He had to think fast. "Tell me, Downing… it is Downing, isn't it?"

"Aye, Capt'n, Bob Downing's the name."

"Well, Downing, before you went into the courtroom, did you have a few mugs of rum?" the captain enquired.

"Oh aye!" Downing replied cheerfully. "We all did! I mean, we only went in for a laugh… and because me wife told me to…"

"Well, there you go," the captain interrupted. "Your eyes are playing tricks on you."

"No, no, it's her, I know it's her! She's with child, ain't she?"

The captain studied the sailor's expression intently.

"As a matter of fact, Downing," the captain remarked. "I also happened to be in court that day and I can assure you that *that* lady, my friend, is not Anne Bonny!"

"Ain't she?" Bob Downing replied, beginning to doubt himself.

"No! So you'd better leave her alone or I'll keel haul you!"

When he heard the last threat, the little man winced as if in pain.

"Sorry, Capt'n," he mumbled sheepishly. "I just thought… aye… I just thought…"

Before he could finish his sentence, the captain turned on his heels abruptly, leaving Bob Downing on the spot mumbling words of suspicion. He knew he was right, that *that* lady was the very same he had seen standing in the courtroom, but what did it matter anyway? After all, they were on a merchant ship bound for Bristol, England, and at the end of the journey he would be handsomely paid. So, why should he care?

Chapter Thirteen
The Cross of Madeira

Back in Nassau, Governor Woodes Rogers was in the middle of an emergency meeting with his councillors to discuss the damaging effects of pirates' activities on the island's economy, when loud voices coming from the corridor interrupted the proceedings.

"I need to see the Governor straight away!" the stranger insisted.

Heavy footsteps approached the Council Chamber and the door flew open.

"I'm sorry, Governor, I couldn't stop him!" the guard apologised.

The Governor stood up and scowled at the man who had forced his way in. It was John O'Malley, the local sheriff.

"What's the meaning of all this?" the Governor barked.

"My apologies, Governor, but I've just had news that Bart Roberts has seized another ship," he blurted out all in one breath.

"Damn!" the Governor cursed.

"A Spanish galleon."

"Oh hell! Damned pirates! With their reckless behaviour, they're going to start another war!" the Governor growled in anger.

The messenger paused. Should he continue while the Governor was in an apoplectic mood? He eyed the Governor whose voluminous body had slumped into his gilded armchair. Now, he seemed more composed. The messenger deemed it safe to deliver the next piece of news which he knew would cause even more anguish. "One of the survivors has informed us that Black Bart raided the whole content of the galleon which was carrying gold coins, silverware and among that lot, the Crown Jewels, including the Cross of Madeira that was especially commissioned for the forthcoming coronation of King Alfonso."

"Good Lord! Damn those stupid fools! Spain is bound to declare war on us now! They're going to think we had a hand in it, and we've only just signed a peace treaty! This simply cannot go on! We've got to act straight away," he decreed. "Right, gentlemen, the only thing we can do is to redouble our efforts to get rid of those damned pirates once and for all! I want to mobilise all the ships fit to sail and we're going to hunt them down until the last of those damned scoundrels is brought to justice and hanged!"

"But, Governor, we haven't got that many ships," a councillor noted.

A long thoughtful pause punctuated his remark. Then a lone voice rose. "There's one thing we could do, though…" another councillor suggested.

All sat up to listen.

"Let's set pirates against pirates. Use the ruffians to catch Black Bart by promising a handsome reward and an instant pardon to whoever catches the villain, dead or alive!"

"I think you might have something there, Cartwright!" the Governor commented. "Well, Gentlemen, let's get on with it. The meeting is adjourned."

Then, turning to his secretary, he ordered, "Gardner, I want you to draft an edict immediately detailing our plan of action and I want it read out in the town square today!"

"Today?" Gardner parroted.

"Yes today… and tomorrow, and the day after until everybody's got the message!" the Governor insisted.

"How much of a reward were you thinking about?"

"Now let me think… one hundred gold doubloons; that should help them bite the bait."

"One hundred gold doubloons! That's quite a substantial amount, Sir!"

"Well, would you stick your neck out for less?"

"Er… well, probably not."

"There you are then, one hundred gold doubloons and an instant pardon, that's the deal."

"Very well, Governor."

***

Meanwhile, out in the middle of the Atlantic Ocean, the *Kingston* sailed on unhindered, pressing the waves and fighting the currents. They had been sailing for two weeks when Captain Jennings noticed some ominous clouds gathering from the west. He observed the cloud formation keenly, calculating the speed and direction in which they moved. He was hoping for an easterly wind that would push the clouds away from them but after a few minutes of intense observation, he concluded that it was a southerly wind and that this wind was blowing a blanket of thick dark clouds straight towards them. Feeling uneasy, he called his quartermaster.

"Connor, I think we're sailing into a storm."

"Don't worry, Captain, at this time of year, they're never stronger than a storm in a mug of rum."

"Nevertheless, I think we'd better get ready for this one. Order the men to furl the foresail and reef the topsails."

With her main sail down, the *Kingston* slowed right down to a gentle cruising speed.

A while later, the ship boy shouted from the crow's nest, "Ship ahoy, ship ahoy! To starboard!"

The captain peered into his long glass and noted, "Humm… I don't like the look of her. We'd better get the cannons ready just in case, and make sure that all pistols are clean and loaded and all other weapons ready for use…"

"Why? We're not going into battle, are we?" Jack Connor queried.

"Not just yet… but you should know the first rule of the sea, never trust a passing ship."

Captain Jennings rushed up the quarterdeck. Pulling out his long glass, he peered eastward and trained his eye on what looked like a brigantine. As the wind pushed them closer still, he tried to read the name on the prow but to no avail. The ship was still too far away. He took a deep breath and put away his long glass. Then, turning to his quartermaster, he enquired, "What do you think, Connor?"

"I'm not too sure, Captain…"

"Neither am I but I sure don't like the look of her!" the captain stated. "For a start, she's not flying a flag, and that alone makes me suspicious. She would only do that if she didn't want to be identified." Then, handing the long glass to his quartermaster, he commanded, "Keep an eye on her."

The captain left and went in search of the only woman passenger. He found her sitting on the prow.

"Mrs Smith!" he called out, feeling odd using her fake name. "There's a storm brewing, I think you should go below deck. You can use my cabin if you like. It'll be safer for you there and you'll be able to rest."

Annabel Smith got up reluctantly.

"I hate this," she grumbled.

The captain looked at her with inquisitive eyes.

"You know…" she continued. "Feeling a great big fat useless lump and not being able to take part in the action."

The captain smiled.

"You're still the wild roving pirate at heart, aren't you?" he teased.

For reply, she gave him a sharp dig in the ribs and looked furtively around in case someone had overheard the jibe. The captain winced.

"Sorry, I was forgetting…"

As she left to seek shelter in the captain's cabin, Jack Connor called. "Captain! I can read her name. It's the *Royal Fortune*."

Instantly, both the captain and Annabel Smith stopped in their tracks for, to the ex-pirates, the name was all too familiar. The captain glanced at his woman companion and repeated his order, "Go! And whatever happens, stay in my cabin… and make sure you take Basil with you."

Annabel Smith hesitated.

"It's an order!" The captain shouted.

***

The captain returned to the side of his quartermaster.

"What speed do you think she's doing?"

"Average, Captain, ten knots at most; we'll easily catch up with her."

"That's exactly what I don't want to do." Then turning to the helmsman, he shouted, "Hastings, give her a wide berth; try to avoid her at all costs."

"Why's that, Captain? She doesn't look threatening."

"Look at her main mast, Hastings. Can't you see?"

"Nope… there's nothing there, Captain."

"Exactly! There's no flag flying… Hastings, bear north!"

"We'll go off course if I do that," Hastings replied.

"I don't care! We've got to avoid her, Hastings!"

Captain Jennings remained on the quarterdeck. He knew that the brigantine was captained by one of the most redoubtable pirates of the West Indies. The thought made him tighten his muscles and clench his teeth. He assembled the whole crew on the main deck in order to brief his men on what they might expect. If a fight was inevitable, Charles Jennings was about to enter battle as captain and leader of his ship for the very first time.

Mindful of his new role, and drawing on the military training he had received during his short time in the Navy, he was anxious to prepare his men for a possible confrontation, in the full knowledge that most of them were not professional soldiers. However, the last thing he wanted was to panic his crew, so he chose his words very carefully.

"Men, we think that *that* ship you see over there belongs to Bartholomew Roberts, otherwise known as Black Bart!" he began. At the sound of the name, an audible gasp rose from the main deck. "As you all know, Black Bart is a pirate, ruthless in his actions and wicked in his deeds, but we may pray that he leaves us alone today and God willing, we shall be able to continue on our journey to Bristol. We must do everything we can to deliver our cargo safely because you all know the deal, 'no delivery, no pay'. So be ready, take your courage with both hands, sharpen your cutlasses and load your pistols. Should we be forced into a fight, the battle will be hard but the rewards will be high. And should you waver in front of the enemy, remember this, you'll be fighting for your right to live, for the survival of your families and for the sake of peace; and after the battle, it will be your glory, not theirs; it will be your livelihood, not their ill-gotten gains. You may not be professional soldiers but in your hearts, you have the same strength and courage as the best of them, so be strong, be fearless and show them no mercy for, together, we shall overcome the enemy!"

At that point, Captain Jennings paused to allow his words to sink in. He had practically shouted the last sentence and after a resolute silence, the shipmates began to stir.

"Aye, Captain!" Dave Warren shouted brandishing his cutlass at the same time.

"Aye, aye! Down with the pirates! Down with the robbers and thieves!" Will Harris chanted.

More loud cheers followed his rallying cry and the men began to chant his words before arming themselves with anything they could find.

Two of the ship boys rushed to the captain.

"Captain! We want to fight too!"

"That's great, lads," the captain replied with a friendly smile, though before he could say anything else, one of the lads cut in, "But we ain't got no weapons."

"All right, lads. Don't worry, go down the gun deck and help the gunners with the cannons."

"Aye, aye, Captain!"

Not wanting to take his eyes off the *Royal Fortune*, the captain rushed back to the bulwark. His heart was pounding hard in his chest. His hands resting on top gripped the side of the ship tightly. At this very moment, he could not tell whether he was shaking with excitement or trembling with fear. Everybody on board knew of Black Bart's reputation. To date, he was reputed to have seized over four hundred ships. No other pirate could claim a higher figure.

Jennings looked up to the sky. The oncoming storm was gathering strength. The prow of the ship was dipping deeper into the sea, bouncing off the waves and splashing the decks with large sprays of water. Able seamen clambered up the rigging to tie up the loose sails. Up there in the crow's nest, ship boy Thomas Parry threw a nervous look at the darkening horizon. He was scared. Fearing that he was about to be thrown overboard by the force of the waves, he swiftly left his post.

Back on the quarterdeck, Captain Jennings peered once more through his long glass. To his horror, he noticed that the wind was pushing his ship towards the enemy. Soon after, the pirate ship manoeuvred herself right behind his own ship, taking the wind out of her sails and slowing down her course. Worse still, thunder clouds hovered ominously above the darkened sky bringing torrential rain that began to lash at the sails and onto the deck, exposing the shipmates to the wild elements and the perilous rocking of the waves.

"Hastings!" he called out. "What are you doing? Get away from her!"

"I can't!" the helmsman shouted back through the sea spray.

The captain looked around.

"Humphreys! Go and help him!" he ordered.

Humphreys jumped to Hastings's help and together, they tried to lock the big wheel using their bare feet as leverage. But the sea spray was relentless, making the deck slippery. They struggled to steer the ship away. Alas, they were powerless against the forces of nature and all of a sudden, the threatening shadow of the *Royal Fortune* was upon them. Captain Jennings prayed for the wind to continue to whip up a storm, for he knew that, while the ships were being tossed violently by the waves, no boarding would be possible. Ominously, the *Royal Fortune* was still sailing close behind them. From that position, neither ship could fire cannons at each other. In that moment, Captain Jennings cursed, if only a violent thunderstorm could come and scare the superstitious pirates out of their skin, or for a thunderbolt to strike and split her main mast in half, or even for a rogue wave to smash her hull and sink her on the spot. But to his horror, he noticed the thick mass of black clouds moving away. The storm was abating though the sea remained choppy.

A battle seemed unavoidable. The captain ordered his crew to remain on the main deck. Now, all could see clearly the other ship at the ready with a prominent figure dressed in a red coat standing on the quarterdeck and holding on firmly to the balustrade while glaring back at them.

Below deck, the gunners were ready. Charles Jennings saw no point in waiting. He gave the signal to Connor who shouted, "Fire!"

The gunners fired their cannons. Jennings watched tensely. The cannon balls missed their target and fell into the sea, throwing up huge sprays of water.

"Reload the cannons!" Connor shouted.

Suddenly, the ship rocked violently. Cries of pain cut through cries of fear. Captain Jennings looked around and shouted more orders. A thick blanket of gunpowder smoke prevented him from seeing his enemy clearly but he knew he had to fire straight back. The ship rocked again. All of a sudden, Jennings's men gasped in horror as the tall and dark silhouette of the enemy ship surged through the thick cloud of smoke like the angel of death spreading its giant wings. Hanging from the rigging, the pirates howled their threats like a pack of crazed hyenas. Captain Jennings glanced at his own deck and saw fear in his men's eyes. He turned his head again towards the *Royal Fortune* and saw the pirates preparing for the onslaught. There was only one thing he could do now. He called 'quarters', for he knew that '*under the pain of death, quarters, whenever called, must be granted*'.

A sardonic laugh followed the captain's call. The pirates pointed at his ship, jeering and mocking. A few minutes later, Bartholomew Roberts boarded the *Kingston* flanked by his opportunist rogues. A tall man with a wild mop of dark curly hair squashed under his large hat, the pirates' captain cut a dashing figure that inspired foreboding and fear, intensified by his haughty air and piercing eyes. Around his neck hung several layers of gold chains. Sparkling among them was a huge gold cross encrusted with a large ruby surrounded by the biggest diamonds anyone had ever seen. It was a magnificent cross, a priceless jewel whose true significance escaped Captain Jennings and his crew, for none of them had any idea that the glittering object they were staring at was the *Cross of Madeira*, the coronation jewel destined for the King of Spain.

Black Bart scoured the deck and seemed to take pleasure in detecting the sheer terror on every man's face. He took his time and remained silent while striding the deck with authority. Suddenly, he stopped, turned around to look at the men and asked, "Who's your captain?"

There was a pause… a long silent pause. Nobody moved. Black Bart continued to scrutinise the sullen faces that were staring back at him without flinching. Then, he heard a slight shuffle and watched a young man take a step forward.

"I am."

"And you are…"

"Captain Charles Jennings."

At the sight of the young captain, Bart Roberts let out a little chuckle. He looked Jennings up and down as if admiring his brave stance. The pirates made a move to grab him but Roberts immediately barred their way with his sword.

"No!" he said. "Leave him to me." Then he paused, taking his time to study the captain. After a short while, he addressed Jennings again and simply declared, "I'm impressed."

Standing in front of the young captain, Roberts scrutinised Jennings's solemn face, his calm resolve, his unwavering courage and the quiet authority he exerted around him.

On the deck, there was complete silence. The atmosphere was tense with every man on board holding his breath waiting to see what Bart Roberts would do next. When he finally deigned to speak, his voice made them jump with fear. "I want you," he declared outright, looking straight in Jennings's eyes.

Charles Jennings looked stunned and puzzled by the ambiguous remark. Everybody knew of Roberts's reputation as a man's man. They also knew that his favourite companion and bedfellow had been Hywell Davis, the close mate who had been responsible for his somewhat irregular situation, the ally whom he loved and admired most until he was killed during the storming of a French man-of-war.

"You're young, strong and fit… I'd like you to be my second-in-command," Roberts continued.

"Never!" Jennings blasted.

Remaining totally impassive, Bart Roberts continued, "Or if you prefer, you could be my quartermaster."

"You go to hell! I've no wish to become a pirate!" Jennings spat with verve.

Bart Roberts let out another little chuckle.

"A man of spirit... I like it," he declared, still keeping very calm. "Unfortunately, my friend, I'm afraid you have not much of a choice..." he added, pointing his sword at the captain's neck.

Suddenly, a loud voice interrupted.

"*He* may not... but I have!"

All heads turned in the direction of the voice and to their surprise saw the woman passenger standing at the top of the stairs pointing a pair of loaded pistols straight at Roberts.

"You let go of him, you go back to your own ship and no one dies!" she blasted.

Roberts turned around slowly to face his adversary.

"Well, my o my! If it isn't..." he stuttered.

"That's right! So you get the hell out of here, either on your two feet or in a dead man's chest! It's your choice but don't take too long, I ain't got much time," the woman threatened.

Bart Roberts let out a nervous laugh. His hands resting boastfully on his hips, he grinned from ear to ear, unable to take seriously a challenge issued by a woman with child.

"Do they know who you are?" he queried with a mocking voice. Without waiting for an answer, he shouted to the whole crew, "Did you know she's a pirate? That's Anne Bonny right here. Yep, that's Jack Rackham's woman!"

The crew stirred a little. Among them, one man showed no great surprise at hearing the news. Bob Downing, who had always sworn that he had seen her before, nudged his neighbours and whispered through the gap in his teeth, "I told that to the capt'n but he wouldn't believe me!"

Suddenly, a loud crack hit the deck just behind where Anne Bonny stood. It had come from the pirate ship. Quick as a flash, she fired back. The pirates took it as a signal to launch the attack. Immediately, Captain Jennings shouted, "Come on, men! Let's get rid of these vermin!"

In a flash, he drew his cutlass and set upon Bart Roberts. Roberts, the more experienced of the two, pushed his adversary towards a spot that would expose him to the line of fire. Jennings was no fool. He lunged forward but Black Bart responded with a quick swipe that struck the captain on his side. Shocked by the sharp pain, Jennings fell to the deck, writhing in agony. There was his chance! The pirate lifted his sword and snarled, "Pity! But so be it!"

At that very moment, a loud crack tore through the air. Bart Roberts's arm froze in mid-air. His body stood rigid. His eyes, as if caught in a trance, stared blankly at his victim. Rendered half-conscious by the pain, Jennings stared back, unable to move. He had heard the shot, but Black Bart was standing above him, his foot pinning him to the deck. Helpless, he watched the sword, waiting for it to fall. He knew his last moment had come. As he let out a resigned sigh, the pirate's body came crashing on top of him where it lay, rigidly still. Shocked, Jennings could barely look at the inanimate body that was slumped on top of him with the diamond cross dangling very close to his own neck. Although in terrible pain, the captain kept his wits about him and before anyone could see, he quickly removed the cross and tucked it under his belt.

Soon after, a handful of pirates jumped onto the main deck and, as if executing a well-rehearsed drill, grabbed Bart Robert's lifeless body and threw it overboard. Once their grim task completed, they hurriedly retreated back onto their own ship, not even stopping to take any of the merchandise with them.

As the *Royal Fortune* sailed away, Jennings managed to smile through the pain. In a spontaneous move, the whole crew broke into a loud cheer. The danger had passed and Captain Jennings, victorious, was ready to resume full command of his ship.

"Humphreys, Warren, Harris, Connor, full sails on! Hastings, back on course!" he commanded with authority, still holding his injured side.

Suddenly, a thought occurred to him. Where was his female companion? His thoughts vacillated between apprehension and fear. He stormed around the decks, searching frantically for her. Just in case, he leant over the bulwarks and peered intently into the sea. She might have gone below deck, he thought, stomping across the deck and down the narrow steps. There, he spotted the four ship boys huddled together in a corner by one of the cannons, visibly shaken. He walked straight towards them.

"It's all right, lads, the battle is over," he declared. "Go on, go to the galley and ask Cook to give you some hard tacks then go back on deck. The fresh air will do you good."

"Aye, aye, Captain!" the boys chorused, smiling with relief.

Having dealt with the boys, the captain made straight for his cabin. No sooner had he opened the door than he heard a heavy thump. He looked behind the door and saw Anne sprawled on the floor. She had fainted. Taking the utmost care, he carried her to his berth and laid her there. Then, he shouted at one of the ship boys to fetch him some water. Young Thomas Parry quickly returned with a full tumbler. The captain thanked him before dismissing him.

Relieved to find his friend still alive, he set about to nurse her. After a while, she opened her eyes. She looked bewildered as if she did not know where she was. The captain sought to reassure her with a smile.

"That was a very brave thing you did," he said.

"Not that brave," she replied. "I was thinking of my unborn child."

"Maybe, but thanks to you, we're now free from that tyrant of the sea. If you haven't already got a pardon, I'll make sure you get one."

"Don't waste your time, Jennings. I'd only need one if I wanted to go back to Nassau, but me, I'm through with all that pirate business. I'm gonna take care of myself and my child," Anne decreed in a tired voice.

"But," the captain continued. "Where did you get to? You really got me worried when I couldn't find you. I thought… I thought…"

"You thought I was dead… or worse, that I'd jumped ship and joined the pirates, didn't you?"

"Well, I never know what you're going to get up to next…"

"Don't be daft, Jennings! In my condition! You must be joking. You better believe me when I say I'm through with this pirate business!"

Exhausted by the events, Anne rested her head on the pillow and looked at Jennings fondly. To her, he was still Boy Jennings, that young man with hay-coloured hair, clear blue eyes and a look that still wavered between the boy he was and the man he had become. Unusually for a man with a rough past, he was blessed with a gentle disposition that belied the time he had spent as an enforced pirate. Searching deep into his blue eyes, Anne could tell that his thoughts were still with Mary. Alas, neither she nor his child had survived and those bitter sweet memories bonded both survivors into a close mutual friendship that had to be kept secret for their own survival.

Anne suddenly noticed blood on his side.

"Jennings! You're hurt!"

The captain shrugged his shoulder and replied dismissively, "Oh, it's nothing."

"But you're bleeding! If you don't get that wound fixed, you're gonna bleed to death. Come on, let me fix it."

As she busied herself tending to the captain's injury, she resumed their conversation.

"Why do you want to rejoin the Navy? What if they find out about your past?"

"Why should they? You're the only person alive who knows about me."

"Oh Jennings, I hope you're right… and I hope you make it."

"And I hope you make it too… you and your child."

Anne smiled. Their common past had become a bond, solid and unbreakable.

"Anyway," the captain reprised. "Ouch! Careful! Don't waste too much rum on that wound!"

"Oh Jennings, don't go back to the Navy. They treat you so badly there, everyone knows that; and the few groats you earn for risking your life for King and Country… it's really not worth it."

"But I have to, because…"

Charles Jennings hesitated. He had clear plans mapped out in his head but beleaguered by superstitions he had collected over the short period of time spent in the company of pirates, he feared that revealing them would only flounder them.

"Because what?" Anne questioned.

"Never mind, Anne…"

"With a bit of luck, the crew'll forget about that little incident with Black Bart. I just hope I make it to our destination," she added with a sigh.

"Of course you will. You're as strong as an ox and stronger than half the men on board. But what are you going to do once we get to Bristol?"

"I've got an address. Tisdale gave it to me. He's got a niece in Cornwall. I just hope she doesn't mind me staying with her until my child is born."

"And then what?"

"I don't know, but I'll promise you one thing, though…"

"What?" Jennings asked intrigued.

"If I ever go back to Nassau, I'll not steal your treasure."

"You know where it is?"

"Mary told me before she died."

"Oh well… I guess I have to trust you." Then, extending his hand, the captain challenged, "Word of a pirate?"

Anne clasped his hand firmly and pledged with a broad smile,

"Word of a pirate."

At that moment, someone knocked on the door.

"Yes?" the captain hailed.

Young Thomas Parry slipped his head around the door, stared at the two adults and, forgetting his business, asked all excited, "You… You're pirates?"

The captain forced a laugh. It made him feel good to laugh. It had been such a long time since he had been able to drop his guard and enjoy the moment, no matter how short.

"What are you talking about, Thomas bach?" the captain exclaimed, betraying his Welsh origins. "It's only a joke, a way of bragging… and anyway, it's very bad manners to listen at people's doors."

"Sorry, Capt'n. I couldn't help hearing."

"All right, what do you want?"

"The quartermaster wants you up there."

"Go and tell him I'm coming. Now, scram it or I'll give you a feel of the cat-o'-nine-tails."

"Aye, aye, Capt'n!" young Thomas replied in mock terror before scrambling up the stairs. In his rush, he ran straight into another sailor, threw a casual "Sorry" and disappeared.

Soon after, there was another knock on the captain's door.

"What?" an exasperated voice answered.

"It's me, Capt'n, Bob Downing."

"What do you want?" the captain asked through the door.

"I thought I might have a word with you…like… if I might…"

The sailor waited for a reply. Just when he least expected it, the door flew open.

"Yes, Downing?"

"It's just like… I wouldn't want anyone to hear… If I might be so bold…"

"All right, Downing, close the door behind you!" the captain said, pushing the sailor inside his cabin. "What can I do for you?"

"Well, as I said, like…"

"Stop faffing about, for goodness' sake, and say whatever you've come to say!" the captain cut in.

"Aye, Capt'n, it's like… you know… the lady here…"

As the sailor struggled to spit out his words, he looked at Anne, greeted her with a subtle bow of the head, muttered "Much obliged" to her, then turning to the captain finally blurted out, "I know she was a pirate like…"

"So?"

"Well, I thought that… if I don't say nothing like… I might get a reward like…"

The captain scowled at the little man and thought for a moment. Then he sat casually on his desk to observe the sailor closely and stated plainly, "As it happens, Downing, as I said before, you are quite mistaken."

"I know I'm not, even Black Bart said so."

"Black Bart may have said so but he's dead so he's not much good to us now, is he?"

The captain paused. Then he cleared his throat before resuming the talk.

"Tell me, Downing, can you read?"

"Well, as much as I can tell me name, Capt'n."

The captain took an official looking document out of his desk.

"I have here a letter from Mr Woodes Rogers." Here he stopped and enquired in a patronising tone, "You *do* know who Mr Woodes Rogers is?"

"Aye, Capt'n. He's the Gov of the Island."

"Quite right, Downing. And in this letter, here… can you see?"

"Well, I can but I don't know what it says."

"Never mind, Downing, I'll tell you what it says. It's a letter of pardon addressed to a certain Miss Anne Bonny, former pirate. See? It's written right here. Now the lady here happens to be Mrs Annabel Smith from Bristol so scram it before her husband hears about your defamatory remarks and has you shot!"

"Your defa… what remarks?"

The captain opened the door and kicked the muttering sailor out of his cabin.

"Scram it, I said!"

***

The voyage resumed with everyone on board relieved to have escaped with their lives. None were more pleased than the captain who knew that, thanks to Black Bart's sudden demise, the *Kingston* would be able to continue its journey in relative safety. Once again, the young captain dreamed about the future and smiled with great satisfaction at the thought that his plans would work out even better than he had envisaged. From the quarterdeck, he scoured the whole ship and studied his crew. Perhaps because of his youth, the older members felt protective towards him and in return, he had shown steely determination to get them out of trouble. All of them had been good and faithful, and watching them minding their stations without as much as a complaint, he vouched that he would give them some form of reward, even if it meant having to give away some of his share. Two weeks later, the ship boy on duty in the crow's nest sighted land, port side. The captain rushed to fetch his long glass and peered over the chiselled horizon. He took a deep breath and watched with delight the jagged cliffs of southern England becoming more and more distinct. It was almost two years since he had last seen his homeland and he rejoiced at the prospect of seeing his family again, at sitting at a proper table without fear of coming under attack and tucking into his mother's scrumptious food without first having to brush off weevils, dust and mites or even the odd worm wriggling out of a rotten piece of meat. Most of all, he looked forward to the heady musty smell of damp earth that rose from an English garden. He could not wait to see the soft carpet of wild flowers blossoming in lush meadows. Staring at the familiar contours of the coast, he reckoned that, depending on the wind, they should touch land early that evening. This would not leave him enough time to go to the Admiralty, but this was the least of his concerns. First, he had to organise his crew to unload the cargo, then pay and dismiss them, writing down the names of those willing to make the return journey with him.

***

When the time came to disembark, Anne emerged from below deck, looked around to see where the captain was and went to stand next to him. They stared at each other for a while, not knowing how to initiate their final goodbye. Their adventures together would live forever, indelibly etched in their memories.

Captain Jennings took a deep breath and put his arm around his companion's shoulders in an uncharacteristic show of affection.

"I'm sailing back in two months' time," he told her. "You're welcome to join us…"

"Jennings! You're going back?"

"I have to. There's someone waiting for me over there. You want to join us?"

"You've met someone? Aw… Who's she?" Anne asked, curious.

"Well, I'd rather not talk about it… anyway… are you going to come back with us?"

"I don't think so, Charles, I've decided to stay on land for a while and take good care of my child. Thanks all the same."

"I can't imagine you staying put anywhere, Anne Bonny. Your soul carries the spirit of the sea, indomitable, tempestuous and totally unpredictable, that's why there will always be a place for you on my ship…"

"Forget it, Charles," Anne interrupted in a gentle tone. "You go on your journey, and I'll go on mine."

As she tried to utter words of farewell, they embraced fondly and remained locked in each other's arms, oblivious to the rest of the crew. For the first time since losing her friend, Anne found herself choked up with emotions. After a while, Captain Charles Jennings lifted her chin gently to look into her tearful eyes and whispered, "Take care, Anne Bonny."

"And you take care too, *Boy* Jennings," she bade, purposely using the familiar nickname as a way of showing her fondness for him.

They finally parted. As they walked away from each other, both were hit by a profound sadness that stuns the heart and weakens one's steps. Would they ever meet again? Perhaps… Fate alone would decide whether they may live a long and happy life or a short and merry one.

Part II
The Cross of Madeira

Chapter Fourteen
Of Charles Jennings's Fate

Watching Anne walk away hurt as much as if the two friends had been forcibly torn apart, and Charles Jennings felt wretched. This was the accidental friend, the formidable and brash woman he had known, courageous and fearless, who liked to shake her long brown locks with utter contempt and who had on occasion exposed her large chest just to shock the enemy. Now, her subdued silhouette moved with an assured step, calm and collected, in the large frock she had borrowed from Mrs Tisdale, the innkeeper's wife. As she blended into the crowd, marching towards an uncertain future, she slowly disappeared into a nebulous mass from where she would re-emerge as an ordinary citizen, soon to be a mother living an uneventful life through ordinary days.

The captain quickly regained control of his thoughts. He had too much to do to linger on a turbulent past. Remembering his mission, he felt the leather pouch hidden inside his jacket to check that the precious *Cross of Madeira* was still safely tucked away. Then he went back on board the *Kingston* to leave instructions with his crew before making his way towards the postal coach.

It took him four days to get to London and he wasted no time to make his way towards the Admiralty Building situated in Whitehall, the very site where Wallingford House used to stand before it was demolished to make way for more lavish headquarters, more befitting to the highly decorated gentlemen of the King's Navy. Once there, he hoped to surprise the stern officials in full-bottomed wigs and thick eye glasses with his account of Black Bart's last and final battle. He also hoped that he would be handsomely rewarded for his efforts. Walking purposefully towards the imposing building on a fine spring morning, he recalled with pride the moment he took the oath of allegiance with his right hand placed on the Bible and his left hand on his heart. And he was in luck for the wars against France, Spain and the Netherlands had taken their toll on the English fleet, which left the Admiralty in desperate need to recruit more able and experienced sea captains.

As he entered the Admiralty building, the captain felt a tremor of excitement. After several irregular months at sea, he could not wait to resume his rightful role as an upright captain of the King's Navy.

He marched to the desk, confident and happy with a beaming smile on his face, and gave his name, "Captain Charles Jennings of the King's Navy!" he ejected with pride.

The official glared at the young officer. Suddenly, he shouted, "Guards, seize him!"

Shocked, Jennings did not have time to react.

"What? What's going on? Let go of me!" he screamed in total shock, trying to free himself from the iron grip of two burly guards.

Ignoring the young captain's protests, the official rushed to an office down the main corridor and returned with Lieutenant Wardell in tow who immediately declared, all in one breath, "Captain Charles Jennings, I am arresting you on charge of desertion and dereliction of duty. You will be taken away this instant and kept at his Majesty's prison until the day of your court martial."

"What? I never deserted the Navy! I was captured! I demand to see the Lord Admiral!"

Lieutenant Wardell looked Jennings straight in the eyes and replied quite placidly, "You will… at your court martial!"

***

Several days later, Jennings was brought back to the Admiralty Building. Standing to attention in front of the Board, Charles Jennings appeared a fit and personable young man, but in view of his dishonourable past, how far could he be trusted? Some gentlemen of the Board were of a view to simply charge him with treason, desertion and dereliction of duty, but the Lord Admiral, a certain Lucius Bond-Balfour, adopted a more charitable view of the young man and whilst his most honourable colleagues debated vociferously over his fate, the Admiral raised his hand to bring calm to the proceedings.

"Gentlemen, gentlemen, please!"

Then, he lowered his glasses and, with his hands clutched together on the desk in front of him, looked at Charles Jennings straight in the eyes before enquiring, lilting his voice slightly to indicate a small remnant of incredulity, "What was your rank when you were allegedly *captured*?"

"I didn't have a rank back then, my Lord. The pirates ruined my plans of getting a commission."

"On which ship were you serving?"

"The *Solient*, my Lord."

"And your captain was…?"

"Captain Harvey, my Lord."

Suddenly, a member of the Board interjected, "This man is a liar!"

"Let's not forget he's a pirate, and perhaps even a spy!" another heckled.

"No," Jennings denied vehemently. "I was never a pirate! I was captured and forced to join the crew of a pirate ship! And that's the truth of it!"

A heavy silence followed his outcry. Squinting eyes focussed sharply on his face, trying to eke out some measure of guilt but Captain Jennings did not flinch once. Gradually, the members of the Board began to stir. They mumbled and whispered to one another, debating over and questioning the young man's integrity. Not entirely taken by the captain's plea, the Lord Admiral wanted to hear more.

"Pray!" he said, rising his right hand to quieten his colleagues. "Let him speak!"

"My Lord, I'm telling the truth and I can prove that my intentions are entirely honourable…! But I need your help," he claimed.

Shocked, the Admiral straightened his pose.

"My help, Captain Jennings?" the Lord Admiral exclaimed, mildly puzzled. "A rather audacious request in view of your circumstances!"

At this point, Jennings thought of surrendering the *Cross of Madeira* as a token of his integrity, but this would leave him with nothing to negotiate a pardon or claim a reward from Governor Woodes Rogers. He thought again and instead decided to play on his knowledge and experience as an ex-pirate.

"I know where some of Bartholomew Roberts's treasure is," he bluffed, "and to prove my innocence, I vouch to bring some of it back to you."

"I say!" someone heckled. "This man's not a pirate, he's a *privateer*!"

His remark caused a ripple of laughter. The Lord Admiral gazed at the young man with suspicious eyes, then after a slight pause, he leant forward and replied very firmly, "I don't want *some* of it back, Captain Jennings… I want *all* of it back!"

Jennings stared back at the Lord Admiral and decided to stake one last gamble.

"I could bring you back the *Cross of Madeira*…" he ventured.

"The *Cross of Madeira*?" The Lord Admiral gasped. *"The Cross of Madeira?"*

"What's the *Cross of Madeira*?" one of the officials enquired.

The Lord Admiral looked at the members of the board and declared in a solemn tone, "The *Cross of Madeira*, gentlemen, along with other precious jewels, was commissioned by the King of Spain for his coronation. Unfortunately, the ship was intercepted and raided by Bartholomew Roberts. If we are able to return the Cross to its rightful owner, we may very well avert another war with Spain." Then, turning towards young Jennings, he asked, "Do you know where it is?"

"I do, my Lord, and if you would be generous enough to finance my next voyage…"

"By the way," the Lord Admiral interrupted again. "What happened to Bartholomew Roberts?"

"He was shot and his body thrown overboard by his own men as was his wish. He didn't want his body to be paraded as a trophy like they had done with Blackbeard's head."

"How do you know so much about Bartholomew Roberts if you were not a member of his crew?" a gentleman of the Board cut in. "You seem to know a great deal for a man who claims to have encountered Roberts 'by accident'."

"My Lord!" Charles Jennings declaimed emphatically. "I'm not a pirate, I never was a pirate! All I have ever wanted to do was to serve my country!"

The Lord Admiral twitched his nostrils as he always did when he became suspicious, and stated unequivocally, "I put it to you, young man, that you were fighting *alongside* that rogue of a pirate when he was shot…"

"No, my Lord!" Jennings protested. "He was trying to kill me when he was shot. That shot saved my life!"

"All right then, tell me, who fired the shot?" the Lord Admiral demanded to know.

Instantly, Jennings clammed up. He could not possibly reveal the identity of the person in question for he knew that she was a wanted woman, even here in England. The very fact that it was she who had shot and killed the most infamous pirate of the West Indies should have secured her an instant pardon. Unfortunately, neither she nor Jennings knew of the deal that had been struck by the Governor of Nassau, and it was almost certain that here, in England, nobody knew of it either. Besides, Jennings was all too aware that, in the officials' desire to deal expediently with pirates, miscarriages of justice had become far too commonplace. Who did not know of the miserable fate of Captain Kid? The man had been seized in the belief that he was a pirate and subsequently tried, executed and his body clamped in a metal cage to be fed to the seagulls after he could not find the Letter of Mark that would have proven that he was a privateer and not a pirate.

"Come on, tell us! Who fired the shot?" one of the officials urged the captain.

"I don't know, my Lord. It happened during the battle… there was a lot of noise…screaming and shouting and all that… I don't know where the shot came from."

Charles Jennings looked at the stern faces in front of him to study their reaction. The gentlemen of the Board threw incredulous glances at each other and remained silent while they pondered over his statement. Then suddenly, one of the officials shot out of his seat, pointed at Jennings and shouted, "This man is a charlatan! We've no way of knowing whether he's telling the truth, except that he's just given himself away by saying, '*as was his wish*'. How would he know it was Bartholomew Roberts's wish to be thrown over board should he be killed in battle, unless *this* man standing here knew him personally? In other words, he could only have known this himself if he was an integral part of his crew. I say hang him!"

"Hear, hear!" several voices seconded.

"No!" Jennings interjected. "I only know this because I heard his men shouting at each other to grab his body and throw it overboard. I heard them say it, that's how I know and that's the truth!"

Following the young man's emphatic plea, there was complete silence in the room. Eventually, the Lord Admiral raised his hand.

"Gentlemen, let's not be hasty. We cannot condemn a man without clear evidence or tangible proof of his guilt. For all we know, he could be telling the truth. After all, he came here out of his own free will…"

"Only because he was hoping to collect some reward!" someone interjected.

"Anyway," the Lord Admiral resumed, keeping calm. "He has committed himself to find the lost jewels of the Spanish Crown, including the *Cross of Madeira*…"

"It could be a bluff to save his neck!" another cut in.

"And I think…" the Lord Admiral continued, ignoring the last remark. "We should at least give him the benefit of the doubt and the chance to prove to us all that he is telling the truth. Let me remind you, gentlemen, right now is not the time to lose valuable officers of our proud Royal Navy."

The Lord Admiral looked at Jennings who declared hand on heart, "My Lord, when I was just fifteen years of age, I swore the oath of allegiance that I would serve my King and Country and I'm ready now more than ever to resume my duty."

The Lord Admiral listened intently to the young man's impassioned plea. He then cleared his throat in readiness to give his verdict. "There is of course one clear solution to all this which would suit us… and you in particular. I've had a communication from Governor Woodes Rodgers of the Isle of New Providence asking for more ships to help him win the war against those wretched pirates. Do you have a ship, Captain?"

"Yes, I do, but I don't own it. She belongs to an acquaintance of mine, an innkeeper who lives in Nassau. Her name is the *Kingston* and I'm due to sail her back in about two months' time. She needs some repairs but she should be ready by then."

"I don't think the Governor can wait that long. What type of ship is it?" asked the Lord Admiral.

"A sloop, quite a large one with three masts…"

"Perhaps you could do with a bigger ship…"

"Oh no, my Lord. She's plenty big enough for me. Besides, I have to return her to her owner."

The Lord Admiral thought for a moment. Then, he eventually resumed, "Well, Captain, as I said, there's no way of knowing if you're telling us the truth; and the only way to find out is to put you to the test. What I'm going to do is to put you in charge of one of our ships and use it as a scouting ship…"

"You mean… a spying ship? But what about the *Kingston*?"

"Didn't you vouch earlier to bring back the King of Spain's jewels?"

"Yes I did but…"

"In that case, you can collect the *Kingston* when you return with the jewels."

"Very well, my Lord," Jennings complied, wondering what on earth he was going to tell Tisdale when he would sail back on board an Admiralty ship and not the *Kingston*.

"You can come and collect her on your return voyage after you've handed over the jewels, I'm sure. But right now, your allegiance lies with your King and not with some inconsequential innkeeper. All I want you to do is to log the position and possibly the name of every enemy ship you encounter, and that includes foreign ships as well as pirate ships. In addition to this, you will be in charge of the safety of two special passengers with the mission to return them safe and well, back to the Isle of New Providence. Once you have reached your destination, you will come under the command of Governor Woodes Rogers and join his fleet. During the voyage, as a reconnaissance ship, you will not be expected to seek out or attack any enemy ships, and you are expressly asked not to fire the cannons unless absolutely necessary. Of course, all this means that you will not see our shores for quite some time… unless you succeed."

"Pardon me, my Lord, but… am I being exiled as a reward for doing my duty?"

"Well, Captain Jennings, there are two ways of interpreting my decision and only your subsequent actions will decide whether you have been exiled or indeed given a second chance to prove yourself as a loyal subject to the King and an outstanding officer of the Royal Navy."

The Lord Admiral paused to catch his breath but also to scrutinise Jennings's reaction. Standing to attention, the young man gave nothing away.

"At this point in time," the Lord Admiral continued. "There is no need for you to know the identity of the special passengers. You'll find out when you take command of your ship which is a schooner called the *Redemption*, a fitting name you might say. It is at present moored in Bristol harbour and you will take over from Captain Thompson who has been injured in battle. She sails on Sunday."

"On Sunday! This Sunday? But that's only three days away!"

"The sooner the better, Captain Jennings! Besides, you look like a man of resources… as I said, you set sail on Sunday… either that or you will be court-martialled for desertion."

"Very well, my Lord... One last thing, my Lord... Please forgive me for being so bold, but would it be possible to give me an advance on my wages?"

The Lord Admiral raised his head and returned a stern look.

"We never give advances on wages... specifically to avoid desertions," he decreed curtly. "However, once you've reached Nassau, I'm sure Governor Rogers will be kind enough to hand over your due reward when you return the *Crown Jewels* safely."

"I understand, my Lord," Charles Jennings replied, bowing his head at the same time. "I shall be ready to set sail at high tide on Sunday."

"Good. I'm delighted to hear it. You are dismissed."

"Thank you, my Lord. Goodbye, my Lord. Goodbye, gentlemen."

With these words, Charles Jennings bowed, turned on his heel and left the room mightily relieved.

Chapter Fifteen
Two Mystery Passengers

When Charles Jennings left the Admiralty, he gathered that the postal coach would take too long to reach Bristol. He had to hurry. Not far from where he stood, he knew of a tavern where horses could be hired.

As he galloped through the English countryside, he hardly noticed the vibrant colours of the new spring. Only the fresh smell of damp earth and the wind carrying with it the sweet scent of trees in full bloom reminded him that he was travelling through lush and green land where the air resonated with the sound of horses' hooves rather than that of crashing waves.

After reaching the small village of Frogmore in early evening, he looked up to the sky. Behind him, the sun was sinking into a red mass of incandescent clouds, throwing a luminous glow over the landscape and smoothing out the sharp edges of treetops and roofs, shaping the countryside into the homogenous mass of a giant asleep.

Jennings estimated that there would be enough light to ride for another hour or so. As he passed the *Boar's Head*, he glanced at the inn. It looked so tempting, so welcoming as it drew in each passing traveller with its hypnotic golden glow flickering from every window, but Jennings decided to press on, knowing that the next village was only another three miles away.

It was late evening when he finally reached the *Black Swan* in the village of Moatcastle. He immediately took his horse to the stable to be fed and watered.

Rather pleased with his progress, he marched towards the secluded inn and bent his head to get through the small and narrow door. However, even before he could put one foot inside, out of the darkness, a cavernous voice growled, "Get out of my way!" at the same time as a powerful fist punched Jennings on the shoulder. The unexpected blow made the captain stumble backwards and threw him to the ground. Angry, Jennings scrambled to get back on his feet, ready to fight back, but, as he did so, his eyes locked on the rogue's belt which had a skull suspended above two pistols. The stranger totally ignored him. Instead, looking straight in front of him, he swaggered away towards the courtyard, crushing the ground with his rugged boots as he went, and disappeared into the crepuscule.

Furious, Jennings brushed himself down. Once inside the inn, he went straight to the innkeeper.

"Who was that?" he asked, still smarting.

The innkeeper kept his eyes on the pint of cider he was pouring, and answered, "Don' know. Never seen him before in me life."

The captain looked around to see if anyone would volunteer some information. There were only half a dozen men in the inn and when they heard the question, they quickly turned their heads away, pretending to be totally absorbed by the chipped corners of their table, the flames of the roaring fire or the blankness of the walls. Guessing that no one would speak, the captain went on to negotiate the price for a bed for the night. Having heard the price, he discovered that he only had enough to pay for a bed and one meal or spend the night in the barn and have enough left for two meals. Choosing sustenance over comfort, he plumbed for the latter option.

Later on that night, as he lay on a bed of hay next to the horses, he pictured in his mind the roguish character who had so unceremoniously pushed him out of the way. Pirates! He cursed. I wouldn't mind betting my last groat that he was a pirate, he told himself. Perhaps not. He had not had time to see his face; it was concealed by a large hat, the kind peasants wear when they work in the fields. Pirates, he mumbled again, meeting them at sea was almost inevitable, but here on land? He felt cursed. Then, his thoughts turned to his friend, Anne Bonny, and he wondered whether she would make it, her and her child. Then, in a semi-conscious dream, pictures of Mary's radiant face fleeted through his mind, but rather than seek comfort in the soothing images, he tried to block them out, refusing to linger over memories that were still too raw, too painful; but the more he fought against them, the more they flooded back. Now, he saw Ned Hornby, bobbing his head to the brisk rhythm of a sea shanty while around him, shipmates hammered the deck with their clumsy feet. Above them, Indigo John appeared, hanging from the rigging, flashing his beautiful white teeth in a fixed smile and waving wildly, while on his chest, rivulets of blood trickled over his pristine blue coat. Then, Freddy Main's face slammed in front of his eyes, half of his skull blasted off. He was snarling and growling, and mouthing muted death threats through his broken teeth, all dripping with blood. The images filled him with such intense terror and fear that he woke up with a start, in a sweat, panting heavily as if someone had tried to smother him.

He sat up and looked about him, bewildered. He could feel his blood throbbing through his veins. His heart pounded so hard that he put his hand over his chest as if trying to slow it down.

Getting over the horror of his nightmare, he shook his head to chase the bad dreams away and focused his thoughts on the day ahead. He wondered how long it would take him to reach the port of Bristol and speculated over the identity of the two mystery passengers before finally giving in. What did it matter anyway who they were? He concluded. Overwhelmed with sleep, he tossed over one more time on his bed of hay and fell into a deep, exhausted sleep.

***

The shrieking cry of a nearby cockerel tore through the dawn. Charles Jennings covered his ears and cursed the animal. The early morning light, pale and grey, filtered through the barn's wooden slats and wooden beams, and shone dully into his eyes. Too excited to go back to sleep, Jennings got up and stretched outside the barn from where he observed the early morning dew rise above the ground mist, sprinkling the fresh blades of grass with pearly drops of rain. The captain took a deep breath and savoured the heady earthly musk of the countryside arising. Now that he was awake, he decided to set off on his journey straight away so as to reach the port of Bristol before the evening.

A gradual change in the light and smell told him that he was approaching the city. He looked for a relay inn where he would be able to leave his horse, and proceeded to the harbour on foot. Once there, he looked for the tide ladder and saw that the tide was in. Good, he thought, that would give him plenty of time to go through the formal handing over ceremony, gather his own crew and, with a bit of luck, grab one last proper meal in a nearby tavern before boarding.

Following the throng of sailors in uniform, he soon located the *Redemption*, climbed the gangplank and asked the first sailor he met on board to take him to the ship's captain. The able seaman looked him up and down with a queer eye and asked, "And who might you be, I might ask?"

"I'm your new captain!" Jennings replied with authority. "So don't waste my time and take me to Captain Thompson this instant."

"Aye, aye, Capt'n!"

A few minutes later, Captain Jennings was standing in Captain Thompson's cabin. The officer looked a lot older than he had expected, given the shock of white hair that extended all the way to his white beard. However, through his weary features, his eyes still glittered with a spark of mischief. Before he got up to greet him, Captain Thompson grabbed a stick and eased himself slowly out of his chair to reveal a wooden peg instead of a left leg. Hobbling over to greet his new colleague, the old captain grunted a few times.

"At last, they're letting me go home… About time, I say! It's fifteen years since I asked to be relieved of my duty and it's fifteen years since they've been telling me that I was more valuable at sea than cooped up in a cold damp office scratching a blunt quill. As a result, I'm left with half a leg, gout in my right foot, a dodgy eye, rheumatism all over my body — or what's left of it — rotting teeth and a stomach… arrgh, you don't want to know about my stomach." Then greeting his colleague with a limp salute, he finally introduced himself in the same tone as he had used to list all his various ailments, "Captain Thompson."

"Captain Charles Jennings, ready to take over command of your ship."

"Welcome aboard, Captain. I'll get the quartermaster to start organising the handing-over ceremony. His name's Dai Griffiths, a Welshman from the Valleys, he tells me. Good and loyal, and extremely reliable. Take good care of him, Captain, there's not many of them left around."

Very soon, the voice of the quartermaster was heard shouting, "All hands, on deck! All hands, on deck!"

All the sailors lined up in neat rows on deck and stood to attention until the ceremony was over. Captain Thompson made a brief speech to thank his men for being a good and faithful crew, and to ask them to give their new captain the same level of loyalty and respect than they had given him; then he prepared to leave.

"Well, that's me off, Captain Jennings!" he hailed, hobbling down the gangplank. "I hope your passengers don't bring you too much bad luck… and don't let those damned pirates get the better of you."

Captain Jennings's head twitched.

156

"What do you mean 'bad luck from passengers'?" he queried, but instead of a reply, Captain Thompson gave a dismissive wave of the hand and declared with a sardonic smile, "It's over to you now. Good day and good luck!"

A while later, Captain Jennings was standing against the balustrade, surveying the crew from the main deck, the young, the old and the infirm, especially the infirm as he did not think it fair that they should be expected to go on another voyage without a proper period of convalescence to give them time to recover. Observing two of them on wooden crutches, another with an eye patch and his lower arm missing, and an older sailor unable to straighten his body and with a foot wrapped up in a thick bandage, he went to speak to them.

"But Capt'n, we want to go!" the one-legged sailor insisted.

"Aye Capt'n!" the others responded with unexpected vigour.

The captain felt heartened by their determination but still, he tried to dissuade them to come on the voyage.

"You've done your fair share for your King and Country and you've paid a high enough price for the privilege."

"Actually Capt'n, I didn't lose my leg fighting for King and Country, I lost it fighting over the treasures of a Spanish galleon... and got ripped off!" He laughed.

His mates sniggered, half mocking.

"Aye! But don't forget, you got a few extra pieces of eight to make up for it," the other one-legged sailor pointed out.

"And so did you and you didn't do nothing for it. You was sleeping on the lower deck at the time we was hit."

"It weren't my fault! Curse those damned pirates!"

"Well, it's up to you," the captain said. "What's your names?"

"Danny Stokebridge, Capt'n!" the sailor replied, saluting the captain.

"Phil Keogh from Cork, Ireland, Capt'n, and that's me mate Cyril Stanway."

As they gave their names, the captain came up with an idea.

"Actually, I have a more important mission for all of you. I need a crew to look after my own ship. Her name's the *Kingston* and she's being repaired. I'd like you to take over and look after her until I return."

The sailors looked at each other.

"And when would that be, that is when you return, Capt'n?" Stanway asked.

"That, I'm afraid, I cannot tell you. But, don't you worry, I shall return," the captain vouched. "So, what do you say?"

"I'll do it," Phil Keogh volunteered. "It'll be an easier job and safer than dodging pirates."

"Aye, aye!" the others acquiesced.

"Good," the captain exclaimed with a smile of relief. "I'm glad that's sorted. Stokebridge and Keogh, I put you in charge of supervising her repairs and when that's done, take over and defend her like she was yours, all right?"

"Aye, aye, Capt'n!" they chorused.

"So, off you go, and I'll see you when I return. In the meantime, I'd better go and get more able seamen."

As he took his leave, he was already thinking about the names of the men he wanted to join his crew, Luke Humphreys, Dave Warren, Will Harris, Jack Connor and other trusted hands who had already sailed with him. What's more, he knew exactly where to find them.

On a cobbled street, not far from the harbour, Captain Jennings heard the raucous voices of men wolf-whistling and hailing anything that went by in skirts. As he turned the corner of the street, the captain found his route barred by a line of merry men, arms locked around each other's shoulders, swaying from left to right like a rogue wave out of control. As soon as they recognised him, the merry men cheered.

"Hi aye, Capt'n!" Dave Warren greeted.

"You... you looking for pi... pirates... because we ain't seen none, have we Warren?" Will Harris stuttered, spitting copiously.

"Nope, we ain't got none and we ain't seen none!" all the mates replied before bursting into laughter.

At that point, Dave Warren disengaged himself from the line and pointed his finger at his mates.

"Owever... Owever..." he stuttered in a drunken slur. Unable to keep his head still, he tried to lock gaze with his mate Will Harris.

"Harris... what was I trying to say?"

"Don't know, mate," Harris replied with a complete blank look on his face. "Maybe... might you be looking for pirates like, Capt'n?" he asked in jest while the others chortled all the more.

"No, but I was looking for you... although I think I've changed my mind," the captain stated, forcing himself to keep a straight face.

"What for?" Luke Humphreys queried.

The captain hesitated for a second, then he replied, "I'm about to set sail and I need extra hands… I mean *able* seamen…" he said, glowering at Warren and Harris.

"Where would we be going?" Connor asked.

"Back to the West Indies, but I won't give you any more information until you agree to join my crew."

"I'll come," Humphreys volunteered. "As long as I get paid the same."

"Me too," Jack Connor echoed.

"You will and you might even get a bonus at the end, depending on the Governor's generosity."

"Why?" Humphreys asked.

"I'll tell you why later," the captain said.

Warren nudged his mate.

"Hey, Harris, fancy a trip at his Majesty's expense?"

"Aye, but I'm more thinking about the rum we're gonna…"

"Forget about the rum, Harris," the captain cut in. "We have a very important mission to accomplish and for this reason, you won't be able to drink your share of rum for the whole trip."

"What!?" Harris exclaimed. "No rum… no beer… no ale… no nothing at all? No thanks, Capt'n."

"Aye." Was all that Dave Warren managed to articulate.

"I don't know why you're making such a fuss because, by the look of you two, you've drunk enough rum to last you for days…"

"For days, aye Capt'n, but not for weeks!" Harris interjected.

"Aye," Warren parroted, shaking his head. "Not for weeks…"

"Very well. Humphreys, Connor, you come with me," the captain said.

"What about us?" Warren asked, with the devastated look of a man who has missed out on one last tot of rum.

"But you said you didn't want to go," Harris reminded him.

"Who said? *I* wanna go, Capt'n, I wanna go! You promised!"

"I know I did but you need to sober up first."

"I… I'm sober… nearly… just give me five minutes, Capt'n."

"No time!" the captain replied curtly before marching off with Humphreys and Connor hot on his heels.

"Capt'n, I'm coming! I'm coming! Come on, Harris, get your clogs here!" He chivvied his friend.

"But... but I thought..."

"Don't think, Harris!" Warren riled. "It'll take too long and we'll miss the boat!"

At these words, all the others laughed and continued to march at a good pace in the direction of the harbour while behind them, Warren and Harris staggered along, moaning and groaning, and begging them to slow down.

At last, they reached the embankment where the *Redemption* was moored.

"She's a nice ship, Captain!" Connor whistled in admiration.

"Aye, very smart indeed," Humphreys agreed.

"Aye!" Warren enthused. "Very beautiful!" he added, looking the other way and smiling woefully, not at the ship, but at two ladies who had just arrived on the scene.

"There she is," one of the ladies noted loudly.

At the sound of the female voice, all the men turned their heads around. Their eyes were met by the sight of two ladies dressed in long plain frocks. They could not see who they were for their faces were concealed underneath large fashionable hats. Behind them, an old porter huffed and puffed away as he pushed along an old creaky cart laden with the ladies' luggage.

Captain Jennings separated from the group to go and speak with the ladies.

"Good afternoon, ladies. I'm Captain Jennings. May I be of assistance?"

The ladies turned their heads at once, and the shadow turned with them revealing their faces to him. When he saw who they were, the captain's jaw dropped with shock. Before he had time to recover, the older of the two ladies greeted him with a convivial smile, "Good afternoon, Captain. I hope you don't mind us joining you on your voyage."

"Well... er..." he stuttered, staggered by the sight. "I was expecting two extra passengers but I had no idea..."

"That's right, Captain. I'm Lady Whetstone Rogers and this is my daughter, Lady Sarah."

The captain looked at Lady Sarah and smiled. She smiled back but neither was prepared to acknowledge a previous all too brief encounter in the draughty corridor of Government House in Nassau. Noting a mutual reconnaissance, Lady Rogers looked at each in turn and asked, "You two know each other?"

The captain took Lady Sarah's hand to kiss and replied cryptically, "How could I possibly forget my charming visit to Government House in Nassau? I am delighted to have you both on board, ladies," he said, bowing his head.

At last, the identity of the two mystery passengers was revealed. Lady Whetstone Rogers, wife of the Governor of Nassau, chivvied her daughter up the gangplank, closely followed by the captain and the rest of the shipmates who pushed and shoved for the privilege of carrying the ladies' luggage.

***

Once on board, Lady Rogers turned to the captain and enquired, "Captain, when are we likely to set sail?"

"Well, the tide is in just now, but we're not ready to go yet, so I'm afraid we shall have to wait for the next tide which should be tomorrow at dawn."

"Good." Lady Rogers breathed with relief. "That'll give us plenty of time to settle in. We might even treat ourselves to a last meal in a local tavern. Would you like to join us, Captain?"

Captain Jennings wanted to take up their offer, but knowing that he was down to his last groat, he was unable to accept.

"I'd love to accept your offer, Lady Rogers, but there are still so many things to be done before we leave…"

"But… that's why you've got a crew… to do all these things for you, Captain," Lady Rogers remarked.

As he listened, the faces of both Warren and Harris flashed before the captain's eyes.

"Hmm… I'd rather be here. That way, I'll know for sure everything's been done properly and correctly. I wouldn't want to put any lives at risk by some negligence, especially with you, ladies, on board."

"I understand," she said, then turning to her daughter, she continued, "Come on, darling, let's go and refresh ourselves. We don't want to keep the captain away from his important tasks."

***

Just as he had calculated, the tide came in at dawn. At last, the *Redemption* was ready to sail. Standing on the main deck, Captain Jennings gave the orders to rig the sails. It was a beautiful and fresh morning with an invigorating breeze blowing over the harbour. The captain looked over to the east where the sun had risen in a magnificent halo of red flamboyance, leaving streaks of dark clouds stretching languorously over a flaming reddened sky. Immediately, the popular saying came to his mind, *red sky in the morning, shepherd's warning.* Far too excited to heed the warning, the captain refused to let some superstitious nonsense dampen his spirit. So he strode about the deck with his shoulders thrown back, his chin up and a fixed smile upon his face.

***

During the voyage, the ladies occupied themselves as best they could, strolling along the bridge, observing the sailors at work, studying the direction of the wind and the movements of the sails, and sometimes even interacting with the crew. But above all, they liked nothing more than to engage in conversation with the captain who was always only too pleased to oblige.

"So," he began. "Why did you undertake such a long and risky journey to go to England?"

"Where else can one get decent material?" Lady Rogers replied.

"So you went to London?" Captain Jennings enquired.

"Oh no, far too dangerous!" she exclaimed in a dramatic tone. "Can you just imagine it, two ladies travelling on their own with the most refined garments, not to mention jewels, in their luggage? We would not have made it alive beyond Richmond! No, I decided that the best thing to do was to have the material brought to us here in Bristol and have our dresses made locally. And I'm so glad we did because we now have a whole new trousseau made to our taste, haven't we, darling?"

Lady Sarah looked at the captain and smiled coyly.

"So," Lady Rogers continued, looking Captain Jennings straight in the eyes. "Your father is a lord… or an admiral?"

"Actually no," Captain Jennings replied humbly. "My father works on a farm."

"Oh, how interesting," she exclaimed with her eyes lighting up. "Would it be a large farm… with a vast wealth of land?"

"Why, yes," the captain acquiesced with a smile.

"So…" Lady Rogers continued, her eyes sparkling with renewed interest. "You belong to that most respectable class of people that we call the landed gentry."

"I'm afraid not," the captain corrected. "My father doesn't actually own the land. He's a tenant farmer."

"Aww," Lady Rogers responded, her interest suddenly waning. "Well, I suppose, there's not much use for land when you spend all your time at sea," she noted with a discreet cynical laugh.

Lady Sarah scowled at her mother. In response, Lady Rogers shrugged her shoulders, turned her nose up and pretended to be wholly absorbed by the magnificent sight of the waves glistening in the sunshine, breathing in great gulps of iodine air and exposing her fair delicate skin to the warm rays of the sun. There was no doubt that, in her mind, the captain had to be made aware in no uncertain terms, that if his present position made him noteworthy, his humble family roots would make him quite forgettable in her daughter's eyes. So she added pointedly, "My daughter is going to marry a commodore who happens to be a friend of ours. Sarah has known him for a long time for he is the Deputy Governor of the Island. His father is a Lord Admiral based in Portsmouth. As a matter of fact, we were staying at their country house just outside Bath, weren't we, darling?" she boasted.

Lady Sarah resented the way her mother bandied about the most intimate details of her private life to ward off any potential suitor, so she kept a stubborn silence. Undaunted, Captain Jennings was quick to offer his congratulations. "A noble choice, if I may say. I'm sure they'll make a charming couple and that they'll be very happy together." He opined with a calculated note of indifference in his voice.

* * *

Drawing on his maritime knowledge and experience, Captain Jennings estimated that the voyage would take roughly one or two months, depending on the weather and the direction of the winds. To fill his time, he planned on reading navigational manuals and maritime law books which had been left on board by his predecessor, for he had gathered that the more he acquainted himself with the regulations and rules of life at sea, the quicker he would climb up the officer's ladder. Indeed, while he was quite content at present to hold the title of 'captain', sole commander of the *Redemption*, he saw his future much higher up in the hierarchy of the Admiralty. To realise his plans, he decided that he needed to mix with the right sort of people, a great deal more sophisticated in their stance and manners than the people with whom he was currently acquainted. From previous social gatherings, he had noted that the favourite topics of conversation in smoking salons invariably revolved around the fast-developing marine technology and engineering, a subject he felt reasonably comfortable with since, talking with the men in charge of careening his ship, he had discovered that naval architects were working on a new type of warship, capable of carrying a hundred cannons or more, called a *frigate*.

But this was not what Lady Sarah wanted to hear for, from the moment the captain intimated to her that he had once been captured and forced to join a pirate crew, she was far more interested in his past and the battles he had fought, than in his present career; and as he recounted all the times he had had to fight for his life, she became totally captivated by the colourful pirates and their daring adventures. She began to spend many hours in the captain's company, listening to his exciting stories and drifting away in the imaginary world of pirates instead of involving herself in the doleful tasks of writing letters, reading the bible, doing a few stitches of embroidery or polishing her French. And as the captain tried in vain to make his excuses in order to get on with his duties, Lady Sarah kept pressing him for more stories, particularly those involving notorious pirates. Had he ever come face to face with Blackbeard? Did Jack Rackham really have two mistresses? And... was it true that Bartholomew Roberts was a real gentleman who never touched alcohol? He sounded quite a man, she sighed rolling her eyes in awe and wonder. Her avid interest in all piratical matters greatly surprised the captain. Lady Sarah, a sophisticated young lady with an air of vulnerability and fragility about her, was suddenly revealing a ruthless streak entirely in sympathy with those lawless cut-throats, in contravention to her very own father's mission to hunt them down. And that was not all. When Captain Jennings casually mentioned the *Cross of Madeira*, Lady Sarah could no longer contain herself.

"The *Cross of Madeira*!" she exclaimed excitedly. "You saw it, you actually saw it? And is it as beautiful as everyone says?"

"Yes indeed, Ma'm, I saw it with my very own eyes and yes, it is the most beautiful object I have ever seen," Captain Jennings replied with an enthusiastic smile.

"Where is it now?" Lady Sarah asked with her eyes firing sparks of excitement.

The captain hesitated before giving his reply, "It's now part of a treasure hunt and my fate rests upon my returning it."

Lady Sarah looked at the captain with a quirky smile.

"Captain! I do believe you have the heart of a pirate," she exclaimed with a little giggle.

"It may appear so but I can assure you I don't. I took the oath of allegiance to serve the King some five years ago and I fully intend to honour my vows."

Chapter Sixteen
The Devil's Triangle

They had only been at sea for three days when one night, the captain caught Warren and Harris trying to get at the rum, so he decided to remind the crew of the rules and regulations on board his ship, then he made a few checks with his quartermaster and finalised the rota for the night shift before retiring to his cabin. There, he picked up a book and settled on his berth to read '*A Précis on Maritime Law*' by Georges Denning. Stumbling over the incomprehensible legal jargon, the captain flicked a few pages hoping to find an easier chapter with which to begin. Unfortunately, almost every page was obscured by an array of Latin phrases and technical terms, as yet incomprehensible to him, so he put the book aside and tried to go to sleep.

Below deck, the crew were settled in their hammocks, disturbed only by Warren's and Harris's loud snores, and by the prow of the ship pounding the waves.

That night, the watchman on duty happened to be Richard Slater, a shipmate known for his nervous disposition, exacerbated by his firm belief in every superstition going round. It was for this specific reason that he did not like pacing the port side of the ship because someone had told him that the word for 'left' in Latin was *sinister*, the side occupied by the devil. So, he always hurried his steps until he reached starboard again which he covered at a more leisurely pace. Suddenly, as he came level with the cockboat, he thought he heard a noise. He stopped and listened. He looked around, behind him, towards the prow... and the stern... but there was nothing, not a trace of a shadow anywhere; so he started to walk again, softly, all the time throwing shifty glances around him. Just as he lifted his head to look up at the sails, the noise started again. He stopped and scoured the bridge. There! This time he saw it. The canvas on top of the cockboat had moved. He did not panic straight away. It could be the wind, he told himself, causing the canvas to move, making a sound that resembled hushed whispers. He stood on the same spot for a while, observing with hawk eyes any movement coming from the cockboat. He may be capable of behaving like a ruthless pirate when surrounded by his mates, but right now, all alone in the oppressive silence of a deserted deck… he was scared. He thought he could see dark shadows moving furtively around the sails… and on the deck. Fearing the devil and an eternal life in hell, he implored the Almighty and begged for redemption as he reflected upon his past crimes.

Yes, he had sinned… many times… he had even killed a man on the highway…

"But…" he reasoned, "it was his fault… he wouldn't give me his money! I wouldn't have done it otherwise…" *The cockboat canvas lifted slightly…* "Aaahhh…" he let out, trembling in fear. "Oh God Almighty…" he whimpered with alarm. "That's it… I'm done for… the devil has come to claim my soul!"

Mustering all the courage he had, pistol at the ready in his shaking hand, he tip-toed along the deck, never taking his eyes off the cockboat. Now levelled with it, he stopped. He hesitated. Then, with his pistol trained on the cockboat, he grabbed the edge of the canvas and lifted it off with a sharp tug.

"Aaaargh!" he screamed in terror.

Right there, two pairs of eyes stared back at him.

"The devil's eyes!" he gasped in shock. As he stood there, mouth baying and paralysed with fear, two small figures stirred in the cockboat.

"Hey!" he exclaimed, all his fears instantly melting away. "Who the hell are you?" he stuttered, quite shaken up. Unable to believe his eyes, he watched two young boys clamber out of the boat.

"By the devil's teeth!" he could not help exclaim. "What are you doing here?"

"'Twas his idea, Mister," one of the boys said, pointing at his friend.

"No, 'twas his!" the other boy protested.

"No, it wasn't!"

"Yes, it was!"

"All right, all right you two," Slater spoke more calmly, hugely relieved that instead of the devil, he had encountered two juvenile stowaways. "What's your names?"

"I'm Jonesie…" the taller of the two boys replied.

"And I'm Jamesie," the younger boy said. Then for good measure he added, "We're brothers." With a cheeky grin on his face. Jonesie looked at him with surprise but said nothing.

Watchman Slater eyed the two boys with the suspicious eyes of a schoolmaster assessing the veracity of their statement. One was tall and slim with long dark hair and deep brown eyes while the younger of the two was short and stocky and had thick and fair curly hair.

"You're brothers?" Slater questioned, somewhat incredulous.

The boys shrugged their shoulders simultaneously.

"Anyway, what you're doing here? You've no business being here. You'd better come with me. I'm taking you to the captain."

"What for? He's probably asleep," Jonesie said.

"You're gonna be in trouble if you wake him up," Jamesie warned.

"Never you mind. This is my watch and it's my duty to report anything untoward."

"But we're not *untoward*, we're brothers!" the younger boy retorted cheekily.

Detecting a hint of mockery in the boy's remark, Slater grabbed each one by the scruff of the neck and growled, "I've had enough of your cheek. You're coming with me to the captain and we'll see what he thinks of stowaways!"

Moments later, Slater rapped on the captain's door and waited… and waited. No one stirred inside the cabin. He tapped on the door again. Eventually, a sleepy voice responded.

"What? Who's there? What's the time?"

"It's two and a quarter, Captain," Slater replied.

"What! Two o'clock in the morning! What do you think you're doing waking me up at this time of night?"

Still speaking from behind the door, Slater explained, "I've found two stowaways, Captain."

"And what do you expect me to do with them? If you can't do anything about it, let them go and I'll deal with them in the morning."

At hearing this, the boys smiled triumphantly at Slater.

"And don't disturb me again unless we're under attack! So get back to your post and take them with you."

"Told you," Jamesie said, smirking.

"All right, all right," Slater grunted, still holding the boys by the scruff of the neck. "Well, there's no room down below so you might as well stay in the cockboat for now."

"Good. I'm rather sleepy," Jonesie declared, yawning widely.

"Me too," His brother echoed.

***

The next morning, at the end of his shift, Slater went to report to the captain.

"Nothing to declare, Capt'n, except of course the pair of stowaways."

"Oh yes, where are those two scoundrels?" the captain queried.

"Asleep in the cockboat, Capt'n."

"In the cockboat?"

"Aye, that's where I found them, Capt'n."

"Are they still in there?"

"Oh aye."

"Right, Slater. You go and catch up on your sleep and I'll go and deal with them."

"Aye, aye, Capt'n."

Captain Jennings went straight onto the main deck towards the cockboat. Inside, he found the two stowaways fast asleep wrapped up in a blanket underneath the canvas. He was shocked. Slater had not told him how young the boys were.

"All right, lads, time to get up!" he said in a loud voice.

The boys produced a few moans but did not stir.

"Come on you two, get up or you'll have no breakfast!" the captain warned, tearing the canvas from them.

At these words, one of the boys sat up.

"Breakfast? What's for breakfast?" he asked.

"I'll tell you when you've told me what you're doing on my ship," said the captain, folding his arms across his chest.

The younger of the two boys looked at the captain with a big grin on his face and trumpeted, "We want to be pirates!"

Captain Jennings let out a little chuckle.

"Do you, now? Well, I'm afraid, you're on the wrong ship." After scrutinising their youthful faces briefly, the captain asked, "How old are you?"

The two boys looked at each other.

"Er... Last time I was told my age, I was ten," the older boy said.

"And how long ago was that?"

"Can't remember."

"What's your name?"

"Jonesie."

"Jonesie? That's not a proper name. What's your real name?"

The boy shrugged his shoulders.

"It don't matter, does it? I've always been called Jonesie."

Then, the captain turned to the other boy. "What about you?"

"You mean, my age or my name?"

"Both."

"I'm Jamesie and he's my big brother."

"You're brothers!" the captain exclaimed, consternated. Then, he continued, "And I suppose you don't know your proper name either…"

"No, but I know my age!" Jamesie stated, smirking with confidence.

"Oh, yes? How old are you, then?"

With a triumphant smile on his face, the young boy pointed at his brother and declared proudly, "I'm younger than him."

The captain shook his head with a wry smile.

"I see. Well, I'd better warn you, if you want to stay on my ship, you're going to have to do your share of chores. Now, go to Cook and ask him to give you some ham and hard tacks. After that, go and get a mop and bucket and start scrubbing the deck."

"Aye, aye, Capt'n! Thanks, Capt'n!" the boys chorused before jumping out of the cockboat.

***

Several days passed without further incidents until…One night, when the sky was lit by a myriad of glittering stars, dark shadows moved furtively around the ship while the crew slept. The wind blew cold and sharp like the breath of evil spirits on the face of the unwary, spreading whispers of doom and foretelling disaster and death. The shadows played and danced in the moonlight, until dawn. Then, at first light, they vanished, as swiftly as they came.

***

At dawn, the crew were woken up by the cook brandishing a wooden spoon and shouting at the two ship boys, "Get out of my kitchen, you little thieves!

170

I'll report you to the captain if I catch you again!"

Jonesie and Jamesie fled to the main deck, giggling, and quickly sought refuge inside the cockboat, their favourite hideout, to eat the hard tacks they had just pilfered.

On the lower deck, another loud voice was heard to shout, "Harris! Have you taken my cutlass?"

"Your cutlass? What would I do with your cutlass? I've got my own and…"

As he spoke, Dave Warren slipped out of his hammock and felt his belt.

"By the devil's teeth! Where's… where's mine? It's gone!"

Further along the crowded sleeping quarters, another shipmate discovered that his own cutlass had disappeared too.

Alerted by the noise, the captain appeared.

"What's going on?" he asked in a firm voice.

"There's a thief among us, Capt'n!" Harris decreed. "My cutlass's gone."

"So's mine!" Warren growled.

"And mine!" Richard Slater complained.

The captain threw a suspicious look at the men. He wondered whether Warren and Harris had been at the rum all night, and in such a state of drunkenness that they had forgotten where they had laid their cutlasses. But that was another matter which he would deal with later. He looked at Slater and asked, "What's going on, Slater?"

"Well… er… we can't find our cutlasses, capt'n," Slater replied coyly as if confessing of a mischief.

The captain looked back at Warren and Harris, and simply stated, "You've probably misplaced them. They can't have just disappeared!"

At that moment, Slater looked up to the sky where heavy cumulus clouds hung menacingly above the ship.

"It's a bad omen," he warned. "We're doomed, capt'n, we're all doomed!"

"Get hold of yourself, Slater! The lack of sleep is clearly playing up on your mind. Go and get some sleep!" the captain ordered, somewhat exasperated.

Mulling over the irrational attitude of his crew, the captain returned to the main deck to survey the sea and catch up with his quartermaster.

Meanwhile, by the stern of the ship, Lady Whetstone Rogers was reading a book while her daughter stared vacantly at the sea. Captain Jennings decided to join them.

"Good morning, ladies. I trust I find you well rested."

"Nearly," her Ladyship moaned. "There's so much noise going on. Men ought not to wear shoes when on board a ship, especially at night," she remonstrated.

"Not many do, Ma'm." Then, after a short pause, he wrung his hands together and asked, "I wonder if I could ask a rather special favour... of your daughter that is."

Lady Rogers smiled and replied, "Well, as long as it's not to ask her hand in marriage..."

It was the captain's turn to smile.

"No, Ma'm, indeed not."

"What then?" asked her Ladyship.

"I have a book I thought she might be interested in reading."

"Is it a poetry book? Because she likes reading poetry. She plays the piano, you see, that's why she prefers the musical cadence of poetic verses to plain ordinary prose. I do as well as a matter of fact."

The captain wondered whether he should continue. Eventually, he said, "No, it's not a book on poetry. I thought she might like to read something different for a change."

"Like what, for example?" her Ladyship enquired dryly. "I do not wish her mind to be corrupted by some vulgar romantic novel."

"My Lady, the book I have in mind is not a novel, has nothing to do with romance and, if anything, will probably improve her Latin."

"Oh, really? Sounds a bit dry to me. I'm not sure she'll be interested, but do ask her. She looks so bored."

Captain Jennings made his excuses and went over to speak to Lady Sarah. At first, she seemed reluctant to take on the challenge, but when the captain intimated that they would need to meet at least once a day to discuss her findings, a spark glittered in her eyes.

"Of course, Captain, it will be my pleasure," she enthused.

And so for the following days, life on the *Redemption* assumed an orderly pace, the ship boys scrubbed the decks, the riggers minded the sails, the gunners polished the pistols, guns and cannons and the rest of the crew helped wherever they could. Those less physically able to help either undertook chores in the ship's galley or took it in turn to be the look out in the crow's nest.

They had now been at sea for several days. During their idle moments, the shipmates chatted and played cards or games of dice and while they played and chatted, the topic that all of them discussed was the disappearance of the three cutlasses.

"We're not far from the devil's triangle," Reg Brown declared, looking glum. "That funny business with the cutlasses gives me the jitters, that does."

"Aye, and I don't mind saying, many a ship has been lost in the devil's triangle and we're gonna be next, I feel it in my bones," his mate Alistair MacKay warned like a prophet of doom.

"Aye, we've got bad luck scratched all over our sails and it's those damned women that does it," Christopher Muldoon riled from the corner of his mouth.

"No, it's not them," Richard Slater intimated with such a weird look on his face and in such a mysterious tone of voice that the others could not help but glower at him. "I've sailed on this ship before and I told them then and I'll tell you now… she's haunted."

At hearing this, Dave Warren, who was smoking a pipe leaning against the bulwark, moved closer to the group.

"Don't be daft!" he cut in. "You always see things when you're drunk."

"But I'm not drunk, am I! And I saw them shadows only the other night!" He swore on his mother's grave. "We've had nothing but bad luck ever since we started on this journey!" Slater reiterated.

"How?" Dave Warren requested to know.

"We've got two women on board, haven't we?"

"Aye!" the group chorused.

"Three cutlasses have disappeared and no one knows where they've gone."

"Aye!"

"And there's another thing…"

"What?" they all asked eagerly.

Slater took a deep breath.

"*The Cross of Madeira*!" he finally whispered ominously.

"What about it?" Dave Warren queried.

"It says that whoever touches it will carry bad luck with him for seven years."

"You're full of bull, Slater!"

Undeterred, Slater continued with his doom theory.

"You should know, Warren!" he spat back. "You were on his ship! And who had it then? Black Bart! And what happened to him? He got shot and now his body's feeding the fish!"

"So, what happened to the cross after that?" Reg Brown enquired.

"Well, apparently, the captain had it for a while… so the rumour goes."

"What? You mean… *our* captain?"

"Aye."

"Has he still got it?"

"Don't know, but he's got bad luck written all over him, that man!"

"You don't know what you're saying, Slater." Warren riposted. "I was on his ship all right and I never saw the damned cross except on Black Bart's neck!"

"Of course you didn't! Because you're always too drunk to notice anything!"

Whilst the men continued to argue, the *Redemption* sailed on. The sea was calm and the sea breeze blew with just enough force to stretch the sails. The sun was so hot that it seemed to pulverize instantly every passing cloud that dared leave a shadow on the clear blue sky. To avoid the searing heat, many of the crew sought refuge below deck where they slumbered in an uneasy sleep.

Then, suddenly, everything changed. An enormous black cloud crept over the horizon from the west, rumbling menacingly like a pyroclastic flow that burns the eyes and smells of death.

The look-out shouted, "There's a storm on the horizon! Storm coming!"

Immediately, all the men rushed to the bulwarks to take a close look at the oncoming threat. Gripping the sides of the ships with their hands, each knew that, as they watched the huge black mass surging forth tossing everything in its path, that the powerful forces of nature would have no pity or mercy on their wretched souls. Some began to pray and begged the Almighty to spare them. Flashes of lightning streaked the tenebrous mass with blinding rays and, seconds later, a series of deafening thunderous claps echoed through the sky spreading terror among the men. As the ominous cloud drew closer, the temperature dropped suddenly. The wind blew harder, whipping and slashing the men's faces. Amid the terror and fear, a voice shouted, "It's the devil's triangle! We're doomed, we're all doomed!"

It was Slater. His eyes bulging out with fear, his face struck the look of a mad man. Panic-stricken, he jerked his head after each bang, flailing his arms aimlessly and jittering on the spot.

Not far from him, the captain was following the path of the storm with a keen eye and soon, his worst fears were confirmed. The storm was heading straight for them. He had to act fast.

"Hastings! Prepare to come about! Humphreys! Get your men up on the rigging to furl the sails. Connor! Go and help him. Warren, Harris, stay with Hastings at the helm! Everybody else, remain on deck and help wherever you can. You, ship boys, go below deck and stay there!"

Then, thinking of his two special guests, the captain strode across the deck towards their cabin. He had to warn them of the imminent danger. On his way there, he bumped into Lady Sarah who was beside herself with worry. Captain Jennings stopped her from going any further.

"What's going on, Captain?" she immediately asked. "Are there cannons firing at us?"

"No Ma'm. There's a storm coming our way. It would be wise if you and Lady Rogers stayed in your cabin until the storm passes over. In the meantime, I must ask you to blow out all the candles."

"But I won't be able to read," Lady Sarah objected.

The captain gave her a wry smile.

"My dear lady, if we hit the storm head-on, you won't be able to sit still, let alone read. My advice is, just stay put and try and remain calm. After all, the storm might just miss us." He hoped, doubting his own words.

"Very well, Captain, if you say so." She complied, returning that instant to her cabin.

***

When the captain returned onto the main deck, the sky had turned molten grey. The sea seemed to have risen by several feet. Huge raging waves swelled up to come crashing down onto the wooden decks. Up in the rigging, the wind howled, whistling through the cables like the wails of banshees calling out to the dark forces of hell. Then the rain came, cold and hard like iced steel rods cutting into the shipmates' hands, arms and necks. A sudden bolt of lightning streaked the sky straight above them and flashed the bare blades of three cutlasses burning and sizzling at the base of the main mast like hot metal on bare wood. Worse still, they were shaped in a triangle. Instantly, cries of terror resounded all around the ship. Amid the general chaos, one terrified voice rose above the thunder.

"That's the devil's triangle! We're gonna die! We're all gonna die!" Slater wailed with rain pouring down his face.

"Shut up! You stupid fool!" Will Harris barked.

However, his words were lost in the howling wind. Suddenly, a loud groaning sound made all the men look up and to their horror, they saw several of the riggers fall into the sea screaming. Moments later, the mizzen mast came crashing onto the deck with an almighty bang. More terrified screams followed… and then… they stopped… dead. Another flash of lightning lit up the deck to reveal several men pinned down under the mast. They were dead, and among them lay Slater with his face frozen in terror while the devil's triangle flickered only inches away from his head.

Immediately, several shipmates rushed to try and lift the broken mast. They heaved it with all the power they could muster but giant waves continued to rock the ship violently, making it impossible for the men to secure a strong foothold. After a while, anxious to spare the men he had left, the captain shouted through the lashing rain, "Leave it! There's nothing we can do for them now. Everyone down the brig! Warren! Harris! Stay at the helm with Hastings! Help him!"

The storm raged unabated for another hour or so, tossing the ship so violently that at times, her sides touched the water.

Desperately clinging on to the balustrade, the captain continued to shout his commands. Then, another flash of lightning struck the sea, ahead of the ship this time. This was the sign all had been waiting for. At last, the storm was moving away. But their relief was short-lived, for over there, flickering in the lightning blitz, the men caught sight of the tall dark silhouette of a ghostly ship dipping into the sea like a blue whale ready to feast.

Chapter Seventeen
A New Menace

From the height of the upper deck, Captain Charles Jennings was holding firm, his eyes permanently fixed on the horizon for he too had seen the jagged silhouette of the mysterious ship. He waited for the next bolt of lightning to light up the sea so that he could catch a better glimpse of the potential threat, but the storm was abating and the thunderous clouds moving east, leaving in their wake a pure and transparent blue sky. As the sunshine returned, the tense atmosphere on board lifted. The captain strode about the deck nervously, checking on the welfare of each of his men while keeping a wary eye on the other ship that lurked surreptitiously only a short distance away.

Humphreys, Connor and their men were busy rigging the sails once more while the rest of the men set about to clear the main deck of all loose debris in preparation for the ceremony to bury the dead sailors at sea. The mood was sombre and the men silent. A few feet away, the two ship boys surveyed the damage to their cockboat.

"It's all broken," Jamesie wailed, on the brink of tears.

"Aye." Jonesie sighed with a heavy heart.

Overhearing them, one of the sailors approached them and put his arms around their shoulders.

"Don't worry, lads," he said in a reassuring voice. "There're a few carpenters among us. We'll repair your boat for you. That'll give us something to do until we reach port. And if you like, we'll show you how to do it as well, because it's always a good thing to know how to put two pieces of wood together."

"Aye, we'd like that. Thanks, Mister," Jonesie enthused.

Walking around the deck, Captain Jennings surveyed the state of his ship and reflected on the effects of the devastating storm. He had never lost any of his men at sea before and he felt wretched. For him, to lose men in battle was unfortunate but inevitable, and rather honourable, but to lose several men in a storm seemed downright reckless. He wished he could have done more to prevent this devastating loss of lives, but he had been too busy saving himself from being dragged overboard by the powerful draught of a twenty-foot wave. It was while he tortured himself with these rueful thoughts that he was accosted by two men. They were Warren and Harris and they had come to consult their captain about the disappearing cutlasses.

"What do you want me to do about it?" the captain asked with slight exasperation, thinking there were more important things to do than worry about disappearing cutlasses. "You got them back, didn't you?"

"Aye," said Warren. "But we don't like the way they disappeared in the first place."

"Aye," Harris cut in. "Someone's playing tricks on us and we want to know who before something else happens."

"Nothing will happen," the captain declared. "It was probably just a prank, a silly little prank, and whoever did it was having a bit of fun, that's all."

"They're after our souls…" a voice quipped.

The three men turned round to find MacKay's dishevelled head levelled with their shoulders.

"What are you talking about?" Warren asked dismissively.

"They're after our souls," MacKay insisted, "because we have strayed into their space. Don't you see? The devil's triangle has three corners, one for evil spirits, one for fallen angels and one for the devil himself…"

Before he could add anything else, the captain cut in, "Stop that bloody nonsense, MacKay! You're talking like a man who's lost his marbles. Have you been at the rum again?"

"You may mock, Capt'n, you may mock" he continued in a weary tone, "but that's the whole damned truth. Legend has it that only a mariner with eight arms will be able to kill the lot in one swipe of a sword and make the devil's triangle disappear forever. That's why they're after us, Capt'n, that's why they want to kill us all!"

As soon as they heard this, the three men burst out laughing.

"A man with eight arms?" Warren scoffed.

"Well mate!" Harris chortled loudly. "That'd make him an octopus, wouldn't it? I'd like to meet that man; I'd be for ever shaking his hands!"

MacKay leered at the three men with a dark and angry look on his face.

"Like I said, that's the whole damned truth of it and I don't mind saying, whoever doesn't heed those words will die a terrible death, mark my word!"

The captain began to feel sorry for poor MacKay. It was plainly obvious that the recent events were playing on his fragile mind. Nevertheless, he was a member of the crew and the captain felt compelled to appease him. In a friendly manner, he patted Mackay on the back and said, "Come on, MacKay, you need to clear your head from all that superstitious nonsense…"

"But it's not superstitious nonsense!" he protested.

"Well, whatever it is, you've got to stop thinking about it before you lose your mind completely, so go back to your chores and I don't want to hear another word of it, understand?"

"Aye, Capt'n, but one day, you'll see, I'll be proved right!"

The captain watched him stride across the deck, still trying to retain his composure. Then he had a thought.

"I wonder… Harris, go and get the ship boys."

A few minutes later, Harris returned holding the two ship boys by the scruff of the neck.

"Ouch! Let go of me!" Jamesie pleaded, trying to free himself from Harris's iron grip.

"Where are you taking us? We done nothing wrong!" Jonesie protested.

"Stop wailing like two mad banshees, the capt'n wants to see you."

The latter was indeed waiting for them, standing with an air of authority about him.

"Well," he started, looking at the boys straight in the eyes. "What have you been up to, lads?"

"Nothing!" Jonesie protested.

"Aye!" echoed Jamesie.

"It ain't us, Capt'n!" Jonesie protested again.

"Aye, we never took them cutlasses."

"So, you do know why you're here, then?"

"Aye. I never moved from the cockboat that night, so it wasn't me," Jamesie protested.

"Me neither!"

"So… the cutlasses were taken during the night, were they?"

"Aye," the boys chorused.

"Hang on a minute!" Harris interrupted. "How come you know so much? You were supposed to be fast asleep." Then, turning to the captain, he said, "I tell you, Capt'n, they done it!"

"I don't like to admit it, but I think Harris's right," the captain concurred. "You seem to know too much about this incident, so you'd better own up or I'll make you scrub the decks three times a day for the next month!"

The boys stared at the captain, then at each other. Finally, Jamesie pointed at his brother and said, "'Twas his idea!"

"'Twas your idea too!" Jonesie shouted in his brother's face. Then, turning to the captain he explained, "We both heard the shipmates talk about the devil's triangle when we was hiding in the cockboat and that's when we decided to play a trick on them. We just wanted to scare them a bit, especially Slater..."

"Why Slater?" the captain asked.

"'Cos he looked so funny when he was scared, with his eyes bulging out like a toad's eyes."

"Well, he's dead now so you won't be able to torment the beggar any more," the captain stated reproachfully.

"Aye." The boys sighed, bowing their heads in contrition.

"Right, well as a punishment, you're both going to scrub all the decks once a day for two weeks," the captain declared, passing sentence on the boys.

"What!" they exclaimed at once.

"Jeez! It ain't fair!" Jamesie moaned.

"You're lucky to get off so lightly!" the captain remonstrated. "But there are far more important things to do than waste time on you two little rascals! However... if you do a good job, I'll give you an extra groat each."

At these words, the boys' faces lit up. "Really, Capt'n? Cheers, Capt'n!" they chorused before rushing to their buckets.

***

"Blast!" Jennings suddenly remembered. "The ladies!"

He rushed across the deck. By the grace of God, he found them quite unharmed, although rather shaken and stirred.

"Mother, Mother," Lady Sarah wailed. "I never want to come on board a ship ever again."

"Don't worry, darling, we'll be fine. See, the captain got us out of it in the end."

The captain tried his best to reassure them.

"It may be of some comfort to you to know that the storm has finally passed. I'll ask Cook to bring you some refreshment. Would Lady Sarah like some cider or some punch, perhaps?"

"I don't want anything. I just want to go home," she replied, snivelling.

"Come on, darling, some cider will do you good." Then turning to the captain, she confirmed, "Yes, Captain, some refreshment would be greatly appreciated."

"Very well, Ma'm, I shall have some sent straight away. In the meantime, I would strongly recommend that you stay in your cabin until I come back to give you the all clear."

"You need not worry, Captain. That's exactly what we had planned to do, but thank you anyway for your kind advice."

Captain Jennings made a detour by the ship's galley before returning onto the main deck. He felt uneasy, for at starboard, the same unidentified ship was still lurking within striking distance while still refusing to declare herself by not flying a flag. This could only mean one thing, she was a pirate ship. Rather a tropical storm than a close encounter with a pirate ship, he thought. He called his quartermaster.

"What do you think, Griffiths?"

"I don't like the look of her, Captain," he stated succinctly.

"Neither do I, but my remit is to log the name and position of every passing ship, not to intercept them or attack them, and that's exactly what I'll do."

From the crow's nest, Ron Martin shouted, "Capt'n, she's heading straight for us!"

"Right!" the captain said determinedly. "Humphreys, Connor, full sails on!" he ordered. Then, hailing the helmsman, he shouted, "Hastings, steer the ship away from her! And make sure you keep a good distance."

"I'll try, Capt'n, I'll try," Hastings replied.

Immediately, the whole crew sprang into action. Shipmates shouted orders to each other while ship boys ran into each other in their eagerness to obey orders as promptly as they could. Once everyone had reached their station, a tense silence fell onto the ship, only cut by the sails flapping, the cables whistling and the waves splashing the sides of the ship.

The sea was calm, but the wind direction favoured the other ship. With his turbulent past still at the forefront of his mind, Captain Jennings had hoped that for once he would enjoy a peaceful crossing, but the more he observed the rogue ship, the more he recognised the unmistakable signs of a piratical enterprise, like the glaring absence of a legitimate flag and the poor state of her sails. As the captain pondered, the unidentified ship finally declared herself by hoisting up a black ensign bearing two crossed pistols underneath a white skull, the very sight of which chilled the whole crew to the core.

"I've seen that flag before. I wonder whose it is," the captain pondered out loud.

"I don't know, Captain, but she sure means business!" Dai Griffiths breathed with great apprehension.

Suddenly, clouds of smoke escaped from the side of the rogue ship, a clear signal that the pirates had fired a broadside. Fortunately, the two ships were still out of firing range which made the captain wonder whether this was a prelude to a forthcoming attack or simply a warning for them to keep their distance. Whichever way, Captain Jennings was in no mood to take any chances.

"Gunners, at your posts! But do not fire until I give the order. Warren and Harris, go with them and help load the cannons. Everybody else, remain at your station and wait!"

As Harris followed the gunners below deck, the captain noted the glaring absence of shipmate Warren.

"Harris, where's Warren?"

By the awkward expression on his face, it was clear that this was a question Harris had hoped to avoid. He looked at the captain, shrugged his shoulders and replied, "Don't know, Capt'n, he might already be down there with the gunners."

Such a vague answer always made the captain suspicious. He turned to his quartermaster. "Griffiths, keep an eye on that other ship!"

Then, he rushed below deck and immediately spotted Warren fast asleep in his hammock. He smelt his breath and just as he suspected, Warren reeked of rum. Furious, the captain grabbed the side of the hammock with both hands and lifted it with a sharp tug. Shipmate Warren went crashing onto the floor where he landed with a loud moan. Blinking furiously, he looked about him and saw the captain standing at his feet.

"Ouch! What did you do that for? Oh… it's you, Capt'n," he greeted limply.

"Stand up, Warren!" the captain ordered angrily. "What did I say about drinking on board?"

"Well… it's just that… I was a wee bit thirsty…" he mumbled.

"Right, you two," he said, pointing at the nearest sailors, "lock him up in the brig and I'll deal with him later!"

Fuming with anger at this blatant breach of discipline, the captain marched out and went back on deck to consult with his quartermaster who noticed the irate look on the captain's face.

"What's up, Capt'n?" he queried, rather concerned.

"Warren's drunk!" the captain answered exasperated, taking the matter as a personal affront. "Which means… he must have stolen the rum."

"Well… you know… there's only one punishment for that crime."

"I know," the captain replied flatly.

Dai Griffiths sensed the captain's reluctance to carry out the punishment.

"You're gonna have to do it, you know that, otherwise you're gonna lose respect from your crew."

The captain bit his lip but did not reply. Instead, he gazed at the sea and to his great relief, noted that the distance between the two ships had increased.

"Good, I see that the other ship only fired as a warning."

"The Gods are with us, Captain. The wind has just turned and it's pushing us away from her."

"At last… a bit of luck… God knows we need it. Right, you deal with Warren while I go and warn the ladies not to come out on deck for a while. I don't want them to witness the awful sight of a miscreant being ripped to shreds; but make sure the ship boys are there, that'll be a good lesson for them."

Captain Jennings left the deck, but not before asking his quartermaster to carry out the unpleasant chore. In his mind, there was nothing more repugnant to a captain than having to flog a member of his own crew, but he had no option; the punishment had to be administered to ensure discipline on board, crucial for the smooth running of the ship.

Chapter Eighteen
Return to Nassau

If fate rested mostly in the lap of the Gods, the shipmates were leaving nothing to chance. Up in the crow's nest, the lookout kept an eagle eye on the horizon while Lady Rogers kept an equally vigilant eye on her daughter. In his cabin, the captain continued to note diligently in the logbook the sighting of every ship, using his sextant to calculate their exact position on his navigational chart.

The tension and suspense on the ship had altogether vanished and the shipmates idled the hours away dozing in her balmy atmosphere. However, as soon as land was sighted, they could feel their nostrils twitch with excitement at the mere whiff of hot baking sand. The distinctive aroma reminded them of life on land, which for them meant no more rules, no more restrictions, no more arduous chores; instead, there would be proper food and an endless supply of beer, punch and rum in the company of buxom women who were always ready to welcome their company and their pieces of four. Already anticipating the good time ahead, they chatted animatedly and bragged about the quantity of drinks and women they would have. Their games became more boisterous, their behaviour rowdier and their laughter more raucous. Meanwhile, closing his ears to the deafening racket, the captain strode about with his hands behind his back, thinking about his own plans and mapping his own future. The sight of his happy crew pleased him immensely and with his mission nearly accomplished, he felt exceedingly proud of them. Their cheerful mood was quite infectious and soon he felt in a celebratory mood too. He assembled his crew and told them, "I would like to congratulate and thank all of you for helping me complete this perilous crossing. Not all of us have made it safely back to port and we pray for their departed souls, but I want to show my appreciation by allowing everyone to take a small share of their rum, and I said 'a small share' for we're not back in port yet!" the captain warned.

Instantly, a spontaneous clamour rose from the ship as shipmates cheered the news by patting each other on the back and grabbing the nearest partner in order to perform a little impromptu dance. Dave Warren and Will Harris jumped to their feet and made straight for the deck below where they knew the rum to be stored. Promptly, but with a quirky smile on his face, the captain called them back.

"Warren! Harris! Come back on deck, you two! Putting you in charge of the rum would be like putting a thief in charge of gold doubloons! And that goes for you too, Jonesie and Jamesie! You stay on deck. You're too young to drink that stuff anyway. Griffiths! Humphreys! Go down and get the supplies!"

"Aye, aye, Capt'n!" the men chorused while Warren and Harris grumbled their way back to the main deck.

Soon after, the *Redemption* sailed past Cove Island. Captain Jennings blocked all thoughts from his past and purposely shifted his gaze onto the elegant silhouettes of the two ladies he had in his charge, who, at this very moment, were standing near the prow of the ship, presently absorbed in watching the shipmates celebrate.

Lady Sarah leant against the side of the ship and let out a big sigh.

"What was that for?" Lady Whetstone Rogers asked, scrutinising her daughter.

"I can't wait to be back home, to sleep in a bed that doesn't rock and to see Father again."

"And Commodore Holloway?"

Lady Sarah did not respond straight away. Then, exhaling another sigh, she simply said, "Yes, of course…" in a voice singularly devoid of passion.

Lady Whetstone Rogers ignored the flat response. As far as she was concerned, Lady Sarah's fate had been sealed long ago. In time, it would be her destiny to take over her mother's role as First Lady of the Isle of New Providence. Commodore George Holloway had been a popular choice from the moment he had met Governor Woodes Rogers, and the ruler of the island already treated him as one of the family. Life seemed so simple, so straight forward, away from the political maelstrom of a Europe always at war. Here in the Bahamas, one could easily imagine being in the most beautiful and secluded paradise on earth, were it not for those wretched pirates, the occasional hurricane and that cursed tropical fever.

In the past, Lady Sarah had been quite content to settle into a life among the exiled nobility of the Admiralty, but after the longest voyage she had ever undertaken, a spark had lit up and stirred her adventurous spirit. All of a sudden, she did not feel quite so ready to settle into the gentle pace of island life. While still on board the *Redemption*, she actively sought the captain's company to hear more of his riveting pirates' stories, in sheer contravention to her mother's wishes.

***

As soon as the ship was sighted, the port master sent for the Governor. As always happened at the news of a ship nearing port, onlookers crowded the quay to welcome the ship, greet the crew and catch up with continental gossip. At last, after several weeks at sea, the *Redemption* glided majestically into the port of Nassau. A few minutes later, preceded by half a dozen drummers, a small detachment of soldiers wrestled through the crowd to clear the way for the Governor and his wife. The drums rolled to a crescendo. Woodes Rogers, flanked by his deputy, stood on the quay in full regalia, his chest bursting with pride and anticipation as he eagerly awaited their ladyships, and of course news from England and the Admiralty.

***

On board the *Redemption*, most of the crew were leaning against the bulwarks, cheering, hailing and waving to the excited crowd.

Captain Jennings gave orders to prepare for landing and reminded the crew that they would have to stay on board until they were paid. Hearing this, Dave Warren and Will Harris winked at each other.

"…Could take days!" Warren whispered from the corner of his mouth.

"Aye!" Harris whispered in return. "…Gives us plenty of time to slip ashore for a pint."

Suddenly, both men jumped when they heard their names being called.

"Warren! Harris! Mackay! Muldoon! Brown! Get the cables ready!" the quartermaster ordered.

Surveying his crew from the upper deck, the captain summoned the ship boys, Jonesie and Jamesie.

"You two," he said, pointing at the boys. "Go and help the ladies with their luggage."

"Aye, aye! Capt'n!" The boys chorused cheerfully, glad to be back on terra firma after such a long journey at sea.

***

A few minutes later, Captain Jennings helped the ladies down the gangplank, with the ship's boys labouring behind, trailing two wooden trunks.

Governor Rogers stepped forward to greet his wife and daughter, and peered at the young man who was standing to attention next to them.

"Captain Jennings," the young man introduced himself, saluting.

"Pleased to meet you," the Governor greeted, saluting back before extending a welcoming hand. Then, giving the captain a peculiar look, he asked, "Have we met before?"

"I don't think so, Sir, but I do need to meet with you urgently to ask for funds so that I can pay my men."

"Of course, Captain, of course, but first you must give me news from England and tell me who's fighting whom."

"Indeed, Sir. As a matter of fact, I have a letter and some documents from Lord Admiral Lucius Bond-Balfour, Sir."

"Ah! I hope you are the harbinger of good news, Captain. How's old Lucius, by the way? Still got problems with his gout?"

"I wouldn't know, Sir," Jennings replied with a quirky smile.

"Why don't you come and have supper with us tonight. We can sort things out then. Come at eight o'clock."

"Thank you, Sir, it will be my pleasure."

The Governor started to walk away. Lady Whestone Rogers turned to the captain and gave her hand to be kissed.

"Thank you so much for looking after us, Captain. It was not always plain sailing but at least we made it."

"It was my greatest pleasure to have you both on board, Lady Whestone Rogers."

It was now Lady Sarah's turn to step forward. As she gave her hand to be kissed, she blushed. The captain took her delicate hand and said, "I hope we meet again, Lady Sarah."

The young girl smiled before being briskly whisked away by Commodore Holloway. Behind them, a servant was busy helping the ship boys put the trunks on a wooden trailer.

Back in his cabin, the captain lay on his berth for a while thinking, deliberating, planning and plotting. He was now a free man with time to wander about as he pleased. His thoughts veered towards his present situation and he wondered how soon it would be before he would become a gentleman of independent means. He knew that Lady Whetstone Rogers would be firmly opposed to her daughter's alliance with a penniless captain and he concentrated all his thoughts on working out how to intimate that he owned a sizeable fortune without revealing the true origin of his sudden wealth. However, at this moment in time, he was most concerned about one major obstacle that stood in his way, Commodore Holloway.

***

As the evening beckoned, the sky slowly turned amber red. The sun sank languorously into the mercurial sea, leaving in its trail the sharp pictorial shadows of boulders and palm trees, as black as ink, silhouetted against the flamboyant sky. As often happened on board a crowded ship, feelings ran high and tempers flared, but the calm serenity of a sea that lay without a tremulous ripple subdued the mariners' spirits and lulled the ship in an atmosphere of relative tranquillity and peaceful harmony.

***

After organising the night watch, Captain Jennings left his quartermaster, in charge of the ship before making his way on foot to Government House, perched on a small hill a few hundred yards beyond the far end of Duke Street. As soon as he spotted the white colonnades of the imposing building, he quickened his steps. Upon reaching the threshold of the colonial house, he looked back towards the sea to take in the splendid views. He immediately spotted Fort Charlotte clearly visible in the distance to the west, and Hog Island stretching just beyond the shore to the north. Behind the Governor's house, however, lay a large piece of land that formed a natural coral ridge nicknamed 'Dead Dog Hill' where many ex-slaves and free blacks lived. Charles Jennings was well aware of the settlements and had always vouched never to involve himself with the slave trade.

His thoughts were suddenly interrupted by someone querying, "Can I help you, sir?"

Charles Jennings turned around. It was one of the servants. His hair may have been grey and his body so frail that he could no longer stand up straight, but he was happy because he was going home for the night.

"Er... why yes. I've come to see the Governor."

"Would you like me to ring the bell for you, sir?"

Before Charles Jennings could stop him, the old man shuffled to the front door and pulled a brass handle. Then he turned to the young man, gave a huge toothless grin and uttered, "They won't be long... the butler will see to you in a minute. He's very nice, very handsome... I know, he's my son. Good night to you, sir."

"Thank you very much. Good night."

Upon these words, the old man shuffled down the path that led to the street; then he turned left at the bottom of the garden and disappeared in a side street that ran alongside the Governor's property. Following him with a distant glance, Charles Jennings quickly concluded that the old man must be making his way over there, towards a settlement that was situated on Dead Dog Hill. Better here, Charles Jennings thought, than anywhere else in the world, poor devil. Suddenly, a voice called out, "Yes, sir?"

Jennings turned his head towards the door and was struck by the sight of a very handsome young black man, resplendent in his butler's uniform. The captain introduced himself. "Good evening. My name is Charles Jennings, Captain Charles Jennings and..."

"Oh yes, Captain Jennings, the Governor is expecting you. This way, please."

The butler led the captain through the house and onto a large veranda which was shaded overhead with long palm branches affixed to thick wooden beams and where a group of formally dressed men and women were lounging in cane armchairs. Further to the left of the veranda, the captain noticed a long rectangular table which had been sumptuously laid with white porcelain plates, crystal glasses and silver cutlery.

"Captain Charles Jennings," the butler announced in a distinct voice. Immediately, the gathering stopped talking to stare at the visitor.

"Ah, there you are!" the Governor exclaimed. "Come and have a drink, Captain, and let me introduce you to everybody."

"I hope I'm not late," he apologised.

"No, no. We just like to relax out here with a drink before dinner." Then starting the introductions, he waved his hand in front of him and said as if he was repeating himself, "I think you already know my wife and daughter…"

"Delighted to meet you again, my ladies," the captain greeted with a broad smile.

"No more than we are." Lady Whetstone Rogers nodded delicately.

"And this is my son, William… my sister Lady Charlotte… you've of course already met Commodore Holloway… and this is Mr Daniel Defoe, a dear friend of mine who's recently published his latest novel, *Robinson Crusoe*. You might have heard of it."

"Well, it's not exactly a recent *ouvrage*," the famous author corrected. "It was published two years ago. Anyway, how do you do."

"How do you do," the captain reciprocated. "It wouldn't be about pirates, I wonder?"

"Not exactly, it's about this poor wretched sailor who finds himself marooned on a desert island."

"I should love to read it," the captain enthused.

Looking at his watch, the Governor butted in.

"Now that we're all here, let's have dinner… And then Captain, you can give us all your news."

Everyone proceeded swiftly to the table. One of the servants showed the captain his seat between Lady Charlotte and Lady Whetstone Rogers.

"Well…" the captain began with a hesitant smile. "Where shall I start?"

"Tell them about the *Cross of Madeira*." Lady Sarah breathed with excitement.

"I'm sure that by now your father must be rather familiar with the story," the captain remarked.

"I'm not!" a feminine voice stated vigorously.

It was Lady Charlotte. The captain turned towards her. She was looking at him with her head erect and her face lit with a mischievous smile. At first glance, it was difficult to tell whether she was a younger or an older sister to the Governor but for someone who had lived on the island for some considerable time, her complexion appeared remarkably smooth and pale, and quite unmarked by the scorching sun.

The captain returned her smile and embarked on the story of the *Cross of Madeira*, sparing no details on the battle against Bartholomew Roberts, with Lady Sarah butting in every time she could fill in a particular detail which the captain, purposely or not, had omitted to mention.

"And tell them about the *Devil's Triangle*!" Lady Sarah insisted.

The very term nearly gave a turn to Lady Charlotte who immediately threw her hand over her heart and exclaimed horror-stricken, "The *Devil's Triangle*! Good Lord, that sounds most horrid!"

Concerned by Lady Charlotte's reaction, the captain turned to Lady Sarah and said, "Actually, Lady Sarah, I don't think these good people would be interested in hearing about a silly little prank."

Lady Charlotte put her hand on his arm and declared quite adamantly, "Don't you believe it, Captain! Of course I am interested! Besides, I'm not superstitious! It brings bad luck!" Causing hilarity around the table.

"Don't take any notice of my sister, Captain! She'll be the first one to scream blue murder while insisting on your giving her every single gory detail!" The Governor chortled.

"Now, Woodes, you're being patronising again!" Lady Charlotte chided. "Anyway, I have found that I always sleep better when I've been entertained with wild stories that frighten me out of my wits!"

More laughter punctuated her remark. Lady Sarah continued, "The scariest part of the journey for me was…"

"The storm!" Lady Whetstone Rogers immediately interrupted.

"Not just that, Mummy! There was also that dreadful pirate who wanted to attack us," she added in a dramatic tone of voice.

"Forgive me, Lady Sarah, but I don't think he wanted to attack us," Captain Jennings corrected. "He just fired some warning shots, that's all."

"And how do you know he was *not* trying to hit us?" Lady Sarah questioned, expressing her doubt.

"It's a question of ballistics, Lady Sarah. From that distance, the pirate — if indeed it was a pirate — knew very well he couldn't possibly strike us."

"Blast! That's all I wanted to hear!" the Governor exclaimed, visibly annoyed. "So there's another pirate on the loose again."

"I thought you'd got them all," his son William said.

"So did I," the Governor replied. "But it would appear that those dreadful miscreants are still intent on making a nuisance of themselves. Commodore, we're going to have to check the whereabouts of this one."

"I quite agree, Sir, and the sooner the better," the Commodore concurred.

"As a matter of interest, Commodore, what do you think he was up to since he seemed unwilling to attack?"

The Commodore shuffled uneasily in his seat.

"It's difficult to tell since I wasn't there…" the commodore was forced to admit.

Seeing that the commodore was struggling for an answer, the captain took over.

"It would appear, Sir, that from the position where his ship was sighted, the alleged pirate might have taken over Black Bart's operations in the slave trade. If that is so, then he might have been transporting slaves which would explain why he didn't attack us because he would have wanted to protect his valuable cargo."

The gathering looked rather impressed with his eloquent delivery. After a short period of silence, Commodore Holloway scorned through his thin lips, "Of course, as an ex-pirate yourself, Captain, you would understand the mind of one better than any of us."

The sly remark brought on an embarrassed silence. Lady Sarah looked at her intended then at the captain, worried about her father's reaction. Then she turned to her father and said, "You were a pirate too, once, weren't you Papa?"

The sudden revelation caused a frozen silence around the table. The governor bristled in his seat and coughed in his plate. He picked up his knife and drummed it a few times on the table as if measuring the tempo of his next reply. Finally, he lined up his knife next to his plate and stuttered, "Well, er… not exactly, I started off as a *privateer* which is not quite the same thing…"

"Not that much different, Father," William cut in. "You plundered ships just like pirates do, with the only difference that you picked on foreign ships, preferably Dutch or Spanish, with the blessing of the King."

Lady Charlotte looked at the guests and exclaimed quite bemused, "It's a wonder you want anything to do with our family, gentlemen. We must sound like a right bunch of reprobates!" She giggled.

"But you are!" William affirmed, referring to his father.

"I'm certainly not, but he is!" his father protested, pointing at the captain. "And I don't recall ever granting him a pardon!"

At these words, Lady Sarah panicked.

"What do you mean, Papa? If you haven't, then you must!" she pleaded.

"Why?" The Governor objected.

"Because Captain Jennings saved us from certain death!" Lady Sarah pleaded emphatically.

Keeping a dramatic tone, Captain Jennings stood up and said, "And because of this!"

A stunned silence followed his remark. Looking rather calm and collected, the captain took an object out of his breast pocket and showed it to the gathering.

"This, Governor, ladies and gentlemen, is the *Cross of Madeira*."

An audible gasp of surprise rose from the table. Ignoring the general shock, the captain placed the precious jewel on the table. Instantly, all eyes focussed on a large cross made of solid gold framed with a thin layer of delicate laces of gold. The whole cross was encrusted with large sparkling diamonds interspersed with lustrous emerald stones encircling the biggest ruby anyone had ever seen, resting like a head on a bed of the most precious gold.

"And this," the captain continued in the same unaffected tone, "I hope, will earn me the much-wanted pardon that will set me free from my most unfortunate past."

With his eyes riveted on the jewel, the Governor very delicately took the cross and whispered in awe, "So this is it… the *Cross of Madeira*!"

Then he turned to the captain and said, "Well done, Captain. You may not be aware of it but by returning this most invaluable jewel, you may just have averted another war with Spain." There he paused, unable to take his eyes off the magnificent cross. Eventually, after a few seconds spent in sheer wonderment, he enquired, "Er… Is there any more where this came from?"

"I'm afraid not, Governor. Bartholomew Roberts used to carry as much jewellery as possible around his neck so a lot of it went down with him when he was thrown overboard."

"I have to say, Captain, I'm extremely curious to hear more about your experiences among those cut-throat pirates."

"So do I," Mr Defoe chipped in. "I am most anxious to learn more about your experiences among those cut-throat devils, especially about those two women pirates everyone is talking about."

The captain did not respond straight away. A look of melancholy briefly passed over his fine features as he stared vacantly at his empty plate.

Memories of Mary Read and Anne Bonny did not sit well with his present situation. No matter how much those women meant to him, they belonged firmly to the past, a turbulent past he was all too keen to forget.

"Come on, Captain!" He heard William chivvy. "Tell us about these two frightful daredevils! After all, you must know them rather well since you sailed with them on the same ship!"

Jennings slowly raised his head and looked directly at William. Then, he smiled… an uneasy smile.

"Maybe another time, William."

"Well, I dare say we all know what happened to that wretched Mary Read," the Governor ventured. "But what happened to Anne Bonny, no one seems to know."

"Do you know, Captain?" Mr Defoe queried.

The directness of the question unsettled Jennings. He took some time before answering, "No I don't," he replied almost truthfully. "And quite frankly, I don't wish to know. But let me tell you this, those two women had more guts, strength and courage than most men I know. It is true that the survival instinct is stronger than fear and pushes men — and women for that matter — to do whatever they can to survive. For women especially, with reduced circumstances, life on land is pretty dire and offers nothing but a miserable existence, so who can blame them if they seek to make a better life for themselves than most wouldn't dare!"

His vehement defence of two lawless women left the gathering stunned. After a prolonged silence, the Governor butted in, "But why did they have to choose to become wretched pirates!" he protested, somewhat pique.

"Because as women, they had no choice. The Royal Navy certainly wouldn't have them… and the women wouldn't want to either… the way naval officers treat their crew!"

As the tension mounted, Lady Charlotte felt compelled to somehow diffuse the situation. So, she turned to Mr Defoe and asked on the most casual tone, "Are you working on another book just now, Mr Defoe?"

The author returned a quirky smile and said, "As a matter of fact I am, it's called, *A General History of the Pyrates*."

A ripple of laughter greeted his reply, though none of the guests were able to tell whether this was a genuine answer or just a way to ease the tension. Enjoying the sudden light-hearted mood, the Governor chipped in,

"Pray I don't feature in it!"

Defoe looked at him and quipped, "Perhaps... perhaps not, my dear friend... though Captain Jennings's experience in these matters would be most valuable to my writings," he added in all seriousness.

Entirely satisfied with the successful turn of events, Lady Sarah turned towards the captain... and smiled, a broad winning smile.

***

After the last course had been consumed, the butler came round with a small wooden box containing the best of Havana cigars and offered them to the men. The Governor took one, smelt it and rose from the table to toast the King before lighting it. The rest of the men followed suit. After a round of port and brandy, the dinner guests departed for an after-dinner walk along the beach, led by the energetic Aunt Charlotte.

Rather than join his sister and his guests for a gentle stroll, the Governor invited Jennings to partake in a brandy in his office. He poured two glasses and came straight to the point.

"Captain," he started. "I have orders from the Admiralty that, in view of your past experience, you should lead the hunt for pirates in our waters."

"It will be an honour to serve my country," the captain vouched sincerely.

"You have your own ship and crew, I understand, on loan from the Admiralty, and I trust they are all well."

"Yes they are, but they are waiting to be paid..."

"I was coming to that... but since you took such good care of my wife and daughter..."

"It was my pleasure, Sir," the captain interrupted.

"...I would like to invite you to become a member of the Council of the Bahamas, which means that you will receive an additional payment to supplement your income."

"Thank you, Governor. I also understand there's a handsome reward attached to the *Cross of Madeira*."

"Ah yes, the *Cross of Madeira*. That should leave you quite well off, Jennings, but fair dos, you did get rid of that villain Bartholomew Roberts. That was a remarkable coup, Captain, putting an end to that terrible menace, very well done... but should you ever, and I really mean *ever* entertain the thought of returning to your previous trade…"

"Sir!" Jennings protested.

"Very good, Jennings, very good! To your good health!" the governor toasted, raising his glass.

"And yours!" the captain echoed. After finishing his drink, he added, "I am most grateful for your generous hospitality, but if you will excuse me, I have to return to my ship. There's one last thing, though, Governor, when can I expect my men to be paid?"

"Ah yes," the governor acknowledged. "Ask your men to come to the treasury tomorrow morning. They'll be paid then. Good bye, Captain, and good luck!"

Upon these words, the Governor rang for the butler.

Shortly after, Captain Jennings walked towards the front door, led away by the young butler.

"What's your name?" he asked out of interest.

"Johnny Canoe," the butler replied.

"Johnny Canoe?" the captain quizzed.

"Yes Sir. I arrived here in a small kind of canoe carved in a tree trunk. I was too young to know my name and my father was too weak to speak, so when the local people found us, they called me 'Johnny Canoe', though my people pronounce it 'Junkanoo'. I don't mind, I like the name."

"Johnny Canoe, hey? Interesting name… You don't fancy joining my crew by any chance, do you?" the captain asked in jest.

"Oh no, Sir." The butler chortled. "I never want to go out to sea ever again. I'm safe here and well looked after, and that's where I'll stay for the rest of my days."

"I don't blame you. All I can say is, they're jolly lucky to have you here."

"Thank you, Captain. Good night, Captain."

"Good night."

The captain descended the path that led to the sea front, eager to rejoin his crew. With the prospect of surpassing his own expectations, he had never felt so driven… and so happy and contented. On his way back to the harbour, he met the Governor's party returning to Government House. Immediately, Lady Charlotte accosted him.

"So you're off, Captain. Shall we see you again soon?" she enquired eagerly.

"Rest assured, Lady Charlotte, you will undoubtedly see me again, but how soon? I cannot tell."

"Well, you take care, Captain. And make sure you come back and visit us soon. William could do with the company of people his own age."

Captain Jennings looked at Lady Sarah's brother and it suddenly occurred to him that they were indeed probably the same age.

"William," he called out. "You're welcome to come and have a look around my ship. Her name's the *Redemption*. Come whenever you please in the next few days. After that, I shall be sailing, probably in two weeks or so after she's been careened."

William Whetstone Rogers greeted the captain's offer with great enthusiasm.

"I'd love to. Thank you, Captain."

"Perhaps Lady Sarah would like to show you around," he suggested with a cheeky smile.

"No thank you," Lady Sarah replied unequivocally. "I don't ever want to step on a boat ever again. I feel quite dizzy just thinking about it."

"It's called a ship, Lady Sarah. Anyway, I'd better get back to my ship before someone takes her away. Good night all."

"Good night, Captain," all replied except one, Commodore Holloway.

Jennings stayed put for a moment to watch the party walk up the hill. Then, as he began his descent down the path, the captain heard the rush of flowing crinoline brush the footpath behind him. Intrigued, he stopped and turned around.

"Lady Sarah!" he exclaimed, surprised.

"Captain!" she uttered, out of breath.

"What is it?" he enquired anxiously, suspecting some kind of trouble but when he looked at her face expecting to read signs of heightened anxiety, all he saw were her deep brown eyes sparkling with the flames of passion.

"Please…" she pleaded with a glorious smile. "Come and visit us soon."

The captain smiled back but did not answer straight away for up the path, he could distinguish the unmistakable silhouette of Commodore Holloway glowering at them.

"Please, Captain… Will you?" Lady Sarah pleaded again.

"I can't promise but I will try," he finally conceded.

Reassured, Lady Sarah smiled again and stole a kiss on the captain's cheek, which took him by surprise.

"Bye, Captain!" she bade, happy, before rushing back up the path.

Stunned, the captain watched her elegant silhouette disappear at a brisk pace. He waved to her knowing that she probably would not see him but just as he raised his hand, she stopped, turned around and smiled again because, there below her, she saw the captain smile.

Chapter Nineteen
Titus's Cave

With extensive repairs to be carried out, it was well over a month before the *Redemption* was fit to sail again. During that time, after paying several social visits to Government House, Captain Jennings discovered to his dismay that Commodore Holloway had been given the very same remit, that of hunting down the last of the pirates. However, still reeling from his recent victory against Bartholomew Roberts, Captain Jennings felt quietly confident in his new mission, despite knowing that Commodore Holloway was in charge of a better ship, a schooner named the *Valliant*, with more cannons on board and a larger crew. And he was already out there scouring the sea and stopping only to search and interrogate all those with a dubious look, a queer eye or a dodgy past. However, for once fate favoured the captain. Indeed, better than anyone else, he knew where the pirates might be lurking, for on board his ship, he still had in his possession the chart on which he had logged the sighting of every single ship. And he knew exactly where to begin, Cove Island.

***

At last, the ship was ready. On a morning in November 1722, Dai Griffiths, the quartermaster, was sitting at a small wooden table at the foot of the *Redemption*'s gangplank, checking in each member of the crew.

"Name?"

"Jack Connor."

"Sign here… Name?"

"Dave Warren."

"Sign here… Name?"

"Will Harris."

"Sign here…"

"Name?"

"Stan Mitchell."

Stan Mitchell? The quartermaster looked up. He had never heard that name before but there in front of him stood a big man with a large head crowned by an unruly mop of thick hair, acres of cheeks and full lips, and right now, the newcomer was staring at him with an inane toothless grin.

"Where have you come from?"

"I was told by me mates here that I could come and sign up," he said with a nod towards the gangplank. "They said it'd be all right."

"Who's *they*?"

"Like I said, me mates here," the big man replied, pointing at Warren and Harris.

The two shipmates had already reached the top of the gangplank, and when they heard their mate calling out to them, they turned around and hailed, "It's all right, Skipper, he's with us."

The new recruit breathed a sigh of relief and continued, "You see, Skipper, me ship's gone down and I've been stuck here doon nothing. Me capt'n gone back to England and I've been trying to…"

"All right, Mitchell, that'll do," the quartermaster interrupted. Then he looked the new recruit up and down before continuing with his task.

"Now, Mitchell, have you got any ticks, lice, nits, wooden eye, missing limbs or any other handicap?"

"Nope," the sailor replied scratching his bottom.

"All right then, sign here."

"Like… I just put a cross here like?"

"Aye, that's your name right here so put a cross next to it."

"Thanks Skipper."

"Next!"

As the next recruit stepped forward to sign his name, the quartermaster watched Mitchell walk up the gangplank. Bloody hell, he thought, he's only just joined the crew and he's already calling me 'Skipper'. However, despite appearing not to be quite the full shilling, there was something likeable about the big man. His voice rumbled loosely inside that huge chest of his though it sounded soft and gentle; and when he had drawn a cross beside his name with his tongue sticking out for better concentration, his hand had held the quill ever so delicately as if afraid to crush it. He clearly could not read or write, which was thankful in a way for his mind could not risk being corrupted by the sort of thoughts that create tyranny and start wars. He was just a wandering sailor with a childlike innocence who was happy to call any ship 'home'.

Spotting the two ship boys playing tag on the quay, the quartermaster called out to them, "Come on, you two, get on board the ship!"

"Not yet!" Jonesie shouted.

"Up to you but if you don't get on board now, I can't mark you down and if you're not marked down, you won't get paid."

"All right, all right," the boys chorused, rushing towards the enrolment table.

"Now, you two, are you sure you haven't another name? I mean... Jonesie and Jamesie... they're not proper names."

The boys looked at each other, then at the quartermaster.

"Well..." Jonesie started. "It don't matter really, but when I were a lad, at home, I was Billy Jones but me mum always called me Jonesie."

"Right," the quartermaster said, relieved at last. "That's all I wanted to know. There, you see, now you have a proper name on the register, sign here."

"But..."

Guessing what the boy was about to say, the quartermaster shook his head and said, "All right, just put a cross right here where my finger is."

Then he turned to Jamesie.

"So, young lad, you must be James Jones, then." He assumed.

The boy looked at Jonesie, then at the quartermaster and sighed, "I'm just James."

"But you're brothers, aren't you?"

There was a silent pause.

"Actually," Jonesie reprised on behalf of the younger boy. "Jamesie used to hang around our house. We used to play together, you see, we're best mates. Me mum used to give him some food when we had leftovers, which wasn't very often. And then, we started going to the harbour and watched the ships coming in. Sometimes we'd beg for food or money. And then one day, we saw all this food being taken on board this ship, you see, and that's when we decided to become pirates because we thought we'd never go hungry again."

"What made you think we were pirates?"

"I don't know... All sailors are pirates, aren't they?"

The quartermaster smiled at the naïve remark. He observed the boys for a moment, then with a look full of compassion, he declared, "Well,

201

Jamesie, since you two are 'brothers', I'm going to mark you down as James Jones, all right? Put a cross here, then."

"Thanks, Mister," Jamesie replied with a big smile.

Having been officially declared members of the crew, the boys sauntered up the gangplank, while the quartermaster shook his head in disbelief before resuming his head count.

By the end of the morning, the whole crew had been checked in, crossed and ticked. Captain Jennings took his position on the upper deck while his quartermaster allocated a station to each member of the crew. Jonesie and Jamesie, the ship's boys, were sitting by the prow playing a game with bits of bones. Dai Griffiths checked the water level and saw that the tide was high. At last, he was able to shout out the orders they had all been waiting for and soon, his booming voice resounded everywhere around the ship.

"All hands, on deck! Full sails on! Slip the cables! Remove the plank!"

***

A few minutes later, the *Redemption* glided out of the port of Nassau with a brand-new mizzen mast, en route to Cove Island. As soon as they were out to sea, Captain Jennings gathered the whole crew to explain the purpose of their mission. He asked for his men's assurance to abide by the rules and obey their commander, and once they had pledged their loyalty and obedience, together they recited the Mariners' prayer which was his very own adaptation to the Pirates' prayer.

> *Thank you, Lord, for opening our eyes to the beauty of this world*
> *For the wind in our sails and the freedom of the sea*
> *Thank you for the water we drink and the food we receive*
> *Let us sail in your faith and pray in your name*
> *And should we stray away from the righteous way*
> *Forgive us all our trespasses*
> *Forgive us our greed and excesses*
> *And let us sail in your faith and pray in your name*
> *Amen*

Then the captain retired to his cabin. for he had some thinking to do. Sitting at his small desk, he closed his eyes for a moment to recreate a mental picture of the island, and straight away he saw the jagged coast overlooking Dunmore Bay and the solid bank of dunes that rose up from the east beach. He saw the hidden creeks, the invisible caves and most interestingly of all, *Titus's Cave*, a dark cavern with an underground passage that linked the west side of the island with the east side and where most of his and his friends' treasures had been stashed away. Allowing himself for a brief moment to be transported back to his tumultuous past, he could once again feel the gentle sea breeze that carried with it the happy banter of pirates at play, toasting their new riches and celebrating their good fortune. But these were nostalgic memories of bygone days which had ended with rotting corpses hanging above Dead Man's Quay. Freed from the shackles of the past, he was now in complete control of his destiny, a destiny that would make him a man of honour and a proud officer of the King's Navy.

Several hours later, the lookout sighted Cove Island. The captain returned on deck and soon he was once again staring at the familiar contour of the western side of the island overlooking Dunmore Bay.

"Weigh anchor!" he commanded. "Humphreys, Connor! Come to my cabin. I need to have a word with you."

Once in his cabin, the captain wasted no time in unveiling his plans. Then, rolling out a large parchment paper, he showed the men a map of the island and pointed at a specific spot where he wanted to land.

"Tonight, after night fall, we'll take the cockboat and row to shore. Then we'll make our way here to *Titus's Cave…*"

The men peered at the map to take a closer look at the dark cross marked on the south-west side of the island.

"*Titus's Cave?*" Humphreys quizzed.

"Yes, it's a small cave where we can hide if we need to, but the main thing about that cave is that it has a small tunnel that leads to the other side of the island where we'll be able to observe discreetly what's going on."

"Wow, Capt'n, how did you know about that cave?" Connor asked in awe.

"Never mind about that," the captain replied curtly. "As I said, we'll go ashore after dark, and with a bit of luck, we'll find a few of those ruffians."

"Aye, Capt'n." Connor seconded.

"Now, the first thing you need to do is to lower the cockboat onto the water ready to be used later. Then put some torches in it."

"Aye, Capt'n," both men acquiesced before returning onto the main deck.

From their vantage point by the prow, the two ship boys were observing keenly the shipmates' movements. As soon as they saw the cockboat being put out to sea, they sprang onto their feet and made straight for the captain.

"You're going somewhere, Capt'n?" Jonesie asked expectantly.

"Just doing a bit of surveillance, that's all."

"Can we come too, Capt'n, please?" Jamesie begged, tugging on the captain's sleeve.

The captain smiled at their youthful ebullience.

"Well, I need to make sure it's safe, first. Then, if you're good, I might take you on the next trip."

"Yeah!" Jamesie clamoured.

"Thanks, Capt'n!" Jonesie effused.

"Now, don't get carried away, boys, I didn't promise anything. Besides, this deck needs scrubbing, so get cracking, boys!"

"Aye, aye, Capt'n!" The boys chorused.

***

The night was still. High up in the sky, the full moon shone with an iridescent glow that lit up the sea and cast dark shadows all over the island. The captain looked over the bulwarks and noted with relief that there was no wind, just a slight cooling breeze.

A few minutes later, the threesome settled in the small rowing boat.

"Got your pistols?" the captain checked.

"Aye."

"Loaded? Just in case…"

"Aye. But…" Humphreys began hesitantly. "I'm not sure about leaving Mitchell on the night watch. After all, he's only just joined us. We don't know if he can be trusted."

"Don't worry," the captain replied. "If Griffiths says it's all right, then it's fine by me. I'd be more worried if it was Warren or Harris and they've been with us a lot longer."

"Aye," Connor agreed. "Rather big Mitch than those two layabouts."

The captain steered the boat towards the very creek that had witnessed much drama not so long ago, and as soon as they reached the shore, the three men dragged the small boat onto the beach. Quickly, they marched through the thick vegetation and headed straight towards a cluster of palm trees among which they soon spotted a small opening deep in the coral rock, *Titus's Cave.*

"Mind your heads," the captain warned as they entered the cave. "We're going to need to light up the torches."

Having done so, the men began to proceed along the tunnel. Behind them, the sound of the cascading waves lapping the shore pursued them for a while like a hushed whisper warning them of unspeakable deeds. The men continued their journey without uttering a single word until they came to a fork in the tunnel.

"Which way, Captain?" Humphreys asked, almost giving himself a fright at the echoing sound of his own voice.

"Left," the captain replied without hesitation.

"Where does the other tunnel go?" Connor enquired.

The captain paused before giving a measured reply, "I don't know and you don't need to know either," he simply stated. "Just keep going and when you hear the sound of the sea again, you'll know we've reached the other side."

They had been walking for about half an hour when Humphreys suddenly stopped and said, "I can hear it, Captain!"

"I can smell burning wood," Connor added.

"So can I which means there are pirates on the island, so we're going to have to move very carefully. Put out the torches." The captain warned in a forceful whisper.

At the end of the tunnel, the exit was surrounded by thick vegetation. Wading through it, the captain led the small party to the knoll from where he knew they would be able to observe the long sandy beach stretching over the whole of the eastern side of the island. As they made their approach, the first thing they noticed was the presence of three ships moored in the bay. As the beach came into full view, the three men caught sight of several campfires burning brightly with people milling around them, some talking merrily, others hailing each other loudly. Some even were singing to the happy jangle of a concertina, a sound that caused Charles Jennings to shudder every time he heard it.

Scurrying among the thick vegetation, he signalled to Humphreys and Connor to stay a few steps behind. The rustling of bushes reassured him that his men were following a short distance away. He turned around to check. Just as he did so, a powerful blow struck him on the head, and he fell heavily to the ground. When he came to, he found himself sitting up against a tree with his mouth gagged and his hands and feet tied together. He strained his neck to look around but found he could hardly see through his right eye for the swelling. Not far from him, he heard some faint groans and guessed that they must be coming from Humphreys and Connor.

Footsteps were approaching. Jennings pricked up his ears. Despite the pain, the fear growing inside him kept him alert and sharpened his senses. Suddenly, four burly men emerged from the long grass. They swore and jeered before untying the men's feet. Then, the burliest of them grabbed the captain while the others pushed Humphreys and Connor in front of them.

"Come on, you lot! Move!"

For a moment, the men struggled to stay on their feet. They staggered along trying to keep up with the pace. They thought they would be taken to the beach and perhaps even onto one of the ships to be confronted by the master villain, but to Jennings's surprise, they were kicked and pushed through the thick vegetation towards the south of the island. A few minutes later, the group arrived at a large clearing which was almost entirely taken up by a vast wooden shack. The spicy smell of pipe smoke greeted their arrival. Then, a figure appeared in the doorway wearing a loose shirt and a pair of oversized trousers held up with a thick leather belt. The ruffian's loose mop of hair concealed a tanned face with surprisingly smooth features. Jennings stared in shock. There, in front of him, stood a woman he knew all too well. The captain could not take his eyes off her, for the woman who was swaggering with contempt in front of him, smoking a pipe, was none other than Annabel Smith, an adventuress whom he knew better under her real name, Anne Bonny.

Chapter Twenty
The Devil's Well

The woman glared at the prisoners and smirked with disdain.

"What have we got here, hey? Remove their gags."

Then, addressing the prisoners, she growled, "Who are you and what are you doing on my island?"

As soon as the men's gags were removed, Bonny looked at each man in turn, scowling heavily, until her gaze fell on one of them. She took a double take and stared at the captain in complete shock. The captain returned her intense gaze, savouring the moment. The silent duel was rudely interrupted by one of the ruffians asking, "What's the matter, capt'n? What's wrong with this guy?"

"Nothing!" Bonny replied, forcing an indifferent tone. "Take the other two to the beach but don't kill them yet. We might need them. As for this one here, I'll take care of him myself. I reckon I can get everything I want to know from him."

The pirates did not move. They seemed more interested in finding out what was going on between their leader and the one particular prisoner than obeying orders.

"What are you waiting for?" Bonny yelled, exasperated. "Go on! Scram! And if they try to escape, throw them down the devil's well!"

No sooner had the small group disappeared down the sandy path, crunching the hot sand as they went, than Bonny turned to Jennings, looked him straight in the eyes and barked, "What the hell are you doing here?"

Her tone of voice had changed. She was now purring like an enchantress rather than barking like an untamed shrew. She threw her head back to flick her hair away from her face and immediately, the heavy frown and scowl that had blighted her fine features disappeared to reveal her smoother and softer lines.

"Anne!" Jennings cried out. "I can't believe you've returned to your old trade. Why?"

"It's fate, Boy Jennings, it's fate," she stated plainly without a trace of emotion in her voice.

"But why? You had managed to get away from it all…"

"I got bored. Life on land isn't for me. I need the excitement… I need that thrill that makes me feel alive, I want to live each day as if it were my last. And besides…" There she paused, bowed her head down as if about to make a confession, then resumed in a much softer tone. "I did it for my son…"

"So… you had a son…"

"Yeah… I had a son," she confirmed, looking as if she wanted to say more.

"Where is he now?" Jennings enquired.

"With Tisdale's niece, a young woman called Lorna Shielding. His name's Angus… Angus Shielding, and she's taking good care of him. He probably thinks she's his mother and that don't bother me because she's probably a better mother to him than I'd ever have been. But whatever you think of me, I don't care, because whatever I do, I do it for him. I've already stashed away a small fortune so that when he comes of age, he won't have to become a pirate and risk his life every day for a pitiful existence."

While she took a pause to catch her breath, Jennings suggested, "You can untie me, you know, we're old friends. I promise I won't try anything."

"Not until you've told me exactly what you came here for."

"Don't worry, I'm not after any of the treasures, and as far as the authorities are concerned, you don't even exist any more. No, a pirate ship has been spotted lurking around these waters and it's my mission to catch it. Was it your ship?"

Anne Bonny answered with a little giggle.

"What's so funny?" Jennings asked pointedly.

"Nothing… It could be… or it could be my partner's."

Jennings shook his head in despair.

"Why are you doing this, Anne. You had the chance to start a new life somewhere where nobody knew about your past… why?"

"I told you! I'm doing this for my son…" she barked in frustration, then she looked Jennings straight in the eyes and added, "*our* son."

Stunned, Jennings was convinced he had misheard.

"*Our* son? What do you mean '*our* son'? I don't have a son," he stated categorically.

"Well, I've a surprise for you, Boy Jennings, my son is your son too!"

Jennings looked at her in a complete state of shock.

"But that's impossible! We… we never…"

"You seem to have forgotten that one night when I seduced you…"

"Impossible! You were Rackham's woman, everybody knew that."

"Ah, Rackham… Poor old Rackham… God bless his soul, but he was useless, totally useless, always laid low with his body awash with rum. He was no good for nothing; but me, I wanted a man, I needed a man and secretly, I envied you and Mary. So one night, when you two had arranged to meet, Mary wasn't feeling too well so she asked me to go and tell you that she was indisposed… and… well… I took advantage of the situation and seduced you. Mind you, there was no moon that night so it was pitch dark, so you could easily have mistaken me for Mary. It was my chance to be with a man, a real man, a decent man…"

"How could you!" Jennings blasted out, in sheer outrage. "You're a despicable woman and I despise you… You were Mary's friend for Christ's sake, how could you have done that to her… and me!"

"Like I said, I needed a man."

"But you could have had anyone else on board!"

"No, I wanted you. Mary had good taste, she picked the best one."

Charles Jennings shook his head and sighed heavily.

"So, Angus's my son!"

"Yep, he's your son."

After the initial shock, Charles Jennings felt an uncontrollable anger grow inside him.

"You devious… evil… two-timing wench!" Jennings blurted out in disgust. "You betrayed the only friend you had, and now you've betrayed me!"

He lunged towards the pirate, grabbed her cutlass and pointed it at her.

"Anne Bonny, I despise you more with every breath I take! You are evil and right now, I shall be your judge and your executioner, and may the Lord have mercy on your soul!"

"You wouldn't kill your very own son's mother, would you?" she challenged him with an arrogant smirk on her face.

"Rather that, than him finding out what a vile creature you were."

"Up to you… but you won't be able to leave this island alive without my help. And who's going to take care of our son then?" she questioned. "Watch yourself, I can hear the others coming back."

While both listened intently to the noise coming from outside, Jennings kept the cutlass firmly pointed at Bonny's chest.

"I'm going to make a deal with you," he eventually said in a rasping voice.

"Well, be quick, Jennings!" Bonny urged him in a defiant stance. "You don't have much time. These guys don't have any notion of 'love' and 'care'. The only thing they know is to shoot to order. No feeling, no emotion and no hesitation."

"All right. I shall postpone your death sentence for now, and in return, you let me and my men go, unharmed! And one other thing, if you ever get to meet our son, I want you to promise that you will never ever tell him who you are, because the only time he's ever likely to meet you will be in a court of law or on the gallows and I don't want him to feel dishonoured, shamed or disgraced by a mother who didn't care enough for him to give up this shameful lifestyle. Is that a deal?"

Bonny hesitated before giving her reply. She seemed hurt, but with a casual shake of her long hair, she dismissed her wounded pride, pushed the point of the cutlass away from her and decreed, "It's a deal... but any funny move from you... and I'll shoot."

"I'll kill you first! With the blessing of the King!" he riposted. Then he looked her coldly in the eyes and added, "And another thing... I hope we never meet again!"

As he stomped his way towards the door, he heard her retort, "Don't worry, we won't."

Surprised by her icy tone, the captain turned around to take one last look at her, only to find himself staring down the barrel of a loaded pistol. Instinctively, he tried to grab it and in the ensuing scuffle, the gun went off. Both stood rigidly still, wondering if either had been hit. No blood was showing. Suddenly, Jennings pounced on her.

"You're losing your touch, Bonny!" he riled.

"And you're still so naïve, Jennings!"

He grabbed her arm, wrenched her towards him and looked at her fixedly. All sorts of conflicting thoughts and emotions ran through his head as he locked his gaze into her eyes, sparkling with murderous intent. Her heavy breathing so close to his face took the semblance of words, unleashed yet unspoken, but full of passion... and hatred. He did not want her dead, but he did not want her close to him either. He reckoned that the only way both would come out of this alive would be by appeasing the wild tigress that was clamouring for blood… his blood. He gradually released his tight grip and said in a softer voice, "Come on, Anne, give up this wretched life and come back with me to Nassau."

Anne looked at him with a long, frozen stare, and all of a sudden, she burst out laughing.

"You must be mad, Jennings! And even more naïve than I thought."

After she had quite calmed down, she looked at Jennings with softer eyes and said in a more controlled voice, "No, Jennings, there's nothing for me there… Besides, too many people know my face."

"I can get you a pardon," he added enticingly, but Anne shook her head and replied in a defeated tone, "Thanks, Jennings, but I'd rather stay here until…"

"Until what? Until you're caught, tried and hanged? Because that's the only fate that awaits you here! Why, Anne, why are you doing this? You were free; you could have made a new life for yourself and your son…"

"Yeah, in good old boring England!" she quipped.

"But you would have been free to take care of your son… our son! What on earth did you think you were doing hooking up with another pirate? Surely, you didn't have to go with him!"

"I didn't want to!" she protested. "But I had no choice! It happened while I was travelling back from England, the ship was intercepted by Black Bobby…"

"So that's his name, is it?" Jennings interrupted.

"Yeah, that's his name!" she replied aggressively. "And when I saw how ruthless he and his men were, I decided, for the sake of my son, that I'd rather side with him and live than fight against him and die. There! That's what happened."

After her outburst, Jennings studied her face, her lips curling with anger, her eyes firing angry sparks while her hand flicked her hair back nervously.

"Just go, Jennings, and leave me be." She finally relented. "Go back to your ship the same way you came here…"

"What about my men?"

"Don't worry, they'll be safe. I'll make sure of it."

"My ship is moored on the other side of the island, in Dunmore Bay and…"

"I know," she quipped.

"You know? You've been spying on us?"

"It's a matter of survival to know," she simply stated.

"Anyway, tell my men I'll wait for them there."

"No you won't. Right now, Black Bobby is busy sorting his loot on his ship; the moment he finds out that you're after him, he's going to hunt you down and let me warn you, he's only interested in prizes, glittering prizes, not dead weight. Trust me, Jennings, I'll look after your men; I'll take them on board my ship back to New Providence myself."

"What about Black Bobby?"

"I don't have to justify anything to him. We're in a partnership, not a marriage!"

"What's the name of your ship?"

"She's called the *Conqueror*. But before you go, you're gonna have to scratch my arm with your knife. I don't want my men to think that you managed to escape without me putting up a proper fight. And don't go and get any fancy ideas in your righteous head... I'm not doing this for you... only for my son!"

Charles Jennings took his knife out and ran his finger over the cold blade, "I've never harmed a woman before..."

As he said this, he grabbed her arm and drew her very close to him, his eyes firmly fixed in hers. His head was so close to hers that for a moment, she thought he was about to kiss her. Then, all of a sudden, she felt the sharp pain of a blade running along her upper arm. Jennings watched her wince and clench her teeth and soon, a thin trickle of blood began to flow. Grabbing her arm, Bonny looked at Jennings and said, "You know... if you hadn't been such a handsome man, I would have done away with you ages ago."

Outside, footsteps were fast approaching.

"Go, Jennings! It's your last chance! Go!"

Jennings seemed to hesitate. He threw one last glance at Bonny, then ran out of the shack and towards the secret passage.

***

Meanwhile, back on the east beach, Humphreys and Connor could not believe their luck. Claiming to be pirates, they had been allowed to join in and presently, they were feasting on wild rabbit. Sitting by the campfire in the company of other pirates, Connor ventured to ask one of them, with his mouth full, "What's the devil's well, mate?"

"You don't need to know," one of the pirates fired.

"It's a hole in the ground," another explained, ignoring his mate's rebuke. "Big enough for any man to fall in, even a fat arse like yours." He chortled.

"Aye, but it's got the sea at the bottom of it and once you fall in, you can't get out!"

"Why is it called the 'devil's well' though?" Connor asked again.

"Cos 'tis so deep and so dark that it's said to end in hell," he added, opening his eyes ever so wide in pretend horror.

At that moment, Connor felt a knee being jarred against his back and the sharp blade of a cutlass pressed against his throat.

"You ask too many questions," a cavernous voice berated.

"Hey!" Connor yelled. "What the hell! Let go of me!" he yelled, struggling to speak.

The man released his strong hold and, with a strong push, threw Connor to the ground. His aggressor was well over six foot, with his shoulders thrown right back to make himself appear even bigger than he was, and over his large frame, he sported a red army coat with all the brass buttons still intact. His jet-black hair was loosely pulled back in a ponytail underneath a moth-eaten tricorn sporting the same logo that was embossed on the buckle of his belt, that of a skull with two pistols crossed underneath it. It was difficult to study his facial features for a beard streaked with grey strands covered the lower half of his face and hung low below his neck. However, his most terrifying feature was undoubtedly his bulging eyes, as black as sin and spewing sparks of malevolence and murder. Nobody knew how he got his nickname but 'Black Bobby' was as fair a description as only the devil could have made himself.

At the first sight of the man, Connor instinctively flinched but Humphreys looked on, unperturbed. He was quite a good size himself and, unbeknown to anybody else, in his early adult life, he had learned his fighting skills from a French master named Jacques Lagardère, a mousquetaire from Louis XIV's royal court whose ship had floundered off the coast of England after a violent storm. Although a quiet man by nature, he had concentrated on improving his fighting skills with the result that, while his appearance remained rough, surly and aggressive, in actual fact, he was a learned, rather sophisticated man and one of the very few who could actually read and write, a fact he was quite happy to keep to himself.

Addressing the two prisoners, Black Bobby barked, "What are you doing eating *my* food?"

Connor looked at the piece of rabbit he held in his hand, then at Black Bobby.

"It's rather nice, you should try some," he jibed, trying to humour the pirate.

However, Black Bobby was not a man renowned for his sense of humour. He brandished his cutlass and with a swift flick of the wrist, swiped the piece of rabbit off Connor's hands. Fearing for his life, Connor jumped to his feet and fled towards the sandy dunes. Immediately, Black Bobby grabbed his pistols, but by the time he realised they were not loaded, Connor had already disappeared on the other side of the hill. He sprinted up the path and through the bushes, never looking back. Behind him, he could hear the horde of pirates chasing after him. Soon, he spotted the hut but as he came level with it, in the distance he caught a glimpse of his captain running in the direction of the tunnel, so he kept going; by now his chest was burning but he continued his desperate run to catch up with the captain. Unaware of this, Jennings kept running faster and faster believing that the runner behind him was one of the pirates. As he came nearer the tunnel, he decided to set an ambush. So he stopped and crouched behind a bush, and laid in wait for his pursuer. As soon as the latter reached him, he pounced on him and wrestled him to the ground. As he looked at the terrified face of the man, he exclaimed in total surprise, "Connor!"

"Captain! Thank God it's you! The pirates are after me! Quick! To the tunnel!" Connor managed to stutter out of breath.

Both men scrambled back onto their feet and sprinted towards the tunnel, pursued by the pirates shouting, "After them! After them! Get them!" The sound of their war cries was immediately followed by the crackling of pistols being fired.

Seconds later, Jennings and Connor jumped through a thick bush before disappearing inside the secret passage. There, they stopped to catch their breath. Outside, the pirates' cries came within metres of them, only to die down again. As soon as he was able to speak, the captain queried, "Where's Humphreys?"

"He didn't run. What about you? How did you manage to escape?"

"There's no time to talk. Light the torches and let's go back to the ship."

***

From the position of the sun in the sky, it was about mid-morning and back on the *Redemption*, shipmates Warren and Harris were stirring up trouble.

"They've been away for nearly a day, now," Dave Warren began.

"Something's happened to them. They've probably been caught and killed by some pirate…" Harris added, slicing his throat with his thumb. "I think we should get out of here," he urged.

"We can't without a captain," Warren quipped. "And I suggest…"

"You'll suggest nothing!" Big Mitch cut in. "I say we wait, and we wait here for the captain."

"But we can't wait around for ever," Dave Warren whinged. "We're going to run out of food and water soon."

"What are you worried about, Warren?" a shipmate heckled. "You only drink rum!"

A chorus of raucous laughter rose instantly from the crew. Suddenly, the loud cries of one of the ship's boys drew everyone's attention.

"There! There they are! They're coming back!" Jonesie shouted, pointing at a small rowing boat.

All heads turned towards the island.

"Are you sure it's them?" Warren asked.

"Pretty sure," Jonesie confirmed.

"Yeah!" the crew cheered.

"I told you they'd come back," Brown told MacKay.

"Hey, look! There's only two of them!" MacKay remarked.

"Which one's missing? Me eyes are not as good as they used to be… Not the captain, I hope."

"Humphreys… It's Humphreys, he's not with them."

Moments later, Captain Jennings climbed the rope ladder and was pulled on board, helped by Big Mitch.

"Good to see you, Capt'n," he greeted jovially.

"Likewise," the captain replied, clearly relieved. "Is everything all right?"

Big Mitch racked his throat. Others followed suit. The captain looked around with a puzzled expression on his face.

"I asked, is everything all right?"

Big Mitch threw a quick glance at the crew and answered confidently, "Aye, Capt'n, everything's fine."

His words soon echoed all around the ship. "Aye, aye, everything's fine."

"Let's go, then! All sails down! Brown and Stevens, raise the anchor! Griffiths, back to Nassau!"

"Aye, aye, Capt'n!"

"What? Without Humphreys?" MacKay enquired anxiously.

"Don't worry about him," the captain reassured him. "He'll be fine. He'll soon be back in the *Cock 'n Bull* for his usual pint! Now go back on the rigging and help stretch the main sail! The quicker we get going, the sooner you'll be drinking something tastier than tepid water!"

Once he had given his orders, Captain Jennings went to stand by the bulwarks to stare at the island. The unexpected news of a son had shaken him hard. For the first time in his life, he no longer felt content to be drifting haphazardly from one adventure to the next. Indeed, not. From now on, he planned to take charge of his own destiny. He wanted to make his own decision rather than let fate decide for him. He thought about Lady Sarah, this truly exceptional young lady who had awakened his wounded heart and filled it with the most exclusive and exquisite of all sentiments, love. With her by his side, he would be able to mingle with the venerable gentlemen of Nassau's high society as a highly respected officer of the King's Navy. However, before he could declare his love for her, he would have to prove his worth by catching the last major threat to blight these islands, a threat that bore the obscure name of '*Black Bobby*', pirate and pilferer of the High Seas.

Chapter Twenty-One
Preparation for Battle

Upon his return to Nassau, Captain Jennings went straight to Government House to ask for an audience with Governor Rogers.

As usual, he was greeted at the door by the young butler Johnny Canoe who welcomed him with a broad smile. In the background, the captain noticed a different kind of noise.

"What's that awful racket?" he asked, half mocking.

"Drums, Captain Jennings. I'm teaching Master William how to play the drums." He chuckled.

"Do you really have to?"

"Yes, Captain, it's for the *Junkanoo*."

"The *Junkanoo*? But I thought he couldn't take part…"

"That's right, Captain, he can't take part because he's not a native but Master William heard me practise and he asked if I could teach him in return for a few groats."

The butler beamed with pride. Suddenly, it occurred to the captain that perhaps…

"Johnny Canoe… *Junkanoo*… Are the two names connected by any chance?"

"Yes, Captain. *Junkanoo* is how my people pronounce my name. We do have a different kind of accent here," the butler confided, smiling. It's my father who taught me how to play the drums, and it was him who started the festival as our way to celebrate the New Year and when he was looking for a name to call it, he used mine — family pride, you see — and that's how it all started."

"Your father is a good man, Johnny Canoe. He's made you someone very special!"

The young butler bowed low with deference but inside, his pride was up high, levelled only with the angels. He then left the captain to wait in the Great Hall. During that time, Lady Sarah happened to come along. As soon as she saw the captain, she smiled and hurried towards him.

"Good evening, Captain." She greeted jovially. "Are we going to have the pleasure of your company at dinner tonight?"

"I'm afraid not. I've come to see your father on business."

"Is it such serious business that you cannot discuss it over dinner?" she asked with a smouldering smile.

"Ah!" a voice hailed in the background. "Captain Jennings! I take it that if you've come, you have some news for me."

"Yes, Governor, as a matter of fact I have."

"Papa," Lady Sarah butted in. "Can the captain stay for dinner?"

"Well, I don't know, Darling. The captain may be busy."

"Please, Captain," Lady Sarah insisted, fluttering her eyelashes. "Will you stay for dinner?"

"You're not in a hurry to go, are you?" the Governor enquired.

"No, but... I wouldn't want to impose..."

"Well, that's settled then. Darling, go and tell Cook there'll be one more for dinner."

***

At the dinner table, the governor requested that the captain be seated next to him in order to facilitate conversation in a discreet manner. Lady Charlotte huffed and puffed, and shrugged her shoulders.

"Men! They think whatever they say is *sooo* important. They always treat us like delicate creatures who have no understanding of the serious business of life and politics."

The Governor rolled his eyes in mock exasperation.

"Charlotte my dear, we all know you're as tough as old boots!"

"Not just me, dear brother, look at those women pirates!"

Captain Jennings bristled uneasily in his seat before quickly changing the subject. "I see Commodore Holloway is not here," he ventured, glancing at Lady Sarah at the same time.

"No, he's not back yet, although we are expecting him shortly," the Governor informed him. "Anyway, what's your news?"

Without prevaricating, the captain decreed plainly, "I've found Black Bobby."

A loud gasp rose from the table.

"Good Lord!" the Governor exclaimed. "So soon! Well done, Captain.

So, tell us where the ruffian is hiding."

"Not far from here actually… on Cove Island."

"How did you find him so quickly? I mean, how did you know where to start, with thousands of islands to choose from?"

"By a judicious use of my past experience, Sir. I've also discovered that he has three ships and the total run of the island," the captain revealed, giving just enough information to avoid any further questions.

However, the Governor was not entirely satisfied. He wanted to know more.

"Who else is with him? How many men has he got?" he quizzed further.

The captain started fidgeting with his knife and fork. He was not prepared to answer the first question and swiftly moved on to the next.

"Difficult to tell, Governor. There were about thirty of them on shore, though I suspect that a few of them stayed on board to keep a vigil. However…" he finally stated vaguely, "he must have some experienced sailors under his command who are skilled enough to sail his other ships."

"Right then, Captain, the sooner we catch him, the better for all of us here."

"That is my intention too, Sir, but I cannot fight him on my own and I was hoping that Commodore Holloway would join forces with me and help me bring that lawless brigand to justice. After all, Black Bobby has three ships, I only have the one."

"You're quite right, Captain," the Governor acquiesced.

"There's one more thing…"

"Yes, Captain?"

"Black Bobby is mostly involved in the slave trade and he's likely to leave for Africa at any time which means the sooner I go, the greater chances I'll have to catch him."

"You can't do that! You might get killed!" Lady Sarah interjected, in a rather distressed state.

"Darling, you mustn't interfere with your father's business," her mother chided.

"But three against one! The captain won't stand a chance!" She protested.

The Governor threw a concerned glance at his daughter before continuing, "You're quite right, Captain. It would be foolhardy to expect you to take on three ships single-handedly. If you wish to go sooner rather than later, then I won't stop you but what I can do is send the Commodore as soon as he returns to assist you. However, we mustn't forget, Captain, that I also have my own ship and I know it's a while since I've seen battle, but Black Bobby is the last of those damned pirates and if I have to go and get him myself, then I shall!"

"Bravo!" Lady Charlotte hailed.

Not all received the news with equal enthusiasm. Lady Sarah, for one, looked ever more alarmed.

"Oh no, Papa!" she objected plaintively. "Not you as well!"

Captain Jennings stared at her with a sympathetic eye but remained firm in his resolve. "In that case, Sir, I shall be sailing tomorrow, as soon as my ship has been provisioned."

"Good man, Captain, good man."

At the end of the meal, Lady Charlotte led the ladies for their usual evening walk on the beach while the men retired for a glass of port or brandy.

"Come and have a cigar," the Governor invited the captain. "They're the best... from Cuba."

The captain helped himself to one of the fine cigars, while still engrossed in his own thoughts.

"As a matter of interest, what's the name of your ship, Governor?" he finally queried.

"Of course, you need to know that, so you don't start firing broadsides at her," he stated with a little chuckle. "Her name is the *Maryland*. Now, don't ask me why because that was her name when I got her and I, for one, won't be changing her name; not that I am superstitious, but it's supposed to be bad luck to change a ship's name." After a short pause, he added, "It's interesting, you know, I used to sneer at all that nonsense... but the older I get, the more superstitious I become. It's silly, isn't it? I'm slowly turning into a befuddled old fool."

"Not exactly true, Sir. Superstition is quite a useful belief. It forces us to think about the consequences of our actions and proceed with caution, making us better prepared to face our enemies."

The Governor stared at the captain, visibly impressed.

"By Jove, Jennings! Who did you say your father was?"

"He's a farmer, Sir."

"With land?"

"No, Sir. He's a tenant farmer."

"Hm… Is that so? Ah well, better your own master and commander than a slave to the land, hey?"

Captain Jennings understood straight away the undertone of the Governor's comment.

"I am not a pauper, Sir. I have enough resources to enjoy a perfectly comfortable lifestyle, which is what I'm planning to do once we've caught Black Bobby."

"You mean… you're planning to retire from the Navy?"

"Not entirely. I'm hoping to secure a position on land."

"Back in England?"

"No, Sir, here in Nassau."

"I'm glad to hear it, Captain. You've a good head on those young shoulders of yours and we could certainly do with people like you around here."

"It's kind of you to say so. Anyway, it's getting late; I'd better go back to my ship. Goodnight, Governor."

"Goodnight, Captain… And please, do keep me informed on that ruffian."

"Certainly, Sir. Goodnight, Sir."

As the captain crossed the Great Hall, he heard a series of hurried steps echo behind him. He turned around and saw Lady Sarah looking rather flustered. When she came level with him, she grabbed his arm and whispered in his ear, "Goodnight, Captain, and please, do take great care." Then she planted a little peck on his cheek before imploring, "Please, come back to us soon."

After these words, she promptly left. Alone again, all Captain Jennings could hear was the rustling of her long flowing dress fade away down the corridor. As he made his way towards the main door, the young butler appeared.

"Goodnight, Sir," he hailed with his usual cheerfulness.

"Goodnight Johnny."

***

The following morning, while his ship was being loaded, Captain Jennings went to pay a visit to Henry Tisdale, landlord of the *Cock 'n Bull*. As he approached the tavern, he spotted Mona Tisdale sweeping the pavement outside the front door.

"Good morning, Captain," she greeted in a loud voice. "What can I do for you?"

"Is your husband home, Mrs Tisdale?"

"Oh aye, he's busy cleaning the bar. Do go in. If you can't see him, have a look behind the bar. Sometimes he hides there to sneak in a quick pint." She chortled.

"I'm not!" a voice protested from inside.

The captain bent his head to cross the threshold of the tavern.

"I hope you haven't come to put a large order in because I'm almost out of ale."

"No, Mr Tisdale. I've come to ask you a very big favour."

"A big favour? Oh… I don't like the sound of that," he stated apprehensively.

"You have a ship, don't you?"

"I had, I had! Remember? You took my ship to England and didn't bother to bring her back!"

"I will bring the *Kingston* back, I promise, as soon as I get the chance," the captain vouched.

"So, why are you asking me to lend you my ship, then?" Henry Tisdale asked, slightly irate.

"I thought you had another one to do local business with…"

"No I haven't," Tisdale denied categorically.

"Yes, we have!" a voice shouted. It was Mona Tisdale.

Henry Tisdale glared at his wife and threw his hands up in the air.

"I'm never gonna win, am I?" he complained. Then, turning to his wife, he berated, "It's only a small sloop and she's made to transport merchandise not to fight battles at sea."

The captain intervened. "Don't worry, Mr Tisdale. I'm not asking you to send her into battle. I just wondered whether I could borrow her as an assistance ship…"

"Out of the question!" Tisdale cut in abruptly. "Where is it you're going anyway?"

"I'm afraid I'm not at liberty to say. All I'm asking is for your ship to accompany my ship so that if we need help, yours can come back here and alert the authorities."

"And that's it? No firing, no fighting, just a trip out there and back."

"Yes, that's all I'm asking."

"In that case… er… no."

"If our mission is successful," the captain insisted, "there will be a large reward…"

"How big a reward?"

"For a start, any bounty found will be confiscated and shared among those who'll have helped capture it…"

"That could be a lot… on the other hand, that could be monkey feed!"

"I can assure you, Mr Tisdale, it won't be monkey feed."

"When are you sailing?"

"I was hoping sometime later today."

"Today! But… but… she's not even fitted yet!"

"But you will let us borrow her when she's ready?" the captain continued undeterred.

"No!" Tisdale refuted adamantly.

"Why not?" his wife demanded to know.

Henry Tisdale looked at his wife.

"Don't interfere, Mona. We've already lost the *Kingston*. We've only got the *Merchant Maiden* left. That ship is our livelihood, if we lose her, we lose everything!"

"Yeah, but if Black Bobby gets her first, we'll lose everything anyway," she argued. "I say, we should help the captain to get rid of that menace."

Henry Tisdale shook his head. "No, sorry Captain, it's too risky."

"Very well," the captain said, turning on his heels. "However, if you change your mind… By the way, Mrs Tisdale, have you had news from your niece lately?"

"Oh, now let me think… We did get a letter from her some time ago… Was it last month…? Harry, was it last month we had a letter from Lorna?"

"Can't remember, dear," her husband answered, looking preoccupied.

Mrs Tisdale rolled her eyes as if to say, well, can he *ever* remember anything? And more to the point, does he care?

"Anyhow," she continued. "She's fine. She's got a son, you know, thank the Lord." Mrs Tisdale declared proudly.

"I know, that's why I was asking."

"I thought it'd never happen with her poor husband being captured by those damned pirates!" Then, Mona Tisdale stopped suddenly and looked askance at the young captain. "You know? How did you know?" she remarked sharply, as if objecting to the fact that he should be aware of such a personal matter.

"Must dash! Bye, Mrs Tisdale."

"Bye Captain... and good luck!"

Then, hitting her sides with her fists, she wondered out loud, "He knew... how did he know?"

Mona Tisdale watched the captain disappear down the street, then she turned to her husband with her fists still dug deep in her hips and exclaimed, "Well, I'll be jiggered! How does he know about Lorna and her wee bairn?"

"You're speaking Scottish again, Mona dear."

"Well, you know what your trouble is, Harry Tisdale, you're nae Scottish... otherwise, you'd *almost* be perfect!" his wife mocked.

At these words, Henry Tisdale pretended to strike his wife and the two chased each other around the tavern screaming and laughing.

"Come here you little wench, so that I can give you a good hiding!"

"You'd better watch out, Harry Tisdale, I've got me broom, but all you've got is that dizzy head of yours!"

After a few minutes of this mad chase, both soon found themselves quite out of breath. Panting heavily, Mona Tisdale stopped and dropped onto the nearest chair. When she was quite recovered, she looked at her husband and said, "Cup of tea, Dear?"

While they were sitting in the kitchen, sipping their tea, Mona turned to her husband and in a low voice asked, "Do you think he knows about the map?"

"Why should he know about the map? The only person who knew about it was the one who gave it to us and she's probably rotting in some jail or dead. Now, Mona dear, I don't know why you wanted to lend our ship to the captain? Had you forgotten we were supposed to go to the island today?"

"Of course I hadn't forgotten but I'm using my head, dear! Black Bobby is still on the loose and of all the islands, that's probably where he's hiding because that's where pirates go to hide their booty — we've got the map as evidence — and I wouldn't mind betting that we're the only people who know that. So, Harry Tisdale, rather than risk our own skin, I say, let someone else take the risk and once Black Bobby's out of the way, hung high and dry, we'll be able to go treasure hunting without fear of being shot and killed!"

Henry Tisdale thought for a moment and saw that his wife made sense.

"In that case, the sooner Black Bobby is captured, the better…"

"That's right, dear, that's what I've been trying to tell you and that's why we have to help the captain. Anyway, I'm gonna go after him and tell him where he should start looking. After all, there's no point in him wasting weeks hunting around when he could catch that murderous thief in a day and make us rich in the bargain."

"All right, but don't be too long, dear. It's nearly ten o'clock and it'll be opening time soon."

Chapter Twenty-Two
The Hunt for Black Bobby

When Mona Tisdale arrived at the harbour, she walked at a brisk pace along the quay in an attempt to spot Captain Jennings's ship, but while searching, it suddenly occurred to her that she did not know her name. So, she began to ask around.

"Captain Jennings's ship? It's that one over there." A sailor indicated helpfully.

"What, the third one along with the two masts?" Mona Tisdale enquired.

"No, not that one, the one that's sailing out to sea right now."

"Oh no, I've missed it!" she exclaimed, disappointed.

"I shouldn't worry, love," the sailor stated. "They don't take women anyway."

Mona Tisdale threw him a cold stare, shrugged her shoulders and promptly returned to the tavern.

***

Meanwhile, on board the *Redemption*, Captain Jennings was busy briefing his crew for the task ahead. He laid out his plan of attack and gave his orders with the assurance and confidence of an admiral. However, he jumped when a large shadow loomed over his head.

"What do you want me to do, Captain?"

The captain turned his head around. It was Big Mitch.

"Ah yes, Mitchell. I've got the perfect job for you."

The captain took him aside and whispered some instructions discreetly in his ear, to which Mitchell replied compliantly, "Aye, Captain."

Late that afternoon, the ship approached Cove Island from the western side. As they had done before, the captain and Connor boarded the cockboat and rowed to shore. This time, the captain also decided to include the two ship's boys in the reconnaissance party for he reckoned that they would be safer hiding in *Titus's Cave* than dodging pistol shots and cutlasses at sea. Just before leaving his ship, however, the captain hailed his quartermaster to remind him of the plan of action.

"Griffiths, you know what to do. Wait till dark though before you do anything."

"Don't worry, Captain. I've got everything sorted and my head's well clear of rum."

"Good, I'm glad to hear it. Best of luck, Griffiths! And keep a close eye on Warren and Harris."

"Aye, aye, Captain!"

Then the captain hailed the ship's boys.

"Boys, you're in charges of the torches."

"Aye, aye, Capt'n!"

Once ashore, the captain led the small party to *Titus's Cave.* No sooner had he reached the entrance of the tunnel than he was hit by an overwhelming sense of foreboding. Still smarting from having been outwitted by a bunch of ruffians who counted more rotten teeth than brain cells, he entered the tunnel with butterflies in his belly.

Inside the dark and dank tunnel, the atmosphere resonated with an oppressive and palpable silence. The clammy walls, covered in a slimy layer of damp, reeked of a pungent musty smell. Without the torches, it was impossible to see what lay ahead, and Captain Jennings was careful to steer the group away from dark alcoves whose contents he did not want them to see. In the confined space, each step they took reverberated like a chilling echo rambling with terror down the tenebrous tunnel. Suddenly, the captain felt a little hand grip his breeches at the same time as he heard a little voice whisper, "I'm scared."

Recognising Jamesie's voice, the captain did his best to reassure him.

"Don't worry, lad. I think it's safe now to light the torches. Once we can see where we're going, it won't be so scary any more."

Jamesie was not so sure. As the flames flickered along the walls, they created eerie shadows that danced and pounced all around them, teasing his imagination and scaring him even more.

The party proceeded with caution down the tunnel. At the slightest noise, the boys jumped but marched on, regardless. Every now and again, a light clatter resounded ahead of them, and sometimes behind them.

"What was that?" Jamesie whispered nervously.

"Don't panic. It's only small clumps of mud falling from the roof."

A while later, the air began to feel warmer against their faces; it was the first indication that they had reached the other end of the narrow passage. Upon reaching the point where the tunnel forked, the captain led the party down the left junction until they got to the outside opening. There the captain gave the signal to stop, and turning towards Connor and the ship's boys, he hushed his orders.

"Boys, we're going to have to move about very carefully. Stay low and keep your eyes peeled and your ears close to the ground. At the slightest noise, stop and wait. And strictly no talking, understood?"

"Aye Capt'n!" The boys hushed.

"At the first sign of trouble, boys, just run back to the tunnel and wait for me there."

"Aye, aye, Capt'n!" the boys whispered excitedly.

The captain threw a few inspectorial glances outside the tunnel before beckoning the others to follow him. The starkness of the sunlight made them blink a few times, but at least, they were glad to be freed from the oppressive atmosphere that hung inside the tunnel. As if emerging from a long sleep, they stood up and stretched to the maximum their bodies and limbs. Connor swivelled on the spot and shaded his eyes with his hand to scan the landscape. The boys watched him, rather bemused.

"What are you doing?" Jamesie asked.

"I'm looking for baddies," Connor mused with self-importance.

The boys guffawed at his reply.

"Shush, you lot!" the captain chided. "Come on, let's go before you give us all away."

Connor and the boys followed the captain who seemed totally absorbed in his own thoughts. He knew exactly how many pirate ships there were and how many pirates occupied the beach. The reconnaissance party walked silently down a path which Connor instantly recognised.

"Capt'n, that path goes to the hut," he whispered.

The captain did not respond straight away.

"Why are we going back to the hut? Is it not dangerous?"

Again, the captain remained silent.

"I think we shouldn't waste time going back to the hut," Connor continued. "We should go straight to the beach, that's what I think."

At last, the captain spoke, "That may be what you think but you seem to have forgotten that there's only one path, and it leads to the hut *and* the beach."

"Oh aye, I'd forgotten!" Connor admitted.

"So stop wittering on and stay behind me!"

It was not long before they sighted the wooden hut. Using sign language only, the captain pointed to the tall vegetation. Connor and the ship's boys scrambled towards it, half crouching. Then they stopped, and waited. Through the tall vegetation, they could just about see the hut. The captain crept outside the hut. Very slowly, he poked his head round the small window.

The hut was empty. Quite unexpectedly, Jennings felt disappointed. For some strange reason, he had hoped to meet up with Anne again, the woman who had unwittingly forged an unbreakable bond between them by giving birth to their son.

On the other side of the path, Jonesie's burning curiosity took the better of him. Disobeying orders, he crawled on ahead and stopped at the top of a dune. From there, he observed the pirates and counted two ships in the bay.

Moments later, the captain rejoined the group.

"Let's go back to the tunnel," he whispered. "Where's Jamie?"

"Right here, Capt'n!" Jonesie hailed in a quiet voice. "I've seen them, Capt'n. There's loads of pirates and two ships out there in the bay."

Furious that Jonesie had disobeyed him, putting his life at risk, the captain grabbed the boy by the scruff of the neck and dragged him back inside the tunnel.

"Jonesie! What did I say? You must stay with the group. It's too dangerous to go out there and the pirates might have seen you!" the captain scolded.

"They didn't. I was really careful," the boy replied, defiant.

"So you saw two ships… only two ships?"

"Aye!"

"Drats!" the captain interjected.

"Why do you say that, Capt'n?" asked Jonesie.

"Because, my lad, if there's only two ships out there, it means that Black Bobby's gone away, probably back to Africa or somewhere. It also means we won't be able to catch him, which is the whole point of us being here."

"But we can catch his crew!" Jamesie quipped.

"And then what?" the captain spat back, somewhat irritated.

"Well, without his crew, they can't sail which means it will be easier to catch Black Bobby," Jamesie argued back.

Captain Jennings looked quite taken aback. The boy made sense. Studying the young lad's proud stance, he declared with a glint of admiration, "I say, Jamie! I do believe you have the soul of a war tactician! Jonesie, how many men do you reckon there are on the beach?"

"I would say around thirty," the boy estimated.

The captain made a quick mental calculation. "Hm… thirty men and two ships… That's not enough to man two ships. There must still be some on board. Right, you three, go back to the ship and at nightfall, bring most of the men back here. We'll set up an ambush and round up the ruffians."

"What about you, Capt'n?" Jamesie asked.

"I'm going to wait here while I work out our next move."

***

About two hours later, Captain Jennings watched the sun disappear over the horizon, sitting on the ground just outside the tunnel entrance. At the foot of the hill, the crescent of Dunmore Bay gleamed under the scintillating light of the sun's dying rays, re-igniting the passionate feelings he harboured in his heart. Closing his eyes for a moment, he took a deep breath to smell the strong aroma of baking sand, and the powerful scent of bougainvillea in full bloom. Lulled by the songs of palm warblers, bananaquits, the odd white ibis that had been swept upon these shores by a recent storm, and the noisy cawing of quibbling parakeets, he fell into a deep reverie. Through the mist of his dream, he smiled at the squabbling nature of parakeets. They're just like a bunch of rowdy pirates, he thought to himself, except that their fate is to hang from trees rather than from a set of wooden gallows.

Now, a different kind of noise filtered through his dreams. He became alert. He sat bolt upright and pricked up his ears. It was the sound of men moving furtively in the undergrowth. Immediately, he jumped to his feet and hid inside the tunnel entrance. He hoped they were his men but the poor light made it difficult to discern accurately the silhouettes. Then he heard a voice, very distinctive in its high-pitched tone; it could only be Jamesie… or Jonesie… anyhow, it was one of the ship's boys. He scrambled down the rocky path but made sure to remain concealed in the tall vegetation until he could distinguish them more clearly. Then, he spotted them. Connor was leading the group from the front, closely followed by the ship's boys. In the distance, they caught sight of a dark silhouette scrambling furtively towards them.

Connor jumped in fear, but quickly recovered as soon as he recognised the captain.

"Jeez, Capt'n," Connor panted. "You gave me a real fright! Please, don't do that again cos me heart can't take that kind of fool mongering." Then, in the same breath, he added, "It's all right, boys, it's only the captain!"

"Why, Connor?" said the captain, surprised at Connor's reaction. "Am I that scary?"

"In the dark, Capt'n, everybody looks scary!" the sailor replied.

Quickly, they all scrambled inside the tunnel. There, the captain spoke, "Connor and Mitchell, take the men to the beach. Once there, you're going to have to work out how best to ambush the pirates. But remember, they've got Humphreys and we've got to rescue him so before you start any shooting, find out where he is and get him out of there as quickly as you can."

"What about us, Capt'n?" Jonesie asked expectantly. "Can we go too?"

The captain looked at the boys, thought for a moment, then said, "No, I've got another job for you two. Connor, Mitchell, you know what to do."

"Er… Capt'n… I'm not sure…" Connor began. "Do we kill them all or do we take prisoners?"

"Use your own judgement; though bear in mind, if you hesitate, you're sure to get killed, so use your head and your pistol, and if you catch them alive, fine, but if you don't, nobody's going to hold you to account. So do what's best for you, for your mates and for your King, all right? Off you go and good luck!"

Connor pondered briefly over the captain's words, trying to make sense of them. Did he say 'shoot to kill' or what? He was not sure. Anyhow, he had a job to do and he was going to do it to the best of his understanding, so he pressed on.

The group consisted of about thirty men. The smell of wood burning guided their steps through the darkness towards the beach where the pirates had lit a campfire. The glow of the flames flickered on their faces from below, making their features more menacing, as they exposed their jagged teeth every time they laughed. Most of them were gathered around the fire drinking, singing or playing cards. A little further away, another group of them were playing dice on a flat piece of driftwood. And among this primitive cohort, lo and behold, there was Humphreys behaving just like one of them.

"By heck!" Connor exclaimed. "Humphreys's turned pirate! He's one of them!"

Suddenly, a shot rang through the air. It came from the other side of the beach. Connor raised his arm and whispered loudly, "That's the signal! Come on! After them!"

**

Meanwhile, behind them, on the other side of the sand dune, Captain Jennings was creeping towards the main hut. Once there, he stopped and listened. Immediately, he detected a different kind of smell from wood burning and instantly recognised the spicy aroma of fresh tobacco. He crept closer to the hut and peered through a small opening in the wall. Inside, Anne Bonny was lying in a hammock smoking a pipe. She was alone. After making sure that there was no one else around, the captain moved inside the hut and crept behind the hammock. Then, swift as lightning, he grabbed her pipe and put his hand over her mouth to stop her from screaming. She immediately fought back but he had a strong hold on her.

"Shush!" he whispered. "It's me, Jennings!"

At the sound of his voice, the woman pirate stopped struggling to take a good look at him.

"Jennings, you stupid fool! Don't you ever do that again. I could have killed you!"

Ignoring her alarm, the captain went straight to the point. "Where's Black Bobby?"

"Gone to hell!"

"I need to know," the captain insisted.

"Why?"

"You saved my life once, now it's my turn to save yours," he briefly explained.

Anne scrutinised the face of the young captain before replying in a tone full of disdain, "You're not really here to save my life. You just want the loot, don't you?"

Jennings took a deep breath and blasted, "They're all out there hunting for Black Bobby and hunting for you!"

"Who's *they*?"

"The Governor's ships, the King's ships. Commodore Holloway's got two ships under his command and believe you me, he has no intention of taking prisoners! You've got to leave the island, fast!"

"Who says?" a voice suddenly boomed.

Both Jennings and Bonny jerked their heads at the same time and saw Black Bobby standing in the doorway, taller and larger than the door itself. He was dressed in a red coat covered in brass buttons and held together by a wide leather belt where he had tucked two pistols and from where a large cutlass hung loosely. Instead of his usual tricorn, he was wearing a black headscarf to keep his wiry black hair away from his face, a small detail that was not lost on Anne for she alone knew that Black Bobby never wore his moth-eaten tricorn when he was about to go into battle.

Jennings squared up to the pirate and pointed his pistol at him. His heart was racing but faced with his enemy, he clenched his teeth and held his pistol firmly with both hands.

"What? You're going to shoot?" Black Bobby riled, half mocking.

"If I have to," Jennings hissed through his teeth.

"What do you want?" the pirate asked placidly.

"I've come for you," Jennings stated curtly.

At the sight of the audacious young man, Black Bobby let out a howl of laughter. Suddenly, an almighty bang shook the island. The battle had begun. Black Bobby whipped a pistol out of his belt and pointed it at Jennings, ready to shoot. In a flash, Bonny grabbed his arm.

"Don't shoot him! Not yet. We need him."

Black Bobby growled.

"Sure we don't!" the pirate replied menacingly.

"Yes, *you* do!" Bonny retorted with bravado. "We can use him to distract the Governor's ships away from us."

"Argh…" the pirate grunted. "Keep him here and if he tries to escape, shoot him or I'll shoot both of you!"

The pirate stormed outside to check the origin of the sudden explosion. Taking advantage of the situation, Jennings made a step towards Bonny.

Speaking in a softer tone, he hoped to placate the tigress.

"Anne," he started. "Come with me before it's too late."

"You heard him! You move and you're dead!" Bonny spat, wielding her cutlass.

Undeterred, Jennings continued, "With Black Bobby, you stand no chance. The whole of the Governor's navy is after him! Come on, Anne, with me, you have a chance to get a pardon and you will be a free woman."

"What do you care about me?"

"I care that you are my son's mother!"

Outside, hurried steps approached the hut and voices shouted, "Capt'n Bonny, the ships are on fire!"

Alarmed, Bonny glanced at Jennings then at the door. She wanted to go outside but she did not want to let go of her prisoner. She pointed her pistol at Jennings and prepared to shoot, but her hand trembled. Jennings said nothing. He just stared stoically at the woman who had never hesitated to shoot in cold blood. He clenched his teeth, steeled his nerves and waited for the bullet to hit. After a few excruciating minutes, Bonny pressed the trigger. Instinctively, Jennings closed his eyes. He felt nothing. He immediately opened his eyes again and looked at Bonny. Her arm was not pointing at him but at the ceiling.

"I have to make Black Bobby believe that I won't hesitate to kill you," she simply said.

She forced Jennings to sit on the floor and tied his hands around one of the wooden pillars. Then, she left.

In the middle of the bay, two bright pyres lit up the sky. The pirate ships were completely engulfed by fire.

Alarmed, Bonny ran all the way down to the beach.

"Damn!" she exclaimed. "We've lost our ships!"

"And the loot!" one of the pirates moaned.

"We've still got my ship!" said Black Bobby. "Hidden in the creek. Come on, let's go!"

"What about him?"

"*Him*? Get rid of him!"

"We can't!" Bonny decreed.

"Why not? Have you lost your nerve?"

"Think about it, Black Bobby! If we get caught, we can use him to bargain with. He might even be a good sailor!"

Black Bobby glared suspiciously at the woman, still unsure as to how much he could trust her. At that moment, another explosion resounded in the distance.

"Come on, let's go!" he ordered impatiently.

"What about the rest of the shipmates?"

"Like the "mousquetaires" say, each for himself and God for all!" Black Bobby stated coldly.

With fear lightening their steps, they rushed back to the hut to get Jennings. Flanked by pirates on both sides, Jennings stumbled through the thick vegetation while behind him, Black Bobby kept a hawk eye on his every move.

The group made their way silently through the bushes towards the south of the island. For a moment, Jennings feared that they were making their way to *Titus's Cave* where the ship's boys were hiding, but a few yards from the entrance, Black Bobby turned the opposite way towards another path leading to a hidden creek. A few moments later, the small group reached the top of a low-lying cliff. At the bottom, a series of rocks and boulders piled high created a natural harbour around a small sandy beach. In the middle of the creek lay an abandoned cockboat. Further out, in the tranquil water, a sloop lulled nonchalantly in the moonlit night. A sarcastic remark suddenly broke the silence.

"A sloop? Is that all you've managed to get?"

It was Jennings.

Black Bobby retorted by punching him in the back.

"Keep your mouth shut and keep walking!"

A few minutes later, the small party clambered aboard the cockboat. As they rowed closer to the ship, Jennings strained his eyes to try and discern her name.

"Oh my God!" he suddenly exclaimed. "It's not… is it? It's the *Kingston*! How… how did you get her?"

Anne Bonny relished the look of surprise on Jennings's face.

"Never you mind! I brought her back here and that's all that matters," she stated wryly.

"But that's Henry Tisdale's ship," Jennings reminded her.

"Aye! Imagine his surprise when he sees his favourite pirate sailing her! Ah! Ah! Ah!" She cackled.

Puzzled, Black Bobby jerked his head back and forth between the two seemingly friend and foe, trying to make sense of their innuendoes.

"What's going on here?" he questioned. "You two know each other?"

Jennings threw a dark look at the woman, daring her to remain silent. In return, Anne sustained his gaze, her features remaining as still as if set in marble, refusing to give away any of her thoughts.

Eventually, she broke the silence.

"We, pirates, all have the same soul, glittering with lust, life and gold," she stated cryptically.

Never one to meddle in poetic thoughts, Black Bobby had no time for all that soul searching nonsense. He, of a more primitive nature, could only express himself through the swiftness of his cutlass for, in his eyes, no man or woman could surpass him in his sword fighting skills. And if the woman who had become his companion by fate rather than by design befuddled him occasionally with airy fairy thoughts, he did not care as long as she remained *his* woman. Hence, not one bit interested in deciphering the cryptic exchange, he racked his throat, spat on the wooden deck and grunted, "Stop that bloody nonsense, you two, and get rowing!"

Moments later, the runaways boarded the *Kingston*, and with no time to lose, Black Bobby immediately gave the orders to sail.

***

Once more, and against his will, Charles Jennings found himself as part of the crew on the very same pirate ship. He could not believe it. What on earth had he done to deserve such persistent misfortune? Unable to save himself from his own fate, he felt helpless against forces beyond his control. But he, Charles Jennings, was not the sort to go without a fight. Should he settle the matter with a duel to the death and die with honour and glory? Perhaps not. After all, he had a son, a young boy who, without him, might suffer a fate worse than his own. To stay alive, there was only one thing he could do, go along with the pirates and play their game.

On the distant horizon, dawn was breaking, streaking the sky with pastel hues of mauve and pink. The sea was calm and on board, those not on quarter watch were sound asleep. In this rare moment of plenitude, Charles Jennings contemplated the early morning scene from the bulwark. He wondered what had happened to his men although he felt quietly confident that they would have got the better of the ruffians. But what about the ship boys? Were they still holed up in *Titus's Cave* waiting for his return?

Suddenly, his attention was averted by the ominous sight of two ships in full sail, skimming over the water towards the *Kingston*. He could not as yet read their names but he knew instinctively that these must be Commodore Holloway's convoy. His thoughts were interrupted by the look-out who shouted with a hint of panic in his voice, "Ship ahoy! Ship ahoy!"

Immediately, the quartermaster shouted the orders, "All hands, on deck! All hands, on deck!"

Almost instantly, the thumping noise of bodies falling out of their hammocks shook the lower deck. Heavy feet stomped along the planks and voices rose. Amid the frantic scene, Black Bobby appeared on the main deck wearing his black headscarf, and to all those present, this could only mean one thing, war. Pressed against the bulwark and holding his long glass, the pirate called his first mate. "Bonny, what do you think?"

"They're too far still. I can't make out their flags but I say, we get ready for battle just in case."

"If they're after us, that's two against one. I'd rather go back where we came from," the quartermaster declared.

"Don't be such a fool, Rashford," Bonny blasted. "No, I say! We remain on course. Merchant ships are often shadowed by a man-of-war for protection, so if we attack the warship first, she'll be ripe for the picking."

Black Bobby could not decide. He turned to Jennings. "What do you say, Jennings, we go after them?"

Charles Jennings immediately sided with Bonny, not because he thought she was right but because he knew the ships to be part of the Commodore's fleet and here was his chance to be rescued. Putting on his most convincing voice, he decreed boldly, "Bonny's right. We should go after them and if one turns out to be a merchant ship, it's only one we'll have to fight, not two."

"Yeah?" Black Bobby retorted. "And what if you're both wrong? I don't like the way you two seem to agree with each other all the time. I hope you're not leaguing against me or planning to steal my ship from me." Then scowling heavily, he grabbed Jennings by the scruff of the neck and blasted in his face, "I don't like you, Jennings, and I don't trust you. I know there's something going on between you two, but don't ever think you can fool me, or I'll skewer you with my cutlass and roast you alive on a spit!"

All the shipmates on the main deck stopped whatever they were doing to watch the scene unravel. Black Bobby was always at his most aggressive just before battle. Before he got too carried away, Anne Bonny stepped in. "Take it easy, Bobby! Whatever he's up to, we need him, so leave him alone."

Black Bobby responded with a swipe of the hand. "Shut up, woman! On this ship, *my* ship, *I* decide and *I* give the orders!"

Anne was quick to respond. Almost without thinking, she drew her cutlass and blasted back, "Actually, this is *my* ship and you're on it because yours got sunk! So, like I said, we go after them and we fight!"

Black Bobby saw red. He had killed before for such an affront. He growled, grunted like an injured beast and drew his cutlass; but before he could make his next move, a cry from the crow's nest made them all jerk their heads.

"The ships are splitting! And there's another one coming!"

Everyone rushed to the bulwarks. During the spat, the ships had got closer. Now, they were sailing in a V formation.

"What are they doing?" one of the shipmates asked.

Jennings observed the ships for a moment and stated confidently, "They're not merchant ships. They're the Governor's fleet and they're moving to position themselves on either side of us in order to attack us from both sides!"

"Quick! Prepare to come about!" Black Bobby yelled to the helmsman.

"It's too late, Captain!" the helmsman shouted back. "They're taking the wind out of our sails. I can't manoeuvre her fast enough."

Anne lost no time in taking over command.

"Gunners, prepare the cannons! Everybody else, prepare your weapons and get your pistols ready! And if you want to live long enough to enjoy your booty, then fight like you've never fought before!"

"There's too many of them; we don't stand a chance!" Rashford stated nervously.

Anne scowled at the shipmate and blasted, "Is that fear I see in your eyes, Rashford? A sign that you've given up, like a shameful coward, before the battle's even started?"

Embarrassed by this verbal assault in front of his mates, the pirate grunted in frustration and walked away.

Suddenly, a loud bang reverberated through the air and seconds later, on the port side, a huge spray of water surged out of the sea a few feet away from the pirate ship. Another soon followed at starboard. The *Kingston* retaliated by firing a broadside but the cannon balls failed to hit their target. In the middle of the mayhem, the helmsman made desperate attempts to steer the ship into a more favourable position but steering one way would only expose her other side even more. They were trapped. He quickly made the sign of the cross, knowing that the end was nigh and as he grabbed the wheel again with both his hands, a deafening boom tore through the ship. Men and wooden debris were tossed in the air and into the sea. Charles Jennings, who at that moment had been standing on the main deck, felt himself being flung through the air. Then, all of a sudden, everything went blank.

***

Despite her extensive damage, the *Kingston* was still floating. When the naval officers boarded her, accompanied by Commodore Holloway, there was no sign of life on board. All was quiet, too unnervingly quiet.

"There doesn't seem to be many sailors on this ship," one of the naval officers remarked. "What shall we do with the bodies, Sir?"

"Throw them overboard. I'm only interested in one, Black Bobby," the Commodore replied dryly.

After an extensive search of the ship, a sailor reported back to the Commodore, "I don't think he was on board, Commodore. There's no sign of him anywhere."

"Check for survivors. Some of them might be able to tell us what happened to their brave captain," he declared in a sarcastic tone. "If he's not on board, it can only mean one thing, the wretched pirate's escaped!"

"Or he could have been blown off!" his lieutenant suggested.

"No... not him... I feel it in my bones. He's still out there... somewhere."

Then, peering at the island in the distance, he ordered, "Set sail for Cove Island. That's the nearest island. They might have tried to swim ashore."

"Er... Sir, pirates as a rule can't swim," his lieutenant remarked.

"I don't care! I know Black Bobby's still alive and we're going to search all over the island until we find him!" he shouted in frustration.

Before returning to their own ship, the Commodore's men checked every corner of the *Kingston* to make sure there was no one left alive. Back on his ship, the Commodore scanned the water and scrutinised the island. He was convinced that the renegades were hiding out there, and he vouched never to rest until he had brought every single one of them to justice. Through his long glass, he observed Cove Island which, in his eyes, looked calm and serene, taking on the allure of an innocent bystander who has no crime to confess.

Reeling with anger and frustration, the Commodore ordered the firing of several broadsides into the *Kingston* until she broke up completely and sank into the sea. Watching her break into pieces gave the Commodore a huge sense of satisfaction. Without a ship to his name, the ruffian could not get very far.

The Commodore decided to stay on board while his men went ashore. Some of the surviving pirates readily gave themselves up rather than being shot while others remained in hiding, among them, no doubt, were Black Bobby and Anne Bonny. The Commodore's men rounded up the pirates swiftly and forced them into the rowing boats.

Now, the Commodore felt ready to return to Nassau. From there, he would go straight to Government House and lay his sword at the Governor's feet, declaring his duty fulfilled and his mission accomplished. Whatever the Governor thought of him, at least he was sure of one thing, Lady Sarah could not fail to be hugely impressed.

Chapter Twenty-Three
An Unexpected Rescue

Meanwhile, not long after the battle, a lone sloop happened on the scene. The crew of five men pressed themselves against the bulwarks to take a closer look at the scene of devastation. So far, they had counted as many as a dozen bodies floating among the debris. Henry Tisdale shook his head in disbelief and whistled in awe.

"Well, I suppose… They asked for it," he remarked, almost in sympathy. "And the less there are of those damned pirates, the better our lives will be."

Suddenly, a loud cry alerted him to the other side of the ship.

"Capt'n! Here! I think that one's still alive!" a shipmate hailed excitedly, pointing at a body floating on a large broken piece of wood. Then, he immediately loaded his pistol. "Shall I finish him off, Capt'n?"

"Hold your fire, you moron! What have you got in that thick head of yours, hey? Think about it, mate, where there's a pirate, there's a treasure, but if you start shooting them all before asking questions, you're never gonna find them treasures, are you, hey? Bring him on board!"

The shipmate threw a rope overboard and with the help of two others, pulled the piece of wood towards the ship. As it was being lifted out of the water, a shipmate noted, "Capt'n, there's letters written on that piece of wood."

"What does it say?"

"I don't know, I can't read," the shipmate replied.

"All right, pick up the piece of wood as well. It's probably the name of the ship that was sunk."

The shipmates lay the body onto the main deck. Henry Tisdale looked at it with a heavy frown on his face.

"By the power of thunder!" he exclaimed. "But that's… that's…"

"Who's he, Capt'n?" the first mate asked impatiently.

"You know pirates?" another asked.

"In my sort of business, one knows everybody! But this guy here's not a pirate, though he looks soundly dead to me. What made you think he was still alive?"

"I thought I saw his arm move."

"It's probably the force of the current that did it," someone suggested.

As they spoke, Henry Tisdale knelt down and put his ear on the man's chest.

"Aye…"

"You mean… he's dead?"

"No, he's still breathing."

Henry Tisdale took the man's hand and felt it to be still warm. Relieved, he proceeded to lift the man's head and slap his cheek to try and revive him.

"Who's he, then?" a shipmate asked again.

"Never mind who he is. Where's that piece of wood?"

One of the shipmates fetched the wood and presented it to the captain. Henry Tisdale squinted his eyes to focus better on the three large letters that had been burnt into the wood, KIN…

"By the power of thunder!" he exclaimed once more. "I can only think of one ship that's got them letters in her name, the *Kingston*! And if I'm not mistaken, that's young Captain Jennings. What was the damned fool doing on the *Kingston*?"

"The *Kingston*? Was that not Rackham's ship?"

"It was but not any more! It was mine. I bought it at auction after that wretched pirate was captured," Tisdale declared firmly, putting the record straight.

"Wasn't he hanged?" one of the shipmates queried.

"Aye…but this fellow here…" Tisdale muttered pensively. "I wonder… Anyway, someone bring me some rum."

One of the shipmates dashed to get a small timbale of rum and handed it over to Tisdale. Ever so gently, the innkeeper poured a few drops on Jennings's lips, and as soon as the liquid filtered into his mouth, the young man started spluttering. He opened his eyes and looked at the faces peering back at him.

"Where am I?" he asked, bewildered. "Who are you? Ouch, my head! I think I must have banged my head or something."

"You did that all right!" Tisdale replied with a small chuckle. "Believe you me, you're lucky to be alive. That was some battle you've just been through. Captain Jennings, delighted to meet you again and if I may say so,

I'm amazed you're still in one piece." Then after a slight pause, Tisdale continued, "What I can't help wondering, what the hell were you doing on the *Kingston*?"

Shocked to hear a familiar name from the past and with his memory momentarily blanked out, Jennings looked back at the man who was speaking to him.

"The *Kingston*? That's not my ship... Where's my ship?" he mumbled, still in shock.

"But you were on the *Kingston*..."

Captain Jennings looked blank. He could not remember a thing.

"My ship's the *Redemption,* and you know that as well as I do!" he stated, baffled by Tisdale's statement.

"Ah," said the shipmate who was standing closest to the captain. "We saw the *Redemption* on our way here, didn't we, Capt'n?"

Henry Tisdale turned to the sailor with a look of surprise on his face.

"I thought you couldn't read."

"Oh, me, I can. It's him who can't," the man replied pointing at his mate.

While they argued as to who could or could not read, Jennings, still looking bewildered, glowered at them and asked with visible apprehension, "You're not pirates, are you?"

"No, we're not, rest assure. It's me Tisdale, you know, from the *Cock 'n Bull,* and this is my crew here, and you're on my ship."

The welcome answer made Jennings feel instantly better. Already, the pains in his body were beginning to subside and he pushed himself up in an attempt to stand up.

"Thank God for that," the young captain stated with distinct relief. "Come on, Tisdale, help me get back on my feet."

"Er... I sure don't want to pry in your affairs, but... what were you doing on a pirate ship?" Tisdale asked again, grabbing the young captain by the arm to help him up.

"Why do you keep going on about a pirate ship?" Jennings quizzed, looking thoroughly confused. Then changing his tone of voice, he protested vehemently, "I'm not a bloody pirate so stop going on about it!"

For all answer, Henry Tisdale took the piece of wood which had been left lying on the deck and showed it to the young captain.

"Well, I thought that piece of wood might have belonged to the

Kingston…"

"The *Kingston*!" Jennings exclaimed nearly choking on the word.

"Well you know, with them letters…"

The sound of the cursed name hit Jennings like another blow on the head. Suddenly he felt strange. Flashbacks of the battle appeared before his eyes, and then… there she was, fighting on the main deck. He shook his head to dispel the disturbing images and without thinking, he asked, "Where is she?"

"The *Kingston*? From what we can gather, she's lying at the bottom of the sea. She was blown to bits, in case you don't know, and good riddance, I say!"

That was not what Charles Jennings had meant although he realised straight away that he should never have asked the question in the first place. However, he needed to know, he wanted to know, although he told himself, whatever the outcome, it should not bother him one way or the other, but it did. Locking his gaze on the distant horizon, he took a deep breath and mustered all the courage he had left to rephrase the question. Hardening his stance even more, he turned towards Tisdale. "Were there any survivors?" he finally asked, dreading the answer.

"Well, if there were, they were taken away, that's for sure. We passed Commodore Holloway's ships on our way here," Tisdale stated in a matter-of-fact way.

This was not exactly what Captain Jennings wanted to hear but he had to remain circumspect. Feigning utter indifference, he continued, "And what were you doing coming this way?"

"We were coming to help you, like you asked. I know I said no, but my wife took pity on you and practically pushed me out to sea!"

The truth was that Henry Tisdale was not in the least bothered about anybody's battle. His main concern was to retrieve his share of the loot before anyone else could get their hands on it and for this purpose, being the shrewd opportunist that he was, he had calculated to arrive on the battle scene well after the last broadside had been fired. What allowed him to keep so well informed on all the major events was the fact that, being a popular landlord, people came to drink in his tavern and while they drank copiously, they often became loquacious and less guarded in their comments. Loose tongues were the most prolific gatherers of gossip. In this manner, our man, with his ears close to the ground, had found out exactly where Black Blobby was hiding, when the Commodore was likely to strike and how many ships had been sent to hunt down the ruffian. Unfortunately for him, however, the tide of fortune had turned against him. Rather than the treasure hunter that he had set out to be, he had become an unwitting rescuer. What would he tell his dear wife Mona?

Unaware of Tisdale's secret plans, Captain Jennings smiled as he pictured Mona Tisdale ordering her husband about and telling him what to do while Henry Tisdale always insisted to whoever would listen that in his own house, *he* was the boss. Offering a helping hand, Tisdale suggested, "Let me help you, Jennings, we'll go to my cabin where we can talk more."

"Talk about what?" the captain questioned, still feeling dazed.

"I'll tell you when we get there."

As soon as they reached the captain's cabin, Tisdale came straight to the point. "I believe she's still alive."

"Who's *she*?"

"You know very well who I'm talking about. When we were on the deck you asked, 'Where is she…?' and at first, I thought you meant your ship but then I realised… you were not talking about her at all, were you? You were talking about *her*, weren't you?"

"What do you mean?" Jennings asked with a worried look on his face.

"Her! Anne Bonny! She's still alive, ain't she?"

"What makes you think that?" Jennings asked, puzzled by how much Tisdale knew.

"The cockboat… there was no cockboat… aye, the cockboat was missing, and I'll bet my last groat that they've absconded, the two of them, her and Black Bobby. I know they're out there somewhere but I'm not gonna risk my creaky old bones to find out. I'll leave that to the Commodore."

Jennings shook his head in disbelief. Then he remembered the ship's boys. "But we've got to go to the island, some of my men are still there. We've got to go back and rescue them!"

"Oh no, not me, Capt'n, I'm not a fighting man and this isn't a battleship. I've done what I came here to do and now, I'm going back to Nassau, to my missus."

"But if they're caught, they might be mistaken for pirates!"

"Aye," Tisdale admitted without showing the slightest concern for the stranded men. Then he left the cabin abruptly and as soon as he was back on deck he shouted orders to the helmsman to set sail for Nassau.

Charles Jennings followed him on the upper deck, feeling uneasy. Overtaken by the events, he felt wretched at being forced to leave his men behind. He hoped Griffiths, his own quartermaster, would launch a rescue mission. Griffiths was a good man and the captain had faith in him; and when he saw the Commodore's ship, he felt sure that Griffiths would join in and help round up those wretched pirates and rescue his men.

The *Merchant Maiden* was now sailing smoothly towards the port of Nassau. Charles Jennings paced the deck nervously. He could not help thinking about the fate of his men. All sorts of bold ideas and wild plans rushed through his head as he plotted and sussed how best to get them back when a loud voice from the crow's nest shouted, "Ship ahoy! Ship ahoy!"

Everyone rushed to the bulwarks but no matter how hard they scanned the ocean, they could not see any sign of a sail.

"Where?" Tisdale asked.

"There!" the watchman shouted, pointing towards the stern of the ship.

And indeed, not far behind them, the crew spotted not a sloop or a schooner in full sail but a small rowing boat with two men on board waving frantically at them. Tisdale took out his long glass to study the pair.

"They're waving at us, but I don't know who they are," he remarked.

Captain Jennings squinted at the pair then asked pressingly, "Pass me the long glass, quick!"

After a brief scrutiny, Jennings turned to Tisdale with a huge smile of relief. "My o my! They're my ship's boys, Jonesie and Jamesie!" he exclaimed. "Tisdale, we've got to rescue them."

Tisdale agreed and immediately shouted, "Tack the ship and let's go and pick up the boys!"

A while later, the two ship boys were safely brought on board, and before anyone could say anything, they both broke into a chorus of thanks and gratitude.

"Thanks Mister!" Jamesie effused.

"Thanks, Capt'n! You won't believe how glad we are to see you again." Jonesie reeled off.

"We thought we was done for! Didn't we?" Jamesie admitted, expressing great relief.

"Aye, we tried to row as fast as we could, but we just couldn't catch you up!"

"Great to have you back, boys!" Captain Jennings said, greeting them with a friendly pat on the back. "But where did you get the boat from?"

"From them," Jonesie answered, jerking his head towards the island.

"Aye!" Jamesie seconded. "We was in the tunnel waiting for you and we heard all the shots and all, so we knew that the battle had started. Then it all went quiet and we didn't know what to do…"

"So I said we should go out and take a look…" Jonesie added all excited.

"No," Jamesie interrupted. "It was me who said that. Anyway, we heard these voices, so we ran back inside and hid in the alcove near where the tunnel forks, and then these two pirates appeared…"

"But thank God they went the other way!" Jonesie quipped in.

"And then we thought, if they're here, then they must have a boat. So we ran out of the tunnel as fast as we could and we found their boat down there, in the creek, so we jumped in and…"

"Well done, lads!" Captain Jennings cheered, congratulating them. "That was very smart thinking of you!"

"'Twas my idea!" Jonesie declared with a triumphant smile.

"No, 'twas mine and that's the truth!" Jamesie refuted.

Captain Jennings could not help but smile at their little squabble.

"Lads, it doesn't matter whose idea it was, the most important thing is that you're both safe and well," the captain said, patting them on the back again. "Anyway, about those two pirates, were you able to see who they were?"

"We kind of saw them but not very clearly…" Jamesie stated hesitantly.

"Except that one of them was a woman," Jonesie added.

"A woman? Are you sure about that?" Tisdale, who had been listening avidly, queried.

"Oh aye, 'twas definitely a woman," Jamesie confirmed.

"But how could you tell for sure? It's pretty dark in that tunnel," Captain Jennings asked dubiously.

"We heard them talk," Jonesie said, nodding his head.

"Aye, we heard them all right and I tell you, one of them was a woman."

Tisdale and Jennings looked at each other but said nothing.

"All right, lads," Captain Jennings said. "Go and get yourselves something to eat from Cook, you must be hungry after all this."

"Hungry?" Jonesie riled. "I'm famished!"

"Me too!" Jamesie added before sprinting below deck.

After the boys had disappeared, Henry Tisdale turned to Jennings and said, "Well there you are, then. Now we know."

"Aye," Jennings replied pensively, scouring Cove Island. "They're still out there… and without a ship."

Chapter Twenty-Four
The Accused

Back in the port of Nassau, the quay was jammed-packed with a bustling crowd. Soldiers and sailors mingled freely with day-trippers who had come to greet their loved ones or cheer any crew that had made it safely back to port. And among them, there were those who had simply come to gawp.

The first thing that Charles Jennings noticed was that the Commodore's ships were already back in port... but not his own ship, the *Redemption*. He was surprised. Suddenly, his attention was drawn by a line of soldiers barging their way through the throng of onlookers towards the embankment. Following closely behind them was Commodore Holloway. The sight filled him with nervous apprehension. What on earth were they up to?

Moments later, the Commodore lined up his soldiers at the foot of the *Merchant Maiden*'s gangplank where he waited with a stern look on his face.

"What's going on?" asked Jennings.

Tisdale threw a quizzical look at him and said, "Let me handle this."

Henry Tisdale marched down the gangplank, swelling up his chest with self-importance, and went to stand in front of the Commodore holding his head up high.

"What can I do for you, Commodore?" he asked.

"Did you rescue any pirates?" the Commodore asked.

"Why, no," Tisdale replied in good faith.

However, the Commodore had just spotted one of the men he was looking for. He pushed Tisdale out of the way and shouted, "Captain Jennings!"

The captain was presently standing at the top of the gangplank, flanked by the two ship's boys, staring intently at his nemesis with his jaws firmly locked. Very calmly, he descended the gangplank at a slow pace. As he came level with the man who had summoned him, Holloway declared haughtily, "Captain Charles Jennings, I'm arresting you on suspicion of being involved in acts of piracy."

Immediately, Tisdale surged forward and squared himself up to the Commodore. "Poppycock! Where did you get that fancy idea from?" he protested. "Captain Jennings is not a pirate. He's... er... he's my associate!"

Holloway threw him an icy stare and decreed firmly, "If you don't move out of the way, I'll have you arrested for complicity in acts of piracy."

"How dare you?" Tisdale spat back, feeling insulted.

Ignoring Tisdale's outburst, the Commodore turned to his soldiers and ordered, "Seize him!"

The first two soldiers in the line pushed Tisdale out of the way with their rifles and grabbed hold of Jennings. At the sight of this, the ship's boys threw themselves on the soldiers and started kicking and punching them.

"Let go of the captain, he's not a pirate! He's our captain!" Jonesie shouted.

"Yeah, that's right and you're not gonna get him, so leave him alone!" Jamesie harked.

Unfortunately, the soldiers were much too strong for them and using their feet, they sent both boys rolling to the ground.

"That's all right, boys," Captain Jennings said. "Let the men do their duty." Then, staring straight into the Commodore's eyes, he added, "I've nothing to hide and my conscience is clear. Let the court decide and justice be done."

Upon these words, the soldiers seized the captain and led him away under the stunned gaze of Tisdale and his crew.

***

The news of Captain Jennings's arrest soon reached Government House. Knowing of her vested interest in the drama, the butler, Johnny Canoe, intimated the bad tidings to Lady Sarah who, left shocked and speechless by the news, stared back at him in sheer disbelief. Minutes later, she stormed into her father's office.

"Papa! Is it true that Captain Jennings has been arrested?"

Governor Woodes Rogers rolled his quill nervously between his fingers. He did not know how to reply. Eventually, he nodded his head several times and said tentatively, "Sarah darling... don't upset yourself with matters that don't concern you."

"So he has been arrested! Why? What has he done?"

"I'm afraid I'm not at liberty to tell you. It's a matter for the court."

"It's that Commodore of yours, isn't it? He's discovered that I'm in love with Captain Jennings and he just wants him out of the way."

"Steady on, Darling, steady on. Don't get all upset…"

"Upset?" Lady Sarah screamed, taking her handkerchief out to dab the flow of tears that was streaming down her face. "Of course I'm upset! Can't you understand?"

"No, Sarah darling, I don't…"

"I love him!" Lady Sarah wailed.

"Well, I'm pleased to hear it since you're going to marry him…"

"No, not him!" his daughter corrected forcefully. "I'm in love with Captain Jennings!"

"Now, Darling…" the Governor said. "I'm sorry to hear that because the plan is that you will marry the Commodore and that's that… It's all been arranged."

Drying her tears, Lady Sarah spoke in a very controlled but firm voice.

"So, Father, it doesn't rattle your conscience that you wish me to marry a man who has no qualms about sending an innocent man to the gallows. According to your own moral code, the best you can do for your daughter is to have her marry a traitor?"

At that moment, Lady Charlotte happened upon the scene. "What's happening?" she enquired with a worried frown, putting a protective arm around her niece's shoulders. "What's going on?"

"Aunt Charlotte… They've arrested Captain Jennings!" Lady Sarah informed her in a trembling voice.

"But you shouldn't get all upset about that… He's only an acquaintance of ours…"

Lady Sarah stared at her aunt in shock. Then, dissolving in tears again, she let her head fall onto her aunt's bosom and wailed, "I love him, Aunt Charlotte, I love him and I don't care who knows it!"

Patting her head gently to comfort her, Aunt Charlotte was about to speak, and had even begun to say, "but I thought…" when she spotted her brother, the Governor, waving his hands frantically in a negative manner and mouthing silently 'no, no!'

As fate would have it, while the Governor was trying to placate his daughter and sister, Lady Whetstone Rogers arrived on the scene. Jerking her head with apprehension, she made straight for her daughter.

"What's happened? What's the matter, Darling?"

At the sound of her mother's voice, Lady Sarah wailed even more loudly, "Mummy, oh mummy, they've arrested Captain Jennings!"

"What?" she said, swivelling her head between her husband and her sister-in-law.

At that moment, the Governor stood up and pleaded, "Please, Darling, take her away. I'll explain later, but right now, I've got urgent correspondence to finish."

**

Later that evening, the Governor and his family were gathered around the dinner table. The whole family was present, except for one, Lady Sarah. William, her brother, glanced around the table with a quizzical look.

"Isn't Sarah coming to dinner?" he pondered out loud.

His father stared back at him while the ladies threw a knowing look at each other. A stony silence followed as each wondered how best to answer his question. Then, Lady Charlotte bristled in her seat, waved to the servant to refill her glass with chilled wine and announced in a matter-of-fact way, "Apparently, Captain Jennings has been arrested."

"Has he?" William exclaimed. "Why? What has he done?"

"The rumour goes," Lady Charlotte volunteered. "He's reverted to his old ways…"

"What? Captain Jennings… a pirate? No way! That's not his style." William declared categorically.

"But he had been a pirate," his father reminded him.

"Just like you had been a privateer," William retaliated. "Why can't the poor man be left alone? After all, it is thanks to him that we averted another war with Spain."

"Well, I do hope so, we've yet to return the cross," his father pointed out.

"All right, but what I mean is if he had really been a pirate, he would never have returned the *Cross of Madeira*. He knew how valuable it was but he did the honourable thing and returned it."

"He may have known how valuable it was, but I'm pretty certain he was not aware of its full political significance. The way I see it, he was damned lucky we believed his Cock 'n bull story about him stealing it from Bartholomew Roberts. You only have to look at him to know that he was never a match against that formidable pirate. He is too green still, too inexperienced."

"But he is a gentleman and gentlemen don't lie!" William retorted in the captain's defence.

"Goodness, William! How naïve…"

"His father is only a farmer… and a tenant farmer at that," Lady Whetstone Rogers threw in casually, using his humble origin as a further proof of his guilt.

"What does it matter?" William sneered.

"It matters to me," his mother replied in an inflexible tone. "I have high aspirations for Sarah and I expect her to get the best."

"Like that manipulative, devious, conniving Commodore? Is he really the man you want Sarah to marry?"

"What's wrong with him?" his father asked brusquely.

"I don't trust him."

"Why not?"

"I don't know… I just don't trust him."

Suddenly, a distant voice quipped in, "Neither do I."

All the heads turned towards the wide-open French doors. It was Lady Sarah.

"Ah, Darling! We were just talking about you," the Governor greeted.

"I know… I heard."

"Come and have something to eat, Darling, you must be quite hungry," her mother urged.

"I don't think I could eat a thing," Lady Sarah admitted plaintively.

"Well, come and join us anyway," Lady Charlotte invited her in a cheerful tone. "Rather here in jolly company than on your own churning up all sorts of dark and horrid thoughts in that pretty head of yours."

Lady Sarah took her usual place at the table and when she was quite settled, her aunt looked at the gathering with the most cheerful look and said, "Now, who wants to join me for the usual constitutional walk?"

***

Two weeks later, the town crier was seen hurrying towards the market square in his full regalia flanked by a young drummer. Soon, the drum reverberated loudly all around the square calling out to the gentle folks of Port Nassau. On the last beat, and with much ado, the town crier enrolled a large parchment paper and made the following announcement, "Oyez! Oyez! Ladies, Gentlemen, Folks of the land and others, on behalf of his Majesty King George I, I hereby proclaim:

"— On 31 December, in the year of the Lord 1722, the trial of Captain Charles Jennings will be held on accounts of acts of piracy.

"— Witnesses able to provide evidence for or against the prosecution are requested to submit their findings at their earliest opportunity.

"— Other witnesses able and willing to testify for or against the defendant are requested to make themselves known as soon as possible.

"— No man or woman shall be allowed inside the courtroom carrying pistols, muskets, cutlasses, knives or any other weapons.

"— No child under the age of fifteen years old shall be allowed in during the proceedings and no eating or drinking shall be permitted inside the courtroom.

"— Here ends the proclamation. Oyez! Oyez!"

During the reading, an excited crowd had formed around the town crier, mainly made up of women, young and old, who had become fascinated by the rumours of a certain rivalry between Commodore Holloway and the dashing young captain. And rightly or wrongly, each and every one of them knew exactly on which port they sided. But they wanted to be sure.

"Is it that young captain that was trading with Tisdale?" one young maiden was heard to enquire keenly.

"Aye! The handsome looking one, is that him?" another one queried.

"Ladies! Ladies! You'll soon find out! The doors will open at eleven o'clock. In the meantime, I've got important things to do so make way, make way!" the town crier declared firmly while wrestling his way through the throng of excited women.

Chapter Twenty-Five
The Trial

Meanwhile, in the depth of a forgotten gaol, a dark silhouette moved furtively along the dank corridors, her long skirts trailing heavily behind her on the damp and putrid ground. At the sound of the light footsteps, Charles Jennings pricked up his ears. Soon, a hooded figure appeared and a voice cried out, "Charles!"

Captain Jennings sprung onto his feet and rushed to the iron bars. He had recognised straight away the sound of the desperate cry.

"Lady Sarah! What are you doing here? You shouldn't be here! This is not a place for ladies!" he whispered.

The young woman grabbed the captain's hands through the bars, struggling to speak but the emotion proved too strong. Eventually, she managed to whisper, "Charles… I'm so glad you're safe."

After a while, regaining full control of her emotions again, she confided, "I've come to say that I'm going to get you out of here…"

"How?" the young captain interrupted.

"My father, of course!"

Captain Jennings looked at the young lady and emitted a long sigh of despair. "I'm afraid it's no use, not even *he* can help. There's only one person who can save me from the gallows but to testify on my behalf would mean certain death for her…"

"Her?" Lady Sarah reprised with a worried frown. "A woman? Who is she?" After a slight pause, she added, "Does she… does she mean anything to you?"

"Only in the sense that she's the only person alive who can prove that I'm innocent."

"Why would it mean certain death for her if she helps you?"

"Because…"

"Go on, Charles. Tell me… tell me why she can't testify on your behalf?"

"Because… she's a condemned woman…"

"But I want to help you, Charles. And I'm sure she'd want to help you too." Then after a thoughtful pause, Lady Sarah added, "Would you like me to contact her on your behalf?"

Charles looked at the young woman standing in front of him, so naïve, so innocent and who had not the slightest inkling of the troubled life he had led so far.

"I don't think she'd be quite prepared to risk her life for me."

"She's a pirate, isn't she?" Lady Sarah deduced.

Charles looked at his beloved straight in the eyes but did not respond. Suddenly, the worried look that had lined the young woman's delicate features disappeared and Lady Sarah became unexpectedly assertive.

"Well, there's only one thing for me to do, but first, I'm going to get Tisdale to send you his best ale and I'll make sure you get properly fed too, even if it means smuggling in my own supper," she vouched, trying to smile at the same time. "Anyway... I'd better go now... though there's one more thing..." she added as if on second thoughts. As she spoke, her facial expression changed and became soft and gentle. Then, in a soft whisper, she declared, "I love you, Charles Jennings."

This was her first open declaration of love for the young captain. Charles Jennings looked at her longingly, unable to reciprocate in words his true feelings for her. This was not the right place nor the right time and with his fate undecided, it was neither right nor proper to commit himself to a young woman who had her whole life in front of her. So he smiled, but it was not a wooing smile, just a smile to acknowledge his gratitude to the young woman who was prepared to risk everything for a few stolen moments with him.

Lady Sarah returned his smile, but the emotion proved too much, and she could not bring herself to say any more. In the subdued light, her eyes sparkled with love and passion, but also with tears. She sighed heavily, and then left as swiftly as she came. Once she had departed, Charles Jennings returned to the wooden plank that was his makeshift bed and as he sat himself down, he could not help noticing that the prison cell seemed darker than ever, as if suddenly, a hundred candles had been blown out all at once.

***

At that very moment, on the other side of town, Henry Tisdale was busy tidying his tavern and spreading sawdust on the floor, ready for opening time. He considered for a moment stopping for a short break to smoke one of his beloved clay pipes but the sound of his wife's nagging voice in the background made him quickly change his mind.

"You're all right, Mona dear?" he asked when suddenly, a knock on the front door diverted his attention.

"Yes?" he said, unbolting the front door.

"Good afternoon, Mr Tisdale, I'm Lady Sarah, the Governor's daughter…"

"I thought you might be… although you don't normally come here… but I'm sorry, we're closed right now."

"I know, but I've not come for myself… I've come to ask for a very special favour, I would like you to deliver some of your best ale to the prison…" she began, lowering her eyes to the ground in slight embarrassment.

"That can be done, but I normally ask for payment in advance."

"I'm afraid I have no money with me… It's for Captain Jennings…"

"Ah!" Tisdale exclaimed. "The captain! In that case, don't worry, love, I'll send the bill to your father…"

"No, no!" Lady Sarah interrupted with the look of panic in her eyes. "You mustn't do that. My father would be furious if he knew…" Then she stopped, unable or unwilling to finish her sentence. During this enforced silence, Henry Tisdale looked at the young woman and felt genuine compassion for her.

"I tell you what," he started again in a softer tone. "I'll just add it to your father's monthly bill; that way nobody'll notice, all right?"

At these words, the young woman's face lit up.

"Thank you very much, Mr Tisdale, thank you so much."

As she bade him goodbye, Mona Tisdale appeared on the threshold just in time to see the silhouette of a young lady hurrying away from the tavern.

"Who was that?" she asked in her booming voice.

"Never you mind, Mona dear. Business is all that counts."

"Aye," Mona Tisdale riled. "I hope you're not chasing young petticoats again, Harry Tisdale!"

Henry Tisdale looked at his wife and replied with a wooing smile. Then he grabbed his lady by the waist and lifted her off the ground in a strong embrace.

"With you around, why look elsewhere?" he declared in jest.

"Only because you wouldn't dare! I know you, Harry Tisdale! Now, let go of me."

But Henry Tisdale was not ready to let go.

"Let go of me, Harry!" his wife begged again without sounding overtly cross.

"I will, Mona dear, but I just want a little kiss first to keep me going!"

Now, Mona Tisdale was laughing. "Behave yourself Harry Tisdale! And get back to work! There's still lots to do before opening time," she scoffed.

Henry Tisdale eventually released his wife and, just as Mona Tisdale found her feet on the ground again, two young women happened to pass by. At the sight of the fractious pair, they emitted a little giggle. Unfazed but rather keen to display a semblance of decorum, Mona Tisdale quickly brushed herself down, thrust her head back, looked at the young women with a glitter in her eyes and exclaimed, "Men!" with a wry smile.

***

By now, the rumour that a dashing young captain was about to be tried for acts of piracy had begun to circle around town. Details of the case were still sketchy, but this did not seem to deter the womenfolk who, quite frankly, were only interested in the fascinating snippets of a sensational story which involved a love triangle. And among themselves, they had already worked out the plot and adjudged the main characters. For a start, there was the handsome, daring, young — but not very rich — captain whose sole crime, as far as they were concerned, had been to fall in love with the Governor's daughter. Then, there was Commodore Holloway whom none of them really knew but who, for the purpose of this gripping tale, was unanimously declared the villain, the instigator, the perpetrator and worst of all, the torturer bent on tormenting two young people in love. As for Lady Sarah herself, well, they did not know her either but by all accounts, she was young and helpless, thus undoubtedly in great need of their support whilst she wrestled with the turmoil presently tearing her heart apart, and as far as the general consensus went, that fact alone made her quite worthy of their full sympathy.

The day of the trial came. Throngs of excited women rushed early to the courthouse to secure the best seats, leaving their men folks alone and helpless, and without any guidance on how to hold the baby, do the house chores or feed their offspring. Opportunistic market traders who had set up stall at dawn hoping for a rich bonanza were left to negotiate their prices with the odd ageing folks stuttering and dithering through their missing teeth, and with other people who had kept their heads about them, indifferent as they were to the drama that was about to unfold. Together, they ambled leisurely around the market stalls unsure as to what they should get but hoping to bag a bargain or two.

Outside the courthouse, the air was filled with the jolly banter and giggling of female voices hailing and greeting each other. Though far too early for the court proceedings to have begun, an animated queue had already formed. The officials found themselves having to wade through a throng of excited women to even get to the door. When the clerk of the court finally unlocked the double doors, they all cheered and then… mayhem descended. Suddenly, the court officials were thrust forward, into the building and pushed unceremoniously to the fore, along the corridors and inside the courtroom by the hysterical crowd of women who could not wait to grab a seat. And there they waited unperturbed by the deafening hubbub, straightening their bonnets, rearranging their long skirts and competing with each other over the best piece of gossip. Within minutes, the courtroom was packed to the seams with many in the gallery choosing to remain standing just so that they could witness the most riveting court case ever to take place on the island.

A good while later, the door of the courtroom creaked in its hinges and a solemn procession of officials proceeded to the bench. Instantly, the room fell silent. All eyes followed the men in their formal attire while people craned their necks to see which one of them was the accused, but a disappointed sigh denoted that he had not arrived yet. Minutes later, Charles Jennings was brought in, flanked by his lawyer, a certain Mr Fenwick. He was led to the front of the bench where, from his pulpit, the judge in full bottom wig peered short-sightedly at him. The young captain felt awkward and ill-at-ease for the man about to decide on his fate was none other than the Governor himself, Sir Woodes Rodgers. He looked to his right and saw

Commodore Holloway who now stood for the prosecution, then to the left where his own lawyer had taken his seat. Mr Fenwick gave him a reassuring nod which the young captain acknowledged before turning his head towards the bench again. Seated next to him was William, son of the Governor who, as a law student himself, was particularly keen to follow the proceedings and had offered to assist Mr Fenwick in this most interesting of cases. Another bystander who had come along just to watch was a certain Daniel Defoe, family friend and highly respected author who hoped to add an extra chapter to his riveting novel recounting the *'General History of the Pyrates'*.

What none of them had noticed, however, was a slight silhouette creeping in discreetly at the back of the courtroom.

When all were finally seated and silent, and the members of the bench had all their papers ready, the trial began in earnest.

The evidence against the defendant was put forcefully forward by the prosecution. After claims and counterclaims, the judge felt it his duty to ask the Commodore if there were any witnesses to corroborate his evidence. Commodore Holloway was forced to admit that none had come forward to testify for or against the defendant. However — and there he laboured the point — he spelt out the fact that Charles Jennings was known to have been on the *Kingston* when that very ship was attacked by his own fleet and therefore, he had to have been in league with the pirates.

"And that very fact alone, my Lord, should be enough to prove that this man here is no less than a lawless, devious, remorseless and tyrannical pirate!" the Commodore declaimed with gusto.

Following this flow of accusations, a huge outcry rose from the gallery.

"This is not true, my Lord!" Charles Jennings protested vehemently. "The truth is that I was captured. I was tied up, gagged and forced to board the *Kingston*!"

"Captain Jennings, you are speaking out of turn. I need to remind you that you are in a court of law and as such you must let your lawyer speak on your behalf. After all, you are paying him handsomely for the privilege," the judge cautioned.

A discreet chuckle rose from the public gallery. Immediately, Mr Fenwick jumped onto his feet and declared, "I wish my client to take the stand."

"Just a minute, Mr Fenwick," the judge interrupted. Then turning towards the Commodore, he asked, "Commodore, has the prosecution finished declaring all its findings?"

"Yes, my Lord."

"In that case, Captain Jennings, you may take the stand."

Once the formalities performed, Mr Fenwick spoke for the defence.

"Captain Jennings," he began. "Could you explain to the court how you found yourself on the *Kingston* at the time in question?"

"As I said," the captain answered without hesitation. "I was captured, tied and ganged and forced to board the *Kingston*. Any member of my crew will be able to vouch for this!"

"Talking about your crew, Captain Jennings, it is a matter of interest to me and to the court that we haven't yet heard from your crew. Where is your crew, Captain Jennings?" the judge asked.

"I'm afraid I do not know, my Lord. They should have been back by now."

"Unfortunately, without any member of your crew to testify on your behalf, I will be unable to pass judgement in your favour."

Suddenly, a loud commotion erupted just outside the court. All heads turned towards the back of the room. The judge sat bolt upright and scowled at the guards standing on either side of the door.

"What on earth is going on? Guards, get rid of these people!" he ordered.

Before they could make a move, however, the door flew open and a group of burly men forced their way inside the courtroom.

"Beg your pardon, me Lord, we're here! We're Captain Jennings's crew!" one man hailed loudly. It was Dai Griffiths, the quartermaster.

"Aye! Aye!" chorused the others.

Charles Jennings breathed a huge sigh of relief and smiled at his men. At the front of the group, he spotted Dave Warren and Will Harris grinning broadly and waving at him. Right behind them, he could distinguish the large figure of Stan Mitchell and as he greeted each of his men with a relieved smile, the two ship boys barged their way through to the front.

"Our captain's not a pirate!" Jamesie shouted.

"Aye! And we've got the proof!" Jonesie declared.

Overwhelmed by the ensuing commotion, the clerk of the court grabbed the gavel and banged it loudly while pleading at the top of his voice, "Order! Order in the courtroom!"

As the noise began to die down, Captain Jennings's men stepped out of the way to let Stan Mitchell through, for in front of him stood an individual, a rough-looking woman sporting long loose black hair and wearing a pair of old slacks and an oversized shirt. At the sight of the dishevelled woman, a loud gasp of revulsion rose from the courtroom. The woman stared at the bench but avoided looking at Jennings. Then, still saying nothing, she went to stand next to the defendant. Again, she did not look at Jennings and instead kept her eyes firmly fixed on the judge. There was complete silence. No one had ever known the courtroom to be so quiet, so still, as everybody, riveted by the unexpected turn of events, followed wide-eyed and mouth-gaping the main characters, afraid to even blink in case they should miss a vital detail. Finally, the woman spoke, "My name is Anne Bonny," the woman declared boldly.

Immediately, a series of hushed whispers ran all around the courtroom. The clerk of the court scowled at the gathered audience and ordered, "Silence in court!"

Then the judge spoke, "I know who you are, Miss Bonny. I seem to remember that we have met before... and not that long ago, if I am correct."

His remark was followed by a loud snigger coming from the public area which forced the clerk of the court to bark again, "Silence please!"

Once the calm had returned, the judge was able to continue, "On what business do you stand in this court, Miss Bonny?"

"I wish to testify on behalf of Captain Jennings, my Lord."

"I'm afraid I cannot allow you to do that..." he began.

In the gallery, people gasped in shock. Charles Jennings threw a worried look at the judge then at the woman standing next to him. Amid the general consternation, only one man seemed to revel in this latest turn of events, Commodore Holloway. Sighing with relief, he sat further back in his seat and smiled... a sardonic smile, while on the other side of the bench, the captain's lawyer sprang onto his feet.

"But, my Lord...!" he protested.

"Sit down, Mr Fenwick!" the judge ordered. "And let me finish." Then he turned to Anne Bonny again.

"As I was saying, I cannot allow you to do that..." he reiterated slowly, leaving the whole room in suspense. "...unless you stand as a witness."

At the sound of these words, a huge sigh of relief rose from the room and people bristled in their seats and cleared their throats as if preparing to make their own speech. At the front of the court, Anne turned to Jennings and smiled but her smile soon disappeared as she prepared to speak again.

"My Lord, I wish to stand as a witness," she requested solemnly.

"Very well, Miss Bonny, take your place in the witness box," the judge invited her. Then, turning to the clerk of the court, "Bring the bible, will you?"

At hearing this, Commodore Holloway nearly suffered an apoplectic attack. He jumped to his feet and rushed in front of the judge.

"But, my Lord, you cannot allow this to happen!" he protested vehemently. Then pointing an accusative finger at the woman, he spat, "She's a pirate! Everybody knows that. The fact that she's a wanted woman, a condemned woman, a fugitive I might add, should disqualify her from giving evidence!"

The judge responded by giving him a stern look. "Commodore, may I remind you that you are in a court of law and that the sole purpose of this court is to ensure that justice is done. Whatever his circumstances, a man has the right to a proper hearing, even more so when his life is at stake," the judge remonstrated. "So, go back to your seat and let the proceedings continue or I shall have you arrested for contempt of court!"

A loud cheer from the public gallery punctuated the judge's remark. Angry and humiliated, Commodore Holloway reluctantly regained his seat while the clerk of the court brought the bible to the witness so that she could take the oath. Having sworn to tell the truth, the whole truth and nothing but the truth, Anne Bonny finally began to give her evidence.

Chapter Twenty-Six
A Formidable Challenge

She began with the capture of Captain Charles Jennings and explained how they had forced him to flee with them on the one remaining ship they had, hidden in the creek. Then, during the battle, as soon as they realised that all was lost, herself and Black Bobby had abandoned ship and escaped in the cockboat, leaving the captain alone to face the attack.

At that point, Commodore Holloway sprang out of his seat to cross-examine the witness.

"The question is, Miss Bonny, did you or did you not know Captain Jennings *before* you captured him?"

Anne Bonny froze in a stubborn silence. Not a sound could be heard in the courtroom while all waited for her reply. Eventually, the judge leant towards the witness box and intimated in a soft voice, "Miss Bonny, you are obliged to answer the question."

Before she had a chance to speak however, Commodore Holloway assailed her with more cross-examination. "I put it to you, Miss Bonny, that you knew Captain Jennings before you captured him because of the very fact that he had previously been a member of the *Kingston*'s crew!" he declaimed loudly.

"Well of course, the ship's name was the *Kingston*," Anne Bonny riled back.

"I'm not talking about this latest incident, Miss Bonny, I am talking of the time when the *Kingston* was captained by none other than the notorious pirate whose name is familiar to all, Jack Rackham!" he shouted.

Instantly, a loud gasp rose from the courtroom but in the witness box, the witness remained locked in a stubborn silence. She looked straight ahead, avoiding eye contact with anyone or anything.

After a few seconds of this, the judge felt it necessary to intervene again. "Miss Bonny, I need to remind you that, as a witness, you are required to answer the questions put to you."

At these words, Anne took a deep breath and clenched her teeth. Then, looking straight at the judge, she declared, "My Lord, I came here risking my own life to try and save a man being hanged for something he hasn't done. Yes, Captain Jennings was a member of the crew but twice he found himself on the *Kingston* because twice he was captured and forced to join the crew. Boy Jennings is not a pirate and never was a pirate!"

"*Boy* Jennings?" the judge quizzed.

"Sorry, my Lord… I mean Captain Jennings."

"But we've only got your word for it!" Commodore Holloway challenged. "For all we know, you could be lying to save this man because… I put it to you that you were… lovers!"

An instant outcry followed his remark. Animated whispers ran all around the courtroom, almost drowning the proceedings.

"How dare you!" Anne protested.

Keen to put a stop to any further inappropriate revelations, the judge summoned the Commodore to approach the bench.

"Do you have any proof of this?" he whispered.

"No, but…"

"In that case, you cannot continue on this line of questioning. It is entirely unethical to cross-examine a witness on pure conjecture."

The Commodore reluctantly regained his seat while the clerk of the court grabbed the gavel again and ordered, "Silence in court!"

Then the proceedings resumed. It was now the turn of the defence to speak and, using the witness's latest testimony, Mr Fenwick put it to the court that Charles Jennings was quite simply a victim of unfortunate circumstances and should be acquitted of all charges. However, Commodore Holloway had not finished. He stood up and protested, "Objection, My Lord! How can we possibly allow a pirate's word to decide on a man's innocence? Is this really what justice has come to, my word against that of a self-confessed pirate? My honesty and integrity against the immorality of a murderer and a thief? This is not justice, my Lord, this is a farce!"

The judge looked at all the parties involved and was about to summarise the case when suddenly, a voice rose from the back of the court.

"My Lord!" the voice called out. "I have in my possession something that would challenge the Commodore's honesty and integrity."

All heads turned to the back of the courtroom and watched a young woman make her way towards the bench with an assured step. The gallery gasped and gawped in complete disbelief as they followed her every step. As for the judge, he nearly fell off his honourable seat for the woman brave enough to speak out when all seemed lost for the captain, was none other than his very own daughter, Lady Sarah.

Approaching the captain's lawyer, she gave him some papers which Mr Fenwick scanned speedily. Captain Jennings threw a quizzical look at Lady Sarah while her father, struggling to regain his composure, stared at her speechless. On the other side, Commodore Holloway bristled nervously in his seat.

"What's the meaning of all this?" he pleaded. Meanwhile, Mr Fenwick continued to scan the papers and when he had quite finished, he prepared to speak.

"My Lord!" he began excitedly. "These papers are letters that show that Commodore Holloway has been secretly trading with pirates. There are even some invoices which show clearly what he has traded with them at bargain prices in return for his co-operation in letting them go free to sell on their ill-gotten merchandise."

The Judge could not believe his ears. He looked sternly at the Commodore who kept mumbling, "You're not going to believe them, you cannot possibly believe them…"

At that moment, Mr Fenwick approached the bench and gave the letters to the judge. As he scanned each in turn, Governor Woodes Rodgers shook his head in disappointment and sheer disbelief. Eventually, he raised his head, looked at the Commodore and ordered, "Guards, seize him!"

Instantly, the public erupted in a loud cheer. Commodore Holloway was swiftly removed from the court amid jeers and cheers. Once more, the clerk of the court was forced to bang the gavel again in order to shout, "Silence in court! Silence please!"

This time, it took a few minutes for the public to calm down. At long last, the courtroom fell quiet again and the trial was able to continue. After a short deliberation, the judge was ready to deliver his verdict.

"Captain Jennings…" There he paused to weigh his words, leaving the whole room in suspense. He bristled in his seat again before declaring, "There is no evidence to support the charges made against you, therefore the case is dismissed. You are free to go."

Immediately, loud cheers greeted the final verdict. Then the judge turned towards the witness and declared, "As for you, Miss Bonny, you are an inveterate pirate and I should have you arrested on the spot… but for the fact that what you have done today, possibly sacrificing your own life to save another so that justice could be done, is an act of bravery that not many would have done. Therefore, with the power vested in me, I am willing to grant you a pardon…"

There he stopped to give time for his words to sink in. Anne's face beamed with a triumphant smile. She looked at Jennings, then at the judge and continued to smile, unable to contain her joy and huge relief. However, the judge had not quite finished.

"But on one condition…"

Here, the judge paused again. Anne's smile vanished as she stared at the judge with great apprehension, wondering what he had in store for her.

"That you help bring back Black Bobby… dead or alive!"

At these words, Anne looked shocked. In the inner turmoil that was twisting her mind, the courtroom disappeared around her and all she could see in her head was the formidable figure of Black Bobby. Of course he was a ruthless tyrant whose thirst for treasures and gold spread nothing but misery around him; but without him, she had no future. She was cornered. Shaking her head to dispel the frightening thoughts, she looked up to the judge with an air of determination on her face; then, throwing her shoulders and head back in a show of confidence, she finally declared, "Yes, my Lord."

However, when all matters seemed to be settled, there was another commotion at the door. A man was seen wrestling with the guards before shouting, "Let me in! I need to speak to the judge."

The judge exhaled a flow of exasperated air and requested to know, "What is it now?"

The man managed to free himself from the guards and, pushing his way through the throng of people, ran up to the bench and pointed firmly at the witness with his arm shaking.

"My Lord," he started. "This woman here is my wife! I've come to claim my wife back!"

The judge looked quite taken aback. At the same time, a huge roar of laughter filled the courtroom as all eyes set on the hapless man brave enough to claim a pirate for a wife.

The clerk of the court barked, "Silence in court, please!"

The judge coughed a few times to clear his throat. He needed time to think. After a calculated pause, he lowered his glasses to peer better at the newcomer, leant over his pulpit and asked condescendingly, "And who might you be?"

The man swelled up his chest, tucked his thumbs under his belt, threw his head back and declared with gusto, "My name is Bonny, James Bonny, and this is my common-law wife, Anne Bonny!"

The judge turned to Anne. "Is this true?"

Anne lowered her eyes and answered with a nod of the head. The judge turned to face the man again.

"Well, Mr Bonny, unless you wish to become a pirate yourself (*more laughter greeted his remark*), I fear you will have to wait until Miss Bonny here has fulfilled her obligations to the court. After that, you will be free to return to this court to lodge a claim for her rightful return."

People sniggered behind their cupped hands. Never in their lives had they seen such a comical display in a court of law, especially as the man in question, in sheer contrast with his presumed wife, looked no more than a weakling in great need of a square meal or two.

With all matters finally resolved, the clerk of the court grabbed the gavel, banged it once on the block and declared with visible relief, "The court is dismissed!"

At the back of the room, the guards opened the door and the courtroom began to empty slowly. The first thing Captain Jennings did was to go and thank the woman responsible for his freedom; but instead of greeting him in a friendly manner, Anne glared at him, and hissed through her teeth, "Don't thank me, Jennings, I had no choice. I couldn't let you hang for something you hadn't done... and don't go and get the wrong idea... I didn't do it for you; I did it for my son."

With these words, she turned on her heels, left the courtroom and disappeared once again out of his life, with her prodigal husband hot on her tail. Charles Jennings was hurt by her curt response but his sombre mood soon lifted when he spotted Lady Sarah advancing towards him, her face beaming with a radiant smile. He still could not believe what she had done for him and all he managed to utter were a few words of thanks. Then the two fell into a warm embrace, with Lady Sarah's face streaming with tears of joy and happiness.

In the middle of all this, the Governor appeared at their sides. Although Commodore Holloway was no longer a contender for his daughter's hand, he was still unsure whether Captain Charles Jennings was really the best man for her. So he had come up with a solution to keep them apart… for a while at least. Addressing the young man first, he began, "Captain Jennings… I have a special mission for you."

"Yes, Governor?"

The Governor took a deep breath and said, "I want you to return the *Cross of Madeira* to the Admiralty."

The unexpected request came as a real blow. The young captain looked at Lady Sarah, then at her father, pursing his lips and wringing his hands as he thought of an appropriate way to respond. Next to him, Lady Sarah fretted and glared at her father with a heavy scowl.

"But Papa…" she protested.

However, driven by his sense of duty, the captain interrupted her.

"I must say, I was hoping to spend some time on land before my next voyage, Governor."

"There's no time for that, Captain. The sooner the *Cross of Madeira* is returned to its rightful owner, the sooner we can avert another war with Spain. You must realise that I am taking a big risk giving you this mission but this will be your best chance to prove that you are what you claim to be, and that is a loyal officer of the King's Navy."

Lady Sarah sighed heavily. "Oh Papa, why him? There are still pirates out there. The captain could get killed… He may never return… Please, Papa, don't ask him to do this. Get the Commodore to do it instead!"

"Sorry, Darling, I don't think the Commodore is going anywhere for a while."

"But it's too dangerous. I may never see him again," his daughter pleaded. "Is there not any other way that the captain can prove his innocence?"

Captain Jennings listened with interest. Such an open display of Lady Sarah's affection for him warmed his heart and confirmed her feelings for him, which pleased him enormously, but he felt compelled to intervene.

"It's all right, Lady Sarah," he said in a soft tone. "If by this mission I can prevent another war, then I shall do my duty. When would you like me to leave, Governor?"

"As soon as you can."

"Very well, Sir."

Suddenly, a voice butted in, "Can I come too?"

They all turned around to see William standing there with a big grin on his face. The Governor immediately objected. "William, you can't! You've got your studies to think about…"

"But, Father, if my clients are going to consist mainly of high sea robbers and pirates, I need to understand their methods of acting and thinking, and the best way to do this is to watch them in action. Wouldn't you agree, Captain?"

"Well, that is true, except that I was hoping to avoid any close encounter with them since, strictly speaking, my mission won't be to chase pirates but…"

"But you're bound to come across some of those ruffians!" interrupted William.

"William, don't argue with me," his father cut in sharply. "You're not going and that's that!"

Lady Sarah looked at the three men with some concern. She was not about to let the captain go just yet, so she tugged on her brother's sleeve and made a discreet sign with her head, hoping that he would understand her meaning. William looked at her, puzzled, and tried to decipher the words she was mouthing. Eventually, the penny dropped.

"Father? Can we invite Captain Jennings to dinner tonight? After all, if he's about to leave for another long journey, it's going to be a long while before we have the pleasure of his company."

"Actually," the captain corrected. "My ship is being repaired and it will be a while before she's fit to sail again."

The Governor scrutinised his son and his daughter, each in turn, suspecting some kind of connivance between the two. However, mellowed by Lady Sarah's pleading eyes, he finally relented, "You will be most welcome to join us."

With his face beaming with a victorious smile, Captain Jennings accepted the invitation graciously.

At that moment, the sound of loud chanting to the rhythm of rolling drums and piercing whistles invaded the street.

"It's the Junkanoo!" someone shouted.

In an instant, all those left in the courtroom spilt out onto the street, where they were met by a large procession of black people dressed up in fancy costumes festooned with large multicolour feathers. Noisily and merrily, they stomped their way through the streets, some playing the drums, others the trumpet and all of them chanting cheerful rhythmic refrains. It was New Year's Eve and the celebrations had begun. At the front of the carnival, Captain Jennings spotted a familiar face. Almost at the same time, Johnny Canoe spotted him too.

"It's Captain Jennings! Hi Captain Jennings!" Then, urging his mates to follow him, Johnny Canoe grabbed hold of the captain and together, they hoisted him on their shoulders, whistling, chanting and stomping their feet even more vigorously. Lady Sarah had just time to hail, "See you tonight, Captain!" before the carnival disappeared down the next alley on their way towards the main venue, Bay Street.

**

Later, when Captain Jennings eventually caught up with his crew, the first thing he wanted to find out was what had happened at the battle on the beach and whether they had been able to locate Humphreys. At the sound of the name, Connor racked his throat, dug his hands deep in his pockets and fixed his gaze on the ground immediately in front of him.

"Well…" he started hesitantly. "It's like… it wasn't like…"

"He wasn't one of us no more," Stan Mitchell, coming to Connor's rescue, butted in.

Captain Jennings guessed straight away what they meant.

"Arrgh, the damned fool! Where is he now?"

"He's good and dead!" Jonesie said.

"Be quiet, boy! We're having a serious conversation here," Connor barked.

"The damned fool!" the captain repeated in sheer frustration. "He was a good man and a good hand, so reliable… I can't believe he did that, not Humphreys…" Then a thought suddenly occurred to him.

"You attacked at nightfall, didn't you?" he recalled.

"Aye!" Connor and Mitchell chorused.

"So none of them could see who was attacking them, am I right?"

"Aye!" the men chorused again.

"So maybe… if he had known who was behind the attack, maybe he would have…"

"Aye, but he couldn't see, Capt'n, it was too dark," Mitchell admitted.

"So really, all he was doing was to defend himself… he was just fighting back to save his own life… and not necessarily because he had sided with those damned pirates!"

"You might have something there, Capt'n," Connor admitted.

"Aye!" they all concurred.

"I knew he was a good'un!" Big Mitch conceded, shaking his head.

With his mind at rest over Humphreys's last actions, Captain Jennings summoned his crew and, from the upper deck, he made the following announcement.

"Fellow shipmates! We have sailed in the wind and rain, we have fought side by side and ridden out many a storm, but most of all we have stood together to fight against a common enemy. We have been given a new mission now, a mission which is not to go into battle and fight, but there are many enemies out there, amongst them pirates who will not hesitate to attack us for whatever they can grab. Therefore, each mission is a dangerous one. Right now, I cannot tell you where we're going, I cannot even reveal the reason why we're about to set sail, but what I need to know from you is whether you'll come with me on this new mission, on this new journey…"

"When will we know where we're going?" someone heckled.

"When it's safe for you to know and that means when we're at sea."

"When are we gonna be sailing?" another shipmate asked.

"When the ship is good and ready, which will be in about a month's time."

"And what about the pay?" several queried.

"The conditions of employment remain the same, and just like this time, although I cannot guarantee it, there is the possibility of an extra reward if the mission is successful. So… who'll come with me on this mission?"

"Me! Me!" the ship's boys shouted excitedly.

"Aye! Aye!" a chorus of voices echoed.

"Then, let five weeks pass and I'll see you back here if you wish to join my crew. One warning, though, do not spend all your groats at once. It has to last you for four weeks at least. And watch out for muggers. In the meantime, enjoy yourselves, but not too much, I don't want to have to bail you out of gaol. Have a great time and see you all in a month's time."

"Aye, aye, Capt'n!"

Most of the men, rendered homeless by a career spent at sea, made straight for the local inns, except for the ship's boys.

"I'm going back home," Jonesie said to his young friend, as they walked down the gangplank.

"What about me? I don't want to stay on my own," Jamesie said plaintively.

Jonesie looked at him. He had become quite fond of his little mate, so much so that it did feel as if they really were brothers. Having spent so many weeks at sea together, it felt odd that they should not be connected in any way. Jonesie was a kid who played in the streets whereas Jamesie was a street kid.

"I'd take you with me but I'm in real trouble myself... Me mum's gonna be furious with me for running away," he said with a sigh. "Why don't you stay on the ship?"

Jamesie looked at him fixedly. His eyes began to well up with tears and his bottom lip quivered with emotion.

"Please, Jonesie... don't leave me... I'm scared."

The sight of his little friend in distress melted his heart and choked him up with emotion. Fighting back the tears, Jonesie put his arm around Jamesie's shoulders in an attempt to reassure him.

"Don't worry, Jamesie. I'll take care of you. And me mum... well... she won't mind. She'll be mighty pleased to see me, before whacking me one for running away! And when she sees I've brought her some money, she'll be fine..."

At these words, Jamesie's face beamed with a grateful smile.

"Captain Jennings gave me some money too. I can give her some. And if you don't have a spare bed, you can tell her I don't mind sleeping on the floor. It's better than in the streets."

Jonesie smiled back and replied cheerfully, "Aye! After all, we're brothers and we'll stay together!"

The boys ran along the quay and disappeared into a side street.

***

Slightly ahead of the boys, another animated conversation was taking place.

"What are you doing here, James Bonny? You've no business of being here, so push off!"

"But I have!" the neglected husband retorted through the corner of his mouth. "I've heard you've got yourself a bit of a fortune. That makes *us* rich!"

"Scram it, I say! I want nothing to do with you!" Anne barked aggressively.

"Actually, you do! The only way to get rid of me, '*wifie*', is to give me a bit of that fortune."

"Don't make me laugh!" Anne riled back. "The only thing you're gonna get from me is a bullet or a divorce!"

As she said this, Anne let out a loud belly laugh and walked away, leaving her disillusioned husband frozen on the spot, reeling with anger.

***

Meanwhile, in a local tavern, Henry Tisdale was busy bemoaning the fact that every time he had tried to retrieve some of the treasure, his plans had been thwarted by some unforeseeable events. And with Black Bobby still at large, he was not about to try again, he confided to his wife, not for a while anyway.

"Never mind, Harry Tisdale, we're managing all right as we are and we're happy because our consciences are clear. But don't you worry, one day you'll get your hands on them treasures and then we'll shut up shop and retire to South Carolina."

"But I want to retire now!"

"What for? You wouldn't know what to do with yourself. Take it from me, Harry Tisdale, stop now and your body'll seize up on you and you'll end up as stiff as a washboard! As for me, I know exactly what I'm gonna do right now."

"What's that?"

"I'm gonna write to our niece, Lorna. I'm sure she'll enjoy reading about all the funny goings on around here… and when he's older, she'll be able to entertain her wee bairn with plentiful tales of what people get up to out here. Aye…" she continued as if agreeing with herself, "that should give her a good laugh. When the drinks in, the wits out, and the till sings! And that means, we're all happy."

The innkeeper returned an affectionate look at his wife, knowing that once again she had spoken sense. This formidable 'wifie' of his may have nagged him a few times, to the point of martyrdom, but inside, he felt mightily lucky to be married to a woman who was not shy of hard work, kept the inn clean and tidy, who possessed a common sense that abided with the law, but above all, who did not squander his money… except to buy a corset or two.

And so, life resumed apace in this rather eventful corner of the West Indies. In his tavern, Henry Tisdale continued to serve his customers as he had always done, chatting, joking and bantering, but always keeping his ears close to the ground. And he had good reasons for doing so, for somewhere, on a desert island, lay a bounty of unclaimed treasures and the race was on as to who would get it first.

Chapter Twenty-Seven
Blood Brothers?

On the other side of town, at the far end of East Bay Street, Jonesie and Jamesie sauntered languorously, hands in pocket, towards Shirley Street, where Jonesie's family home nestled among banana trees. Kicking the odd stone along the dirt track, he could not remember when he had last said goodbye to his mother, promising to return before sunset. Looking cool and composed on the outside, inside he fretted. What would his mother say when he would finally re-appear without warning, with a new 'brother' in tow?

Ahead of them, they spotted several street kids milling outside a small general store. These kids often swarmed around shops on the off chance of finding some loose change or small items of food that a customer might have inadvertently dropped. Sometimes, they felt bold enough to simply beg. On that day, there were five street kids, of Jonesie's age, or perhaps slightly older, hanging around that particular store. With a wary eye, they watched our two boys enter the shop. As soon as Jonesie and Jamesie stepped across the threshold, the boys rushed to the window to spy on them. They could not see very much through the thick dust caking the windowpane, but the very fact that the two boys had entered the shop meant that they had money.

When the boys came out of the shop, the street kids formed a tight line in front of them. Jonesie and Jamesie threw a glance at each other and decided to ignore them. They had just spent weeks at sea dodging bullets and cannon balls and the sight of five snotty kids squinting with envy at their bags of candies was not about to unsettle them. Avoiding any eye contact, the boys made a few sideway steps in order to walk past them when suddenly, the biggest of the street kids shouted, "Grab them!"

Immediately, the rapacious brats threw themselves on the boys and wrestled them to the ground. Despite putting up a good fight, the boys were soon robbed of their candies and all of their money. The dirty deed done, the street kids all fled in different directions, sniggering wildly.

The boys got up and brushed themselves down, fuming with rage. Jonesie cursed and stamped his feet several times on the ground while Jamesie wielded his fists at them and yelled, "You dirty thieves! We'll get our own back!"

Just about recovered from their ordeal, they resumed their walk towards Shirley Street. Soon they reached Jonesie's home. However, before coming to the door, Jonesie stopped.

"I think you better wait out here. Things are different now that I can't give me mum any money. But don't worry, whatever me mum says, I'll come back for you. I promise."

The house was no more than a wooden shack. Narrow at the front, it was sheltered by thatch supported by wooden beams that jutted out from the roof and served as a canopy to shelter the house from the heat of the sun and the odd tropical storm.

Jamesie waited outside patiently, kicking loose stones with his feet along the dirt track. He was surprised not to hear any voices coming from inside the house. A few minutes later, Jonesie reappeared.

"My mum's not home," he said straight away. "In fact, there's nobody else either so they must have gone to town; it must be market day. Come on, come on in and let's get something to eat from the larder."

"I'll be glad of that." Jamesie smiled. "I'm famished!"

The door gave straight inside the main room which was furnished with an old sofa, a decrepit armchair and a rocking chair. Pushed against the wall were a table and four rickety chairs. The back of the house was divided into two halves. On the right, there was a bedroom and on the left the kitchen.

Jonesie went straight to the larder which turned out to be a cupboard with wooden shelves sparsely filled with dried beans, some rice, an old piece of cheese and some bananas. Jonesie took the piece of cheese and cut it in half while Jamesie helped himself to an overripe banana.

"Who sleeps in there?" he enquired with his mouth full.

"My parents."

"So, where do you sleep?"

"Upstairs, in the attic. Come on, I'll show you."

Leading Jamesie back into the main room, Jonesie pointed at a hatch in the ceiling.

"There, that's the attic," he said. Then, he propped up a wooden ladder against the hatch and began to climb the rungs, urging Jamesie to follow suit.

At the top of the ladder, Jamesie popped his head through the hatch and quickly scanned the dark space around him. The room was totally bare except for four palliasses that lay directly on the dusty floorboards. A small window at the far end of the wall provided the only light inside, chiselled by wooden beams that served as a depository for the few belongings the children had. The sight dismayed him. He had never seen such a poor home before. This was not much of a home, he thought, getting down the ladder again. No wonder Jonesie wanted to try his luck by going out to sea. The thought made him think of his own circumstance. He had never talked about his past or even how he had found himself alone in a strange place, and worst of all in a strange country. He was surprised that Jonesie had never asked him about it, but his adopted brother was probably worried about his own situation, fearing the wrath of his parents when they would discover that he had run away. On the other hand, they might never find out. Jonesie always had a good repartee to explain away whichever irregular situation he happened to find himself in, just like that time when he had declared on the spot that they were brothers, lest they be separated.

"Come on," Jonesie said, interrupting his thoughts. "Let's go to the market. We might be able to catch a bread bun or an apple that just happens to roll off a stand as we pass by." He winked at his little friend.

Together, they sauntered down the street and made their way towards Market Square. They ambled leisurely around wooden trestles groaning under the weight of enticing displays of edible and sometimes live merchandise. With their eyes bulging with hunger, they devoured the mouth-watering pyramids of fruit and candy. They licked their lips as they imagined a bread roll, a juicy apple or a piece of candy crunching noisily between their teeth. As they passed the baker's stand, Jonesie made a subtle nod of the head and winked. Jamesie understood the signal straight away. The boys started fighting on the spot. In a deliberate move, Jonesie pushed Jamesie towards the alluring display and in a simultaneous gesture, both boys extended an arm and swiped a round loaf of bread each before sprinting away. Within seconds, the baker was on to them.

"Thieves! Thieves!" he shouted. "Arrest those boys!"

At that moment, Constable Hardy, the local policeman, happened to be walking around the food stands wondering what his wife had prepared for his tea. Immediately responding to the baker's cries, he raised his head and rushed in the direction of the two boys. In no time at all, he had collared them and was shaking them like a brace of prized rabbits.

"Well, boys, what have you been up to, hey?"

The baker wagged an angry finger at them and answered on their behalf, "They've stolen my bread! Give me my bread back!"

Quick as a flash, Jonesie took a big bite out of his loaf and said, "There, you can have your rotten loaf back!"

Jamesie did exactly the same with his loaf.

"And you can have mine back too!"

Disgusted, the baker came right up to Jonesie's face and spat, "You're gonna pay for this!"

"I ain't got no money!" Jonesie replied with a cheeky smile.

"Me neither!" Jamesie trumpeted.

"All right, you two," said Constable Hardy. "To the station with me!"

Alerted by the commotion, a crowd of curious onlookers had gathered around them. In amongst them, a woman was seen barging and elbowing her way towards the fractious group. To her shock, she spotted her boy. She hit her hips with her fists and shouted, "Billy Jones! Where have you been all this time?" Then, turning to Constable Hardy, she asked, "What has he done this time?"

"He's stolen a loaf of bread, Ma'm."

At these words, Mrs Jones grabbed Jonesie by the ear and scolded, "You're coming home with me, young man, and this time, I'll make sure you don't go anywhere!"

"Ouch! Ouch!" wailed Jonesie.

"What about my money?" the baker requested.

"You'll get your money when my husband comes home!" she replied sharply before dragging away her wayward son.

"What about me?" Jamesie cried out. "Jonesie! Jonesie! Please don't leave me!"

The policeman, still holding the young boy firmly, said in a deep voice, "You, young man, you're coming with me."

"No! No!" Jamesie cried, kicking wildly and punching the policeman with his little fists to try and free himself from his strong grip. "I want to go with him... he's my brother!"

Constable Hardy looked askance at the boy. He had dealt with the Jones boy before and he knew for a fact that he did not have a brother that looked like the little beggar he held in his hand. However, he wanted to be sure.

"Mrs Jones!" he hailed. "Is this lad one of yours?"

Mrs Jones stopped dead in her tracks, still holding Jonesie by the ear, threw a backward glance at the constable and decreed quite flatly, "I've never seen him in my life. Of course, he's not one of mine."

"Right, my lad," Constable Hardy stated firmly. "It's to the station for you."

***

The plight of the ship boys soon reached Captain Jennings's ears. Without a minute to lose, the captain made straight for the police station.

"I understand you're holding a member of my crew here."

"We've got several ruffians in our cells today, if that's what you mean. I don't know," he added, shaking his head in slight exasperation, "as soon as they hit port, they don't seem to be able to control themselves; they drink too much, start fights and make a bloody nuisance of themselves. Anyway, what's his name?" the policeman on duty enquired.

"Jamesie… his name's Jamesie."

"Is that his first or second name?"

"I don't know… I only know him as *Jamesie*."

"So, he's a member of your crew but you don't know his name… You should take better care of your men, Captain."

"He's not a grown-up man, he's a ship's boy, about nine or ten… Apparently, he was caught stealing a loaf of bread…"

"Ah!" the constable exclaimed as if he had suddenly seen the light. "We've got a little ruffian that fits the description. Are you his father?"

"No, but…"

"Have you come to pay his fine, then?"

"A fine? How much is the fine?"

"It's not for me to say. The court will decide."

"The court?" the captain exclaimed. "You're not going to drag that poor little kid through the courts for stealing a piece of bread."

"It may be a piece of bread to you, Captain, but to Howard the baker, it's his livelihood."

"All right. How much do you want? One piece of four?"

The constable shook his head and sneered.

"Okay, I'll give you five."

The constable was beginning to lose patience.

"Are you trying to bribe me, Sir?" he asked in a mildly threatening tone.

"Of course not, Constable," the captain replied while swiftly rummaging through his pockets. He took a coin out and put it on the counter.

"There!" he ejected. "It's a piece of eight."

The constable peered at the coin. He was tempted. As he went to pick it up, the captain slammed his hand down with his own hand.

"You want it?" he asked enticingly. "Then, go and fetch my ship boy."

After a few seconds of consideration, the constable left his desk. Moments later, he returned with the boy. Without waiting for the captain to speak, he quickly snatched the gold coin that was still lying on the counter and put it in his pocket.

"Captain! Captain!" a little voice greeted him.

"Well, Jamesie. You're lucky the constable was in good humour today or I might not have been able to get you out of here." The captain said in a reproachful tone. "Come on, Jamesie; let's get out of here before he changes his mind."

"Aye, aye, Capt'n!"

Once they were outside, the captain asked, "Why did you do it?"

"I was hungry."

"But you could have paid for the bread. You have money, haven't you?"

Jamesie shook his head.

"What happened to the money I gave you?"

"That's just it, Captain. On the way to Jonesie's house, we stopped at the local store to buy some candy and these boys saw us pay with real money. So when we came out of the shop, they jumped on us and robbed us of everything."

"Well, that was bad luck. What have you learnt from that, though?"

"Not to carry my money all at once?"

"That's right. Put most of it somewhere safe, and only have two or three coins in your pockets at a time. That way, if you get mugged again, the muggers only get away with small change and you're still left with most of your money to live on. Anyway, where's Jonesie now?"

"His mum took him home."

"*His* mum? So, you're not brothers, are you? I always suspected you were not brothers. You're too different, you speak differently and you behave differently. I bet you're not even from Nassau, are you?"

"Well... er... no."

The captain shook his head in disbelief.

"Where are you from, Jamesie, and where are your parents?"

Jamesie shrugged his shoulders. He seemed reluctant to speak about himself and in order to avoid further scrutiny, he answered the captain with another question.

"Capt'n, will you take care of me? I'm scared to be on my own."

"Well, I'll have to now, won't I? And the first thing you and I are going to do is to go to a tavern so you can eat a good meal."

At the prospect of a proper meal, Jamesie's face lit up with a beaming smile.

"Thanks, Capt'n."

The captain took Jamesie to the *Cock 'n Bull*.

Already busy in the kitchen, Mona Tisdale heard someone call.

"Good afternoon, Mrs Tisdale."

"Ah, it's you, Captain Jennings!" she replied jovially. "What can I do for you?"

The captain pushed Jamesie in front of him and said, "This young lad is in desperate need of food. What have you got cooking on the range?"

"Well, you're in luck. I've got a delicious rabbit stew on the go, and to make it even tastier, I've even added some sausages I had left over. Would you like to try some?"

"That sounds delicious," the captain replied.

"All right, dinner for two, then. Some ale, Captain?"

"Well, for me, yes, but some cider for the young lad."

Mona Tisdale noted the order before disappearing into the kitchen.

When she returned, the captain held her back.

"Mrs Tisdale, could you do me a huge favour, please?"

Mrs Tisdale rolled her eyes, hit herself on the side with her fist and said, "Captain, why do you always come to me when you need a favour?" she asked in mock exasperation. "I hope you're not after the *Merchant Maiden* because she's being refitted, and we're still waiting for you to bring us back the *Kingston*."

"No, I'm not after one of your ships, Mrs Tisdale. I've got this young lad here who needs somewhere to stay until my ship's ready. Would you mind looking after him? Now you don't need to worry about money, I will pay for his keep."

Mona Tisdale stole a quick look at Jamesie and said, "I'm sorry, Captain, I've already got half of your crew staying here. I don't have any room left."

"I'm sure he won't mind sharing."

"But I can't. There's already four in each room as it is."

Jamesie looked at her with pleading eyes, and in those eyes, Mona Tisdale saw a little boy who could have been one of her sons. So, after a brief moment of reflection, she conceded, "Well, I suppose, there's the attic. Mind, it'll cost you… two groats a day for his food and lodging."

"That's a deal, then?"

"Aye, payable in advance, if you don't mind, Captain!"

The captain threw his purse on the table which Mona Tisdale immediately grabbed.

"What about the *Kingston*, Captain? When are we going to get her back?"

The captain stared at the innkeeper, lost for words. He could not bring himself to tell her that her ship lay at the bottom of the ocean, fiercely guarded by a pool of nurse sharks.

"Don't worry, Mrs Tisdale," he tried to reassure her. "You will get your ship back. I'm due to sail in about a month's time and once in Bristol, I shouldn't have too much problem recruiting a new crew to man the *Kingston*."

"Well, make sure you pick your crew carefully, Captain. I don't want some unscrupulous brigands stealing her from me."

Chapter Twenty-Eight
Old Shack of a House…

A month later, almost to the day, Captain Jennings surveyed his ship with an easy eye. The *Redemption* looked splendid with her new mizzenmast. Around him, the quay heaved with people, mostly sailors and mariners in charge of refitting their own ships. Savouring to the last the buoyant atmosphere, the captain smiled with delight at the sight of the hustle and bustle that always preluded an imminent departure. Standing on the prow of his ship, he listened with pure joy to the shipmates whose cries mingled with the loud hailing of men checking cables, sails and other essential equipment. Their voices were often drowned by the deafening noise of barrels being rolled along the cobblestones, and the rumbling and creaking of wheels from rusty carts busy ferrying misshapen bales and mysterious cargos.

Now, it was time to round up his crew for he hoped to set sail in the next few days.

"Griffiths!" he hailed. "Have we got most of the crew counted for?"

"Almost," the reply came. "We're still missing Warren and Harris, though…"

"Well, there's a surprise! Mitchell, go and see if you can find them!" the captain ordered.

"Aye, aye, Capt'n!"

At that moment, Jamesie rushed to the captain with a worried look on his face. "Capt'n! What about Jonesie? He's not here yet. We can't go without him."

The captain smiled at the boy. "Don't worry, Jamesie. We're not about to go yet. There's still plenty of time for him to join us."

Not satisfied with the captain's answer, Jamesie decreed in a determined voice, "I'm gonna go and get him!"

Anxious about his friend, Jamesie turned on his heels and ran noisily down the gangplank. When he landed on the quay, he waved to the captain.

"Capt'n! Don't leave without us!"

"In that case, make sure you're back before the end of the week!"

"Aye, aye, Captain!"

***

Jamesie walked down East Bay Street, confident that he would be able to find Jonesie's house again, even though he had only been there once before. When he spotted the small general store, he knew that he was on the right way to Shirley Street. He walked on nervously. There were no street kids hanging around the store. He let out a huge sigh of relief and proceeded down the street with an easy heart and a spring in his step, already rejoicing at seeing his brethren again. Halfway down the street, he stopped outside a house which had the overhang around its walls and a small window on the first floor. That's the attic's window, he recalled. He knocked on the door. There was no answer. He knocked on the door again, louder this time, and waited. Still, nothing stirred inside the house. Taking a few steps back, he looked up to the attic's window and shouted, "Jonesie! Jonesie! It's me Jamesie! Are you coming out?"

At the front of next door's house, an old man was dozing in an old creaky rocking chair. When Jamesie shouted his friend's name, he woke up with a start.

"What do you want, kid?" he grumbled.

"I've come for my friend, Billy Jones. Do you know where he is?"

"You're wasting your time, kid, they've gone."

Jamesie stared at the old man, unsure of what to make of his reply.

"Gone? You mean… they've gone somewhere for the day…"

"No," the old man cut in. "Gone away."

"Gone away? But where? When are they coming back?"

"They've gone back to good old England. Aye, that's what they said."

Jamesie could not believe his ears. He looked at the deserted house and sighed heavily, then threw a quizzical glance at the old man again, wondering whether to believe him or not. There was no doubt about it, the house stood silent and empty. No point in hanging around, he thought. He gave a little wave to the old man.

"Thanks, Mister."

Devastated, Jamesie dug his hands deep in his pockets and started walking back towards the harbour, his head bowed low, dragging his feet and kicking loose stones all along the way. For the second time in his life, he felt terribly alone. A painful pang of loneliness hit him right in the stomach, a sensation he had experienced once before, when he had missed his ship and been left behind, by accident. Indeed, nobody had noticed him sneaking out of the ship to buy one last provision of candies before the long voyage back to England and when he had rushed back to the harbour, he had stood there, in total shock, clutching his paper bag of sweeties against his little heart. The ship had gone… and she had gone without him. At first, he had been too dumbstruck to react, and when he had tried to speak, his lips had let out muffled calls of desperation and despair. After the initial shock, his voice had returned and he had stood on the quay, screaming and shouting at the people he loved, "Mother! Father! Wait for me, wait for me!" But to no avail. His frantic calls had remained unheard, deafened by the wind and drowned by the sea that now stood like an abyss between him and the protective cocoon he had always known. For what seemed to be ages, he had stood there, silent, with only tears running down his pale cheeks.

Then, just as he felt the loneliest boy in the whole world, this young lad had accosted him.

"Hi! You like looking at ships? Me too. One day, I'm gonna be on one of them ships."

Young James quickly wiped his tears and looked at the lad. He was a tad smaller than himself, and his long dark hair, tussled by the wind, revealed tanned features and big brown eyes sparkling with excitement.

"My!" the stranger exclaimed. "You been crying?"

"Of course I've not been crying! I've just got something in my eye!" James retorted rather aggressively.

The boy smirked.

"I can tell you've been crying… you little sissy!"

Immediately, James put up his little fists and spat, "I've not been crying and I'm not a sissy!"

"Hey!" the lad exclaimed, raising his hands as a sign of surrender. "Take it easy. I was only teasing. Anyway, what's your name?"

"What do you care?" James growled.

"Well, I'm Billy Jones but everyone calls me Jonesie," the lad said, tendering a friendly hand.

James scowled at the lad, not knowing whether to accept his kind

286

gesture. Eventually, after a moment of hesitation, he extended his hand too and said, "I'm James."

"Oh, great! You can be Jamesie," the lad declared with a beaming smile.

At that moment, a distant church bell struck the hour.

"Damn it!" Jonesie cursed. "I've got to go. See you!"

Immediately, young James panicked.

"When? Where?"

"At the harbour! I often come to the harbour. Bye!"

As good as his word, Jonesie returned to the harbour almost every day and when he realised that his new friend did not have a home to go to, he felt sorry that he could not help for they were rather poor themselves. However, he was not about to let down his new friend and the two spent a lot of time together watching mouth-watering provisions being loaded onto ships. And when they were not busy pilfering food from awaiting cargos and being chased by angry porters, they talked excitedly about sailors, mariners… and pirates… yeah, pirates with their plentiful tales of glittering gold and fabulous treasures. Then one day, both came up with the same idea at the very same time. Why didn't they board one of the ships? After all, with all that food being hoarded on, they were sure never to go hungry again. And so, before they could be spotted, they climbed on board the *Redemption*, declaring with bravado to the stunned Captain Jennings, "We want to be pirates!"

This last thought made him smile. His fears began to subside and suddenly, he started running like the wind, determined not to stop until he had reached the safety of the harbour.

As soon as he caught the familiar sight of the forest of masts denuded of their sails, his spirit lifted. The exciting buzz of the frantic activities going on around the tall ships made him feel that he was no longer alone, and when he spotted the *Redemption*, he felt an overwhelming sense of belonging. Young *Jamesie* was no longer the accidental orphan, but a fully-fledged member of Captain Jennings's crew and suddenly, he felt a warm glow enwrap his lonesome heart, a wonderful feeling that made him smile.

Chapter Twenty-Nine
The Wooden Box

Meanwhile, Captain Jennings had one more important errand to do before setting off for England. As the evening beckoned, he began to make his way to Government House for one last time.

The striking colours of a late April sky, all streaked with ribbons of red and black clouds, shrouded his thoughts in a mellow mood. It had been a whole eighteen months since his timely escape from Cove Island and at this particular moment, despite all his misfortunes, he felt blessed and lucky to be alive. He had long stopped thinking about Mary, afraid that thinking back on his pirate days would only bring him more bad luck and misfortune. So, he looked firmly ahead, thinking about his next voyage, planning his next mission, and more importantly, hoping for his safe return, here in Nassau where he would be able to start a new life, on land, with a refined young woman at his side. As he thought about it, he saw Lady Sarah's smiling face fleeting before his eyes which instantly brought back that wonderful feeling of a warm heart filled with love. He quickened his step to reach the house as fast as possible.

At the door, he was greeted by the young butler, Johnny Canoe, who could not hide his joy at seeing the captain again.

"How lovely to see you again, Captain!" he welcomed with his usual beaming smile. Then, he tilted his head sideways, towards the inside of the house, and declared in a hushed tone, "Lady Sarah needs cheering up. She's so lonesome."

The captain understood. He smiled.

"Thanks, Johnny."

The butler led the captain towards the veranda. On their way there, their path was crossed by Lady Charlotte who had just swept down with great affectation from the marble staircase.

"Ah! Captain!" she hailed as soon as she spotted the captain. Then, she turned to the butler. "Leave the Captain with me, Johnny. I'll show him in," she said, dismissing the young butler.

Johnny Canoe bowed his head and replied "Yes Ma'm," before withdrawing to his own quarters. As soon as he was gone, Lady Charlotte resumed, "Thank goodness you're here, Captain! We're in desperate want of cheerful company. You see, my brother is constantly cooped up in his study sorting out diplomatic affairs and at loggerheads with William who's determined to leave home, my sister-in-law is in complete despair over her daughter's refusal to cheer up and as for Lady Sarah herself… well… what can you do with a young head intent on listening to her heart and nothing else?"

The captain nodded with sympathy and gave a convivial smile, but said nothing.

"I don't know," Lady Charlotte continued. "This is all getting ever so boring for me." Then, she looked at the captain with a cheeky smile. "You wouldn't have a spare bunk on your ship, would you?" she asked in jest.

The captain let out a small chuckle. "I'd love to have you, Lady Charlotte, but I fear the primitive conditions on board and the company of grunting men lusting after your venerable self would probably prove too much for you," he proffered.

"Good Lord, what a picture!" The grand dame chortled, rolling her eyes in mock horror. "I suppose I am forced to resign myself to my singular status… for ever till eternity. There are not many men worthy of my station on the island. However, one has to be thankful for small mercies and thank goodness we have you, Captain."

"It's extremely gracious of you to say so, Lady Charlotte."

"Don't be mistaken, Captain. I'm not being gracious at all; I'm simply speaking out the truth. You seem a man of principles to me, and it's not an easy thing to be on an island like this one, where it's a free for all. Anyway, you're staying for dinner I hope."

"I'd love to but…"

"Well, I'm delighted to hear it," Lady Charlotte interrupted, refusing to hear anything beyond a contrary 'but'. "I'm so glad you're here. I'm sure you have a few more riveting stories to tell us."

Without bothering to pause to catch her breath, she called in a high-pitched voice, "Johnny! Johnny!"

"Yes, Ma'm," the butler responded, emerging from a side door.

"Make sure there's an extra place set at the table for the captain. He's having dinner with us," she informed him.

"Yes, Ma'm!" Johnny replied with gusto, clearly pleased to see the captain welcomed again at Government House.

Overtaken by the events, the captain could do nothing but smile. With Lady Charlotte bustling with excitement by his side, he walked pensively towards the veranda where William was already enjoying a pre-dinner drink, ensconced in one of the cane armchairs.

"Good to see you, Captain," he immediately greeted with a welcoming smile.

"Likewise," the captain reciprocated, shaking his hand.

Lady Charlotte looked around.

"Where's everybody?" she enquired.

"Father is finishing some correspondence. Mother's gone to see how things are progressing in the kitchen and Sarah's gone for a stroll in the garden. Cheers," he greeted, raising his gin.

Captain Jennings threw a quick glance around the garden, then turned to Lady Charlotte and asked, "Would you mind if I went into the garden?" "Not at all, Captain. Please, do," she replied cheerfully. "Johnny will ring the bell when dinner's ready. Now then, I think I'm going to have a gin too. William dear, would you mind pouring my drink?"

***

Outside, the temperature was still hot. Captain Jennings stood on the edge of the veranda, looking out for Lady Sarah. Everywhere, the garden was shaded with banana, lemon, grapefruit and stumpy palm trees which emanated a fusion of aromatic scents that assaulted the senses with their bitter sweet smell. At the far end, towards the most exposed side of the garden, a cluster of avocado trees, devastated by the last hurricane, lay with their uprooted trunks leaning against the garden wall, still waiting to be salvaged. The ground was covered in thick plush grass that extended all around the house. Just as he was about to step into the garden, a familiar voice called, "Good evening, Captain! Lovely to see you again, though I understand it won't be for long."

The captain turned around and smiled.

"Good evening, Lady Whetstone Rogers. Delighted to meet you again," he greeted warmly.

At that moment, the bell rang.

"Goodness!" Lady Whetstone Rogers exclaimed. "I didn't have a chance to get my pre-dinner drink. Never mind. Come on Captain, come and sit next to me and tell me all about your next expedition."

"Thank you, my Lady."

The captain bowed and prayed Lady Whetstone Rogers to step before him. She seemed unusually welcoming and talkative, considering the reservations she had for him. On the other hand, he could not help noticing that the more he talked about his imminent departure, the more she seemed to perk up.

Behind them, a sudden rush of crinoline made them turn their heads.

"Ah, there you are, darling," Lady Whetstone Rogers greeted cheerfully. "We have a lovely surprise. Captain Jennings's here and he's going to have dinner with us, isn't that nice?"

Lady Sarah threw a shy glance at the captain and smiled. Then, the party took their places around the table. There was one notable absentee, however, the Governor.

"He probably didn't hear the bell." William deduced. "He seems to become more and more hard of hearing these days, especially when I ask him for money."

Far from sympathising with her absentee brother, Lady Charlotte declared in a loud chuckle, "I told him before he should get one of those brass gongs; that way he'd be sure to hear it!"

Lady Whetstone Rogers smiled delicately, dabbed her lips with her serviette and called, "Johnny, would you mind calling his Lordship? He obviously does not realise it's dinner time."

"Yes, Ma'm."

A few minutes later, the Governor appeared, grunting under his breath. He threw a quick glance around the table and said, "Sorry, I'm late. All this State business is getting far too complicated. I'm supposed to get rid of those wretched pirates but I haven't got enough ships or enough hands for that matter that can be trusted not to steal the ship!"

William looked at his father and ventured, "Well, as I said before, I wouldn't mind going myself…"

"Going where?" Aunt Charlotte interrupted, cocking her head to one side to facilitate hearing.

"Going out to sea, Aunt Charlotte. Do you realise that I've been living on this island all my life and I've never been out to sea except for a quick paddle around the bay. Even my sister's been further than I have!"

"And I wouldn't recommend it, William, believe you me!" Lady Sarah quipped.

"That's right," their mother acquiesced. "It's far too dangerous. Besides, you've got your studies to think about."

"What good is it to have my head buried in books when we have a bunch of lawless brigands threatening to take over the place?"

"That's exactly why you should learn all about law and order, Son," his father reprised sternly. "You have to learn to do things by the book because the rule of law will give you the power to act. Without it, you'll be no better off than those lawless scoundrels."

William slouched back in his chair and grunted in frustration. Quite flustered by the uneasy tension, Aunt Charlotte looked around the table with an inconsequential smile and declared, "Well, I think I'm going to have another glass… more wine Johnny!"

**

After dinner, the Governor and the captain disappeared into the office. Coming straight to the point, the Governor unlocked a draw concealed under his desk and retrieved an oblong casket made of mahogany and secured with brass edgings and corners nailed into the wood. On top of it, there was also an ornate brass cross embedded into the wood.

"There you have it, Captain, the *Cross of Madeira*. It looks a bit like a wooden bible, doesn't it?"

The captain picked up the box to examine it.

"As you can see, it's completely sealed," the Governor continued. "No one can open it to see what's inside, not even me. I had the box especially made by a very skilled craftsman who worked down the cellar here in complete secrecy and before he sealed all the panels together, I placed the cross inside the box myself. You see it looks just like one solid piece of wood, very clever, wouldn't you say? So, it's over to you now. Your mission is to take it to the Admiralty who will arrange for its safe return to the King of Spain. However, should anyone steal it from you and replace it with a copy, there is an easy way to tell whether it's the genuine article or not. May I?"

The Governor took the box back from the captain and explained,

"Underneath one of these metal brackets, the name of the cross is engraved into the wood and only you and I know this — and of course old Smithy who designed the box for me, but I know I can trust him — so it will be very easy to detect a forgery, should you lose sight of the box."

"Rather smart of you, Sir."

"Well, I wish I could claim credit for it, but it was old Smithy's idea," the Governor conceded. "Now, you're probably aware that you will need to explain how you came upon it to the gentlemen of the Admiralty... and you must expect their next question which is bound to be, where's the rest of it?"

The captain grabbed the box and said, "I know. Unfortunately, there's not much I can say about it other than what I've already told them."

"Well, whatever you say, you're going to have to come clean. We don't want the Admiralty to think that we are part of a conspiracy to defraud the King of Spain... or you'll never make it back to these shores."

"I'm fully aware of that, Sir. I've already experienced their rigorous style of questioning, which is all the more reason for me to make sure I can justify each of my actions. In the meantime, I shall look after the cross as if it were my own..."

"No, Captain, not as if it were your own... but as if it was your *life*," the Governor cut in.

"Well, I suppose it is," the captain agreed with a wry smile. "Good night, Sir."

"Good night and goodbye, Captain. I wish you the best of luck."

In a hurry to return to his ship, the captain made his excuses and left the Governor pacing his office anxiously. Before leaving the house, however, he made his way to the veranda. It was deserted. On his way out, he met Johnny Canoe along the corridor.

"Ah, Johnny!" he hailed with relief. "Do you know where everybody is?"

"They've gone for their after-dinner walk."

"To the beach?"

"I can't be certain but that's where they usually go."

"Thanks, Johnny. Goodbye, dear boy."

"Will we see you back soon, Captain?"

The captain was already rushing down the main path.

"Who can tell...? Take care of yourself, Johnny."

"Will do, Captain."

As he turned around to wave goodbye, the last thing the captain saw was Johnny Canoe's beaming smile.

***

The captain pondered for a while whether he should search for the ladies, but at the last minute, he decided against, for in his mind, he wanted to leave with a picture of Lady Sarah happy and smiling rather than sad and forlorn.

Back on the *Redemption*, the first person he came across was young Jamesie who was sitting on the deck, throwing bits of bones at random.

"Hi, Jamesie. Glad to see you back on board."

The boy smiled then sighed. Noticing his less than enthusiastic response, the captain looked around and asked, "Where's your mate, Jonesie?"

"Don't know, Capt'n. I went to his house but he wasn't there."

"So, he's not coming, then?"

"But he wanted to. I know he did, he told me so."

"Well, if he doesn't turn up soon, we'll have to leave without him."

"Oh no, Capt'n. We can't do that! When are we leaving?"

"Sometime tomorrow, depending on the tide and the wind."

"Can't we wait one more day, just in case Jonesie turns up?"

"I'm afraid, Jamesie, it's not entirely up to me. One day you'll understand that with sailing, you have to go with the wind, not with the crew, that's why it's so important to be ready and prepared, always."

Jamesie let out an audible sigh, then carried on throwing the pieces of bone nonchalantly. He wanted to stay on the deck in case he spotted his mate. Alas. it was getting late and he struggled to keep his eyes open. Every now and again, he felt his head fall on his chest, heavy with sleep. Eventually, unable to stay awake any longer, he gave up his night vigil and dragged himself to the cockboat. He lifted the canvas and was about to step in when he noticed a dark shape curled up inside. His heart jumped. Barely able to contain his joy and excitement, he tentatively poked the sleeping mass.

"Jonesie!" he cried out.

The body moaned and stirred.

"Jonesie! Wake up, it's me, Jamesie!"

"What?" a sleepy voice answered back.

"What are you doing here?"

Looking bewildered, Jonesie sat up and stared back at Jamesie, rubbing his eyes.

"Why did you wake me up?"

"I thought you were not coming. I went to your house but there was no one there, and the old man next door said you'd gone back to England."

"What?" Jonesie exclaimed, thoroughly confused.

"Aye! That's what the old man said."

"My parents haven't gone to England. It's too far. They've gone to South Carolina to look for a job there."

"And you didn't go with them?"

"Well, obviously not," Jonesie replied in a sarcastic tone. After a brief pause, he finally confessed, "I ran away."

"Good on you, Jonesie!" Jamesie enthused, so happy to be reunited with his brethren. "We're sailing tomorrow."

"I know. That's why I'd like to get some sleep."

Jamesie clambered inside the cockboat and fought for a piece of the blanket.

"I'm so glad you're here, Jonesie. I was beginning to feel quite lonely without you."

"Shut up and go to sleep!"

Chapter Thirty
En Route to England

The following morning, the first thing Captain Jennings did was to ask Griffiths, his quartermaster, to check in the crew. A short while later, Griffiths was ready to report back to the captain.

"There are thirty-five hands on board, Captain, including the two ship's boys."

"*Two* ship's boys? So Jonesie's turned up. That's good. Thanks, Griffiths. Now, get some men to check the amount of provisions, drinks and water… and please, don't ask Warren or Harris to check the spruce beer, you know what they're like; and don't bother looking for rum; there should be none on board and if you find any, confiscate it at once and pour it overboard. We have a very important mission to accomplish and I don't want it sabotaged by some drunken idiots."

"Aye, aye, Capt'n."

***

The *Redemption* left port just before midday, in late June 1723. Lost in deep thoughts, Captain Jennings stood on the poop deck while he stared at the vanishing coastline which gradually faded into a distant piece of land, small and barely noticeable in the vastness of the sea. He watched Hastings, his helmsman, manoeuvre skilfully through the treacherous waters, knowing that shallows and submerged sandbanks had not always been accurately marked on the navigational charts, sending many a ship to an early watery grave. Thanks to the strong westerly wind, the voyage from Nassau to England often took a week less than the opposite route, and the captain reckoned that if the wind kept up, they should reach mainland England in about a month's time.

On board, Connor was in charge of the rigging, seconded by Big Mitch; Hastings steered the big wheel; old hands checked and cleaned their weapons while supervising the new hands carrying out essential chores to keep all the decks clean and tidy. Down below, the gunners checked and polished the cannons, giving them women's names, like 'Mabel' and 'Gertrude'. Among the shipmates hard at work, Warren and Harris swanned around with authority, nose in the air and hands in pocket, like a pair of self-elected marshals surveying a suspicious crowd. As for the ship's boys, when they were not running around playing tag and making a nuisance of themselves, they could be found snuggled up in their very own private abode, the cockboat. Right this minute, just when the boys ran past two shipmates busy scrubbing the deck, upsetting a pail full of water in the process, an irate voice called, "Jonesie! Your turn in the crow's nest!"

The boys stopped dead in their track. Both looked up and saw the quartermaster standing next to the captain on the poop deck. They waited for the captain to show some sympathy but all he did was to say, "Do as you're told, boy."

"And you, Jamesie!" the quartermaster blasted again. "Join these two and start scrubbing the deck."

"Jeez, it ain't fair!" moaned the young lad, dragging his feet and picking up the nearest scrubbing brush.

During the voyage, they passed several ships, each one looking perfectly legitimate with her flag floating proudly and vouching for her port of origin. Only one gave them cause for concern. She began to hoist a Dutch flag, but half way up the mast, it was hurriedly furled down and replaced by another, a French flag.

"Strange," Griffiths remarked to the captain.

Captain Jennings remained silent while keenly observing the movements of the ship. She was moving away from them, heading north-west towards South Carolina and her louche behaviour usually meant one thing, whether a merchant ship or a pirate ship, she wanted to steer clear of trouble. There could only be one reason for it, she was carrying slaves. Relieved by the evasive action taken by the rogue ship, the captain took a deep breath and prayed for the voyage to remain trouble free.

***

A week after they had been at sea, a shipmate went to the captain.

"We're just off Bermuda Island. Are we going back to England?" he enquired.

When he heard the question, the captain realised that he had not yet informed the crew of the purpose of the mission. He summoned the crew on the main deck.

"Gentlemen," he began. "We are engaged in a very special mission, a mission that was entrusted to me by the Governor of Nassau, a mission that is so important and so crucial to the peace-making in our country that if successful, we will be directly responsible for averting another war with Spain."

A loud gasp followed the captain's announcement.

"What do we have to do?" a shipmate asked with a certain degree of anxiety.

"You, as part of the crew, have the vital task of bringing this ship safely back to port. That's all I'm asking from you. So, work hard, look after each other, remain alert and above all, always be ready and prepared to defend our ship against any enemy. We don't want any trouble and we're definitely not looking for war, but should we come under threat, we shall not hesitate to defend ourselves to the last, which is why you must keep your weapons clean and the cannons ready at all time. Is that clear?"

"Aye, aye, Capt'n!" a chorus of voices chanted.

"Where are we sailing to?" a lone voice asked.

"To the port of Bristol."

A murmur of perplexed voices rose from the deck.

"If we're just sailing from one port to another, what makes this voyage so special?" a shipmate ventured to ask.

"That, I'm afraid, I cannot tell you. It's one of those cases where the less you know, the longer you'll live. So, return to your chores and think no more of it. Let us hope for a smooth voyage and may God help us make this mission successful."

At the end of his speech, the captain left the poop deck and retired to his cabin.

Soon, there was a knock on his door.

"Capt'n."

"Yes? Who is it?"

"It's me, Bob Downing."

"What do you want?"

"I've got something to tell you, Capt'n."

"Come in, Downing."

The shipmate came in just as the captain was stowing away something in his trunk. Downing's sharp scouring eyes had caught a glimpse of the object. More to the point, he had seen the glitter of a brass cross encrusted on top of a small wooden box and it took him no time to figure out what it might be.

"What is it you want, Downing?" the captain asked with a little sigh of exasperation.

"I think I know what our special mission is," he started.

"So, what of it?"

"I hope you don't mind me saying…"

"What?" the captain asked curtly, already losing patience.

"Well… You know them rumours that you took the jewels from Black Bart, well me mates reckon that you've probably still got it and that's it there in that box, because we all know that Black Bart raided the galleon that carried the King of Spain's treasure and there's been no trace of it since. Well, like I said before, Capt'n, I've got eight children to feed…"

"You said five last time," interrupted the captain.

"Well, I've been busy, you see…"

"You can't have been *that* busy. You've been at sea most of the time!" the captain reminded him.

"Well, like I said, Capt'n, I've got eight children to feed and I thought… I thought that if I keep my mouth shut about the cross… that perhaps you'd give me…"

Before he could finish his sentence, the captain cut in abruptly. "You're obsessed with that wretched cross! What makes you think I've got it?" the captain shouted in frustration.

"But that's it in there, in'it?" Downing said, pointing at the trunk with a knowing smile.

"Tell me, Downing, if you're that interested in gossip, why didn't you stay on land where's there's a lot more going on, rather than enrol aboard my ship and bloody pester me all the time?"

"Well, I really wanted to get away from me wife… but I thought I'd let you know, Capt'n, there's lots of rumours going around about you and I'd like the opportunity to put them gossipmongers right."

"Get out of here, you scheming little swab, before I give you a feel of the cat o'nine tails! But let me warn you, Downing, I don't want to hear any more bilge about some missing cross or next time we reach port, I'll make sure you never board my ship again, understood? So get out of here or I'll give you fifty lashes for dissention, insubordination and dereliction of duty!"

At the thought of being flogged, Bob Downing beat a hasty retreat and scurried off back on deck, mumbling words of impending doom. "That cross is cursed, Capt'n... and don't say I didn't warn you!" he shouted from the wooden steps.

***

On the main deck, everything was calm with most of the men engaged in rigging the sails, polishing pistols and cutlasses or catching up with their sleep before taking their turn on the nightshift. With the absence of rum on board, Warren and Harris sipped their ration of spruce beer in sheer disgust, lamenting the serious lack of much sterner stuff and arguing among themselves as to which tavern served the best ale or rum. All the while, Downing listened. With his eyes swivelling from side to side, and his shoulders hunched above his neck as if trying to hide his head inside it, he mumbled to himself words he had overheard, just in case they were clues to some invaluable secret.

The Island of Bermuda had long disappeared into the ocean mist and as the *Redemption* entered the north Atlantic drift, the air temperature dropped sharply and the waves, more forceful than ever, pounded the hull, throwing up a cold icy spray upon the decks.

Suddenly, a loud voice from above shouted, "Ship ahoy at stern!"

This was not the first time they had sighted a ship on their voyage, and only a handful of shipmates bothered to move in order to take a look. Griffiths, however, took the long glass to observe the ship which was still several leagues away from them.

Up on the rigging, Connor remarked, "She seems to be gaining on us!"

Griffiths looked again through the long glass and said, "I think I'd better fetch the captain."

Summoned on the poop deck, the captain took a long look at the ship that was trailing behind. Next to him, Jonesie and Jamesie waited for his verdict with bated breath.

"Is it a pirate ship? Is she going to attack us, Capt'n?" Jamesie asked with slight apprehension mixed with great excitement.

The captain did not answer straight away. He kept his eye trained on the unidentified ship until he could discern some detail that would give her away. Was she a harmless merchant sloop or a rogue ship looking for trouble? Finally, still unable to identify the ship properly, the captain nevertheless concluded, "I don't think she's fully laden because she's going too fast for that. So she could be a merchant ship on her way to collect provisions or, I fear, a pirate ship; and if she is, boys, then there's your chance to become pirates," he said in jest. The boys scowled back at him. "I tell you what…" He continued with a wry smile, "we'll trade you in exchange for a safe passage to England, what do you say?"

"You can't do that, Capt'n!" Jonesie exclaimed, quite shocked. "We only said that because we thought most ships were pirate ships…"

"Aye. All we wanted was a bit of adventure," Jamesie cut in.

"All right, lads," the captain said. "We'll see what happens when she gets closer. In the meantime, go back to your chores or you'll have no supper!" he threatened half-heartedly.

"Jeez, it ain't fair. We've always got to work so hard for our supper." Jamesie moaned under his breath.

Overhearing him, the captain quipped, "It'd be far worse if you were on a pirate ship."

Jamesie turned to the captain and shrugged his shoulders. "Well, like I said, I've changed my mind about that."

The captain gave him a friendly pat on the shoulder and declared, "Jamesie, you're not a bad lad, but whether on a pirate ship or any other ship, there's no place for malingerers, so get back to work. However, if you do a good job, I might have a little surprise for you later."

"Oh really? What kind of surprise?"

"Well, if I told you, it wouldn't be a surprise, would it? So, get back to work."

"Yeah… all right."

The captain watched the young lad run back onto the main deck where Jonesie was waiting for him; after which, he turned to Griffiths, handed him the long glass and said, "You take over. Keep a close eye on her and as soon as you detect something, send for me, will you?"

"Aye, Capt'n."

***

It was not long before someone came knocking on the door. Without waiting for a reply, Griffiths popped his head round and said, "I can just make out her flag, Captain, though I cannot identify it."

"All right, Griffiths. I'm coming."

***

Peering intently through the long glass, Captain Jennings quickly caught sight of the flag. What's more, he knew exactly whose it was.

"Good grief! It's the Governor's flag!" he revealed with some excitement.

"You mean… the Governor of Nassau's flag?" Griffiths reprised.

Wholly absorbed in the observation of the ship, the captain stated, "It could be a ruse, though. Those miscreants will stop at nothing. Griffiths, give the order to everyone to stand by their posts."

"What about us? Where should we go?" Jonesie enquired with trepidation.

The captain thought for a moment. He took another look at the other ship, scoured his own main deck and decreed, "The safest place for you two, boys, will be in the crow's nest. That way, you'll be above the firing line, so at the first sign of trouble, I want you to get up there, all right?"

"Aye, aye, Capt'n!"

Following this, the sound of orders being given out echoed all around the ship.

"All hands, on deck! All hands, on deck!"

Immediately, the decks rumbled and groaned as hammering feet thundering on the salty wood shook the tranquil air. Men hailed each other with a sudden note of urgency in their voices. Among the total mayhem, the ship's boys stood in the way of sailors rushing to their stations. Then, when a semblance of calm returned, they heard a voice call out to them. It was Warren who was at present leaning against the bulwarks.

"Come here boys!"

"Why?" Jamesie queried.

"You're in the way there. Come here, I'm going to teach you how to fish."

"Why?" Jonesie asked. "We don't want to fish. It's boring."

"You want something for your supper, don't you? Besides, you're gonna get even more bored standing around for hours doing nothing. Come on, come here. I'll show you what to do."

Warren handed them a fishing line.

"What's that horrible thing at the end?" Jamesie asked with his mouth upturned in disgust.

"It's a fish head. Why? You want it?" Warren joked.

"Yuck!" Jamesie reacted.

Ignoring the boy's reaction, Warren continued to coach them.

"It's better if you both hold on to the rod because if a big fish grabs the bait, it'll pull the rod clean off your hands or take you with it, so make sure you both hold on tightly to it, and when you feel something bite, put your feet against the bulwark to get more leverage, all right lads?"

"Aye, aye, Sir."

"*Sir…*" Warren parroted with a proud smile. "They called me '*sir*'. I like it," he said, ruffling the boys' hair with a rough hand.

On the ship, all was quiet. The captain and his quartermaster stood firmly on the stern, in silence and with their eyes fixed on the ship that was following behind them. Connor and big Mitch bustled around the rigging, checking the sails and the positions of each rigger. Hastings concentrated wholly on steering the ship. Down in the galley, Cook was busy checking his pots and pans to make sure no food would be spilled, should there be a rough encounter. On the gun deck, the gunners loaded the cannons and stood at the ready, next to them. Everyone else not assigned to a particular post clustered around the main deck, waiting for the next order, with among them Bob Downing, the racketeer, and Alistair McKay, the prophet of doom.

All of a sudden, the sound of a struggle came from the bulwark.

"There's something on the line!" one of the boys shouted.

"Reel it in. Come on, reel it in!" Warren shouted back.

"We can't. It's too heavy!"

"Right, let me help."

Warren placed himself behind the boys. With both hands, he grabbed the top of the rod and pulled as hard as he could, reeling the line in at the same time.

"Come on, lads, you need to pull harder!" he said through his clenched teeth.

"We are! We are!"

Suddenly, the line gave in, sending the trio crashing onto the deck at the same time as a huge wriggly creature flew through the air and landed squarely on Mackay's head. Everyone burst out laughing, it was a large octopus.

"Get that thing off! Get that thing off me head!" McKay screamed in terror, jittering on the spot in total hysteria.

Rather than feeling sorry for the poor beggar, Warren stared at him bemused. Then, rolling his eyes wide and adopting a dramatic tone of voice, he chanted, "It's the man with eight arms. We are doomed, we're all doomed!"

The slimy creature slid off Mackay's head and slithered onto the deck helplessly. At this point, the captain intervened.

"Warren! Get that thing off the deck and throw it back into the sea."

"Why me?"

"Don't argue. Just do it," the captain told him firmly.

Attracted by the bizarre spectacle, the shipmates formed a wide circle around Warren. From there, they egged him on to pick up the hapless creature, with his mate Harris shouting louder than anyone else, daring him to use his bare hands, but Warren would have none of it. Using the end of the fishing rod, he prodded the octopus in an attempt to pick it up but each time, the slimy body slipped and slithered back onto the deck. Exasperated by his clumsiness, big Mitch pushed his way through the spectating crowd, grabbed hold of one of the tentacles and hurled the sea creature high above the men — who instinctively ducked their heads — back into the sea. Cheers of approval welcomed the swift removal of the animal.

Relieved, the captain shouted his orders.

"Right, everyone, the show's over. Back to your stations!"

Immediately after, he returned to the stern to resume his observation of the pursuing ship. She was now less than two leagues away. Griffiths stood impassively next to him.

"I can't see any signs of threat," he admitted.

"No… but that's the pirates' tactic, isn't it? I've even seen them dressed up as women to avoid suspicions. Best be on our guards, just in case, because if she turns out to be Black Bobby's flagship, we're in for a good fight."

"God I hope it's not." Griffiths sighed.

Several hours later, the ghost ship sailed a mere league away in the wake of the *Redemption*. Captain Jennings took another look through the long glass and decided to hold firm his orders.

"Griffiths, go round the ship and make sure everyone is where they should be, and tell the gunners to be ready to fire. Jonesie and Jamesie, up the crow's nest, now! Connor and Mitchell, get your men down here and make sure they're all armed! Everybody, check your weapons!"

"Are we going into battle?" Bob Downing asked.

"No. We're getting ready for the Mardi Gras carnival," the captain riled sarcastically. "What do you think? Come on, get a move on!"

"Aye, aye Capt'n!" Downing answered, running back and forth, trying to remember where he was supposed to be.

Back on the stern, Griffiths noted, "If she gets any closer, she's going to cut the wind off our sails, and before we know it, she'll be onto us. The good thing though is that from that position, she can't fire at us."

"Neither can we," the captain remarked bluntly.

Suddenly, both men strained their eyes at the same time on the other ship for, on her prow, they thought they had spotted a figure gesticulating wildly.

"What's that?" Griffiths queried.

"Quick! Pass me the long glass!"

The captain peered into the long glass, then passed it straight back to his quartermaster. "Griffiths, take a look."

"By the power of thunder!" he exclaimed. "It looks as if someone's waving at us."

"That's what I thought. But don't be fooled, Griffiths, it's all part of pirates' tactics."

"I can read her name, Captain. It's the... *Ma-ry-land*."

"But... but that's the Governor's ship!" the captain exclaimed. He grabbed the long glass from Griffiths. "Good Grief! Would you believe... I think... er... that looks like William... yes, it is William!"

"Who?"

"The Governor's son. Right, Griffiths, tell the men they can relax now and give the orders to reef the sails so that she can catch us up."

***

A while later, the *Maryland* sided with the *Redemption* and planks were thrown across their bulwarks so that both crews could exchange greetings.

"Captain! Can me and Jonesie go and explore the *Maryland*?" Jamesie asked.

"Wait a minute. I need to speak to her captain, first."

Before he could make a move, however, William had already crossed the plank and was this minute jumping on board the *Redemption*.

"Hi, Captain Jennings! Great to see you!" he enthused, grabbing the captain's hand and shaking it energetically.

"William! What are you doing here? Your head should be buried in your law books!" the captain remonstrated with a smile.

"I know. But I'm old enough to make my own decisions. Father told me about your special mission and I thought you could do with an escort. Come aboard, I'll introduce you to our captain."

The two men jumped aboard the *Maryland* where a tall figure stood proudly by the main mast. As soon as he saw him, the captain stopped dead in his tracks and stared at the man in total shock.

"Why! Er... Hum... Humphreys?" he stuttered, unable to believe his eyes. "Is that really you? But I thought..."

"Nice to see you again, Captain Jennings," Humphreys greeted with a broad smile. "And no, you're not dreaming. It's really me, Luke Humphreys."

William stood, mouth baying, with his head jerking between the two men.

"You two... know each other?"

Leaving William somewhat puzzled, the captain continued, "But everyone told me that you... that you'd..."

"A mistake easily done. I was badly injured and sure enough I was left for dead."

"But how did you get off the island?"

"When the government ships came looking for pirates, they found me and took me back on board with them. It took a hell of a job to convince them that I wasn't one of them cut-throats. Anyway, the surgeon took care of my wounds and then, I was forced to take things easy for a while. That was the worst part of it. I was itching to get back on my feet and go out to sea again."

"Well, I can hardly believe it. It's really good to see you again,

Humphreys… Sorry, Captain Humphreys!"

"Likewise, Captain Jennings, likewise."

Taking advantage of the pause, William addressed the two old friends and said, "So, I take it you don't need any introduction."

They all laughed.

"I suppose we'd better get going but before we do, I'm sure your old mates would love to see you. Come on, on board, I can't wait to see my men's reaction when they see you. Incidentally, Humphreys, sorry, *Captain* Humphreys, I have two young lads who'd love to explore your ship…"

"Bring them on board!" Humphreys invited straight away. "I'll give them a private tour myself."

A short while later, merry scenes of rejoicing shook and stirred the *Redemption.* Connor repeatedly patted Humphreys's back, just to check that this man standing next to him was well and truly his old mate and not a ghostly apparition. Unhindered by the lack of rum, the sailors clinked merrily tankers full of spruce beer as all celebrated the sudden 'revival' of Luke Humphreys, with Jonesie and Jamesie running riot and stealing a sip here and there.

***

And so it was that the *Redemption* and the *Maryland* sailed together for the rest of the voyage and a good few days later, both sighted the unmistakable contours of good old England.

Chapter Thirty-One
Mail Coach to London

Before touching land, Captain Jennings retired to his cabin to plan his journey to London. With all the highway robbers lying in wait at every corner, travelling by himself was totally out of the question. So, he began to make a list to decide who would accompany him on the perilous journey, and he knew exactly who would be first on his list.

"Griffiths and Connor, you stay behind to look after the ships and the crews which, by the way, *does* include Warren and Harris! Start fitting her for the return journey… and remember to check her sails. Also, when you start counting the provisions, try not to have double vision. Mitchell, you go with them. I need a strong man to keep an eye on them."

Just as he started to move away, a little voice squeaked, "And us, Capt'n? What about us?"

Jamesie was standing behind the captain with a sorrowful look on his face.

"Ah, yes!" the captain said as if remembering something. "I did say I had a surprise for you. Well, I've decided to take both you and Jonesie with me. I think a bit of time on land will do you good. And then, Jamesie, maybe, you'll decide you'd like to go back to your own home."

Jamesie shrugged his shoulders in a resigned manner. "I can't remember where my home is… and I don't care because I'd rather stay with you, Captain."

"But surely, there must be something you remember about your home… or your parents?" the captain asked searchingly.

Jamesie felt uncomfortable. Being forced to think about his present circumstances did nothing but revive the acute pain he felt at suddenly finding himself all alone in this world and he fought hard against it, against his feelings and against his past. He looked at the captain with steely eyes and asked in a rather detached tone, "Captain, how long does it take to go to London?"

The captain understood. He put his arm around the boy's shoulders in a fatherly gesture and replied, "It greatly depends on the state of the roads, and the weather and… whom we meet en route."

"You mean like highway thieves and robbers?"

"Maybe. But don't think too much about it. I wouldn't want you to lose any sleep over it."

"It doesn't bother me," Jamesie declared, immediately squaring himself to the captain and making swift chopping motions with his hands. "They can come, I'm ready for them!"

Jonesie stared at him and burst out laughing.

"You wouldn't be able to kill a fly!" He chuckled.

When he heard this, Jamesie launched onto his brethren and wrestled him to the wooden deck. The captain immediately intervened.

"Hey! Hey! Stop that you two or I'll make you scrub the decks three times a day until we reach port!" he scolded.

Still holding Jonesie by the scruff of the neck, Jamesie turned his head and asked, "For a few extra groats?"

"No!" The captain replied emphatically. "You cheeky little monkey. Go and get your scrubbing brush."

"Jeez, it ain't fair," the little miscreant moaned, kicking with his right foot some invisible object on the deck.

***

The moment they reached port, William left his ship and boarded the *Redemption.* As soon as he heard of the captain's plans, he insisted on coming too. The captain was hesitant, but William insisted.

"I have to visit a few relatives I haven't seen in a long while, so since I'm going that way myself, I might as well come with you."

"All right then, but you know how risky the roads are," the captain agreed before quickly adding, "By the way, while travelling on land, we need complete anonymity so it's better if you don't call me 'Captain'. Just call me Charles… and you, boys, from now on, I want you to call me 'Uncle'; I'll be Uncle Jennings, all right?"

"Aye, Captain!" Jamesie hailed cheerfully.

Immediately, Jonesie nudged him.

"It's not 'Captain'! it's 'Uncle' Jennings!"

The captain added, "We'll take the mail coach to London. It might take longer but it'll be cheaper than hiring horses."

"In that case, I'll go and find out when's the next coach," William volunteered.

A short while later, William returned with the information.

"The coach leaves tomorrow morning at five o'clock, from the *Three Sails*."

The *Three Sails* was one of the better inns, located in the main street, just half a mile from the harbour.

"We might as well spend the night on the ship, then," Captain Jennings decided.

William rather fancied somewhere a little more salubrious.

"If you don't mind, Captain, I'll stay at the *Three Sails*, but I hope you'll do me the honour of joining me for a late supper."

The captain welcomed the idea of a good hearty meal after spending weeks at sea eating stale meat and dried biscuits that had no doubt been nibbled by mice, weasels and worms.

***

At around ten o'clock at night, the captain returned from his night out at the *Three Sails*. The atmosphere around the harbour was calm and unflustered. A pale ray of moonlight beamed across the bay, playing with the shadows of ships whose bare masts criss-crossed the sky. The usual clatter created by the frantic activities going on around the harbour had completely died down. On board the *Redemption*, Jonesie and Jamesie slept soundly in their cockboat, curled up in a blanket under the canvas. Without the usual sound of waves splashing against the hull, there was an unusual quietude around the ship.

Reg Norris, the night watchman, paced the empty decks with long assertive strides. All was quiet on the waterfront. The sound of a light shuffle made him jerk his head. He saw nothing. He made a few steps towards the middle of the ship, stopped, pricked up his ears and scoured the deck with hawk eyes. Nothing moved. He went past the cockboat to check on the boys. They had not stirred. Reassured, he resumed his round and made for the poop deck from where he had an overview of the ship and of the door that led below deck. There, he sat down and waited... and waited... till dawn. He struggled to keep his eyes open, jerking his head up as soon as he felt it droop down, but, as hard as he tried, his head stooped a few times before finally coming to rest on his chest.

A nearby church bell chimed and hallowed the still silence that reigned over the town. Reg Norris woke up with a start and stared straight in front of him, bewildered, trying to work out what time it was. Was it three or four chimes he had heard? He was not sure, but he had to make a move; too much was at stake. He could not risk the captain missing the mail coach so he decided to go and wake him up. On his way down the steps, he caught sight of a small shadow slithering silently down the corridor. Thinking that he had just seen the man in charge of the next watch, he strode fast to catch him up. The sound of the steps scurrying away even faster arose his suspicions. He quickly caught up with the dark figure, grabbed him by the shoulder and forced the man to face him. A gasp of surprise came out as he stared at the little man's face, it was Bob Downing. What on earth was he doing creeping about at this time of night?

"You're not on the next watch?" Norris asked, almost as a statement.

"No," Downing replied. "I just went for some fresh air cos I got a bit of indigestion."

Norris leered at the little man with suspicion, but he had urgent business to attend, so he let go of Downing, and made straight for the captain's cabin. As soon as he knocked on the door, Norris heard the captain stir, so he left and went straight to the hammock of the mate who was due to take over the next watch.

What Norris had not seen, however, was that inside the cabin, the captain was frantically searching for something. He had emptied his trunk once already, checked among the books, searched every shelf and every gap, no matter how small, but still, he could not find it. How could it have simply vanished when no one, apart from him, had access to his cabin? Except… except, he suddenly recalled, the only man on board to have seen the precious box was that little pest, Downing, and the more he thought about it, the more he became convinced that Downing had to have something to do with it.

Immediately, Captain Jennings left his cabin to investigate. Outside, the church bell chimed the half hour. There was still time. He went up on deck and asked the watchman to fetch Mitchell and Downing, while he himself went over to the cockboat to check that the ship's boys were awake. And they were.

"Boys," the captain said in a hushed voice. "Get your things and wait for Mitchell. He'll take you to the *Three Sails.* Once you get there, check that William is awake, and wait for me there. I'll be with you shortly."

"Aye, aye, Capt'n!"

They did not have long to wait before Mitchell appeared. Once Mitchell and the boys had gone, the captain returned below deck with only one thought in mind, to search Downing... right down to his pantaloons if need be. At the bottom of the corridor, he saw the watchman push Downing in front of him.

"Come on, move! The captain wants to see you."

"Why?" Downing grunted. "I ain't done nothing!"

"Stop!" the captain hailed. "Downing, take me to your hammock."

"Why?" Downing repeated. "I ain't got nothing and I ain't done nothing."

"We shall see about that."

Reluctantly, Downing led the captain to a hammock suspended from a wooden beam in the central section. There was nothing in it except for a blanket and a grimy piece of clothing folded in the shape of a pillow. The captain grabbed the blanket and shook it thoroughly. Nothing fell out. Then, he seized the piece of clothing. Again, nothing. Meanwhile, the minutes were ticking away. The captain took a quick look around the hammock and up and down the thick wooden beam. He was looking under the hammock just as his eye caught sight of a shiny object shoved in a small niche carved at the base of the beam. He immediately grabbed it.

"What's that, then?" the captain asked reproachfully, showing a small mahogany box encircled with brass brackets.

"I don't know," Downing replied, pleading total ignorance. "It don't belong to me," he lied.

"Right, Downing, when I come back from London, you'd better not be on my ship."

"Why?" Downing protested. "I've never seen that thing before in my life!"

The captain stared angrily at him and riposted, "You know very well it's a complete lie! And you're bleeding lucky that I don't have the time to deal with you right now."

With minutes to spare, the captain rushed back to his cabin, grabbed his bag and ran, hoping to reach the mail coach in time.

From the quayside, the captain ran as fast as he could all the way to the main street. Above, in the brightening sky, a church bell began to chime the hour. The captain ran faster still. His chest was burning but he kept going for in the distance, he could see the two ship boys jumping on the spot and waving madly at him. Next to them, a red and black coach stood at a standstill.

Now he could hear the boys… and William.

"Come on, Captain! Quick, the coach's about to leave!"

As quickly as they could, the five of them jumped into the coach, with the captain still struggling to catch his breath. The driver cracked his whip once and soon, the sound of the horses' hooves clattered noisily along the cobblestones, reverberating through the silent walls of the long and narrow sleepy streets.

Chapter Thirty-Two
Adieu, mon Ami

Once the coach reached the outskirts of Bristol, the boys asked if they could sit next to the driver. Permission granted, they scrambled up onto the small bench and squeezed themselves on either side of Ralph Allandale, coach driver and postmaster. The boys stared at him intently, giving him the once over as if to gauge their safety against his ability to scare off any potential robber, a prospect which both excited and scared them in equal measure. The driver seemed oblivious to their inquisitive eyes and drove his coach with blind determination through the muddy ruts, potholes and loose gravel. As for the boys, reassured by his robust frame and stocky build, they moved on to scrutinise his face, half-concealed by a thick reddish beard. His bushy eyebrows protruded above his eyes like an oversized set of awnings. It was great comfort for the boys to feel part of a formidable team that consisted of the driver, the captain and William, a team that would not hesitate to jump to their defence and fight against any enemy that might be lurking behind every tree, every hillock and at every turn.

Ralph Allandale had the quirky habit of grunting in his beard for no apparent reason which made the boys giggle in their cupped hands. And when the driver asked, "Well boys, where are you off to then?" in his thick West Country accent, Jamesie was instantly gripped in a fit of giggles that rendered him powerless to answer back. On the other side of the bench, Jonesie's shoulders shook with laughter too, despite the boy's desperate attempt to regain control of himself. Eventually, Jonesie dropped his hand away from his face, coughed a few times and replied in a hiccup fashion, "We're off to London."

"To do what?"

By now recovered from his laughing fit, Jamesie trumpeted, "We're going to the Admiralty because I want to join the Navy!"

"Oh my, really? Well, rather you than me, boys!" the driver spluttered with surprise.

"Why? We like sailing. It's great fun," Jonesie stated, unabashed. "And

Captain Jennings's really nice. He's going to buy me a commission and I'm going to sign my name in proper handwriting on a proper piece of paper."

Jamesie watched for the driver's reaction; then, feeling in a mischievous mood, chipped in, "Not me, Mister, not me cos I'm gonna be a pirate!"

It was Ralph Allandale's turn to laugh. "A pirate!" he exclaimed in a loud chuckle. "So, you're gonna be fighting each other, hey?"

"No," Jamesie protested. "We're gonna go treasure hunting together. Ain't that right, Jonesie?"

The driver stared at Jamesie, rather bemused.

"But you're only a little titch! Who's gonna be scared of you?"

"You don't get it, Mister. They're not gonna have time to be scared cos I'm gonna shoot them all, ain't I? Bang! Bang! Like that!"

Having just shot through the air with his invisible weapon, Jamesie brought his hand to his face and blew on his two outstretched fingers like he would on a smoking gun.

Mercifully, Jamesie had no need to put on his scary face for most of the journey went by without any major incident to declare. The weather stayed dry and the roads firm, easing the way for the wheels of the laden coach.

After four days on the road, and just before reaching the small town of Richmond, the coach stopped outside the *Black Swan* Inn. The boys asked if they could take their turn to sit inside the coach as it was beginning to rain, but at that very moment, two refined-looking ladies emerged from the inn, each carrying a cloth bag in one hand and a lace parasol in the other.

"Sorry, lads," the coach driver said. "Too late. It looks as if these ladies are in need of a lift as well. But don't worry; we're stopping here for lunch anyway, so the clouds might clear before we leave."

Ralph Allandale jumped down from his seat and went to the aid of the ladies. He took their luggage and put them in the wooden box at the back of the coach.

"We'll be leaving after we've had a bite to eat," the coach driver informed them. "You might like to wait inside the inn so that you don't get drenched."

***

When they were ready to leave, the driver opened the coach door and gave the ladies a helping hand so that they would not miss the small and wobbly wooden step. Behind them, the boys were pleading with the captain.

"Can't we sit inside the coach? We're cold and tired."

"I don't think there's enough room now that there are two extra passengers."

Seeing the boys' distress, one of the ladies intervened. "I'm sure it'll be all right. The boys won't take up much room and I'm sure we can make ourselves as small as possible to make room for everyone."

"Thanks, Lady!" Jamesie effused gratefully. "If I was rich, I'd give you a big handful of groats."

"That wouldn't be much," William teased. "Your hand's only small... but that's a nice thought, though."

Jamesie frowned heavily.

"Why does everybody keep telling me how small I am?" he groaned.

"Because you are," Jonesie stated. "And when you become a pirate you'll be known as 'Titch the Scary'!"

Everyone laughed.

"All right everyone, we're leaving!" the coach driver hailed.

The boys quickly settled between William and 'Uncle' Jennings, and soon the rhythmic movement of the coach lulled them into a deep sleep. Opposite them, the ladies observed the boys with a maternal smile.

For most of the journey, they remained silent and the men, for fear of invading their privacy, did not feel bold enough to ask any questions. So the passengers nodded politely to each other, none wanting to be the first to break the rules of courtesy.

During the journey, the ladies could not help staring at young Jamesie. William and Jennings looked at each other, somewhat puzzled. The ladies noticed the awkward glances and the older of the two finally broke the silence.

"May I introduce myself?" she initiated with a friendly smile. "I'm Lady Martingale and this is my daughter Eunice."

"Pleased to meet you," the captain greeted jovially. "I'm Charles Jennings, and this is my dear friend William Woodes Rogers..."

When she heard the name, the young lady's eyes opened wide.

"Oh? You wouldn't be related to Sir Woodes Rogers by any chance?" she asked with great expectation.

"As a matter of fact, I am. He's my father," William declared with pride.

The young lady fluttered her eyelashes and smiled demurely, but before she could ask anything else, her mother looked at the captain and enquired, "And these two boys, are they your sons?"

"No, Ma'm, they're not... they're...er... they're my nephews."

Lady Martingale looked puzzled.

"Since when?" she asked without thinking.

Startled, the captain stared back at her in mild shock.

"Pardon me?"

"I'm sorry. Forgive me, Mr Jennings," the lady responded with a little embarrassed chuckle. It's just that I thought..."

"Mummy," her daughter quipped. "The gentleman's just said, the boys are his nephews."

The captain glanced at the lady then at Jamesie who was still fast asleep with his head resting heavily on his arm.

The rest of the journey passed in silence and by early evening, the mail coach reached London.

William alighted from the coach first to give a helping hand to the ladies. As he took Lady Eunice's delicate hand to help her down the step, he whispered with a wooing smile, "Delighted to have met you."

Lady Eunice raised her head and returned a coy smile. After which, the ladies collected their luggage and promptly departed.

Moments later, the boys emerged from the coach rubbing their eyes. They yawned and stretched and were awake again. While searching for lodgings as close as possible to the Admiralty building, they followed the captain closely, like two lost puppies, sniffing anxiously for something familiar to behold.

The following morning, the party discussed their plans for the next few days. William would be off visiting some relatives. The boys were granted leave to go to the park just across from the Admiralty Building while Captain Jennings went inside to do whatever he had to do.

A meeting with the Lords had been fixed for ten o'clock that morning. Captain Jennings put his best clothes on and braced himself to face the gentlemen of the Admiralty.

Straight away, he noticed two or three new faces among the panel but chairing in the middle was the same good old Lord Lucius Bond-Balfour.

Wasting no time, the captain handed over the box and the accompanying letter entrusted to him by Sir Woodes Rogers of New Providence.

"I hope it will be a pleasure to see you again, Captain Jennings," Lord Bond-Balfour began. "I see from the letter from my dear friend Woodes Rogers, that you have with you the *Cross of Madeira*."

"Yes, my Lord," the captain replied with confidence. At this moment, he felt his pockets. He checked the inside of his waistcoat, patted his chest a few times, but still, he could not find the cross. He began to panic.

The Lord Admiral watched him patiently.

"My Lord," Captain Jennings finally breathed in a blind panic. "I don't understand... I cannot find the cross," he muttered, frantically searching his whole person.

"Arrest him!" an officer shouted.

"Send him to the Tower!" another heckled.

"Guards! Seize him!" a commanding voice barked above the noise.

"My Lord! My Lord!" Jennings pleaded. "I did have the cross! I must have mislaid it, or... someone must have..."

He wanted to say 'stolen it' but could not quite bring himself to say the words as no one travelling with him could possibly have been guilty of such a despicable crime.

One of the officers jumped out of his seat and pointed an accusing finger at Jennings. "Don't give him another chance, my Lord! He's already used up all his lives and now he's bluffing his way out so that he can escape!"

At these words, the Lord Admiral stood up and glared at Jennings. "Captain. The matter is now out of my hands. You were entrusted with this one important mission and by failing you have shown that you are no more than a lowlife pirate and a common thief! Guards!"

His call was immediately followed by a loud commotion outside the room. Suddenly the doors flew open. To the general dismay, the guards entered the room holding on with a firm grip two young boys.

"What's all this?" the Lord Admiral remonstrated firmly.

A stunned silence befell the room while the young boys, screaming and shouting, freed themselves from the guards and rushed inside the room.

"Capt'n! Capt'n!" one of the boys hailed. "You dropped this!"

Lord Bond-Balfour stared at the boys.

"What have you got there? Bring it to me here, boy!" he ordered.

Jonesie approached the official desk and triumphantly placed a medium sized wooden box on top of the desk.

"My Lord!" Jennings exclaimed. "That is the box that carries the *Cross of Madeira*!"

"You mean to say that the *Cross of Madeira* is inside this box?"

"That's right, my Lord." Jennings replied emphatically.

The Admiral peered at the box with a suspicious look.

"And… how do you open it?"

"You can't, my Lord. The only way to open it is by chiselling very carefully the top of the box."

The Lord Admiral turned to his left and whispered a few discreet words to his colleague. The Second Lieutenant quickly left the room. A few minutes later, he returned carrying a small handsaw and chisel. After breaking the brass tongues, the officer sawed the box open and immediately handed it over. When Lord Bond-Balfour set his eyes on the priceless jewel, he gasped in awe and wonder.

"Good Lord!" he exclaimed.

As he lifted the Cross in a ceremonial manner, his eyes remained riveted on the magnificent jewel. Around the chamber, lit by dozens of flames flickering with an iridescent glow, the diamonds threw sparks of brilliance that reflected in everyone's eyes while the gold glittered, rich and yellow, like a golden halo.

Still holding the Cross aloft, the Lord Admiral declared in a solemn voice, "Gentlemen, you are looking at the symbol of peace."

"Hear, hear," all responded, banging loudly on the wooden tables as a mark of approval.

With the utmost care, the Lord Admiral was replacing the precious jewel back in its box when suddenly… he lifted his head, narrowed his eyes, leant forward and murmured in complete surprise, "James?"

Instantly, the boy's face lit up.

"Granpa?"

"James Francis Balfour?" the Lord Admiral repeated, just to be sure.

At the sound of his name, ignoring all protocol, the young boy ran into his grandfather's arms.

"Granpa!"

Unable to believe their eyes, the other members of the Board stared speechless at the extraordinary scene. For a few minutes, the true purpose of the meeting was completely forgotten. Equally lost for words, Jonesie came to stand next to the captain who kept shaking his head in sheer disbelief.

"James! Where have you been? We thought we'd never see you again."

"The captain took really good care of me, Granpa!" he trumpeted proudly.

The Lord Admiral glared at Jennings. "What I dearly would like to know is what is my grandson doing in the company of a wanted man?"

The captain was lost for words.

"It's not his fault, Granpa!" Jamesie intervened. "And Captain Jennings's not a pirate! I was left behind by accident in Nassau and Captain Jennings's looked after me all this time. He didn't know who I was and I didn't want to tell him because I knew I was in trouble, so I pretended to be a runaway."

Then, the boy turned to Jonesie, grabbed his arm and added, "And this is my mate, Jonesie. Now *he*'s a real runaway!"

A discreet wave of laughter spread around the room.

"But James!" the Lord Admiral reprised. "Have you any idea of the terrible anguish you've caused to your mother and father?

Jamesie bowed his head in contrition. "Yes, I know, Sir."

"And how did you come about this?" he asked, lifting the box from the table.

"The captain dropped it when he ran to come here because he was late. So we picked it up and…" Jonesie volunteered.

"And when we arrived here," Jamesie interrupted. "The guards stopped us because they wouldn't believe us. We had no idea it was so important cos for us, it was just a piece of wood… yeah, just wood."

"Young man, you have just saved the captain from a miserable fate." The Lord Admiral said.

"By the way, Captain Jennings," he reprised. "At our last meeting, I specifically stated that I wanted all of the treasure back. What happened to the rest of it?"

"I'm afraid, my Lord, it is not going to be possible to retrieve the rest of the treasure. When he realised he was going to get caught, Black Bart blew up the tunnel where the treasure was hidden. Unfortunately, all the pirated treasures were hidden there too, including the King of Spain's jewels."

"Good Lord!" the Admiral exclaimed. "Why didn't you stop him?"

"Because he did it before we could reach the tunnel."

"I suppose you expect me to believe this nonsense?" The Lord Admiral grunted. "I am in good mind to arrest you on the spot!"

"No, Granpa!" Jamesie shouted. "Captain Jennings is telling the truth!"

"Yeah," Jonesie seconded. "The captain's not a liar. It's true what he said!"

Jamesie turned to his grandfather and asked with youthful aplomb, "And anyway, the captain should be rewarded. After all, he saved me!"

Lord Bond-Balfour paused for a moment. He looked at his grandson with a set expression on his face, betraying neither feelings nor emotions. Then, he straightened himself up in his chair, put his hands together and declared, "Right, gentlemen. The Board is dismissed. I need to have a private word with Captain Jennings."

The gentlemen of the Board filed out of the chamber, mumbling to each other words of surprise and consternation. When they had all left, the Lord Admiral turned to his grandson and said, "Right, young James, the first thing we need to do is return you to your parents."

"But I want to stay with the captain."

The captain was about to answer when the Lord Admiral cut in, "It's time for you to go home, James."

"No, no!" Jamesie protested. "I want to stay with the captain!"

"Listen, James," I Lord Admiral continued, striving to sound like a grandfather rather than a haughty admiral. "This is what I suggest. You go back home, go back to school and when you finish school, I'll get you a commission and I'll make sure you serve on the captain's ship."

"I hate school! I don't want to go back to school!"

"But if you want to be a leader of men, you need a good education," his grandfather argued.

Jamesie turned to the captain with his eyes full of tears. "Please, Captain…"

The captain shrugged his shoulders and conceded, "I'm afraid I cannot go against your granpa's wishes, Jamesie. Besides, your granpa is right. If you go back to school, you'll be better equipped to understand what it takes to be a leader of men. And when you earn your commission, I'll be more than happy to have you back on my ship."

With his face streaming with tears, Jamesie turned to his friend and asked, "What about Jonesie? What's going to happen to him?"

The captain patted Jonesie on the back and said with a reassuring smile, "Don't worry. I'll take care of him and when you're ready to join us again, he'll be there, he'll be waiting for you, won't you, Jonesie?"

"Aye," the boy uttered, too choked up with emotion to give a fuller reply.

"Well, that's settled then," Lord Bond-Balfour said with some relief. "Come on, James, let's go home."

Jamesie looked at his friend one more time and said, "You'll wait for me, Jonesie, won't you?"

"Aye, Jamesie, I'll wait for you." Then, forcing a smile, he added, "Pirate's honour!"

Lord Bond-Balfour looked on, shocked, as his grandson shook his friend's hand and vouched back, "Pirate's honour! Bye Jonesie... Bye Captain! And remember, I'll be back!"

Jamesie gave one last wave, and then... he was gone. The sudden silence that followed his departure fell hard and hit them like a stone. The captain looked at Jonesie, put his arm around his shoulders and said in a subdued tone, "Come on, Jonesie, let's go."

For all response, the boy let out a big sigh, keeping his gaze firmly fixed on the parquet floor. Eventually, he raised his head, looked fixedly at the door ahead and replied in a mournful tone, "Aye, Captain, let's go."

Chapter Thirty-Three
On the Way back to Bristol

Back at the lodging house, William was busy packing his new purchases. In between the layers of fine materials, silk stockings and lace, he tucked in several handwritten missives which had been given to him for friends and relatives back in Nassau. Almost ready, he could not wait to set off on the return journey to Bristol, mainly to escape the terrible stench that permeated through the walls of every street in London. They had been in the capital for three days now, and quite beside the stench, the smog made him feel rather unkempt and unclean. So it was with great relief that he saw the captain finally return with Jonesie in tow. Straight away, he noticed the absence of the younger boy.

"Where's Jamesie?"

The captain affected a detached tone and replied, "You won't believe this, William. That little titch of a rascal who always bartered for an extra groat turned out to be no less than the Lord Admiral's grandson!"

"Good Lord!" exclaimed William in complete shock. Then, after a short pause, he added, "Come to think of it… I did notice the ladies in the coach looking at him as if they recognised him. I wonder why they didn't say anything, though."

"They probably thought they were mistaken," the captain speculated. "Seeing the boy hanging out with us lot didn't exactly hint to the prestige of his family ties."

"Speak for yourself, Charles!" William retorted, putting on an air of supreme superiority.

"Anyway, I've got everything I came here to get," I captain continued.

"So have I," William quipped in.

"In that case, I suggest we have an early night and catch the first mail coach back to Bristol."

"That's all right by me. The sooner we get out of this place, the better I'll feel," William articulated with feeling.

***

Just after dawn, the trio set off to catch the mail coach. It was a beautiful sunny morning with the fresh crisp air cutting through the stagnant malodorous haze.

Soon, they arrived at the coach inn near Hammersmith, and to their surprise found the same driver in charge. Ralph Allandale gave them a second look, grunted noisily and greeted jovially, "Ah! It's you again! You didn't stay long in town."

"We didn't need to," the captain explained.

The driver looked around them and asked in jest, "Where's Titch the Scary? Is he not coming?"

"Not this time, he's gone back home."

Without further delay, everyone took their seats and the coach departed. There were three other passengers with them inside the coach, two men and one woman. Their modest clothes and humble manners gave no grave cause for concern to the party.

William had always felt that once the coach had clattered past Richmond, he was well and truly on his way home. He bristled in his seat with trepidation and stared at the landscape where the grimy blocks of sandstones from decrepit buildings had melted into fresh green pastures and where the repugnant atmosphere of the capital floated away, leaving behind a more fragrant and earthy aroma. Sitting next to him, Charles Jennings would have been experiencing the same feelings of sheer relief and pure content, were it not for the fact that he felt nervous and apprehensive, for hidden somewhere in his luggage were his men's wages. He knew that the journey would be fraught with danger as the road to Bristol was notorious for attacks by highway robbers who preyed on travellers returning from the city. For this very reason, Jennings could not relax. Every now and again, he checked his pistol under his coat, making sure it was still firmly attached to his belt.

After two days of travel, the coach driver decided to make an unscheduled stop at the small town of Chippingham to change one of the horses which had become lame. Charles Jennings alighted from the coach to stretch his legs and consult with the driver. He felt uneasy at the extra time spent on the road and wanted to press on, but Ralph Allandale had no choice. There was no other horse available. At the news, Charles decided to go on foot in search of a farm which might have a horse and cart for hire.

"I'll come with you," William offered.

"No, it's best if you stay here to keep a close eye on the luggage," he whispered discreetly.

It was mid-afternoon and by early evening, a cart pulled by a horse was seen churning clouds of dust not far from the inn with Charles Jennings at the reins.

"Come on, hop on," he hailed.

William and Jonesie threw the bags in the cart and covered them with the blanket, just in case it should rain. Then they took a seat on either side of the captain and departed promptly. No sooner had they reached the countryside that Jonesie began to shiver.

"Brr... I don't like this," he muttered, throwing furtive looks around him.

"You're scared?" William asked.

"A bit."

"Don't worry," said Charles, trying to reassure the boy. "We'll soon be there."

Then, he launched into a little ditty to cheer up Jonesie.

Three big fat cows grazing in a green meadow
Had their big fat buttocks facing Pete's widow
With their paintbrush tails squashing the flies
They cooed and smooched... and made mudpies.

Jonesie sniggered. William turned to Charles and riled, "That song doesn't make sense!"

"It does to the milkmaid!" Charles chortled.

"Where did you learn that song, Capt... sorry, Uncle?"

"I learnt it when I was a lad. You're probably not aware of it but I was actually brought up on a farm."

Suddenly, as they were travelling through a sparsely wooded forest, their conversation was interrupted by the sound of hooves at full gallop coming from behind. All three of them turned around at once and watched a rider hurtling towards them. They exchanged looks but said nothing. Charles drew his pistol and placed it next to him. Under his coat, William kept a firm grip on his.

"Quick, Jonesie," Charles called quietly, "get inside the cart and hide under the blanket."

"Aye, Capt'n," he said, taking the captain's pistol with him, just in case. The captain did not notice for his attention was entirely focused on the rider approaching fast. Charles whipped the horse who immediately launched into a fast gallop. William turned around.

"He's catching up." He breathed anxiously.

"I know," Charles muttered through his clenched teeth, feeling the hair on the back of his neck bristling.

In the crepuscular light, William kept his eyes fixed on the dark silhouette that grew more menacing as it got closer. Before they knew it, the rider had pulled alongside the cart and was ogling the two men. He wore a black cape and a black tricorn but they could not see his face for it was hidden behind a black scarf. Quick as a flash, he grabbed hold of the reins to try and force the horse off the track. William immediately whipped out his pistol but the rider threw his elbow into William's face and the pistol flew out of his hand.

"Your money! Give me your money!" the rider shouted at the same time as trying to gain control of the cart.

"Get your filthy hands off my horse!" Charles screamed, cracking his whip on the horseman while desperately trying to find his pistol.

From under the blanket, Jonesie waited anxiously, holding nervously the captain's pistol. He had never shot a man before but fearing for the captain's life, he threw the blanket off, steadied himself in the rocking cart and pointed the pistol straight in front of him.

"You heard what my uncle said!" he shouted with bravado. "Let go of the horse or I shoot!"

At that moment, one of the cartwheels hit a large stone. Jonesie was thrown backwards and knocked unconscious just as a loud bang rang out, reverberating through the forest. Startled, the horse bolted and began to tear down the track at high speed. The highway robber, who had been holding firmly on to the reins, was thrown off his horse and dragged under the cart. In a flash, Jennings picked up the reins and swiftly regained control of the horse. Confused, the robber's horse kept pace with them for a while. Meanwhile, a long way behind, on the deserted track, the robber lay lifeless on the dirt track. All three let out a huge sigh of relief.

"I don't think that vermin is going to trouble anyone for some time." William remarked drily, breathing more freely.

Jonesie opened his eyes.

"What happened?" he asked, dazed. "Where's the robber?"

"Don't worry, Jonesie. He won't be troubling us for a while," William replied, looking quite chuffed with himself.

"You stay where you are, Jonesie," the captain said in a caring voice. "William, you take the horse, and I'll drive the cart."

A few miles down the road, they came across a lugubrious building. The ornate sign above the entrance door pictured a white horse with underneath it two words painted in black, *Relay Inn*.

As soon as he spotted the sign, Jonesie fretted on his seat.

"Capt'n, please, can we stop here? I'm starving," he pleaded.

Jennings did not respond straight away. He seemed totally absorbed in his own thoughts. Eventually, he turned to William and shouted, "We're stopping here."

"Thank God for that. It's getting too dangerous out here!"

"Wait here, I'll go and find out what they've got."

A few minutes later, Jennings re-emerged from the tavern.

"Yep!" he said, keeping his companions guessing. "They've got food… mutton stew."

"Mutton stew? Yeah!" Jonesie cheered.

"Come on, lad, help me with the bags."

A few minutes later, the three of them were sitting at a long wooden table waiting for their supper to arrive. The room was filled with roughly a dozen local folks shrouded in a thick plasma of pipe smoke. The walls were whitewashed and bare, and the floor was covered with large flagstones which had been dusted with a thin layer of sawdust, dampened so as to stop it flying everywhere and getting up the patrons' noses.

Suddenly, the front door swung open and a tall man dressed in dark clothes swaggered in. His tanned face was marked with deep lines and his deep-seated eyes looked dark and sinister. His square jaw was swamped by a thick black beard that let out a ray of light through his menacing grin. The inn fell silent. The stranger threw long glances around him, all the while testing the atmosphere by breathing deeply through his enlarged nostrils. Then he stopped and stared at the bar. A sharp intake of breath resounded from one corner of the room as he reached for his belt, but all he did was to tuck his thumbs in without touching his pistols. Wondering whether this was the highway robber they had encountered earlier, Jonesie kept his hands clutched tightly together to stop them from shaking. Then, suddenly, in the tail of his eye, he spotted something that unsettled him even more.

"Capt'n!" he hushed.

At the sound of the word 'captain', the stranger jerked his head and leered at the threesome. He marched purposefully towards the table, with his eyes firing murderous glances at the trio. Before he could see him, Jennings lowered his hat to conceal his face.

"Captain?" he growled. "Did I hear the word 'captain'? Which one of you is the captain?" he demanded to know, looking at each in turn.

Both William and Jennings did their best to ignore the stranger while Jonesie, paralysed with fear, could do nothing but stare at the man with terror in his eyes like a naughty child waiting for punishment.

At that moment, the waitress arrived carrying a large tray. Oblivious to the tense suspense, she threw a casual "'Scuse me, sir" as she passed the stranger and deposited the tray on the table announcing in a clear voice, "Three mutton suppers!"

Behind the bar, the innkeeper hailed, "Yes, gentleman, what can I do for you?"

The stranger continued to glare at the silent trio for a while before turning on his heels and heading for the bar where he mumbled his order. Instantly, the tension dropped and the conversations returned. Downing his drink as if feeding it through a funnel into a barrel, he slammed his empty pewter tankard on the bar, wiped his beard with his sleeve and left.

As soon as he was gone, Jonesie bristled on his seat, turned towards the captain and hushed, "Did you see? Did you see his belt?"

"Yes, I did."

"So… it's *him*, isn't it?"

Charles Jennings knew the answer to the boy's question for he was the only man present who had ever seen that face before, and it belonged to none other than Black Bobby himself.

"Who? What? What did you see?" William enquired anxiously.

"His belt!" Jonesie replied, somewhat agitated.

"His belt? What about his belt?" William asked, mystified.

"The buckle had a skull and two pistols on it," Charles explained.

At these words, William looked shocked.

"Oh no, you don't mean…?"

"Yep, I'm afraid so!" Charles replied, shaking his head.

"Let's get out of here!" Jonesie hailed in panic.

"And into the wolf's mouth? No, we're staying here for the night. They've got one room left. We can draw lots later to decide who's going to get the bed."

Chapter Thirty-Four
The Last Farewell

The following morning, the threesome resumed their journey just after dawn. The sky was clear and the air crisp. Tired after an uncomfortable night spent on the floorboards, Jonesie wrapped himself up in the blanket that was lying next to him and sat with his back leaning against the front of the cart. Scanning the landscape, he watched the ethereal mist roll over fallow land, fields and marshes. He smelt with relish the earthy aroma of fresh grass sparkling with crystal beads of the early morning dew, something he had never experienced before. For a brief moment, he dared think that perhaps, once he had made his fortune at sea, he would return to England, settle in the countryside and work on the land. On the land? Away from the sea? Perish the thought! He suddenly perked up, turned to the captain and hailed, "Capt'n, when are we sailing?"

"Depends on the tide, lad!" the captain shouted above the clatter of the moving cart.

Of course it depended on the tide, any sailor knew that. What he really wanted to know was *when*, as in today or tomorrow at high tide. The thought of being back on board a ship sprung up pictures of Jamesie's cute little face and his unruly locks being battered by the sea breeze, and as the nostalgic pictures unfurled in his head, a sharp pang hit him in the stomach. God knew how much he missed his little brethren. Nothing would ever be the same without his cheerful and cheeky little companion. But he was going back to sea and the mere thought of it was enough to cheer him up. In the distance, a church bell chimed the hour and a short while later, they reached the outskirts of Bristol. Jonesie lifted his nose up in the air, took a deep breath and, although he could not yet smell the cold refreshing sea breeze, it was as good as if he was already there.

It was eleven o'clock. The sight of the port bustling with porters, sailors and adventurers waiting impatiently for their next departure lightened the young boy's heart. The hustle and bustle of people rushing, carts creaking, ships groaning and men hailing each other created an atmosphere so electric that it heartened even the most reluctant of sailors who had been press ganged to take to the sea. Taking in big gulps of salty air, Jonesie could not help walking along the quay, grinning from ear to ear, all the time telling himself, My! It feels so good to be back.

***

Walking silently alongside him, Captain Charles Jennings was sharing the same sentiment. He soon spotted the *Redemption*. Not far from her, moored at the far side of the quay, the *Maryland* waited resolutely for her next voyage. Captain Jennings needed to move swiftly. Having checked the tide ladder, he reckoned that he had roughly three hours until the next high tide. It might just be enough time.

"William, could you go on the *Maryland*, check the provisions and send her crew over here, on the *Redemption*; I need to reorganise the crews."

As soon as the captain set foot on the *Redemption,* his crew greeted him with a huge clamour and resounding cheers.

"All right! All right!" He responded with a big smile. "Nice to see you all again! Now, there's no need to push and shove, you'll all get paid, just give me a chance to organise myself. Griffiths! Come and give me a hand!"

"Aye Captain!" the quartermaster replied cheerfully.

Once the official business was over, the captain assembled all the men on the main deck.

"Men," he began in a solemn tone. "We are about to embark on our next voyage with not one, but two ships, which means I need to split the crew. Griffiths will take command of the *Maryland* and I shall stay here on the *Redemption*. I shall need some volunteers to sail on the *Maryland*..."

Before he had even finished his sentence, several hands shot up in the air, among them, those of Dave Warren and Will Harris.

"No." The captain immediately reacted with a wry smile. "You two, I'd rather you stayed with me so that I can keep a close eye on you."

A loud chuckle greeted his remark while the two mates looked at each other and grumbled under their breath.

"Mitchell, you go with Griffiths. You'll be in charge of the rigging."

The crews had now been sorted and split. Predictably, William and Jonesie opted to stay with the captain. However, there was one notable absentee. Just as the captain had expected, Bob Downing was nowhere to be seen.

***

At last, the moment came to reel in the ropes, weigh anchor and stretch the sails. As for Jonesie, his first priority was to check out his sleeping quarters, the cockboat. William enjoyed the dubious privilege of sharing his cabin with some of the cargo. There was not much room in his cabin and he practically had to leap into bed, but at least, it was a darn sight better than having to sleep in a hammock with scores of his malodorous companions.

An overwhelming sense of excitement spread all over the ship. Finally, the *Redemption* glided out of the harbour, closely followed by the *Maryland*. The men were too busy cheering and singing to notice the sun sinking prematurely into the choppy seas.

Captain Charles Jennings watched the harbour lights fade slowly away. He had planned this voyage to be his last, for some time at least. With his chest swelled up with pride and mixed emotions, it felt exactly as if he were going home. Already, at the end of this long journey, he dreamt of a long and happy life in a small and exquisite corner of the world surrounded by palm trees swaying gently in the tropical breeze. All around the ship, he could feel the electric buzz heightened by his men overjoyed to be sailing again. From the upper deck, he surveyed his happy crew milling around for a while, unable to believe that he, Charles Jennings, ex-pirate, prisoner, fugitive and outlaw, could be so lucky to escape the gallows, not once but twice, and that he now stood as a respectable sea captain in charge of his own fleet. Standing erect by the balustrade, he took a deep breath, cleared his throat, called out to his crew, and together, they recited the sailors' prayer.

Thank you, Lord, for opening our eyes to the beauties of this world
For the wondrous light of the sun and the freedom of the sea
For the wind that steers our ship and the food that we receive
Let us sail in your faith and pray in your name
And should we sin in pursuit of honour and glory
Forgive us all our trespasses
Forgive us our greed and excesses
And let us sail in your faith and pray in your name

***

They had been at sea for about a week when the lookout spotted a schooner sailing two or three leagues away behind them. Captain Jennings grabbed his long glass and rushed to the stern to take a good long look at the other ship. There was nothing unusual about crossing another ship in these waters. After all, this was one of the main commercial routes for ships returning from the Americas. However, the schooner seemed to be going in the wrong direction. She should have been sailing east towards England, but instead, she was sailing west, just like the *Redemption.* Several days later, perhaps aiming for the calmer waters of the West Indies, she was still pursuing the *Redemption*, her sails looming and looming larger still like a sinister shadow creeping surreptitiously through the dark waves of the sea.

Each day, she gained on Captain Jennings's fleet while keeping enough distance to remain anonymous. The captain was intrigued. It was either a merchant ship seeking protection from other ships or a rogue ship waiting for an opportune moment to pounce on its prey.

At this very moment, sitting on the main deck, William was involved in a game of poker with Warren and Harris, using their rations of rum and spruce beer as stakes. The captain strolled towards the trio and said, "William, I take it you are aware of the rules regarding gambling on board."

"Don't worry, Captain," William replied cheerfully. "We're not playing for money. It's just a game to pass the time."

"Aye!" Warren seconded with a smirk on his face. "By the way, Capt'n," he added. "When are we gonna be able to have a wee drop of rum? We've had none since leaving port and I'm beginning to feel mightily thirsty."

Captain Jennings stood akimbo with his fists dug deep in his hips and let out a small chuckle.

"Warren, when have you ever *not* been thirsty? I don't know how you can still claim to be feeling thirsty when you're downing your share of spruce beer as if your tongue had completely dried out."

"That's the thing, Capt'n," Warren grumbled. "It feels just like it and I fear that if I don't have a wee bit of rum soon, I'm gonna dry out and end up looking like a dried old fig."

"Dried old fig?" Harris chortled. "I don't know what you're worried about, mate. You've always looked like a dried old fig!"

They all laughed heartily at Harris's banter, and, as the captain was moving away, Jonesie arrived on the scene.

"Hey, can I play too?"

"No!" Warren cut in sharply, vexed by his mates' reaction. "It's for grown-ups only. Besides, you don't have any shares of rum."

"No, but I've a few groats!"

The captain caught the last remark and immediately turned on his heels.

"Oops!" Warren exclaimed.

"Lordy lord!" Harris mumbled, shaking his head.

"What?" Jonesie wondered with apprehension. "What have I said?"

The captain glared at him and said, "Jonesie, time for you to do a bit of reading. Go and get a book. Actually, I have a fascinating book on the theory of sailing that you might find useful. It was commissioned by the King of France, Louis XIV, so that he would have the best ships in the world."

"But I don't like reading. I don't like books…" he protested.

"You might enjoy that one. Go on, give it a go," the captain replied firmly. "You see, if you don't read, you won't learn anything and you'll end up scrubbing decks for the rest of your life. So, what do you want to do?"

Jonesie leered at Warren and Harris and declared, "But they're having fun, why can't I?"

"Because they're lost causes and you're not."

Seizing the opportunity to get rid of the youngster who had no shares of rum to stake, Warren riled, "Aye, Jonesie, we're lost causes, but you do as the captain tells you and maybe one day, *you'll* be the captain."

"Jeez, it ain't fair," Jonesie moaned before making his way to the captain's cabin to fetch the book.

At that moment, William called him and said, "Jonesie, I have a book you might enjoy better. It's called '*Robinson Crusoe*' and it's about this poor fellow who's marooned on an island, and he ends up befriending a native called Friday."

"What's interesting about that?" Jonesie asked rather blasé about an all-too-common topic.

"Well, it's fun to read, and if you finish it, I might even introduce you to the author."

"My! You know him?"

"Yes, he's a friend of my father's."

"All right, I'll give it a go." Jonesie complied grudgingly.

***

Meanwhile, the captain was back on the stern of the ship looking through his long glass. He scoured the *Maryland* and saw Griffiths wave to him, so he waved back. Then, he moved his long glass away from the *Maryland* and pointed it directly onto the mysterious ship. She was shadowing them a mere two leagues away.

***

Having reached mid-Atlantic, Captain Jennings turned his attention to the weather. A clear blue sky was not always the best indicator as to what lay ahead. Far more reliable was the swell of the water which would rise unexpectedly, sending a warning in the form of brisk ripples that had come straight from the eye of the storm. The captain grabbed the long glass and scoured the horizon chiselled by enormous waves. The wind was picking up. Anxious, the captain gave the order to reef the sails, an order which was immediately replicated by Griffiths on the *Maryland*.

Suddenly, the tenebrous mass of a huge black cloud, heavy with rain, crept over the horizon. Following the wind direction, it was heading straight for the ships. Immediately, the captain issued his orders, ready to face the storm head on.

Standing by the bulwarks, William watched, mesmerised, the great mass moving ominously, throwing a mantel of impenetrable darkness as far as the eye could see, as it rumbled above the waves. William could not tell whether he felt excited or scared. Perhaps he felt both. He remembered his sister Sarah describing the sea storm. With patronising aplomb, he had readily mocked her, declaring that women were too easily scared by a bit of wind and the odd sea spray splashing the ship. However, fate has a way of teaching the unwary. Still gripping the bulwark hard, William could not keep his eyes off the ominous cloud. Was he about to suffer the same frightening circumstances of a freak storm at sea? He wondered uneasily.

The dark mass was now hovering straight above them and Captain Jennings hoped and prayed that they would come out of the storm unscathed. Then he had a shock. The mysterious ship was right behind the *Maryland* and the captain could see both ships being tossed violently by the storm. He feared for Griffiths and his crew for there was only one reason why a ship would not declare itself, if it be a pirate ship. But the gods were on his side for the sea was too rough for the pirates to attempt any boarding. Still, he now had to face not one, but two enemies, the storm and the pirates.

The powerful eastern wind was far too strong for the helmsmen to steer their ships away from each other. Nevertheless, they battled on. None could see clearly in which direction they were being battered. Then, in between the waves crashing onto the decks and the sea spray splashing the men's faces, Captain Jennings thought he had caught a glimpse of an even darker mass at port. He wiped the sea spray off his face and struggled to stay upright to look. He was right. A few leagues away, he had just spotted land and if his memory served him right, it was the contour of a small island which, he felt sure, was none other than Cove Island.

The ships drifted dangerously towards the sandbanks and moments later, one of the crews heard the unmistakable groaning sound of salty wood floundering on a shallow. It was the rogue ship which had been pushed irrevocably onto the sandbank and now, she was listing badly. Fortunately, the *Maryland* managed to stay clear and she carried on her course and headed straight for Cove Island. Realising that Griffiths was seeking shelter from the storm, Captain Jennings followed suit.

After a long struggle against the wind, rain and choppy seas, both ships made it to the calmer waters of Cove Island where they waited for the storm to abate.

Captain Jennings waved frantically to the *Maryland's* crew, wanting reassurance that they were all right, but to his surprise, no one responded. Standing next to him, Jonesie, looking rather pale, begged, "Capt'n, can we go on land, please, I'm feeling really sick."

The captain looked at the ship boy, ruffled his hair and asked with a quirky smile, "What have you been pilfering this time?" Then, noticing the boy turning greener and paler, he conceded, "All right, Jonesie, get the mates to put the cockboat to the water. I think everyone could do with a break."

"Thanks, Capt'n," Jonesie enthused, already feeling better.

Immediately, the captain organised his crew to be transported to the island in shifts, leaving only a skeleton crew on board. Then, he turned to

William and said, "William, go with the first lot. Jonesie, you stay on the ship."

"Why? I want to go too. I want to fight!" Jonesie protested. "William, please, tell the captain."

William turned to Jonesie and said, "Jonesie, the first rule of a good shipmate is to be able to obey orders. It's too dangerous out there and you're not big enough to fight yet. You be a good boy and wait for us here."

"Jeez, it ain't fair!"

As the cockboat was rowed back and forth to the island, Captain Jennings waved to the *Maryland*'s crew to do likewise. They seemed slow to respond but eventually, as the captain took his turn in the cockboat, he saw the *Maryland*'s own cockboat being lowered into the water. Good, he thought, he would be able to catch up with Griffiths and find out at first hand if there were any casualties among the crew and if the ship was in any way damaged.

When Captain Jennings landed on the beach, he smelt the warm iodine air rising from the hot sand just freshened up by the storm. He stood erect taking deep breaths while scouring the island. The contour of the beach, the trees and the thick clumps of vegetation clinging onto the sand dunes, all looked exactly the same. Loathe as he was to be reminded, his life was encrusted in every inch of this small island like an imprint of all things past. Fate kept tossing him about like a light piece of driftwood that would inexorably end up on a shore, *this* very shore. Determined to erase memories of his tumultuous past, he sought refuge in the serenity of the island, in its staggering beauty, in the soothing sound of the sea breeze blowing through the palm trees. Lost in meditative contemplation, he took more deep breaths, scanned the beach and was about to advance forward towards the dune when behind him a loud voice boomed, "So, we meet again, 'Uncle Charles'… or is it Captain Jennings?"

Charles Jennings did not turn around straight away. He had heard that voice before and he knew that the man who had just greeted him so brazenly did not belong to any of his crews. He turned around slowly and saw that the man was pointing a pistol at him. The first thing he noticed about the stranger was his buckle which bore a skull with two crossed pistols carved underneath it. Then, their eyes met and all Charles Jennings could see were the black satanic eyes of Black Bobby.

"It *is* Captain Jennings, isn't it?" Black Bobby riled sarcastically.

The captain threw swift glances at the pirate, then at the *Maryland*.

"What have you done with my crew?" he asked, seething with anger.

"Don't worry, they're quite safe. They're looking after my ship, over there, see? She's listing badly and I thought your crew wouldn't mind looking after her while I attended urgent business. I regret to say that you may have lost one or two of your mates during the boarding, cos you see, the waves were quite rough during the storm but it was the only time we could jump ship without you noticing. Now, I'd like you to come treasure hunting with us because I know that your old mates never had a chance to come and collect their prizes, God bless them, so we might as well have their share of things, don't you think? It would be such a waste to leave them to rot in this damn place."

"You go to hell!" Charles Jennings blasted defiantly.

"Wherever I'm going, you're coming with me!" Black Bobby retorted with a ferocious smile.

Behind him, Black Bobby's crew were still disembarking. He turned around and called out to them.

"Come on, get yourselves here!"

The pirates started running. Taking advantage of this brief moment of distraction, Jennings drew his cutlass and took a big swipe at the pirate, knocking his pistol out of his hand. Black Bobby reacted swiftly. He took his other pistol from his belt and pointed it straight at Jennings, and shouted, "You do that again and I'll shoot you!"

"That would be a foolish thing to do, Black Bobby. Without me, you won't be able to find the treasure," Jennings retorted, knowing pertinently that the treasures were for ever buried under tonnes of rubble.

"Don't you worry yourself!" he riposted. "It's not that big an island, Captain. Sooner or later, we'll find it."

By now, the other pirates had caught up with them and, forming a semi-circle around the two foes, they listened intently to the heated exchange, their eyes opened wide with vision of pearls, silk and gold. Then, Jennings noticed a figure barging its way towards the front. Straight away he knew who it was, but he was keen not to divert his attention away from Black Bobby.

"All right," Jennings said. "I'll fight you for it. I challenge you to a duel using cutlasses only."

The pirate swelled up his chest to the size of his ego and retorted with bravado, "Fine! If that's what you want. The quicker I can dispose of you, the quicker I'll get my hands on those damn treasures!"

Straight away, he replaced his pistol into his belt and shouted to his men, "Someone pass me a cutlass!"

Immediately, the nearest pirate to him stepped forward and threw a cutlass to Black Bobby.

"Take mine!"

Jennings looked on in horror for the pirate who had just spoken was none other than his old friend and foe, Anne Bonny.

"And go for the kill!" She shouted with gusto, leering at Jennings with intent.

***

A few meters away, Griffiths had managed to land his crew, and right now, he and his men were scurrying discreetly away behind the creek.

Meanwhile, out to sea, a sloop sailed purposefully towards the island, unaware of the drama that was unfolding. Henry Tisdale had set sail that very morning, determined to grab his share of lost treasures with the help of Anne Bonny's map.

***

Back on the beach, Jennings and Black Bobby circled each other, wielding their cutlasses. The pirates took a few steps backwards to allow for extra space around the duellists. In the middle, Black Bobby growled and snarled like an enraged beast. Growing impatient, he lunged forward a few times to force Jennings to react, but the young captain was in no rush to die. Keeping his nerve, he studied the pirate, assessing the pace of his steps, the swiftness of his moves and whether he favoured his right or left foot to lunge and strike. Black Bobby was in no mood to wait. He charged once more, letting out a spine-chilling roar, and hit Jennings's cutlass with a loud clang. Light on his feet, Jennings ducked, dodged and side-stepped the pirate, returning blow for blow. Both cutlasses crossed and clashed fiercely, with neither man gaining the upper hand.

Suddenly, sharp shots rang through the air. Instantly, a mad scramble followed as the pirates took position all along the beach to return fire.

Jennings threw a swift glance towards the dunes. They were his men. Making the most of this unexpected diversion, Black Bobby took his chance. In that split second during which Jennings had been distracted, he lifted his cutlass and went for the kill. But Jennings was too fast. With one powerful hit, he blasted the cutlass out of the pirate's hand. Red with rage and fury, Black Bobby threw his whole weight on top of Jennings, twisted his right arm and pushed his face firmly into the sand. With his mouth full of sand, Jennings struggled to breathe. He could feel Black Bobby's iron grip pushing his head into the sand. He tried to move his head sideways to catch a breath of air but the pirate held him down firmly. Jennings began to panic as he felt his strength desert him. Everything was turning black. Resigned to his fate, he felt himself go when he heard the sharp crack of a pistol shot. Another immediately followed just above his head. Then, there was a third and suddenly, the heavy weight that kept his head firmly buried into the sand fell to one side and he was able to breathe again. Gasping for air and spitting sand, he raised his head and looked about him. Next to him, Black Bobby lay on his back with blood trickling out of his mouth. On his chest, there was a large gaping hole from where the pirate's blood spewed out onto the pink sand. Jennings looked ahead where he thought the shot had come from, but all he saw was Anne lying in the sand. With great effort, he staggered onto his feet and threw himself next to her. Her eyes were closed. Jennings could not tell whether she was unconscious or dead for on her chest, a bright red patch glistened with fresh blood. Gently, he lifted her head and rested it on his lap, stroking her forehead and uttering words of comfort. Slowly, she opened her eyes and when she saw Jennings, she smiled, but straight away, she winced with pain.

"Jennings…" she murmured.

"Thank you for saving my life," he immediately said.

"I did it for my son… our son…"

She struggled to speak and each word she uttered increased the pain and made her wince all the more. Her breathing quickened and at that moment, Jennings knew he would not be able to save her. Looking at him fixedly with desperation in her eyes, Anne managed to utter, "Take care of him, Jennings… promise me you'll take care of him…"

Overwhelmed with emotion, Jennings bit his lips and fought back the tears before replying, "We both know he's in good hands just now, but I promise I'll look after him."

Anne smiled, then turning her head away from Jennings, she scanned the island and the sea.

"It's a beautiful world, Jennings, but through my own foolishness I shall no longer be part of it. Don't ever tell my son the truth about me... He must never know."

She turned her head towards Jennings again and whispered, "I love you, Jennings... I've always loved you but I couldn't..." At this moment, gripped with pain, she stopped to catch her breath, and just managed to say, "...goodbye, Jennings."

No sooner had her last words left her lips than her head fell to the side and her arm slid limply onto the sand.

Jennings closed her eyes. He looked at Anne's face, consciously blocking his emotions. She was no more, and with her, she had taken away Jennings's past.

As if by command, the shots immediately ceased firing. All Jennings could hear now were footsteps crunching the sand. The steps stopped. Jennings raised his head and saw William standing next to Henry Tisdale. They were staring at him in a mournful silence. Griffiths rushed to the scene and knelt next to the captain.

"Griffiths, get the men and round up the rest of the pirates."

"Already done, Captain."

The two men stared at each other for a while, locked in a mournful silence. Henry Tisdale surveyed the scene with a sad expression on his face and said in a soft tone, "You've done your job, Captain..."

"Not quite... There's one more thing I want to do for her... that is to give her a Christian burial."

"Not possible, Captain. The rule is, no requiem for a dead pirate."

"I don't care! This one will!" the captain cried out with feeling.

Tisdale understood the captain's pain. He wrapped his arm around the captain's shoulder and said very calmly, "We can always give her a decent burial at sea, Captain."

Tisdale waited nervously for the captain's rebuff, but Jennings was too shattered and devastated to argue.

After the pirates had been swiftly rounded up and thrown into the brigs, the ships sailed into the sunset. On board the *Redemption*, all united to recite the sailors' prayer.

Thank you, Lord, for opening our eyes to the beauties of this world

For the wondrous light of the sun and the freedom of the sea
For the wind that steers our ship and the food that we receive
Let us sail in your faith and pray in your name
And should we sin in pursuit of honour and glory
Forgive us all our trespasses
Forgive us our greed and excesses
And let us sail in your faith and pray in your name
Amen

At the end of the prayer, Anne Bonny's body was consigned for ever and ever to the infinite kingdom of the clear blue sea as Jennings muttered words of sorrow whispered in the wind, "Please, Lord, have mercy on her soul."

***

To this day, somewhere in the West Indies, there is a beautiful island where the fine sand scintillates in a soft shade of pink, rendered so by the blood spilt by pirates and sparkling with crushed precious stones from the fabulous treasures of these desperate men, not knowing that the only treasure worth chasing is the one that resides in our hearts.

One astute young lady knew. Lady Sarah had no doubt that she had found that immensurable treasure deep in the heart of the dashing Captain Jennings.

Despite her mother's stern protestations, she had declared, quite without flinching, that her future happiness lay with the captain or in a convent. At these words, Lady Whetstone Rogers panicked. Fearing that she would never see her daughter again, she finally relented.

A year later, the lavish wedding brought the main street of Nassau to a standstill. Delicately dabbing her tears with an exquisite lace handkerchief throughout the ceremony, Lady Whetstone Rogers followed the happy couple outside the church, flanked by her Governor husband. As she waved off the newlyweds, she wailed, "I had such high ambition for our daughter…" She sobbed. "His father is only a tenant farmer…"

Quite unperturbed by his dear wife's remark, the Governor took a deep breath, put a comforting arm around her shoulders and declared with a certain rectitude, "Now, Sarah darling, we all have to start somewhere."

PART III
(Ten Years Later)

Chapter Thirty-Five
A Family Secret Revealed

Angus Shielding stood at the top of the hill, lost in a daydream. Below him lay Chelmouth, a small Cornish village perched above a rocky path that led to a low-lying cliff. Powerful breakers of storms past had burrowed tenebrous caves deep into the land through which smugglers carried their stolen treasures.

Often, when the wind howled through the crags like the haunting wails of long departed souls, young Angus would steal away and sit in one of those dark and dank caves re-enacting battles at sea, pirates raiding ships, counting pieces of eight, singing victorious and sharing jugs full of rum.

The young lad, barely in his fourteenth year, had always loved the sea. Taking large gulps of fresh air to fill his lungs in the manner, he imagined with hands on hips, of a sea captain, he often scanned the horizon, but instead of seeing the rough seas and grey skies that were so familiar to him, he always pictured blue skies separated from the emerald sea by a gleaming horizon chiselled with palm trees. It was a recurring dream that one day he was determined to fulfil.

The cold wind whipping his face forced him to return home. As he watched his mother push back the cast iron bracket that held a pot of beef stew over the hearth, he decided to tell her of his plans. However, he hesitated for there was nothing better on earth to convey those feelings of comfort and joy, than the exquisite aroma of food cooked with love. He sat at the table, deliberating how best to begin. The first thing he would tell her was that neither the land nor the city could ever fulfil his dream. His bright future could only be contained in one simple frame, that of the sea.

The fire crackled under the cauldron and the flames jumped to lick its base. Outside, the sun had already sunk into the sombre sea. Dark crepuscular clouds were already shading the jagged arm of the scrawny piece of land that stretched all the way to Land's End. Through the small windows, divided into four misted squares, Angus could just about perceive the silver glow of the waves shimmering under the icy moon.

Lorna Shielding had noticed the preoccupied look on her son's face in the past few days. She knew instinctively that the time had come for her to speak. She pulled her chair closer to the fire and sat herself down, still holding the long wooden spoon she had been using to stir the stew.

"Come here, Angus, and bring the small stool with you," she summoned. "I have something very important to tell you."

Angus threw a quizzical glance at his mother. It was a strange tone of voice she had used, not one that hinted apprehension or sadness tainted with doom or foreboding, but one that was calm and resolute as if she were about to impart words of wisdom. Sitting upright with her back to the hearth, her tired features looked younger and smoother in the subdued light of the fire glow.

"What is it, Mother?"

"Angus, my son, I know what's bothering you. You're still a boy but I can tell you're restless, that the sea will always have a stronger hold than me. You probably think you're old enough to fend for yourself and that soon you'll want to leave. My love for you is stronger than my resolve which is why I won't stop you. But beware, the sea is a treacherous friend and, by the grace of God, the next time you cross this threshold, you will be a man. It is therefore time for me to tell you the truth about your past…"

"What do you mean, Mother?" Angus interrupted.

"Before I say anything else, I want to make sure that you understand that as far as I am concerned, you will always be our son and will always love you as such…"

There, Lorna Shielding paused to keep her emotions in check.

"You see, Angus," she reprised, stroking her son's head tenderly and ruffling that little patch of bleached hair that had suddenly appeared when he was a toddler. "The fact is… your true origin lies elsewhere."

Her words hit the boy like a thunderbolt. He felt his body tense up. It was a truth he had suspected long ago but which he had adamantly refused to acknowledge. His intense gaze directed to his mother seemed to beg her to say no more. He understood too well the words she had forced herself to articulate, noting her pain, her anguish. Whatever she might say, in his mind and in his heart, he was the son of Robert and Lorna Shielding and nothing, not even a blatant truth, could ever change this. As a matter of fact, whenever he was in town, he could never walk down the main street without someone hailing, "He's just like his dad, tall and handsome! A real chip off the old block!" despite the fact that, unlike both his parents', his eyes were of a clear blue that did not reflect his Shielding parentage.

Still in shock, the young lad asked, "So… who are my parents? Are they dead?"

"That's what I want to talk to you about, son. I want to tell you the story of how you came to us and, God be my witness, for this is true… this is *your* story."

Chapter Thirty-Six
The Storm That Brought More Than Fear…

"It was the year of the Lord 1721. Spring had arrived though you wouldn't know it for a fierce gale was blowing, crashing the ocean waves over the harbour wall. Your dad was away at sea and, God the Lord knows, I was praying that his ship would find shelter in one of the coves along the coast.

"It was very dark outside… yes, very dark. I stoked the fire one more time before retiring to bed. I was already half-way up the stairs when I heard some banging outside the front door. I froze on the stairs, staring at the front door, too scared to go and see what was making that noise. All alone in the house, isolated as it is, I was pretty nervous, though it's not in my nature. The wind was howling outside, so I thought maybe one of the shutters had broken and was hanging loose on its hinges. But then, the banging started again, louder this time. I knew I had to fix the shutter or I wouldn't be able to catch a wink of sleep that night. So, I grabbed my shawl and steeled myself to brace the storm. I tell you, and God be my witness, I never said my prayers so loudly and so fast. I think I was trying to chase away demons. Anyway, when I opened the front door, I nearly had a heart attack. Right there, on the doorstep, there was a body. I bent down and saw it was a woman. She was barely conscious. She kept mumbling something… God knows what… so I knelt down to help her and that's when I heard her say, 'Please, help me… help me… I'm with child…'

"I didn't know what to do… me on my own… and anyway, she was far too heavy for me to carry, so I ran through the rain to fetch your uncle Archie, the carpenter, and we brought her in. It was funny, though, because when she said 'I'm with child', I forgot about the poor wench for a moment and thought *that's good because I'll be able to use the crib that Granma Shielding had given me, hoping for some wee bairns, but with your dad being away so much…* Anyway, your uncle Archie went back home to fetch one of the old palliasses he keeps for family when they come to visit, and he put it in front of the fire. You see, the poor wretched woman was frozen to the bone. She stayed there and didn't wake up for two days! It was in the morning of the third, as I was putting more potatoes in the broth, that I heard a faint moan behind me. I turned around. The woman was staring at me. 'Who are you?' she said with fear in her eyes. 'Where am I?'

"She was so weak, she could hardly sit up on the palliasse. So I went to her and tried to reassure her. 'Don't worry yourself, dear. You're gonna be fine. I'm looking after you...'

"But then, she screams at me, 'Who are you? Don't come anywhere near me!'

"I didn't react. I kept calm so that she would stop panicking. 'I'm Lorna Shielding...'

"Then, she notices her shift. 'That's not my dress! Where are my clothes... I must have my clothes!'

"'Don't worry. They're drying by the fire. In fact, they should be dry by now,' I says, trying to sound as calm as I can. I bring her the long skirt and immediately, she snatches it from me as if I were a thief trying to steal it from her.

"'Please, don't tell anyone I'm here!' she suddenly begs. 'Don't tell anyone or I'm as good as dead!'

"'Don't worry yourself,' I says, thinking she was delirious. She had a fever, you see. 'You're quite safe here. Nobody's gonna come for you.'

"Then she grabs my hands, both of them, squeezes them really hard and says, 'My baby... my baby's gonna come soon... will you take care of my baby? I'm a condemned woman... I cannot stay here... I don't want to be caught again... I'd rather die...'

"'Caught?' I says. 'Why? By whom?' And she starts sobbing.

"'Never mind,' I says, 'don't you worry yourself, love, you're quite safe here. No one will come after you, I'll make sure of it.'

"Anyway, some weeks later, she's delivered of a son... I think it came early..."

"Was that me?" Angus asked eagerly.

"Yes, my son, it was you," Lorna Shielding replied with the sweetest smile. "She was ever so pleased that it was a boy... ever so pleased... 'he's just like his father' she kept saying, and that's the only time I saw her smile proper." She added, looking tenderly at her son.

"Did she choose my name?"

"No, I did. I wanted you to have a Scottish name like your granpa."

"So, what did she do after?"

"She stayed for a while... until she was sufficiently recovered, although she was always worried to be found out, so I tell her, 'Don't worry, I'll say you're my cousin from Ireland.' She felt a lot better after that. Then I says, 'What shall I call you, then?'

She thinks for a moment, then she says, 'Annabel... call me Annabel.'

'Just Annabel?'

'Yeah, just Annabel.'

"Then, one day, I can sense she's restless. She comes to me and begs, 'Please, will you take care of my son... there's not much I can give you... except... except for this.'

"She fumbles frantically through the pleats of her long skirt. So I says, 'Don't be silly, I don't want anything from you. I don't mind helping you... I had been longing for a child of my own...'

"But she insists. 'You don't understand. You must take it... for my son... so he has something to remember me by.'

"She takes my hand and put a small object inside. It was a large gold ring with a huge blue stone inserted in it. I really didn't want to take it from her, thinking she could sell it for a few groats, but she insists. 'Please, my son must have it. It used to belong to his father.'

"So I have to take it, don't I, and I says, 'I will look after it and I'll make sure he gets it when he's big enough to wear it... your wee bairn is so bonny.'

"When I says this, she twitches nervously and stares at me with her big brown eyes. So I says, 'Sorry, it's Scottish. I'm from Scotland, you see. Anyway, I'm gonna wear the ring round my neck and never take it off until your son is ready to have it.'"

Angus looked at his mother and pointed at her neck.

"So... is that the ring there?"

Lorna Shielding lifted the ring between her fingers, looked at it briefly and replied, "Yes, Angus, this is it... this is your father's ring. Lots of people have asked where it comes from, because they know very well I could never afford a ring like that. I always says it was a present from my cousin. Because it's too big, I wear it around my neck.

"Anyway, your mother still hadn't told me who she was or where she'd come from. Every time I tried to ask, she'd be quite shirty and abrupt. Then, all of a sudden, she became more talkative. I remember, it was one evening. She had put the wee bairn into bed. I had just finished the dishes and I was sweeping the floor. She comes to me and says, 'Lorna, I want to tell you something.'

"'Come and sit at the table, then.'

"'I don't know what to do,' she starts. 'But you've been so kind to me, I feel I owe you the truth. You see… my name is not Annabel…'

"'I'd guessed that!'

"'My name… my real name is Anne… Anne Bonny…'

"She stares at me as if she expected some kind of reaction, but her name didn't mean anything to me. Why should it? I'd never seen her from Adam, but when she realises that I've no idea who she is, I can tell she's in a quandary, and that, perhaps, she needn't tell me no more. So I says, 'You're not from these parts, are you?'

"Now, she's eyeing me suspiciously.

"'Don't worry,' I says. 'You don't have to tell me anything you don't want to. As far as me and everyone else is concerned, you're my cousin, so I'm quite happy to leave it at that.'

"'Thank you,' she says. 'Thank you. I'll remember this…'

"'Actually, it's been quite nice to have company for a change. As you can see, my husband is away at sea a lot and we don't have any children… yet. So, you can stay here until you're well enough to go home.'

"She looks at me with those pleading eyes again. 'That's just it, you see. I don't have a home.'

"'What? No home… anywhere? What about the wee bairn's father?'

"She turns her eyes towards the window. For a moment, she seems so far away; she doesn't say anything. She looks so sad, so pitiful, so I says, 'Has the little one no father?'

"'No,' she says. 'It's better if he doesn't know anything about him.'

"Then she stops and glowers at me, and I can tell she's wondering whether she's said too much. So I reassure her. 'You've nothing to fear from me. I'm just a fisherman's wife and I have no connections whatsoever with the authorities.'

"She sighs with relief… or sadness; it was hard to tell. 'Where have you travelled from?' I asks, thinking she was gonna say the 'Isle of Wight' or somewhere like that. I've never been there myself, so I don't know what the local folks are like.

"Now she's laughing and when she's quite calmed down, she hails, 'Nassau!'

351

"I nearly fell off my chair. I was so shocked that I remember just staring at her, speechless. I mean, her travelling all alone from Nassau... in her condition... with no sign of a man to take care of her. Nassau isn't exactly next door, is it? To think I thought she was from the Isle of Wight. I should have guessed, though, with her tanned skin... you don't get that kind of tan minding home in these parts.

"'What a coincidence!' I says. 'My uncle lives in Nassau. He runs a tavern called *The Cock & Bull.*'

"'I know. It was him who gave me your address. He knew you would be able to help. But I don't want to say any more. I don't want to put you in danger.'

"'In danger? Why? I haven't done anything wrong.'

"'You don't understand... but if I don't make it, tell my son...'

"'Don't you worry yourself, young lady! You'll be fine, mark my word. I saw that fine frame of yours when I changed your dress. You've a strong body, stronger than any woman I've ever seen. I mean, I don't know how a woman can get arms like yours... and your hand... when you squeezed mine... I've never felt such a strong grip on a woman, so whatever you were doing over there in Nassau, it certainly wasn't keeping house, that's for sure.'"

Anne Bonny looked at the young lass with a hint of envy. For a brief moment, she wondered what it would be like to lead a simple life, tranquil and carefree, to have that solid friend with whom to go through the most perilous moments in life that fate forces upon you, to laugh about them and share that huge relief the minute the dangers have passed. She suddenly thought of Mary. She would have made the ideal companion, though Lorna, with her astuteness, inner strength, kindness and generosity would have made a good candidate too. But life is an ongoing challenge and if she, Anne Bonny, was destined to go through it alone, then so be it, she concluded with a firm resolve.

"You're right, Lorna. I can see why your uncle thinks well of you. You're kind and generous and you have a heart of gold, that's why I feel I can trust you to look after my son."

"I stared back at her not knowing what to say. I was quite flattered, really. Besides, I longed for a child though I always believed it would come from my own flesh and blood. I never thought... But I had to ask, 'When will you return for your son?'

"'I don't know... I really don't know.'

"There was some kind of finality in her words; I sensed it and I was right. She never came back; that's how you became my son, my dear son."

Angus shuffled uneasily on the small wooden stool as his mother continued to unravel the mystery of his past. His mother looked at him tenderly, her hand stroking his face gently, reaching out for his heart and tightening up the maternal bond she had weaved, ensuring that it would never be broken.

"You see, my darling boy, the truth is... both your parents were engaged in... what d'you call it... illegal trading at sea."

Angus's face froze in shock.

"You mean... they were pirates? *Both* of them?"

"Yes, I'm afraid they were..."

Instantly, his eyes lit up and sparkled with excitement and unhinged pride.

"WOW!"

Lorna Shielding noted with some alarm the excited reaction of her son.

"Now, young man," she chided. "Don't you start getting funny ideas in that handsome head of yours!"

"Please, Mother, tell me more about my parents. What happened to them?"

Lorna Shielding hesitated.

"Well, I suppose, you're old enough to face the truth. Your father's ship was caught and all on board were trialled and hanged. But your mother escaped the gallows because she was with child. I'm the only one who knows what happened to her because she turned up here."

"Where is she now?"

"That, I'm afraid I don't know. Once she got better, she said she had some unfinished business to sort out, so she left."

"And she didn't say where she was going? Didn't you ask?"

"Oh yes, I did, but she wouldn't say. Too dangerous, she kept saying."

After a long pause, Angus looked straight into his mother's eyes and declared touchingly, "I love you, Mother. You are and will always be my mother... but what was my real mother like? Was she as beautiful as you?"

Lorna Shielding let out a little chuckle.

"I don't know about me, but she was very young, a very handsome woman with dark hair, dark eyes..."

"But I don't have dark hair and my eyes are blue!"

"Well, maybe your father had blue eyes."

"Would you know her if you saw her again?"

"It wouldn't matter if I didn't because I could always spot her from the scar she had on her left shoulder."

"A scar? What kind of scar?"

"A straight line it was." Using her thumb, Lorna Shielding drew a line on her own shoulder.

"How did she get it?"

"From a cutlass."

"A what?"

"A cutlass. It's a weapon, you know, all pirates have them — well, that's what she said — a bit like a short sword."

"What else did you find out about her?"

"Not much. She wouldn't say much. But, never mind about that; I want you to promise me one thing, darling, promise me that you'll never ever become a pirate."

"Mother!" Angus protested.

"Please, darling, promise me," his mother insisted, anxiously.

"Of course I promise. I've never wanted to become a pirate, so don't worry, Mother."

"Thank the Lord!"

As she hailed the Almighty, Lorna Shielding crossed herself. After a short pause, Angus looked longingly at the ring hanging around his mother's neck and finally asked in a soft voice, "Could I try the ring on, Mother?"

At that very moment, all Lorna Shielding could think of was that she was not ready to let go of her son. She cupped her hand around it and held it firmly.

"Another time, darling... another time..."

Chapter Thirty-Seven
The Call of the Sea

At the end of the narrative, Lorna Shielding paused. She looked at her son, trying to decipher the meaning of his perplexed expression, his furrowed brows, wondering if, at that moment, she had lost him to a perfect stranger, to a woman he had never met and was not likely to ever meet for she had learnt of her passing in a letter from great aunt Tisdale.

"Angus?" his mother called anxiously.

The boy turned to his mother but did not respond. Lost in another world, he now understood why he kept dreaming about an emerald sea bordered with palm trees, why he longed to travel to the end of the world, and why the flapping of sails stirred up in his heart more emotions and excitement than any other noise he had ever heard before. He turned his head away from his mother for a moment and let his gaze rest on the log fire crackling in the hearth, and suddenly, as if awakening from a long sleep, he felt detached from the fire, from the stones that surrounded it, and from the whole room. Sweeping the wide-open space with his big blue eyes, he looked at the whitewashed walls, the beamed ceiling and the small windows from where a crepuscular glow threw dark shadows across the room. How could he reconcile himself with the thought that both his parents had been pirates? He was confused, though right now, he was clear about only one thing, he loved the woman who had taken him in as a baby, he loved her face even when her straw hair hurriedly pinned up rested like a vandalised nest on top of her head because she was more concerned about looking after him than herself. He loved her voice, her smile, the way she fussed frantically around him as if it were a constant matter of life and death, ordering him about and even nagging him at times; but above all, he loved her because in his heart, she would always be his mother.

He looked at his mother again.

"Is she… is she still alive…?" he asked tentatively.

"No, sweetheart, she's not, but your great uncle Henry said she was a brave, very courageous woman and died killing a notorious pirate…"

"Killing a pirate!" Angus interrupted. "But…"

"I know it sounds odd when she was a pirate herself, but your great uncle Henry will be able to explain to you exactly what happened when you eventually meet him. But mark my word, she was a remarkable woman and you have inherited the best of her, Son, don't you ever doubt it," his mother replied firmly.

Angus returned a quirky smile. He looked at his mother and at the ring hanging from her neck, the sole memento that linked him to his lost parents.

"The ring, Mother, can I keep the ring?"

Lorna Shielding hesitated. She became fearful that by giving it away, she would sever the strong maternal bond that existed between herself and her son. The very thought made her fret. Wriggling her hands nervously, she looked at her son with renewed intensity and noticed that the whole of his face had changed. His usually calm expression had hardened. He pinched his lips, sat up straight on his wooden stool and declared in a very determined voice that his mother hardly recognised, "Mother, I want to go out to sea."

The words she had been dreading for so long, delivered in such a clear and precise tone, hit her like a blow on the head. Following the initial shock, Lorna Shielding threw herself at her son, grabbed him, hugged him and began to sob uncontrollably.

"I know, son…" she cried. "I've always known that… that's why I've been desperately trying to find ways to stop you… to divert your thoughts away from the sea… to show you the marvels of the land, the stunning colours of each season, the richness of the soil, the work that would bring you good earnings for you and your future family. All these years I've tried to teach you land skills that would keep you away from the sea… Even Uncle Archie wanted to take you on as a trusted hand, and also because you're not afraid of hard work; he had plans for you… we all did…"

"I know, Mother, but the sea is in my blood, I feel it right here," Angus explained beating the middle of his chest where he felt his heart beat with renewed vigour.

Lorna Shielding shook her head in despair.

"I've failed," she sobbed, letting the words escape from her quivering lips like a death sentence.

"No, Mother, you haven't!" Angus contradicted fiercely. "You've made a man of me and it's thanks to you and the strength you've given me that I feel ready to face my destiny. I shall return, Mother, don't you ever forget that, and when I return, I shall be a better man, a grown-up man and a gentleman of the sea, I promise you that, Mother."

Using her apron to dry her tears, Lorna Shielding raised her head and smiled at her son. "Come on, Son, it's very late… We'll talk about it in the morning. You go on to bed while I put the fire out," she said kissing her son on his forehead.

***

Early the following morning, Lorna Shielding went out to fetch some milk and eggs to prepare Angus's breakfast. The air was crisp and fresh, and the sky streaked with red flamboyant clouds. "Red sky in the morning, shepherd's warning" she automatically told herself as she hurried towards her brother-in-law's farm.

When she returned, Angus was standing on the threshold taking deep breaths and looking distantly at the sea. As soon as he spotted his mother, the young boy's face broke into a broad smile. He rushed to help her.

"Let me carry this for you, Mother," he said cheerfully, taking the milk pail from her.

"Thanks, Angus."

"I'm famished," he declared, hurrying towards the house.

Lorna Shielding smiled back at her son. Admiring his large frame, his confident step and his handsome face, she was not bothered that he did not look a bit like herself because, whatever his circumstances were, he was her son, an undeniable fact that always filled her with pride.

As they tucked into a hearty breakfast, Lorna Shielding began to speak.

"You know, Angus, and I've told you that many times before, the reason why I wanted you to be able to read and write is because I knew it would help you later on. I could tell from early on that you had a good head on your shoulders, and I told myself back then that I shall always make sure that you have the best. You see, Angus, most people can't read or write so with that precious skill, you will be able to rise above ordinary men and if one day you wanted to go out to sea, as I thought you might, I didn't want you to go as a common sailor; after all, better be a commander than a cabin boy, hey?"

Angus looked intrigued.

"I know, but how can I become a commander? I've no connections and no money to buy a commission."

"Well, that may be so but before you give up on the idea, I've a letter for you and who knows, there may be something in it that might help you."

"A letter? For me?"

"Yes, it arrived several years ago. I never opened it because it's addressed to you."

"To me! Who from?"

"I don't know. I'll go and fetch it."

Lorna disappeared into her bedroom and soon re-emerged holding a yellowish document symmetrically folded and sealed with a dark red seal. She gave it to Angus who snatched it from her.

The lay out was very ornate with big fancy letters at the head of the document indicating that its provenance was from some sort of high office. After a tense moment, Angus exclaimed, "Mother, it's from Nassau, in New Providence!"

"Nassau?"

"Yes, Nassau! It's written there at the top of the letter."

"Oh! What does it say?"

"Let me read it to you, Mother."

Nassau, on New Providence, January 1722

Dear Mr Shielding,

You may find it odd that a complete stranger should write wanting to help you but I have very good reasons to do so which I shall explain when we eventually meet, for I do hope that one day we shall meet.

Being somewhat well acquainted with the circumstances of your birth, I suspect that one day your wish will be to go out to sea. Should you wish to and be prepared to do so, after you have gained sufficient knowledge and experience in the craft of sailing, I am in a position to help you financially to buy your first commission to become an officer in the King's Navy.

When you come of age, may I suggest that you take the next available ship bound for New Providence, although be prepared, the voyage may be more eventful than you might expect but once you are safely delivered there, come to Government House in Duke Street, Nassau, so that we can arrange a meeting to discuss your future career at sea.

Yours truly,

Captain Charles Jennings OKN

P.S. Be sure to bring this letter with you.

At the end of the letter, Angus paused, stunned by what he had just read.

"Who's Captain Charles Jennings?" he asked, showing the letter to his mother.

"I don't know, Son, I've never heard that name before, but if I'm worth my weight in groats, I'd guess that he must have something to do with either your *other* mother or father, or even both perhaps."

Angus remained silent for a while. He was so excited at the prospect of going out to sea but felt compelled to conceal his true feelings so as not to upset his beloved mother. Perhaps she should come with him.

"Oh no, Son," she replied. "I like the sea, the clean fresh air, but there's nothing I love more than watching the sunset go down over the beautiful bay, sitting outside the house with a nice cup of tea in my hand and my feet resting on firm ground. I know what you're thinking, Son, but you don't need to worry about me, I'll be all right here. I'll just carry on helping your Uncle Archie on the farm. What I'll do, mind, is to go as far as Bath with you; I'm sure your uncle Archie won't mind taking us in his horse and cart. I would have preferred to go all the way to Bristol with you but your uncle Archie can't stay too long away from the farm and I know how dangerous the roads are so I wouldn't want to travel back on my own. But you'll be fine; you'll be on the postal coach with other people and when you get to Bristol, I'm sure someone will be able to help you find The *Crown & Anchor*. It's the closest inn to the harbour. You'll be able to stay there until you find a good ship that'll take you on as a ship boy. It shouldn't be too difficult. Ships are always looking for extra hands."

Angus looked at his mother and smiled.

"So you don't mind?" he asked, greatly relieved.

Lorna Shielding rolled her eyes and shrugged her shoulders.

"Mind? How can I *not* mind, you silly beggar!" she scolded gently before continuing. "Now," she said, "there's two things you're going to have to hold on to as if your life depended on them. The first is the ring. For that, I've sewn a little pocket inside your sash and that's where you're going to keep it because, mark my word, anybody who sees that ring is going to want to steal it from you, so keep it hidden in that little pocket around your waist and nobody will know about it, and do not wear it until you're old enough to fend for yourself. The second is that letter and in my mind, the letter is even more important than the ring, so I've sewn a double pocket inside your jacket which I've sealed with a few stitches so that it doesn't fall out. The only thing though, you're going to have to try not to get it wet otherwise it will be completely ruined and you won't be able to meet that nice gentleman who says he's going to look after you. Now…" she continued hesitantly, "I think I've thought of everything so all I need to do now is to sort out the transport. Let's go down to the farm and sort it with Uncle Archie."

Chapter Thirty-Eight
Sailing to a New Life…

It was spring in the year of the Lord 1736, in the reign of George II.

Three weeks had passed since the fateful conversation between mother and son had taken place. As dawn was breaking, Lorna Shielding helped her son pack his few belongings and after loading a loaf of bread, a good chunk of cheese, some cured ham and some apples in a separate bag, they set off for Uncle Archie's farm where the one-horse cart awaited them. Both mother and son walked side by side in complete silence, keen as they were to hide their heightened emotional state. Then, unable to control her emotions any longer and feeling the tears welling up, Lorna Shielding looked up to the skies and latched onto the one topic of conversation that helped her soothe away her tortuous and painful thoughts, the weather.

"Clear skies, son," she stated with a big sigh.

Angus understood immediately the underlying statement that had not been able to pass his mother's lips. In an affectionate gesture, he put his arm around his mother's shoulder and gave her a gentle squeeze.

When they arrived at the farm, Uncle Archie's cheerful greeting dispelled in an instant the overbearing mournful mood. Addressing his sister-in-law, he stated, "I've put some food in the cart and some blankets just in case you get cold on the journey." Then, turning to Angus, he added, "I'm also taking my hunting rifle as a precaution. Have you used a gun before?"

"No," Angus replied succinctly.

"Well, do be careful when you handle it, it's loaded. Come on, in you get!"

***

The journey began on a beautiful spring morning. Uncle Archie was in good form, in good voice and in good spirit, and to lift the sombre mood of his sister-in-law, he launched into a repertoire of his favourite ditties.

***

During the whole of the journey, Angus looked keenly around, at the mottled fields speckled with cows and sheep grazing and the ragged peasants working on the land. He let his gaze roll gently up and down the low-rising hills and tried to imagine what lay beyond them, a busy harbour, a sea horizon chiselled with ships in full sails, the palm trees of a tropical island or perhaps even some other feature he had never seen before.

A while later, when Uncle Archie heard in the distance a church bell chime midday, he stopped the cart to give his horse another well-deserved break. The threesome alighted from the cart to stretch their legs and consume a frugal lunch. Biting into a nice big green apple, Angus sauntered along the deserted road looking at the earth-bitten track and feeling the ground that seemed too hard and too heavy under his feet. He could not wait to reach their final destination and brushed aside any thoughts of a long-drawn-out farewell that would leave him, and his mother especially, feeling wretched and devastated for days to come. All through the journey, Angus repeated to himself that it would not be a final farewell, just an extended goodbye for he felt he had fate on his side. Yes, he thought crunching into his apple, he would return, just as he said, as a gentleman, an officer and perhaps even a commander. The very thought cheered him immensely and he turned around to catch a glimpse of his mother. She was standing silently, lost in sheer contemplation and deep thoughts with her strong frame blending into Uncle Archie's shadow. Suddenly, he felt the urge to go to her, hug her and plant a kiss on her cold cheek.

"What was that for?" she asked, startled.

"Nothing," Angus replied with a tender smile.

"Come on, back on board everyone," Uncle Archie chivvied. "We'd better get going if we're to get to Bath before sunset."

***

As they were travelling through a sparsely wooded forest, they heard the hooves of a horse at full gallop coming from behind. Curious, the three of them turned around to throw a casual glance at the rider hurtling towards them, a fairly ordinary sight in these parts which gave them no reason for

362

alarm, but when they looked, they felt unsettled for the hurried silhouette stood against the crepuscular sky like a figure of doom, dark, mysterious and lugubrious. Instinctively, Uncle Archie felt his belt which had a pistol on either side. He looked at Lorna and told her to hide under the blankets at the back.

"Angus, do the same," he muttered through his clenched teeth.

"But…"

"No buts, just do it!" his uncle cut in sharply.

By now, the rider had caught up with the cart and was giving a good look at the driver. Then, quick as a flash, he grabbed hold of the reins to try and force the horse off the track. But the highway robber had not reckoned with Uncle Archie, whose commanding stature would have scared off a charging bull. Using his horse whip, the farmer lashed out at the mystery rider who immediately whipped out his pistol and demanded, "Your money! Give me your money!"

"Get your filthy hands off my horse!" Uncle Archie riposted, cracking his whip as hard as he could on the horseman's back.

Angus wasted no time to come to his aid. He took his uncle's hunting gun and, making great efforts to steady himself, pointed it at the rider.

"You heard what my uncle said! Let go of the horse or I shoot!" he yelled at the same time as pulling the trigger. The power of the shot threw him backwards and he fell into the moving cart. Instantly, the mystery rider let go of the reins and galloped away in the opposite direction. Seconds after, Uncle Archie brought the cart to a standstill.

"Well done, lad!" he exclaimed, getting carried away and patting Angus's back rather too enthusiastically. Then turning to his sister-in-law, he hailed, "Well, Sister, I don't think you need worry too much about this young lad of yours!"

After which, Uncle Archie got off the cart and went to pat his horse on the neck to calm and reassure it.

Having given the horse a few minutes to recover, the threesome eventually resumed their journey and finally reached Bath early in the evening with no further incidents to declare, although Uncle Archie had prudently advised to keep a firm hold on the gun, just in case. As for his mother, she had remained in a petrified silence during the whole episode and it was only afterwards that she managed to utter, "You see what I mean about the ring…"

The first thing Angus noticed about the small provincial town of Bath was its smell, rancid, musty and at times downright revolting. Having never been in a town before, to him, it was like standing in the middle of a field that had just been fertilised with a good spread of muck. Not entirely enamoured with the place, he stared with cold detachment at the Tudor-styled buildings with their exposed dark beams compacting tightly the loose brick and mortar.

Uncle Archie manoeuvred the cart through the narrow streets and soon they reached the main town square. Spotting a red-brick archway, Uncle Archie steered his horse towards it knowing that it led to a backyard. The ornate sign above the entrance door pictured a white horse with underneath it two words painted in black, *Relay Inn.*

"'Tis to hope that they've got room for us. You stay here, I'll go and enquire."

A few minutes later, he re-emerged from the building with a winning smile. "Yep!" he said. "And for supper, they've got rabbit stew."

"Rabbit stew? I love rabbit stew!" Angus cheered.

"Come on, lad, let's get a move on if you want a bit of that rabbit stew."

Without further ado, Angus slung his cloth bag over his shoulder with one hand and took his mother's small carpet bag in the other before making his way towards the backstairs that led to the rented rooms upstairs.

A few minutes later, the three of them were sitting at a long wooden table waiting for their supper to arrive. The room was filled with thick pipe smoke, a somewhat distinctive smell that Angus found most agreeable and far more preferable to the acrid stench that lingered on outside. The walls were whitewashed and bare, and the wooden floor had been dusted with the usual thin layer of dampened sawdust. Angus could not help let out a little chuckle when his uncle explained that it was necessary to dampen the sawdust to stop it from getting up people's noses.

Suddenly, the front door swung open and a tall man dressed in dark clothes swaggered in. His tanned face was marked with deep lines and his eyes looked black and sinister. Immediately, the inn fell silent. The stranger threw long glances all around the room, all the while testing the atmosphere by breathing deeply through his twitching nostrils. Then he stopped. He made two steps towards a particular table and glowered at the man, the woman and the young lad sitting there. Anxious to avoid his glare, Angus kept his eyes fixed on his uncle.

Fortunately, at that very moment, the waitress arrived carrying a large tray of food. The stranger sniffed it and growled, "I'll have that."

Totally oblivious to his menacing stance, the waitress deposited the tray on the trio's table while addressing the stranger, "Just give me a minute and I'll fetch you one."

As the stranger did not respond, the tension dropped instantly, and the conversations resumed. Looking around the room with an inspectorial glance, the stranger propped himself on the bar while waiting for his order. Downing his drink like a man in a hurry, he slammed his pewter tankard on the bar, wolfed down his meal still standing, and then left.

"Uncle!" Angus whispered as soon as the front door closed. "Did you see?"

"Don't worry, lad, I know exactly who he was."

"So you recognised him too?"

"Oh yes, and next time, I'll be ready for him."

"I don't think there'll be a next time for you, Uncle. I think he's going where I'm going."

"What makes you say that?"

"I think he's a pirate."

"Well, my boy, if that's so, you might as well get used to it because at sea, the greatest danger is not the waves or the storms but those darned pirates." He declared in a matter-of-fact way, then turning round he called, "Waitress!"

"Just a minute!" she answered back before rushing to their table. "Yes, gentlemen, what can I get you?"

"Two ciders and a pint of ale. By the way, can you tell us when the next postal coach is due?"

"On Saturday, sir. It always comes on a Saturday unless it's been held up by some robbers or something. Will that be all?"

"Just one more thing, who was that man that came in earlier?"

"You mean the man who…"

"Yeah, that one."

The waitress pulled a face, shrugged her shoulders and said, "Don't know really, but he comes here every so often. He never says anything and people are too scared to talk to him. Somebody might know who he is but I'm not gonna be the one to ask, that's for sure. It's none of my business and I don't want to stir up no trouble so, as long as he pays his bills, I really don't care who he is. Will that be all, sir?"

"Yes, thank you."

The waitress left to fetch their order while Uncle Archie resumed the conversation.

"Did you hear what she said, Angus? The robber is a regular which means he's *not* a pirate! Anyway, the coach's coming on Saturday. Unfortunately, we cannot hang around here for that long; I've got too much to do on the farm. Your mother and I will take our leave first thing tomorrow morning. Right now, though, it's time for bed. Off you go lad and get as much sleep as you can, you're going to need it!"

***

When Lorna Shielding heard the bell tower of the nearby church chime the early hour, she felt a sharp pain hit her in the stomach which made her feel faint in her head. Having to say farewell to her beloved son was the worst torture a mother could endure. As the momentous hour approached, she felt quite sick just thinking about it. Thank goodness she had Archie on the return journey who would be able to comfort her.

Chapter Thirty-Nine
A New Beginning

The postal coach arrived several days earlier than expected. There were already quite a few passengers on it. The coach driver jumped on the cobble stones and disappeared inside the inn carrying a small sack. A few minutes later, he returned with several packages and letters which he stacked up in the wooden box purposely built in at the back of the coach.

Lorna Shielding cupped her hands around Angus's face to take a good long look at her son, logging in her memory every minute detail of his face, the two beauty spots on his right cheek that marked his otherwise faultless skin and the small tuft of bleached hair which she liked to ruffle. What kind of a man would he eventually become, she could not help wondering? This was the one question that dug deep into her heart. And there were many others swirling around her head. When would she be able to admire again these great big blue eyes, his fine features and that unruly mop of fair hair that she kept flicking away so that she could see his angelic face? He was her gorgeous adorable little boy and she feared that a spell out there in this wild and cruel world would spoil his gentle disposition, his soft manners and his ready smile. However, underneath that delicate layer, she knew him to be strong and determined and to possess an iron will that would one day make him a leader of men. Her thoughts were brutally interrupted by the coach driver shouting, "All aboard!" Immediately, she grabbed her son, one last time, to hug him tightly. She tried to speak but her words remained unheard, silenced by a stream of tears. When she finally let go of her son, choked up with emotion, she managed to whisper, "Bye, son... dear beloved son... look after yourself. God bless, darling... and don't forget to say your prayers!"

The coach driver wrapped himself in his long cape and settled in the driving seat grabbing the reins.

"Come on, lad, in you get. You can come and sit next to me if you like."

Angus looked up to the driver and smiled.

"Oh, yes please!" he replied enthusiastically before hugging his mother one more time.

"Bye, Mother. I promise to look after myself... and I'll send you my news whenever I can," he vouched sincerely, planting a kiss on her forehead.

All choked up with tears, his mother was unable to reply but she was determined to leave him with a happy face so she forced herself to smile. Noting that his sister-in-law was struggling to speak, Archie took it upon himself to speak to the driver, "Please take care of him, he's going to Bristol, to the *Crown & Anchor* by the harbour."

"No bother." The coach driver replied in a deep voice. "I know where that is. It's not far from the terminus."

***

Angus waved to his mother until the coach disappeared down one of the cobbled streets. In the distance, he could not see his mother's face streaming with tears, just her slight silhouette propped against Uncle Archie's chest. Catching one last sight of his mother, he finally turned his head away and looked fixedly ahead with a heavy scowl on his face. Then he let out a long mournful sigh. The coach driver began to chat to lighten up Angus's sullen mood.

"So... Where are you off to, lad?"

"I'm going to join the Navy."

The driver spluttered in surprise.

"Rather you than me, son!" he exclaimed.

"Why?"

"I don't need to tell you, son, you'll soon find out for yourself. So, who are you meeting at the *Crown & Anchor*, then?"

"My great uncle Phil."

"Would that be the landlord, Phil Tisdale?"

"Why, you know him?" Angus asked, aghast.

"Well, only by name. I sometimes go for a pint there with me mates."

Suddenly, Angus straightened himself up and declared with youthful aplomb, "He's going to help me find a good ship to sail on and one day, Mister, I shall be captain of my own ship."

The driver let out a little chuckle. "Well, let me know when you get there and when I get fed up pulling this cranky old coach on those bumpy roads, I'll take a long voyage at sea. It's bound to be smoother for a start. So, when you've got your own ship, remember me, my name's Silus Blanchford."

"And my name's Angus… Angus Rackham!" the boy decreed with intent.

"Rackham? I've heard that name… It rings a bell," the driver muttered. Then he took a long look at Angus. "No… it can't be… you've never been at sea before, have you?"

"Nope."

"I thought not… no, it can't be…"

"Can't be what?" Angus asked impatiently.

"You know, lad, the best thing about going to the *Crown & Anchor* is not just for a nice pint of ale but also for the stories you hear, especially there in Bristol. In fact, sometimes we hear about the conclusion of battles even before the old Admiralty does."

"Really? Wow!"

"I hope you know how to fight."

"My uncle taught me how to use a sword and pistols, and on our way here, I even fought off a highway robber with his hunting gun."

"Did you, now? Well, you'll be all right, then."

***

The coach was now rambling along the outskirts of Bath and Angus was once again able to take deep breaths of the clean fresh country air. Although the sky looked overcast and grey and the atmosphere felt damp, his nostrils twitched with great anticipation and excitement as he smelt the wonderful earthy aroma of the open countryside. Soon, however, he would be breathing a different kind of smell in a very different kind of atmosphere. In his head, he was already picturing the port of Bristol, busy and exciting, bustling with dock workers, travellers, fishermen and mariners with the odd immaculate navy uniform milling among the ragged-looking people. And one day, he told himself, that uniform would grace his handsome shoulders, a thought which filled him with immense pride and joy, and boundless trepidation.

Upon reaching Bristol, he went straight to the port to look at the ships. Just as he expected it, the port was bustling with people. He walked along the quay, overwhelmed by the sight of so many masts streaking the clear blue sky. As he continued to walk, he heard someone hailing, "Hey! You boy! Are you looking for a ship?"

"Aye, Sir! I'm looking for Captain Jennings."

"Come aboard! I think I might be able to help you."

Barely able to contain his excitement, Angus ran up the gangplank.

"Hi!" the sailor greeted. "What's your name?"

"Angus, Sir," the boy replied, removing his cloth cap.

Just as he did so, the sailor's jaw hit the floor. Wide eyed, with a note of incredulity quivering his lips, he kept looking at the boy's face, at his big blue eyes, at his fair hair with the tuft of bleached hair on the left-hand side of his head.

"What did you say your name was?" the man asked again, as if coming out of a trance.

"Angus, Sir, Angus Shielding. I have a letter here in my pocket from Captain Jennings..." he replied, increasingly puzzled by the sailor's countenance.

"May I see the letter?"

The boy hesitated.

"Well... er... it's for Captain Jennings."

"I am Captain Jennings..."

"You are? Really? I have the letter right here, inside my jacket, but I can't get it out because my mother's sewn it in."

The captain turned towards the main deck and hailed, "Jonesie, get me a knife!"

However, the young man was busy sorting out cables, so he hailed, "Jamesie, get a knife for the captain!"

"I can't right now! Ask Warren or Harris!"

"What! Those two layabouts? I'd rather go and get it myself."

"It's okay, Master James, I'll go and get it," Big Mitch volunteered.

Once the letter was retrieved, the captain scrutinised the boy.

"Who are your parents?"

"Well, my mother is Lorna Shielding, but she's not my real mother. I'm not sure about my real mother, but my mother told me that my real father was a pirate."

"No, son. Your real father was not and never was a pirate. I am Captain Charles Jennings and I *am* your father."

The shock of the news hit Angus with the same force as a loose cannon. The boy stared at the captain dumbstruck.

At that moment, the two young men whom the captain had been hailing came onto the scene. They took one long look at the boy, then at the captain.

"Jeez, Captain! He's the spitting image of you. He's even got that tuft of bleached hair just like you have. Who is he?"

"Gentlemen…" There, the captain paused, measuring his reply for the fullest effect. "This is my son," he finally declared with panache, choking with pride, before continuing, "Angus, meet the crew, James Balfour, otherwise known as Jamesie, he's the second in command; Billy Jones here, that's Jonesie, and he is the quarter master."

"Hi!" the young men returned with alacrity. "Welcome aboard the *Redemption*!"

"Angus, there is someone else I would like you to meet."

Turning to his second in command, the captain hailed, "Jamesie, go and fetch the ship's boy!"

"Aye, aye, Captain."

A minute later, a young boy appeared. He was about ten years old, if a day, had fair hair, blue eyes and a small tuft of bleach hair on the left-hand side of his head.

Angus could not believe his eyes.

"Hi!" the little chap greeted quite forwardly. "I'm Nicholas. The captain's my papa."

"Hi!" Angus replied, all excited. "The captain is my pa too!"

"Wow!" both boys exclaimed at the same time, laughing at the news. "We're brothers!"

"Come on, Angus!" Nicholas urged his new brother. "I'll show you around the ship."

Overwhelmed by this unexpected turn of event, Angus could not stop smiling. He felt an instant connection with his younger sibling. What's more, he was happy, deliriously happy… aye… for he knew from the bottom of his heart that he had finally come home.

Still standing on the same spot with his arms folded across his chest, Charles Jennings watched his young sons with the undiluted satisfaction of the proudest of fathers. The very sight of the two boys together reminded him of Jonesie and Jamesie when, emerging from the cockboat at roughly the same age as his younger son, they had declared with bravado that they wanted to be pirates. The nostalgic memory made him smile. No such desire had yet troubled his own sons, and with more and more pirates being hunted down, their future at sea seemed more secure, more exciting and a great deal safer. He had no doubt that one day, just like him, they would become proud officers of the King's Navy with the promise that they would treat their crew with more sympathy and… with a great deal more compassion. But for now, it was down to him, Charles Jennings, to instil these values into his sons and indeed, into his own crew.

The surface of the sea was beautifully smooth, cut only by the occasional wake of a small boat rushing back to port…

It was the year of the Lord 1736, in the reign of George II.

***

Pirates roamed the seas for many more years
And so did Captain Jennings and his righteous men
Together, with strong resolve, courage and prayers
They would overcome many of those ruthless rogues.
May the Lord have mercy on them and redeem their souls
For there would be no requiem for these wretched men.
The End

Lightning Source UK Ltd.
Milton Keynes UK
UKHW041044190722
406059UK00002B/51